Gathering of the Titans

The Tol Chronicles II

by Robert G. Ferrell

ZETABELLA
☆ PUBLISHING ☆

For Ady

ISBN 978-1-927384-28-2

Published by Zetabella Publishing
Toronto Canada
Printed in the US.
zetabella.com

Acknowledgements

This novel was pounded out, as were all of my previous works both great and small, in precious odd fragments of time in the evenings and on weekends. It is the final piece of writing I will ever produce under those circumstances, a generous Providence willing, as I am now officially retired from my 'conventional' career and devoting myself entirely to life as an author. My wonderful, talented, patient, wise-as-Solomon wife Adrienne is solely responsible for my being able to make such a bold and frankly terrifying move; I and anyone who reads and enjoys my work are deeply indebted to her for allowing me this freedom.

It can be difficult to compose acknowledgements: there are so many people who contribute in one manner or another to helping me get nominally coherent words into a readable format. For this go-around I am especially beholden to David Watson—the inspiration for Oloi—who also educates and entertains me; Jenice Amber Dean, whose connection to one of the characters in this book should be obvious to anyone who reads it; my Facebook Author page fans, who encourage me on a daily basis; the literary track coordinators and other con organizers who invite me to be a guest author and/or serve on panels at your cons (I really enjoy that); Martha Wells and Elizabeth Moon, just for being there for me to admire and emulate; and lastly the graphic novel artist Paul Taylor, though I have never met nor even corresponded with him. Over a period of three days I read the entire 13 years of his Web comic "Wapsi Square" in conjunction with editing this book. I let myself read four or five strips as a reward for another page of editing completed: his storyline is just that good. This is not a rapid and efficient way to edit a manuscript, but it sure is a heck of a lot more fun. Thanks, Paul.

Here's hoping no one will have to wait eighteen months before my next novel ever again.

Cheers,

Robert G. Ferrell
La Vernia, TX, USA
September, 2014

Maps

ESMIA

Sea of Fleriz

L'Son

Branbolong

Vokkala

Correg

Frespiola

Malaman

Evcolla

Uexafa

Paltor Strait

Coesta

Noclet

Bar

Grosyer

Litr

Spleroste

Homma

Strait

Terimpu

Yiks Island
Moonfish Bay

Hhvidz

ge

Ustrad Sea

↑ N

LITRIA

Hellehaelle

Esmia

Tragacanth

Galanga

Lardonita

Quinés

Asmagon

Paradiddle
Islands

Natio

Aspolia
Sea of Fleriz
Tebmol
Rublosq
Hagfar
Rillwe
Turmia & Bazgush

TURMIA BAZGUSH

Chapter the First

in which the rebirth of a nation is chronicled and an old adversary returns

The Royal Engineering Corps had their job cut out for them. There had been damage reported in every Ferroc, ranging from minimal disruption of services and some minor structural impairment affecting outlying villages in Ferroc Loca to widespread, severe destruction in Ferroc Norda, where 70% of the second-largest city, Fenurian, was destroyed and uninhabitable. While repairs in Ferroc Loca were handled by normal maintenance crews, in the other four provinces a senior or master engineer was appointed to spearhead the infrastructure rebuilding effort. Senior Engineer Beyya Corresca was assigned to Ferroc Oria, where there was light to moderate damage. Master Engineer Eglas Qaglo was sent to Ferroc Sutha, where the damage was moderate to heavy, with several villages demolished and several more severely damaged. Senior Engineer Hin-Lim Varpen traveled to Ferroc Osta, which saw heavy to severe damage, with multiple villages impacted and some damage to Cladimil's less well-constructed buildings. Master Engineer Koxo Nilred was entrusted with the most intense effort, in Ferroc Norda.

His Majesty Aspet consulted with local leadership in each damaged area and approved the plans for reconstruction. He had personally signed the Writ of Confiscation nationalizing Pyfox Consolidated Industries and turning over all of its current and future profits to the Royal Engineering Corps for use in the rebuilding effort. Since there would be no more static portals for accessing The Slice, no dedicated facilities where mages need congregate for such access were necessary. They could be multi-use buildings now, serving as magical conduits when required and then reverting to public spaces like art museums or vaccination clinics at other times.

Five master talismans had been created, one for each Magineer, from which lesser artifacts could be cloned so that no mage had to travel far for a direct pipeline to The Slice. The plan was that eventually every community with an active Lodge of Mages would receive one of the lesser talismans. As with most any sea change, there was resistance to the new schema. Several local mages' associations complained loudly regarding the talisman concept, but they really had little recourse but to adopt it nonetheless.

In the end everyone had to accept CoME's authority whether they liked it or not, as CoME held all the cards. Privately, the Magineers worried what effect the revised system would have on their own prestige and power. Under the historical regimen, while all mages had access to The Slice through their own personal specula, the amount of manna that could be drawn thusly was limited to that usable by a single mage. Only at the Dubers were the manna pipelines spacious enough for tasks that required great magical energy flows.

Now that the physical location of the Dubers was more or less irrelevant, since the major talismans were easily portable, the question of the expense of maintaining the ornate structures arose. While they could yet serve their original function, and were well-suited for it, the fact was that now any location at all could theoretically serve that purpose. In the Dubers' defense, they already had the proper facilities for handling magical energy and, of course, high-bandwidth fiber connections to the RNet. For any project that required access to both arcane energies and digital processing, the Dubers were still the best choice available. Eventually it was decided to retain the Dubers, as much for their symbolic value as their practical.

Forced rebuilding does offer some opportunity for improvement of, or correction of flaws in, previous architectural designs. His Majesty Aspet had essentially opened the Royal Treasury for the reconstruction effort, so the Royal Engineering Corps after consultation with former tenants and local officials were able to go about restoration efforts carefully and methodically. For every building restored or rebuilt, a comprehensive historical profile was assembled, along with suggestions for changes in the new version and desired additional features. The cost estimates were then compared with the final idealized structure and compromises were made when necessary to keep the project within budget.

Once construction began, it proceeded in most cases fairly rapidly. Virtually every construction firm and team in Tragacanth, a small number from Galanga, and even a select few from as far away as Lardonica, were fully engaged in the effort. The highways, carriage lines, and ports thrummed with activity around the clock. While the vile attacks by Namni and Pyfox were horrific in terms of loss of life and property, they were good for the Tragacanthan economy and by extension the economy of Esmia in general.

As with most any large-scale undertaking, there were setbacks. One of these was the discovery, during excavation for a new high-rise building foundation and basement on the extreme eastern edge of Fenurian, of the dome of what appeared to be a gigantic mausoleum. The architectural style of the structure did not match that of any known civilization, past or present; it was therefore deemed of highest cultural significance and all work halted.

At length it was decided to relocate the high-rise entirely and designate the plot where the dome was found an Ancestors' Graveyard. Archaeologists were afraid to penetrate the dome for fear of offending the race whose ancestors were buried here. The only alternative for scholarly study was to excavate all the way down to the entrance. It was not known on which side of the structure this entrance would be located, and there simply was not enough money available given the current climate to fund such a significant dig. So the mystery, for now, remained.

The construction effort in Tragacanth was conducted on a grand scale: so grand, in fact, that laborers from all over N'plork jumped at the opportunity to join in. The tremendous influx of temporary workers took its toll on the limited number of Border Permeability Reduction agents. While the vast majority of people coming in were honest, hard-working folks who just wanted to better the lives of themselves and their families by taking advantage of this once-in-a-lifetime opportunity, there were enough ne'er-do-wells and slackers, and unfortunately a small number of predatory opportunists, that edict enforcement had to double their shifts in some areas to deal with the ones who got past BPR.

One of the least savory of all these opportunist immigrants was a half-ogre who went by the sobriquet 'Sticker.' He was, as the moniker suggests, rather adept with and fond of the use of weapons with sharp points. He kept half a dozen on his person at all times and reveled in their cleaning, polishing, and display to any and all. He being no fool, however, the knives were cleverly concealed when any of the edict enforcement persuasion was about: except on the very rare occasions when one of those was his target. This generally was followed by an immediate and hasty relocation to less hazardous climes.

It was one of these bloody encounters that triggered Sticker's visit to Tragacanth, in fact. He had until recently kept residence in the balmy southern port city of Prilzondra in Asmagon. After a tête-à-tête turned sour with a beach cop on the take, Sticker buried a 20cm planar concave blade between his opponent's shoulders. Whether the cop lived or died, Sticker did not know, or care. What he *did* know was that hanging around would be bad for his health in either case, so he and his close associates jumped aboard a tramp freighter headed up the coast and hopped off again at Qoplebarq, the last port of call before the freighter turned east for Zilond in Spleroste.

From Qoplebarq they made their way at last across the breadth of Tragacanth to the outskirts of Fenurian, where enormous tent and skid-cabin settlements had sprung up to house the workers virtually rebuilding the city from the ground up.

"Whatta we doin' in this dump, boss?" asked one of Sticker's henches: Dross, a kobold.

"We gotta raise some cash for a scheme I got worked up."

"What kind of dough you think we can score in a place like this?"

"Calamity brings recovery, my friend, and recovery means money. Tons of it, all flowing in at once and so difficult to track. All we have to do is put ourselves in the path of that money and pick off a bit here and there. Not enough at a time to raise any alarms. After a while it will add up."

"What we gonna do with all that dough?" asked his other lackey, a hobgoblin named Slag.

"We are going to use it to buy some...equipment that will net us a very large haul. The largest ever, in fact. It will enable us to steal a very well-loaded armored dray."

"An armored dray heist! I ain't been in on one o' them in years!"

"Ah, but the money in the dray is only a side benefit," said Sticker.

"I ain't following. We gonna sell the dray to somebody for even more or somethin'?" asked Dross.

"No, no. I will be placing something else in the dray for safekeeping that we will ransom for a staggering sum. Enough to allow us all to retire in luxury."

"What are you going t' hork that's worth that much dough?"

"Not what, *who*. A cop, by the name of Tol."

"Why would anybody pay that much for a *cop*?"

"He also happens to be a Knight of the Crimson and, more germane, the king's brother."

"We're going to *snatch* the king's brother? Ain't that a little risky?" asked Slag.

"All enterprises of true worth involve a modicum of risk. The risk here is yet small in comparison with the payoff."

"You got somethin' in partic'lar against this cop?"

"Oh, yes. His interference cost me the best operation I ever ran. It was in South Sebacea, Goblinopolis. I had an outfit that repaired betting machines in casinos: all types. We set them up in a special way such that they would only jackpot when someone carrying a tiny transponder pulled the handle or whatnot. The best tech I had—the one who came up with the idea for and built the transponders—was a gnome named Buzzy. That little smekker could build anything. If it involved technology he did it, and did it well. He didn't ask no questions, neither: just did his job."

Dross shrugged, "So what went south, boss?"

"As time went on, I paid Buzzy better and better, 'cause he was raking in the dough for me right and left. Some nights we'd bring in 50K. I guess I paid him too well, though, because somewhere along the line he developed an expensive drug habit. I think it was lickin' some smekkin' toadstools or whatever they do down in those Lardonican border towns. Anyways, one day he got totally stoned on his little gnomish butt and wandered into a casino we didn't have a contract with. He had one of the transponder sets with him and tried to force open a machine so's he could stick the coin slot trigger in there and collect. Of course they caught him and called the cops. This Tol smekker shows up and not only collars Buzzy, but figures out my whole scheme in, like, twenty minutes. I had to drop everything and run for the border toot sweet. Buzzy got six years; out in three, but somehow he got cleaned up in the joint and went to a polytechnic after he got sprung. He's a smekkin' engineer in one of those secret factories in the mountains, last I heard."

"How you gonna get this Tol in the right place to snatch 'im?"

"I'm still workin' on it. By the time we scrape enough cash together here, I'll have it all mapped out."

"So, what's the scam gonna be?" asked Slag, who had wandered off to proposition some nearby females without success and just limped back up.

"Well, you see those supply drays comin' in?" answered Sticker, "They are crammed full of valuable commodities that will fetch a tidy sum on the black market."

"I ain't seen no black market here, boss."

"We're about to start one. We do that by buying off one of the drivers to drop his load in a place more...convenient for our purposes. I leased a small warehouse over there about a kilometer. Once we get a steady supplier, we'll expand into larger quarters and start raking in some serious dough."

"You sure this'll work, boss?" asked Dross a little doubtfully.

"Of course it will work. I've set up this identical operation after two major sea storms in Lardonica and a wildfire I started myself that burned a sizable swath of the southern coast of Asmagon. Nothin' to it, once you get your rhythm."

He put his arms around the henches' shoulders, "There's a world of meaningful profit waitin' for us here, my friends. Let us now reap that which we did not sow."

Chapter the Second

in which Tol and Selpla discover one another in depth

The cherish-fruit wine was delicious. Most everything about that evening was delicious, to be perfectly honest, and what wasn't delicious was intriguing. The intriguing part was that Selpla actually *did* have some additional information on Morianella—information that seemed to corroborate part of what Plåk had told them.

"I came across this small collection of copies of manuscripts pulled up in a chest by some deep-sea fishermen dredging the sea floor for slime rays: you know, the kind they use to make industrial adhesives," she said, as they curled up together on the sofa in her parlor.

"I heard tell that in Litria—mostly Grosyem, I think—they cut the eye stalks and fin warts off those things and eat them with seaweed," Tol interjected, "Charge a ridiculous amount of money for them, too. I'd rather snack on my own fried toe fungus,"

Selpla wrinkled her nose. "I don't find either very appetizing. Anyway, these manuscripts were apparently ledgers and journals from the government offices in Morianella. One of them, which I have a second-generation copy of here, actually has the minutes of a meeting taken by the city council, or whatever they called themselves, shortly before the disaster. I had an ancient languages scholar translate it to Goblish for me; that's the part written in red."

Tol held sheets up in the light and read out loud. "Archmage contracted to remove harbor debris asked for a score of days to accomplish, due to safety concerns. Council inquired if any quicker methods existed, as two large vessels were on their way from Spleroste and would have to wait offshore for an unacceptable period if the clearing took that long. Council voted seven to two to approve faster procedure, with understanding that it posed more risk."

He laid the papers on a table. "Wow. Looks like things did go down the way Plåk said. I guess I'll have to downgrade his case file from murder to unintentional people-slaughter."

"That will be a great relief to him after nine hundred years, no doubt."

They both laughed.

"Nine hundred years," Tol continued after a moment's silence, "It's always amazed me that he remembers anything at all from that long ago. I've only lived five percent that long and my brain is already so full of memories I don't think there's room for much more."

Selpla got that look on her face all males, no matter the species, innately recognize. "I hope you have room for at least one more," she said in a low, husky voice while pulling her pretty laced chemise over her head. "I'll try my best to make it worth the storage space."

Tol picked her up by the waist and carried her effortlessly over to the strategically-positioned daybed nearby. "I've already evicted some useless stuff about my first-grade teacher's bad fashion sense to make room."

The next morning found Tol still there. After breakfast they both decided that if this was to go on any longer they'd better do the 'getting to know you' thing and be done with it.

"I'll start, I guess," Selpla announced over the rim of her cup, "As you probably are already aware, being a detective and all, my father is a wealthy architect named Erminian. He designed a lot of the larger buildings in Goblinopolis, Cladimil, and Dresmak, not to mention Xovcastra in Asmagon, Erolossma and Woklopen in Solemadrina, Zilond in Spleroste, Yiks Island in Frespiola, Rebrugge in Hividz, and a bunch more. He even designed the newest wing of the Royal Complex for your brother."

"Ah yes, the 'Aspet loves Tragacanth' wing. It's got dioramas of historical events, famous places, busts and paintings of famous people, and so on. It's sort of secondary schola history class all in one shot. Or so he tells me. I haven't actually been there."

"I heard there's a diorama devoted to you shutting down Namni and Pyfox, too."

"Really? Who would want to see that? All I did was smash an ugly statue that deserved to die."

"Apparently it was heroic enough to get you knighted. Must have been pretty significant."

"You were there, too. How heroic did it appear to you?"

"I couldn't really see much over Kurg and Lom."

"Oh, well," Tol shrugged, "Those are the breaks. So, how did you get from spoiled rich kid to celebrity reporter?"

"I have three brothers, all older: Ikren, Fatuhl, and Basik. All three of them became architects—graduated from Tropsalla Technical College, up the street. They're spread out all over the world now: Ovinis, Rublosq, and Spleroste, respectively, last I heard: all doing their thing quite successfully."

"You didn't feel the urge to design buildings, eh?"

"I tried my hand at it, believe it or not. I am just not the architect type. My buildings looked like something that might spring up out of the cesspool in The Effluent: oddly-shaped and probably impossible to build."

"I'd be willing to bet you're better at that sort of thing than *I* am. I can't draw a straight line with *two* rulers."

She giggled. "Straight lines played no part in my designs, I can promise you. So anyway, I was the black woolbeast of the family in several ways. I was the only female, as my mother died when I was four; I was the only non-architect; and I was not at all a good student, whereas my brothers were Dean's List all the way. I did attend universitas on and off for years—I went through most of the majors in the catalog, in fact—but I think it broke my father's heart when I finally decided to take my degree in journalism at Loca Arts Institute instead of mathematics or one of the sciences at Tropsalla Tech. He did pay for my college, true, but my graduation party was nothing like the ones my brothers got. There are a lot of architects in my father's contact database; not so many journalists."

"Not a real happenin' scene, eh?"

"Mostly elderly friends of the family and relatives who didn't think I could stick with anything long enough to finish a degree. It was over in an hour, and that includes the photo op."

"Bummer. I'll bet I could have spiced things up."

"My father would never have invited a common edict enforcement officer. Of course, now that you're a Knight of the Crimson and brother to the king you're on the 'A' list."

"Funny thing, snobbery. So, what was your childhood like?"

"We spent a lot of time after mother died in places like Aspolia and Terimpu, although Goblinopolis was always our home base, as it were. The different cities sort of blur together for me: I've memories of people and buildings and such, but I can't tell you exactly what city we were in at the time they happened. I really didn't have any close friends because we moved around so much. Father had to drag us along wherever his job took him, although we did have a live-in nanny and teacher. I got to see him a lot more that way, though, so looking back I can't really complain. Also, I had been around the world by the time I was ten."

"I went to Fenurian once," Tol said, a trace of irony in his voice.

"There's not a lot left of it, I hear. That's a shame. There were nice galleries and workshops there. It was something of an artists' colony, or at least that part that wasn't high tech factories, anyway. I hope it doesn't lose its personality when it gets rebuilt."

"Personality comes from people. As long as the people are still there, the buildings won't matter that much. It may evolve or revolve or convolve, but it will still be recognizable as Fenurian."

"I hope you're right. I was rather fond of the old city."

"So, your childhood was spent globe-hopping from one exotic port of call to the next. How did you get interested in journalism?" Tol asked, taking another piece of toasted flokmeal dough.

"Our house, wherever we lived, was always full of people in the social register. I got to know a lot of them and hear their stories. Gradually I came to realize that investigating and retelling those stories was something I enjoyed and had a talent for. At first it was just the glamorous people who interested me. When I started asking questions and getting more proficient in background profiling, however, I found that there was always something in every person's life I didn't expect; some sad or tragic or scandalous event that made the investigation at least as interesting as the story itself. I always loved the videoz newscasters, too. When I got into college and discovered that the way you became one of those was to major in journalism, everything just fell into place for me, career-wise."

"You always seem pretty relaxed on the news."

"Actually, I still get nervous in front of the camera. But we have teleprompters, acting coaches, and a whole bunch of tech stuff to keep us from crashing and burning *too* often."

"Yikes. All that support just to read the news. Must be harder than it looks."

"Well, the difficulty is that you only get one chance to read it and make it sound good, because even though the broadcasts are usually delayed, we don't have the luxury of multiple takes most of the time. That *is* a lot harder than you might think. Especially when there are difficult-to-pronounce names of people or places. Most of the work, though, is investigating the story and putting all the facts together in some form that is interesting. There are also a bunch of people behind the scenes: camera operators, directors, copy writers, fact checkers, editors, proofers, gaffers, light techs, sound techs, and a whole lot more.

"How do you *pay* all those people?"

"Advertising, mostly. Those ads for cereal and prams and razzle that annoy or entertain you cost the advertisers a lot of money, depending on the length of the ad, where we run it, and how often. Without them there wouldn't be any videoz, like it or not."

"I suppose I never thought much about it."

Selpla poured them both another mug of stankabru. "So, enough about me. Let's hear your story. Up until the Pyfox thing, I mean."

Tol took a long sip and sighed. "Compared to your hoity-toity exotic locales and celebrities in the bathroom childhood, it ain't much. Growing up I was the jock and Aspet was the geek. I played sports and he spent all his time futzin' around with circuit boards and gizmos with dials, switches, and little green screens. Now, of course, he's the smekking King and I..."

"You're the Premier Knight Protector of the Crimson! For the love of Hork, that's mighty impressive by itself."

"Maybe, but who gave that to me? My brother the geek. My point is that I thought he was wimpy and worthless, albeit very smart, when we were kids and look how wrong that turned out to be."

"You were the older brother. You were probably just mad because he didn't want to play sports with you."

"A little, I guess. I was also mad because I wanted to do some of the stuff *he* was doing, but I didn't understand it. I sort of took that out on him."

"You're kidding. Really?"

"Yep. Used to sneak in and mess around with his electronic stuff when he wasn't home, but I could never even figure out how it worked. It made me angry."

"Too bad you didn't have any sisters. They would have realized what was going on and probably helped you two to communicate."

"There...there *were* two sisters, once."

"Two sisters? What happened to them?"

Tol stood up and walked over to a window to look out at the bright sunshine shimmering and dancing over Selpla's flower gardens. "Ever hear that childhood vaccinations can be harmful?"

Selpla thought for a moment. "I remember some fear-mongering about that a few years back, but it was all disproven."

"It isn't all malarkey; they just spread the wrong alarm. I had two sisters, twins, named Resu and Vesu. They were the youngest.

There was a really tough strain of yample beast fever going around—one of those that had spread to goblins—and mother had taken the twins in for their vaccinations. They were about a year and a half old at the time. A feverish yample beast actually came crashing through the wall of the clinic and trampled nearly everyone in the waiting room. My sisters were the only fatalities. After the death rituals we were never again allowed to speak of yample beasts or the twins around the house. Any mention of either set my father off in a fit of pique. My mother refused to discuss them at all."

"That's simultaneously the most tragic and yet darkly amusing family story I believe I've ever heard," Selpla said, taking his hands in hers in sympathy. Tol shook his head, as though to clear it of the memories, and then continued. "Aspet the brain won a full academic scholarship to Mernalview Polytechnic and majored in..." he pulled a laminated card out of his beat-up old wallet and read it with some effort: "Digital Technology, with a minor in Cultural History."

"It's so sweet that you carry a copy of his diploma around with you," Selpla said. Tol ignored this.

"When I finished secondary schola I'd had it with books and classrooms, on the other hand. I enlisted in a Tragacanth Inland Guard regiment and served most of that four-year hitch at Fort Ullglava in the absolute middle of smekkin' nowhere."

"Oh, yeah, I visited there once on a follow-up about a soldier who got into a fight on the GRUC. Not exactly a social destination. Laudable grain fields, though," Selpla smirked.

"The farmers' daughters were about the only perk. After I got out I went through the EE academy in Goblinopolis and I've been doin' that ever since."

"Where were you born?" Selpla asked, sipping her stankabru.

"On Berquin Avenue in South Sebacea. A couple blocks north of the corrections facility."

"Hard to think of a tougher neighborhood than that."

"True. Except that even the street thugs seemed strangely respectful of children. I don't remember any kids getting snatched or even particularly harassed by anyone but other kids. Of course at the time I thought that was normal, but as my cop career progressed I found it more and more atypical of rough neighborhoods. Being an adult on Berquin was a daily crap shoot. Being a kid was not. I don't know why. I do remember the heavy, concertina wire-topped fences around the scholas and the armed crossing guards, though."

"Depressing."

"The nice thing about being a kid, as I said, is that you think whatever is happening to you is normal so you don't worry much about how everyone else does it. My first girlfriend lived on Berquin, too: three houses up from us. Her name was…Ki…Kim… Kimia. Haven't thought about her in years. How about you? Long string of jilted lovers?"

"Not really. Most of the guys I met were society jloks who lived in their own little cocoons of wealth, insulated from the real world. That was acceptable when I was the same way, but after I became a reporter and found out how most people live—scrabbling day to day just to make enough money to eat and pay the rent— their shallow self-absorption turned me off. I'm not sure whether I could make it on my own if I suddenly got tossed out on the streets myself, but I find people on the outside of the golden curtain to be much more genuine and trustworthy in general. By that I mean verbal contracts and such are more prevalent and more likely to be honored among the common people. Many of them still believe that a goblin's word is his bond. You won't find any of that in the society pages. It's written contracts for every little thing, and woe betide any who leave the tiniest loophole."

"So, no serious relationships, then?"

"Depends on what you mean by 'serious.' If you mean 'relationships that moved into the pre-nuptial stage,' I've had several. I've been engaged to be married at least six times, in fact; I've lost count. If, on the other hand, you mean relationships where I actually intended to spend the rest of my life with someone; no. The engagement game is just another high society convention: you give a girl an expensive ring and in return you get to call her your fiancé for a while. It doesn't really change your relationship, and when she gets tired of you and another goblin offers her a nice ring, the players change places on the stage. The play, however, never stops. How about you? Any near-missus?"

"Nah. I had a few short-term girlfriends here and there: mostly waitresses, shop clerks, and one animal control tech, but I never felt like I could offer much of a life to them on a beat cop's salary. When it became obvious I wasn't going to propose anytime soon they wisely decided to look elsewhere. Plus, being a cop's mate means you never know whether your spouse is going to make it home from work in one piece. That additional constant worry is too much for most girls, and I can't blame them for feelin' that way. It takes a strong goblin to be the mate of a street cop."

"Is it really that common for a girl to 'shop around' like that?"

"Don't misunderstand: it's not that they are overly material or superficial; it's just that being married is often the easiest way to survive out there. Combining your efforts and incomes can mean the difference between living on the street and living in a nice little house. Girls are looking for husbands for a variety of reasons, romantic love certainly included, but they can't afford to waste their prime child-bearing years courting, or being courted by, someone who is not mate potential. I've never had a problem with that; pragmatism is an essential survival skill."

"That's a lot to think about. Thanks."

"No prob. Wanna grab some lunch somewhere? We can go to one of your favorites around here; if I can afford it, anyway."

Selpla laughed, "Let's hit Eske's. It might have been a little steep for a Sebacea street cop, but it's well within the means of a Crimson Knight Special Investigator with an office in Justice Hall. I happen to know between your EE salary and your Crimson stipend you're doing quite well for yourself these days."

"Oh, yeah. I forget about that sometimes."

"When are you going to move out of your little bachelor pad in Sebacea and into something more suited to your new station?"

"I dunno. Hadn't given it a lot of thought. That's my home. I guess when I'm no longer a bachelor, if that ever happens."

They sat at Selpla's favorite table in Eske's, an upscale bistro in the heart of Tropsalla, across from the Rococo entrance to Tropsalla Leisure Club and Gardens. Selpla ordered a green salad with crumbled Askadeon curds while Tol picked at his artfully-arranged grilled filet of growling-beast with fresh bumpershoot vinaigrette.

"Am I supposed to eat this or compose an incisive essay about it?" he asked.

"I doubt it matters to Eske, so long as you pay for it at the end, Tol." Selpla replied, giggling. A sudden thought struck her. "Where did you get the name Tol-u-ol, anyway? Doesn't really sound very traditional to me."

"In fact, tradition was what got me here. I was named for my grandfather Tol-u-mez and my grandmother Olona in the family tradition started by my great-great-grandfather, who was lousy at picking names but fond of hyphens. He thought they sounded all high-falootin.' How did you get yours?"

Selpla pushed a curd crumb around her plate with a fork tine. "My father designed a resort on Yiks Island off the coast of Frespiola called the 'Sellestra Placidum.' At the time it was his most elegant and famous creation; it essentially cemented his reputation as a world-class architect. I had the fortune, or misfortune, to be born two weeks after the ribbon-cutting, when his name was being bandied about by every major architectural review magazine in connection with said resort." She shrugged, "I am named in honor of that achievement: Sel-Pla for Sellestra Placidum."

Tol ruminated over this for a moment. "Well, I've heard a lot worse reasons for peoples' names. I ran across one street kid whose name was Denova Here. He told me he was named that because when they gave the birth registration form to his father, he saw the blank line that said 'Baby's Name Here' and thought he was just following instructions."

Selpla almost spit her Semia-leaf infusion all over the table. She reached for her notebook. "I've *got* to work that into a story somewhere." She stared out the window for a moment. "What about your parents? What were they like?"

"My mom was from a farming family. She grew up on a mixed-grain spread in the northern Espwe foothills. She and dad met when she came into Sebacea with her parents on a supply run. Dad was the assistant manager of *Furgo's Feed 'N' Seed, the largest feed store in the Goblinopolis municipal area*, as he was fond of telling people."

"Did you work there as a kid?"

"Yep. I liked stocking the shelves in the supply room best. There was something about making sure every item was on the correct shelf and displayed properly that I found satisfying, I guess."

Tol paid the check and reached across the table for her hands. "I have to go soon. I have a meeting at two back at Justice Hall." He smiled his best smile. "So, are we go for another date?"

Selpla beamed back at him. "I think I can work that into my schedule. I get to pick this time."

"Fair enough. Got anything in mind?"

"Oh, yes. Rock-climbing. Northern Bungash."

"*Rock*-climbing? As in, climbing up the side of big rocks?"

"Of course, silly. It's a blast. I've been doing it since I was a teenager."

"Rock-climbing...Well, as long it's with you, I'll do just about anything. Rock-climbing it is."

"Great. I'll meet you tomorrow at your office right after work and we'll go gear shopping. There's an excellent extreme sports store two blocks from Justice Hall.

"Extreme sports, eh? Sounds like just another day on the beat."

Chapter the Third

in which Sir Tol-u-ol answers a summons and meets a real live titan

The northern margins of the Bungash Mountains form one of the hotspots for rock-climbing in Tragacanth. The three northernmost peaks, Bikosh, Basgule, and Bejlog, were each uniquely suited for the sport in their own way. The northwestern approach to Bejlog was perhaps the most difficult of them all, as it involved two significant overhangs, the uppermost of which sported a good ten-meter undercut. This approach, nicknamed "The Hanging Judge," was the one Selpla chose for their second date.

Tol was a genuine tough guy, with a reputation for tackling anything and anyone that needed tackling, but as he stood at the base of Bejlog and stared up past the two overhangs to the summit, he wondered why anyone would climb this thing voluntarily. To rescue someone, yes. For fun, no. Yet, that's what the little videoz reporter standing next to him was cheerfully suggesting. She must be tougher than she looks, Tol thought.

Tol couldn't see any point to it, but if it was going to happen he would do it right. He'd been forced to do a fair amount of rappelling in the military, as technical rescue had been one of his specialties, so he figured he could at least grasp the basics of getting down. Getting up would be somewhat more problematic.

Selpla was an experienced climber, and she turned out to be quite adept as an instructor, as well. She gave Tol an intensive hour-long lecture on equipment, procedures, and safety, followed by some hands-on instruction—which led to something else for a while—but eventually they got back on track.

Properly equipped and rigged, they started up the mountain. After about a quarter hour of hard climbing, Tol's comm suddenly started beeping. He couldn't answer it right away, so he let it go to messages. When they took their first breather, he listened to the messages. Sliding the comm back into its protective case, he turned to Selpla. "We have to go down. Now. I've been ordered to report to Fenurian.

"I thought you were on leave," Selpla pouted.

"I am. It has been rescinded."

"Rescinded by whom?"

"By the king, to whom I owe a knight's fealty. He's more than just my brother and my king now; he represents the Crown to which I have sworn my life, and as a common jlok I take my oaths very seriously. We have to go. I'll drop you off in Goblinopolis and hop on the train to Fenurian."

"I want to go with you!"

"I know you do, and I'd love to have you along. But this is an official Crimson Deployment, which means battle may be imminent. No civilians allowed, for safety reasons."

"That's not fair!"

"Fairness has nothing to do with it. We have a responsibility to protect civilians from potential injury or death. A Crimson deployment could well involve that sort of threat."

"I could use my press pass."

"That's between you and the Crimson Knights Public Affairs Officer. If you do show up and put yourself in danger, though, you may distract me, which could get *me* killed. Think about that."

"Okay. I don't want you to get killed. That would be a very bad thing."

"I have to agree."

"At least tell me what's going on in Fenurian."

"I honestly don't know. All the message said was that I was to report to Fenurian immediately by the most expeditious means available and that a briefing would be supplied on arrival. That probably means that whatever is going on is state secret. In peacetime most of our missions are state secret, in fact."

"I accept that, but I don't have to like it."

"No, you don't. I'm kind of happy that you don't, actually." He kissed her. "Don't worry; it's probably just some investigative thing where the actor or actors have already fled. As a Knight Protector I don't actually get involved in purely military matters. I'm sort of the king's personal cop, really."

"Yeah? Well don't forget that you're my personal cop, too."

"*You* just like the handcuffs."

Selpla blushed furiously. "No comment."

Tol and Selpla raced all the way back to her house in Goblinopolis with Tol's light bar flashing. He dropped her off and headed over to the carriage station.

"I need a ticket for an express to Fenurian as soon as possible," he told the ticket clerk.

"The only express to Fenurian doesn't leave until nine tonight."

"Then I'll need a private carriage."

The clerk looked at him and frowned, "We don't dispatch private carriages just because someone asks for one, sir. It isn't that easy."

Tol flashed his Crimson Knight badge. "Understandable, but I'm not asking."

"Wha…what time would like to leave, Sir Knight?" the clerk stammered.

"*Now* works for me."

"Please have a seat. I'll arrange it. Departure will be in about fifteen minutes."

"See how *easy* that was?"

Even with a private express carriage benefiting from Crimson right-of-way, it still took the rest of the day to get to Fenurian. The carriage terminal had been destroyed by an aftershock; there were a couple of military tents serving as the station for the time being. A driver and two officials met Tol there. Koxo Nilred of the Royal

Engineering Corps and Dosk Belbomit of the Royal Society for Cultural Antiquities sat in the back of the government diplomatic pram with Tol to brief him on the situation.

"Apparently," explained Koxo after introductions had been completed, "One of the magically-induced quakes opened a chasm along a major fault running parallel to the Masron Mountains near the northern end. A child had fallen into the chasm and, while not seriously injured, required a technical rescue team to extricate. The team had glimpsed what appeared to be evidence of non-natural structures further along in the chasm and notified the RSCA, who dispatched Bosk, here, to investigate. The next day a trio of titans suddenly appeared and claimed the area inside the chasm as their own, on the grounds that it was an ancient titan city that contained a burial site and was therefore subject to the Ancestors Graveyard edict." He motioned for the other passenger to continue.

"The RSCA does not look favorably on this petition, for obvious reasons: the area contains a potential treasure house of antiquities and must be explored and catalogued with that in mind. Preliminary reports are that it consists of multiple large underground complexes, each filled with who knows what manner of historically valuable artifacts."

Nilred finished up. "The titan position does not appear flexible and more of them arrive every day. This has the potential to turn ugly, so we asked the king for help. He sent these sealed instructions for you."

Tol broke the Royal Seal and opened the single sheet. It read:

Greetings, Sir Tol-u-ol, from His Majesty Aspet I.

You are hereby assigned to a high-priority diplomatic mission, the essential details of which should have been revealed to you by now. I want the titans handled with utmost respect and diplomacy, but bearing in mind the almost inestimable historical value of this newly-discovered site at the same time. Find a compromise acceptable to all, and don't get yourself or others hurt in the process. I do not trust anyone else with this mission, which is why I yanked you in off leave. Selpla will get over it.

Any supplies or personnel you need for this mission will be handled by Crimson Logistics. You have an unlimited writ, but please spend with discretion. The writ is unlimited; the treasury is not.

Thank you for your service, Knight Protector. You have my respect and affection, always.

Aspet I, King of Tragacanth

Tol folded the missive and tucked it into his overjack pocket. There was something else in there. It was a pocket he hadn't used in a while; he wondered what it could be. He felt around and realized it was a pen. Not just any pen, though: it was Eyejay. He chuckled. "I thought you were sent back to the Quartermaster's Office when I got promoted." There was a pause as the long-dormant audio systems came back online. "No such good fortune," was the somewhat shaky reply. Tol smiled. This assignment just got a little more interesting.

Titans were semi-mythical to most of Tragacanth. Everyone knew about them, but very few had actually laid eyes on one, despite their enormous size. Titans grew anywhere from three and a half to five meters in height, yet they were offshoots of the same ancestral prototypical species on which all the other races of N'plork were based. For whatever reason, they began to grow larger and larger, leaving the other races far behind. Other than that they were ridiculously tall and, legend had it, capable of quite a lot of destruction when riled, no one knew much about these giants. That was all about to change.

Tol had never seen a titan before, so he didn't really know the proper way to greet one. He wasn't very good at formal, so he decided to go casual but polite. It's difficult to be casual when you are accustomed to being thought of as a big, intimidating person and suddenly you're shaking hands with something that could probably crumple you up and dribble you like a bouncerball. The polite part, though, comes quite naturally.

By the time Tol and the others rolled up, there were two dozen titans and twice as many government workers milling about. He stared in mute amazement at the sheer size and physique of the giants. He definitely did not want to make any of them mad. He only hoped they were sufficiently intelligent that they could be reasoned with. The legends made them sound like mindless brutes. He gathered his wits and approached with what he hoped was not too obvious trepidation. He held out his hands in friendship.

"I Tol-u-ol. I friend."

One of the titans looked at him and shook his head. He turned to another one and said, "I don't see how they expect us to negotiate when they keep sending over morons. This one doesn't even understand basic verb conjugation."

Tol dropped his hands. "I was trying to communicate at some minimal level in case you didn't speak much Goblish. I can see now that won't be necessary."

The first titan sighed. "Thank the gods. We were beginning to wonder if the rest of Tragacanth was inhabited by idiots."

"Well now that you've taken a whizz on my diplomatic approach, I'll just drop it. I'm not much of a diplomat, anyway. Getting down to brass tacks, what are your demands?"

"We haven't demanded anything. We are petitioning for the right to occupy this underground urban complex, built by our ancestors but lost in our surviving historical records, under the terms of the Ancestral Graveyard Edict."

Tol's detective sensibilities kicked in.

"If the city was lost, how did you know we'd found it?"

"You tripped the burglar alarm."

"I don't hear any alarm. Besides, titans are still arriving: that means some of them were days away when the entrance was violated. How could you hear anything from that far off?"

"Ultra-low frequency pulses," the titan replied, "They can travel for hundreds or even thousands of kilometers. Since we have lived for millennia in small, isolated colonies, we developed the ability to hear and communicate with ULF pulses."

"How do you generate them?"

"Most often by Tympanum Majorum. That's a huge two-headed drum where the tension on one head is adjustable with a foot pedal. As the drummer hits the Tympanum with large, soft-headed mallets, he changes the timbre, pitch, rhythm, and tempo according to a code we developed millennia ago. The recipients, once alerted, wear odd-looking ear coverings that filter out everything else to increase the signal-to-noise ratio of the pulse. To a goblin it would sound something like a faint distant *throom*."

"How did you come up with the idea for that?"

"Sea Behemoths taught us. They have built-in Tympana and use them to communicate clear around the world underwater with ULF pulses."

"Sea Behemoths..." Tol replied thoughtfully. He wasn't sure he was buying that explanation, but he would give them the benefit of the doubt for now. The titan, whose name was Tartag, took Tol over and showed him the large Tympana colored to look like stones and mounted in natural-esque stone towers taller than the surrounding landscape. They were set to vibrating by strong puffs of air directed up through tubes from a pressurized chamber somewhere, presumably as a result of the intrusion by the lost child or his rescuers.

"That's very clever," Tol said, "You heard that from how far away?"

"Me personally? Only about fifty kilometers, in the north-central Masrons—but some of our kin from as far away as the Tudmash Marsh are expected to answer the summons.

"Wow. That's about as far as you can get from here and still be in Tragacanth."

"Indeed. It is quite feasible that titans from other continents could even hear the alarm, but they will wait for those of us who live here to send out invitations once the city has been reclaimed. It is our way."

"You mean this sort of thing has happened before?"

"Yes. Twice, according to our records, has an ULF-pulse been employed in summons. Not from this location, however."

"Begging forgiveness for my inexcusable ignorance, but what it the normal lifespan of a titan?"

Tartag seemed pleased at Tol's humility. "Ignorance is inexcusable only when no efforts are made to correct it. We live on the order of 150-200 turnings of the seasons, normally, although a few of the great elders claim to be over 300. Without verifiable records we cannot be certain. I am recently turned 112; of that I *am* certain."

"Titans are longer-lived than goblins, then. That is interesting, given that the scholars say we came from the same stock."

"Indeed, our wise also say that we are all cousins. Titan folk belief is that our longevity is due to the fact that we eat meat only on rare occasion. This is not so much for religious or ethical reasons, but more due to the difficulty in obtaining enough meat for our large appetites. However, there is no scholarly evidence to support this; only anecdotal."

"Titans sure don't seem to want to mingle with the rest of society. Why is that?" Tol asked.

Tartag hesitated before answering. "As you have already alluded to, Titans are rather different from the other races. We have found that these differences seem to cause anxiety amongst non-titans. We don't wish to be the source of anxiety, nor deal with its negative consequences. As a result, we've found that isolation is the most comfortable course; the path of least resistance, if you like."

"You seem to be highly civilized and cultured. I'm certain any distrust or dislike would dissolve rather quickly once contact was made. We are not barbarians or brutes, at least for the most part."

"Alas, isolationism is now so deeply rooted in titan society that removing it would be a significant undertaking."

"I would certainly be willing to help titans reintegrate into society if they decide to do so. In the meantime, let's see what we can negotiate regarding your claim."

"I find you a most reasonable person, Tol-u-ol. I can see why your king dispatched you specifically to handle this situation. He must know you well and trust you."

"Yeah, I suppose he does, although there are times when I don't understand why."

"Sometimes the wise see in us that which we cannot see in ourselves."

"I can't argue with you there."

"So, while we understand the titans' desire to reclaim this magnificent city, the law is very clearly on RSCA's side here," said Bosk Belbomit. "Allow me to quote: 'Places of habitation which have been declared abandoned by dint of no occupation and no registered claim to ownership within the last thirty diurnal cycles are subject to review by the Royal Society for Cultural Antiquities, who are charged with discovering and preserving such artifacts as have historic value prior to releasing the site for new ownership. If the site itself shall be considered historically important, that site and sufficient right-of-way to provide access to it shall become the property of the Tragacanthan government, subject to RSCA management.'"

"Yes," countered Tartag, "But under the 'exceptions' clause later in the edict it states: 'Nothing in this Edict shall be construed to interfere with or supersede the Ancestors' Graveyard Edict, wherein any site containing bona-fide remains interred in a facility or area dedicated to that purpose shall be the sole property of the extant race who occupied it formerly, at such time sufficient claim shall be laid.'"

"So, you are formally claiming this entire site as an Ancestors' Graveyard?" asked Bosk.

"Not exactly. We are petitioning that no excavations or removals take place until it has been established precisely where the interments lie, so that no defilement of our ancestors occurs. Once that petition has been granted we will make a decision as to the extent of our occupation claims."

"The RSCA does not feel this to be necessary. We have scholars who specialize in removing artifacts carefully and with great respect. If and when those scholars encounter any remains or ritual artifacts used in the interment process, we will notify a representative of the titans so that they may take possession after cataloguing has been completed."

"Your idea of 'great respect' and ours differ significantly," said Tartag, with some visible agitation, "You would notify us only after our ancestors had been defiled, at which point the damage is done and irreversible. This we cannot accept."

Bosk stood and seemed about to pound the table with his hand. Tol decided this had gone far enough and was about to intervene when a swirling, shimmering manifestation appeared directly in front of him. It resolved into an odd-looking smooth-skinned biped with longish fur all over its head. Tol rolled his eyes. The others stared in frank amazement.

"Greetings, Plåk," said Tol, "What brings you to the middle of an important negotiation? Did you want to try another earthquake spell to liven things up?"

"Nice to see you, too, Tol. Bite me. I just dropped by to tell you that I've poked around in that huge hole and I think the answers to your questions are all down there."

"So, you think we should mount an expedition?"

"If you want to get all fancy-schmancy. I'd just go poke around."

"Yes, well, you aren't subject to being pummeled, asphyxiated, or lost, so 'poking around' is a bit more practical for you."

"As you like. Gotta split." He sparkled into oblivion. Tol turned back to the table as though nothing had happened.

"Thank you both for your input, gentles. As you may know, the Crown of Tragacanth has sent me here to negotiate a fair and equitable settlement…"

"Which cannot ignore the enormous cultural value of this site!" Belbomit shouted, having completely forgotten about Plåk in his agitation.

Tol put on his best edict enforcement scowl and glared at the RSCA representative until he sat down again meekly. When he was once again firmly in charge, Tol continued.

"Now, as I said, I am here to negotiate a settlement that is satisfactory to both sides. I won't be ignoring anyone or anything germane to the issues." Tol reviewed what he had just said and marveled at how unexpectedly lucid it was.

"I propose to begin by forming an exploratory party whose purpose it is to establish whether there are titan remains to be discovered and, if so, where precisely they are located."

"Wait," said Koxo, "You're taking the advice whatever that thing was?" Tol glared at him and continued. "This party shall consist of myself, a representative of the RSCA, a representative of the titans, and a representative of the Royal Engineering Corps as they have jurisdiction here until such time as the further disposition of the site has been determined."

"And who is to make that determination?" demanded Belbomit.

"These lands belong to the King of Tragacanth; I am His personal representative here. As a Knight of the Crimson and a member of the Tragacanthan Royal Family, *I* will decide that matter, subject of course to review and confirmation by His Majesty and CoME. Is that clear to everyone?"

Tol seemed to have grown almost to titan size during his speech. Everyone, even the titans, nodded their mute assent.

"Good. Now, if I can get representatives from all concerned parties to meet with me here in ten minutes, we will plan the exploratory expedition. Mr. Nilred, may we requisition supplies from you for the expedition? I have an open Treasury writ for that purpose."

"Certainly, Sir Tol-u-ol. I will bring a manifest of the available gear for your selections."

An hour later Tol, Nilred, Episk Grato (for RSCA), and Tartag stood at the edge of the crevasse that led into the underground city, carrying full packs and hung with ropes, hooks, lanterns, and other assorted tools of exploration. They synchronized timepieces and comm units with those remaining at the surface. "Keep one of these comms tuned to arcane and one to conventional," instructed Tol, indicating two commercial comm base stations, "That way we can use either encryption channel without having to pre-arrange it."

"All right gentles, we're ready to get started. I would like for Mr. Nilred to take the lead, as he is primarily concerned with our safety in respect to the structural integrity of the caves and associated formations. Please follow any instructions he may give in that regard. If we get separated, the smaller party stays in place while the larger searches. Do not wander off on your own or take any side trips without reporting your intentions to me first. The authentication slash covert trouble code word is *Tropsalla*. That means if you need help but can't say that out loud or want to verify that who you're talking to is really one of us, use that word or ask us for it."

"Why would we need precautions such as these?" asked Episk.

"Hopefully we won't," Tol replied, "But when heading into an unknown tactical situation it's best to be prepared for any reasonable eventuality. Gear up!"

With Tol and Koxo in the lead, the explorers stepped down into the crevasse.

Chapter the Fourth

in which Boogla uncovers an ongoing crime and the King travels to an unusual woods

"Good morning, Your Majesty," Boogla said in a sleepy voice, rubbing her eyes, "Did you sleep well?"

Aspet ran his fingers down her arm. "I always sleep well after... that. How about you?"

"Like a baby. I had no idea how fulfilling married life was going to be."

Aspet laughed. "Nor did I. I'm looking forward to fulfilling you for a long time to come."

She grinned. "Don't get me excited or you won't get any work done this morning, my king."

"I guess I better watch myself, then. The Solemadrina trade delegation talks start today."

"You've got a Minister for International Commerce. He can handle them just fine."

"Yes, I know, but the formalities have to be observed, and that includes the monarch formally opening the meetings. Goameel would never forgive me if I deviated on a point of protocol."

"He is a bit of stuffed shirt, isn't he?"

"I can't really blame him. Some of the trade delegations he deals with are downright rigid about that sort of thing. He needs to be that way in turn to keep face. If he's seen as weak or out of favor they will tear him apart in negotiations and that hurts the entire country. If I can keep the price of woven baskets, dray wheels, and trolda sprouts down just by showing up wearing the crown, I think I owe that to the Tragacanthan economy."

"Oh, very well. Duty calls, and all that. There will be tonight."

"Indeed there will. I have the string quartet scheduled for eight to nine, on the terrace."

"Oooh," she squealed, "That's so romantic. I think I love you."

"Glad to hear it. Keeps the rumors down, you know?"

Goameel Jigha was a distinguished career bureaucrat who accepted the Minister for International Commerce position when the previous MIC retired upon Aspet's ascension. He was not a goblin of particularly strong wit or good humor, but he was solid, competent, and a tough negotiator who knew the vagaries of Tragacanthan industry and its economy inside and out. He had given Aspet no reason to doubt his suitability for the cabinet position.

Aspet opened the meetings in his own style; he was quickly becoming known on the world stage for his razor-sharp wit and ability to herd even difficult parties down the negotiating trail, making it look much easier than it actually was. In many ways he was born to be king, a fact not lost on CoME.

After the formalities were concluded, he retired to the Royal Chambers for some paperwork while the trade negotiations got underway for real. The trade treaty between Tragacanth and Solemadrina had been in place for centa, but by statute had to be renegotiated and renewed every deca. This would mark the fourth time Jigha had been involved, although the first as Minister. His role was to offer concessions, negotiate new and existing contracts—in short accomplish everything except actually signing the treaty renewal. Only the Sovereign could enter into or renew international treaties. Jigha had at his fingertips every conceivable metric regarding commerce, industry, and production in Tragacanth, as well as a staff to manage it all. He always went into negotiations of this sort exquisitely well-prepared.

The meetings were set to happen over a period of three days. The first day went quite well, and a fair amount of progress was made. So much, in fact, that Jigha reported to His Majesty that the treaty signing might need to be moved up to the morning, rather than evening, of the third day. That would involve a little Royal schedule juggling, but Aspet said it could be achieved if necessary.

The morning of the second day brought dawn showers quickly giving way to sunshine. The delegates gathered after breakfast in the conference room and were pouring glasses of water for themselves and going over notes before the formal continuation of the meetings when Jigha suddenly put his water glass down and slumped over. At first no one really paid any attention, but when the time to start the meeting came and went without any response, or indeed movement at all, from the Minister one of his aides tapped him on the shoulder. Jigha slowly raised his head and everyone gasped. He was bleeding from the corner of his mouth and unable to talk.

The Minister was rushed to the Royal Infirmary and His Majesty notified via comm.

"Looks like Goameel has taken suddenly ill. Suspiciously ill. Think you can handle negotiating a trade treaty?" Aspet said to Boogla over breakfast.

"I... don't know. With enough background material, I suppose."

"Great. All the material you'll need will be in the conference room. Goameel always takes a veritable library with him to these things. I'll go introduce you and ask them to postpone the meeting for an hour to so you can read some papers and talk to his aides. Let's go before the Solemadrinans get restless and decide to raise their prices."

Everyone on both sides of the negotiating table was skeptical of the Magineer Liaison's ability to navigate the intricacies of a trade agreement on so little notice, but as usual Boogla surprised them all. She took virtually every bargaining chip Goameel had brought along and employed them to their fullest extent—even one over which no one had expected to achieve an agreement. By the last break of the day, she had gotten every single concession Tragacanth had sought and two more in addition. There was one session left, the purpose of which was to summarize and confirm the agreements made so that the formal treaty could be drawn up overnight to be signed in the morning by both sides.

Boogla sat at the conference table going through a stack of ledgers, looking for data on a particular military-related materiel acquisition program when she noticed some odd entries. She studied them for a while, correlating the debits against actual equipment requisitions and discovered that there was a considerable discrepancy for several pieces of valuable equipment, both technological and arcane. It appeared as though someone was purchasing more technology than the acquisition vouchers stipulated.

Boogla called in her Edict Enforcement Liaison and showed her the anomalies. She made copies of the relevant documents and departed. Then she brought the evidence over to the head trade delegate from Solemadrina, Deputy Minister of Trade Relations Wabeno Utna. As she went over the discrepancies with him, a minor member of his delegation who had been seated nearby quietly left the table and the room. Boogla watched her go.

Deputy Utna agreed that the numbers had been falsified for whatever reason and corrected them on the requisition tickets. Boogla watched him closely with her social engineer's expert eye. He was telling the truth: he did not know the origin of the attempted theft, for that is what it amounted to. She made a mental note to audit past years' ledgers looking for similar falsifications.

The treaty was signed the next morning and the Solemadrinans took ship back to their homeland. Boogla noticed that the delegate who had slipped out of the conference room was not among the passengers debarking. "She has family here and will be staying a few extra days to visit with them," Deputy Utna explained. Boogla didn't believe a word of it, but she smiled congenially and wished them a safe journey nevertheless.

That night she was up late examining ledgers and uncovering a systematic theft of dozens of pieces of sophisticated military and civilian equipment over the past four years. She asked the head of His Majesty's Secret Service to come in: not as Magineer Liaison, but Royal Consort. She used that title and position only when absolutely necessary; in this case it was.

Principal Special Agent Hobert Akkina was a goblin of breeding and sophistication who also possessed some of the finest detective and martial arts skills in the kingdom. She showed him the evidence she had amassed and then a list of trade delegate names. The only one that appeared every time thefts were documented was Esfina Frem. Akkina looked concerned.

"Your Highness, Ms. Frem is a known underworld operative with strong probable ties to organized crime. I was not aware she remained behind when the ship sailed. This is worrisome; I know of no family of hers here. I will speak to the RPC about doubling your guard for a while."

"Doubling my guard? Why, do you think she'll be targeting me?"

"Quite possible. From what I read you not only uncovered her theft operation, you instituted a new contract that will make it more difficult for her organization to participate in the black market. She may well find you an unacceptable threat to operations. Be vigilant."

When Boogla finally came to bed Aspet was already asleep. He was leaving for the Kopyrewt Forest early in the morning to oversee the dedication of Tragacanth's first protected natural preserve. The RPC would fill him in on what was going on during the carriage trip, most probably. She kissed him tenderly on the forehead and crawled under the covers next to him.

She was barely awake when got up, dressed, and kissed her goodbye.

Twenty kilometers to the west, in a small inn on the outskirts of Goblinopolis, a deal was being made between a female goblin and scrawny hobgoblin dressed in military fatigues.

"It is agreed, then," the goblin said, "Ten thousand up front and another ten when the job is completed."

"Provided you do indeed have the currency up front, it is agreed."

The goblin swung a heavy case up onto the table and snapped it open. "Count it yourself," she commanded. The hob did.

"Everything appears in order. The contract will be carried out within forty-four hours."

"The remainder of the money will be dead-dropped at the location we discussed previously within an hour of confirmation that the contract was fulfilled. Don't get caught; the penalty for high treason in Tragacanth is particularly nasty and unpleasant."

"If I get caught there will be no complications." He smiled and showed her a dark purple capsule hidden securely in a cheek pouch. "Nivril bean powder: highly purified. Kills within fifteen seconds."

"Be certain you have no physical evidence on you that could lead them back to us."

"I am a professional, madam. It shall be so."

"I have engaged the services of a well-respected organization to deal with the supply chain problem. Yes, the arrangements have all been made. Within forty-four hours. I will be waiting in Cladimil for the shipment to be released. Yes. The stockholders needn't worry; the merchandise will be delivered on time or at worst a little late. Yes, that contingency has been covered. No, no further delays are anticipated. Goodbye."

The Royal rail carriage took Aspet as far as Port Zog, where he had to make a decision: he could stay on the rails around to Lumbos and take the Northeast Coastal Highway up to Kopyrewt, or get off here and follow a series of smaller roads to the forest directly. He consulted with the RPC director to get his views on the relative safety of the two routes. The Lumbos route was significantly further in distance, but the roads were better and Aspet could be whisked away by fast ship if some emergency arose. The direct route was shorter, but the roads were less reliable and the country along the way largely uninhabited. Too many good ambush spots; Coastal Highway it was.

Kopyrewt is a vast, mostly pristine temperate rain forest that averages over 200 cm of precipitation a year. Until fairly recently it was virtually untouched, but the ever-increasing demand for wood products to satisfy a growing population began to nibble away at the edges. While sustainable forestry practices were now widespread in the industry, environmental groups had been lobbying energetically for some form of protection for the unique rain forest biome. Aspet had taken an interest in the forest and its hundreds, if not thousands, of unique species and decided that one of his legacies would be a Tragacanthan National Preserve system.

He was here in the heart of the forest, therefore, to declare the formation of Kopyrewt Natural Preserve, to be overseen by the Tragacanthan Natural Resources Administration, also being created today by Royal Proclamation. As this was an historic day for the nation, the number of dignitaries and members of the press in attendance was greater than usual. That meant that the RPC had to bring more agents than customary, as well. The ceremony took place an hour before mid-day on a dais carved from the trunk of a skytoucher tree downed by one of the vicious cyclones that occasionally brush along the northeast edge of the forest. Before Aspet could get on with the declarations and proclamations, however, a small band of dwarves in ritual costumes asked if they may speak with His Majesty.

"Majesty Tragacanth, we beseech you today, in the midst of this noble and much-needed protection of our great forest, to grant protected religious status to a small grove deeper in the woods which serves as the central shrine of our faith."

"I bid you welcome, noble monks. By what name does your faith call itself?"

"We are known as the Sect of H'esh'tuk, Your Regal Majesty."

Aspet consulted privately with the RPC director, Dolmax, as the Corps tracked all manner of organized groups throughout the kingdom.

"They are registered as a religious order, Your Majesty. Their spiritual leader resides in a small church in Dockside, Goblinopolis and is known as *The Exalted One*. His race is unknown; we have no record of any similar creatures anywhere on N'plork."

"Interesting. He presents no threat, though?"

"We have had him and his sect under routine surveillance for a number of years and they have never taken any actions that would be contrary to their stated purpose. They are rated as a level two threat solely due to his indeterminate origin."

Aspet nodded. He returned to the dwarves. "I am minded to consider your proposal, but I will need a little more information regarding the shrine and the grove in which it is located."

"It is not far along the path behind your dais, Your Majesty. We invite you to come and see it for yourself."

The king looked around and shrugged. "Who wants to take a little walk with me?" he asked, and stepped down off the dais. Soon a bureaucrat and media parade had formed: the dwarves and Aspet surrounded by a cloud of RPC, followed by dignitaries and press in no particular order. They walked perhaps two hundred and fifty meters into the deep forest along a path that seemed to be made of living roots and plants that formed a springy but easily navigable walkway. The path led to a clearing, in the center of which was built a small bulb-shaped shrine that came to a point far above them. It did not appear to be crafted by dwarven hands, nor goblin, but rather by enormous roots from the giant purple skytoucher trees that surrounded the small meadow. They swirled in from all sides and spiraled up until they met in a vertical braid that was a lofty as any of the trees themselves.

The effect was that of a tree-root vortex that swirled away into near-infinity. It was spectacular to behold. "Did you somehow train these tree roots to form this beautiful structure?" Aspet asked the dwarves. "Not as such," answered the spokesperson, "Rather, we asked the forest spirit to sanctify this spot, and it responded in this manner."

"Why *this* spot, precisely?"

"It was here that our spiritual leader, H'esh'tuk the Exalted One, first materialized on this plane, Your Majesty."

Aspet glanced meaningfully at Dolmax, who was writing in a notepad. "Materialized, you say? From where?"

"No disrespect intended, Your Majesty, but that is a question much better answered by the Exalted One himself. He has asked me to extend his open invitation to meet with you at your convenience to discuss himself and the Sect."

"I will most certainly take that under consideration and, if our schedules permit, take him up on this offer at some point in the near future. Please convey my gratitude for his most gracious invitation."

"Your Majesty's reputation for courtesy and wisdom seems most well-founded," replied the dwarf, "I will relay your message, of course."

Aspet shook the monk's hand and turned to look at the shrine once more. He walked around to the far side, admiring the way the roots came together seamlessly, when he turned to say something to Dolmax. He suddenly shimmered and vanished with a confused look on his face. Dolmax threw himself onto the spot where Aspet had been standing as though trying to cover him but there was nothing to cover. The king of Tragacanth was utterly gone.

Chapter the Fifth

in which Tol and his party discover Hellehoell and a less-than-cordial welcome

At first Tol was not very impressed with the supposed artificial structures in the crevasse. There were a few pillars and some low stonework walls, yes. Nicely done, yes. Worth all this hoo-hah? Not even close. If the titans really wanted this place, Tol's vote was to give it to them, lock, stock, and barrel. Then they rounded a narrow corner.

There before them was a huge arch, at least twice as tall as the titan. It was framed with intricately carved and polished stone that shone with a mirror finish. There was a gate and portcullis blocking the way, but Tartag walked over to one side and pulled a hidden lever none of the rest of them could have reached without a ladder, much less spotted, whereupon the beautifully carved gates swung open and the portcullis raised effortlessly. Tartag stood in the center of the arch, looking in at the darkness. He turned and addressed them. "Gentles all, welcome to Hellehoell: my ancestral homeland."

They entered and found themselves on polished marble floors. From a rack near the door Tartag removed a long pole with a torch on the end and set it aflame; as they passed each wall sconce he lit the torch inside. Every torch he added showed more and more of the utterly magnificent interior. After a while it became apparent that they were in a complete underground city, and not a small one. Massive support pillars had been left in the native rock every ten meters or so, with the distant ceiling arched between them.

"This is a magnificent city, Tartag," Tol said after a while, "You must be very proud of your ancestors for creating such a marvel."

"Actually, this is probably just one of the outlying communities. If the legends our people tell of Hellehoell are accurate, there are nine cities in total, in a wheel formation with the largest at the center. It took several thousand workers over a centum to carve it all out. 'Hellehoell' translates to Goblish roughly as 'the world beneath the rock.' Eventually the plan was that all titans on N'plork who wished could live here."

"That plan was cut short by whatever closed off the entrance, eh?"

"Apparently. The records from that time are confusing and contradictory. They speak of a great enemy who tore off the mountain top and poured it into the Valley of Welcome—Daludobris—which was formerly located on the west side of the complex, supposedly so that invaders who attacked at dawn could not use the rising sun to hide themselves. I've searched that area and while I did find evidence of a massive slide that filled in a ravine, I can't conclusively prove that ravine was Daludobris."

"Thank you for that information, Tartag," said Episk, "The RSCA will be glad to assist in excavating Daludobris once it has been positively located."

"I will pass that kind offer along to the Council of Elders who will be deciding policy for Hellehoell once it is reestablished," Tartag answered cautiously. Tol noted the subtle shift in his rhetoric.

They wandered down countless avenues, boulevards, and narrower streets, marveling at the wonderful architecture and expert stonework. Tartag was spiraling them in toward the center of the complex, because that was where Titans historically built their mausoleums, to make it easier for all residents to honor their ancestors. While Tartag did the navigating from the mental map he'd made of what little was known of the complex layout, Tol was viewing the city from a cop's perspective. He looked down blind alleys, along rows of closely-packed townhomes with connecting balconies, and at isolated mercantile shops on broad avenues with dense residential areas close by and realized that either titans were impeccably honest or they had a substantial crime rate in this city. It was almost designed with larceny in mind: and don't get him started on all the classic ambush points.

As if on cue a titan voice suddenly rang out: "Stay where you are. Put your hands in the air and keep them there. You are trespassing in the suspended law city of Hellehoell and are under order of confinement."

Tol looked around and saw bows drawn all around them on rooftops and in windows: a dozen or more. He wished he'd brought along that amulet of proof against missiles that Oloi had given him as a token of friendship, but no such luck. Wait... no such luck...

They had asked Tartag to step forward and explain, giving Tol the chance to whisper into his pocket without attracting too much attention. "Eyejay, are you powered up? This is a bit of an emergency. Can you scan the area around us for other infrared signatures? There are only four in our immediate party."

There was no response at first, then through bone induction he heard, "I count fifteen other forms, all titans, in a semicircle ranging from eight point four to thirteen point six meters in your forward direction. And I told you not to call me 'Eyejay.'"

"I have to call you something shorter than 'PDWA/AI Model 36.'"

"I am, as you might put it, speechless that you actually remember my full designation. Knighthood seems to have changed you for the better, Tol-u-ol. If you must shorten that, how about PeeDee?"

"Great. Petey it is. Next question, Petey: how many of these could I reasonably expect to take out with my disruptor before one of them got me?"

"Ordinarily that would depend on the availability of cover, your personal agility and marksmanship, and the titans' unknown archery skills, but in this case the point is already conceded, as your disruptor battery is only at three percent of total charge."

"Smek me! I thought I charged it up on the carriage."

"You did plug it in on the carriage, but that receptacle was shorted to the carriage frame and inoperable."

"Why didn't you alert me? Wait, I know: I didn't ask, right?"

42

"Correct. I have been in hibernation mode for almost three months. Did you wish to activate me fully?"

"Yes. I am going to need your help in the near future, I expect."

"It is good to see that some things are resistant to change. All functions online."

They were disarmed and the goblins marched to a holding cell a block further on. Tartag was allowed to remain free, but closely watched. In the cell, the other goblins were outraged.

"Under what authority do they purpose to incarcerate officials of His Majesty's government? A Knight of the Crimson? Unheard of and unacceptable. We must get free from here and report this immediately," said Koxo.

"I must concur," agreed Episk, "This is unprecedented and a criminal act."

"Hang on to your monogramed handkerchiefs, gentlegoblins. While this city is technically underneath lands owned by the King of Tragacanth, the precise provenance of Hellehoell is debateable. If this city existed prior to the establishment of the lands under which it rests as part of the Kingdom of Tragacanth, they may have some claim to Sovereignty, at least until His Majesty makes a formal Proclamation of Annexation, which they can then either ratify or deny. If they deny it, His Majesty may or may not decide to force his claim militarily."

"I'm impressed, Sir Tol-u-ol," said Koxo, "You have a broad knowledge of not only police matters, but law and statecraft, as well."

"I'm a...quick learner, Mr. Nilred."

No one but Tol could hear Petey laughing maniacally.

Tartag came to visit them often. He had been allowed to explore the entire complex, with a guide, and was quite energized about it. He could picture this as the center of all titan civilization, as it must have been millennia ago before the catastrophe. Tol thought this was a grand idea, as well.

The other goblins were still indignant about their captivity. They wanted to break out, or at least file some sort of formal complaint. Tol reminded them that their mission was a diplomatic one.

"I'm not here for diplomacy; I'm here to secure this area for the RSCA," said Episk somewhat belligerently.

"I agree. I'm here to assess the structural integrity of this area, which is difficult to do from a cell. We need to find some way out of here."

"All right, gentlegoblins, allow me to rephrase. I'm the leader of this expedition because I am a career edict enforcement officer with thousands of hours of urban combat experience. I'm also brother to the King of Tragacanth, which means any offensive actions taken against me by the titans will be considered an attack on the Royal Family; the response to those tends to be swift and overwhelming. Just cool your heels; we'll be released once the titans are certain that our intentions are peaceful and not contrary to the best interests of the titan community. Remember, this little troop is probably all that's left of a once huge population. They've held on to their legacy through famine and sickness and who knows what else just so that one day titan society can once again be whole. I applaud their tenacity and I don't blame them for treating cautiously with us."

With that he wandered off into the darkness at the rear of the cell. Petey had told him that the chamber they were in penetrated fairly far, and he wanted to see what was back there. After a few minutes of exploration he came to a heavy wooden door framed by a splendid arch. He expected it to be locked; it wasn't. He swung the big portal open on hinges that protested their long years of non-use and stepped cautiously inside.

There were rows of niches in both walls, stretching back into the distant gloom. He had found the elusive mausoleum! Examining one of the niches closely, he determined that it did indeed host remains. They had located the evidence they needed to pursue Tartag's claim.

Tol returned to the others and made his announcement. "So, we can settle down and relax. Sooner or later they'll release us and we can carry the news back to surface. It won't make Belbomit very happy, but I'm sure we can work something out."

Just then a figure shimmered into existence again, but this time it was not Plåk. It made no social overtures whatever.

"Tol: your brother has disappeared."

"Well met, Oloi! What do mean, 'disappeared'?"

"I mean he was visiting a dwarven shrine in the center of the Kopyrewt Forest when, in the presence of dozens of witnesses, he suddenly vanished. I've checked all the magical and quantum pathways and he has not traveled any of them. This is a wholly new dimensional transport mechanism. In other words, I can't track him."

"What measures are being taken?"

"The RPC are ripping the place apart, or trying to. Every time they damage anything it heals itself almost instantly. Ballop'ril is on his way there. I'm heading back now and I think you should come with me."

Tol stood in thought for a moment. On the one hand, he owed something to these people as the leader of the party. On the other, his brother and Liege-lord was in need of him. There really wasn't much option.

"Is there any way you can transport my companions to the entrance of the tunnel?"

"How about if I just create a distraction that will draw the titans away and let them make a run for it?"

"That works for me. You gobs in?"

"I'm not certain how well I can run," said Koxo, "But I'll give a shot."

"If we are injured in any way, I will hold you personally responsible," said Episk.

"Yeah, you do that," Tol replied, rolling his eyes. "Okay, Oloi, let it rip!"

After a few seconds there was a bright light accompanied by a rumbling noise and crashing sound somewhere in the opposite direction of the entrance. The alarmed titan guards all ran to investigate. Oloi opened the lock and the two other gobs ran for all they were worth toward the surface.

"Do you think they'll make it out?" Oloi asked.

"They'll be all right," replied Tol, "They both can use the exercise, anyway. I am a little worried about Tartag, though. If the other titans think he was somehow involved in this, he might get a lot of grief."

"Tartag is much more important and powerful than these isolated titans know. He is the last surviving member of his race: the Storm Titans."

"Storm Titans? I thought those were just mythical figures invented to make little gobs behave: 'if you don't eat all of your globeroot soup the storm titans will get you.' That sort of thing."

"No, they're quite real. Or at least they were a millennium past. When the titans dispersed they of all the kin groups fared the most poorly; Tartag is the sole remaining member."

"What makes a storm titan different from a regular titan?" asked Tol, scratching his chin.

"In appearance, nothing; although they tend to be a bit taller. Contrary to certain folk beliefs that they have no arcane abilities, Titans are in fact creatures of elemental magic, meaning they are able to employ magic naturally, without any study. Each kin group specializes in a different form. The storm titans actually absorb energy from atmospheric disturbances and store it within themselves. When necessary they can channel that energy into feats of almost unbelievable strength and endurance. Since titans respect strength above all other attributes, storm titans were always elected as the leaders of Hellehoell. They are luckier than they can imagine to have one available for the reunification. We must go now."

Tol walked over and re-locked the cell door. "That might confuse them a little and buy the gobs some more time. All right, let's blast."

Chapter the Sixth

in which an assassination is narrowly averted

Boogla sat at her desk in the Royal Palace poring over the details of the recently-signed trade agreement with Solemadrina. Every outgoing shipment had been thoroughly inspected before being allowed to depart, as a result of the hanky-panky she had uncovered. Only one ship had failed inspection; it was being held in port in Cladimil until the disposition of its cargo could be decided. Some of it was proscribed military technology, including upgrades and accessories for secret devices and systems, which implied that they already possessed the base units and wanted to increase their utility.

She wondered how long this technology leakage had been going on. She decided to draw up a proposal for increasing the security of programs that produced intellectual property not intended for foreign use. She took a new sheaf of paper from a drawer just as an RPC guard came in.

"Quarter hour check, Your Highness."

"I am well. Thank you."

"Acknowledged."

Since Hobert had recommended an increase in Boogla's protective detail, RPC were required to check in on her every fifteen minutes around the clock while she was alone, in addition to the heavy perimeter and interior security present in the Palace at all times. She had finally come to terms with being constantly under protection and even found it somewhat reassuring now. She returned to her work and was soon engrossed in it.

The Royal Palace of Tragacanth was an elongated "u"-shape with the throne room and receiving halls located at the center of the bend. The Royal Residence occupied two-thirds of the right-hand wing; offices, conference rooms, and similar spaces filled out the rest of the right-hand and all of the left-hand. There were private underground tunnels connecting the Royal Residence with the most frequently used areas of the remainder of the Palace, as well as nearby buildings. The tunnels had both rail carriages and pedestrian walkways, so the Royal Family had an option for traveling them.

The downside of this convenience was that the tunnel system provided additional difficult-to-secure avenues of access for all locations thusly connected. While the RPC were aware of the vulnerability, the existence and exact mapping of the tunnels was a state secret, known only to those with need for the knowledge. The Royal complex was vast, and the RPC had only so many agents.

When Aspet was in the Palace, Boogla most often ate lunch with him; either in his office or in one of a half-dozen private restaurants scattered around the complex reserved for the Crown, high officers of State, and their guests. When she was alone, however, she preferred a working lunch, brought to her by a member of the Royal Household staff, all of whom were closely vetted by the RPC. Today was no different. She ordered a mixed-greens salad with leggen nut oil dressing and a cup of steaming herbal infusion from the Royal menu. Ten minutes later there was a knock on the door.

She waited for the security card to slip into the slot, which would tell her on the view screen next to the door who was knocking. Even the maids had those. She had very specific instructions from the RPC not to open the door without that confirmation. The very highest-echelon RPC agents could open the door from the outside in an emergency with their access cards, but protocol was that they announced themselves this way first if circumstances allowed.

After ten seconds when the automatic confirmation screen had not activated, she walked over the panel beneath it and turned on the camera outside manually. It was blank: either the camera itself was dead, or someone had intentionally blocked it. She wiggled it back and forth; the blurred image did not respond relative to the movement, meaning that it was a static piece of fabric or parchment taped over the lens.

She hurried back over to her desk and hit the panic button hidden underneath. That would put the Palace on lockdown and mobilize a whole lot of RPC. She waited for the alarm status on the screen to turn red. Nothing happened; somehow it had been sabotaged. Boogla was on the verge of panic herself, which in her case was good: that's where she thought the most clearly. With every nerve fiber active and her adrenalin at peak levels, the world seemed to slow down for her, such that she saw and could react to every action appropriately.

She knew something was going down outside: something dangerous. The RPC had everything in the Palace wired with sensors and under surveillance at all times. If this threat was real and not just some colossal systems failure, she might not have anyone to rely on but herself. She stood against one wall and waited.

Suddenly there was a buzzing noise at the door and sparks began to fly from the space inside the door frame. That convinced her once and for all that this was an active threat. She walked over to a painting on the wall and pulled it down and over with a strong jerk. A nearby bookcase slid to the right and she slipped into the narrow hallway it revealed, securing the escape entrance behind her. She quickly followed the tunnel to a ladder that led down. At the bottom there was another tunnel with several branches. She was heading for RPC Central Security Station, where there were at least a dozen agents on duty at any given time.

All RPC agents were heavily armed, as well as experts in one or more martial arts disciplines. She had surprised them once at an inspection by revealing her own third degree black belt in correcting the technique of a particular takedown being taught. Much to Aspet's initial concern, sliding smoothly into amusement, she then went on to spar and easily hold her own with both of the instructors. The Royal Consort was not without her own defensive resources.

She was running almost full out now, every sense straining for information. She heard a faint sliding noise that brought her up short. She stopped just before a tee intersection and waited in a crouch. After two seconds a hobgoblin clad all in black shot around the corner and leapt at her with some sort of weapon. She met him with a strong, braced kick to the sternum that knocked the wind out of him audibly. He staggered back and she followed through with a hand thrust to the neck that fractured his trachea. As he gurgled with hand over throat she elbowed his face and when he fell she slammed her foot on his neck, fracturing it fatally.

She left the hob dying in the hallway and kept running. There was now no doubt that the RPC security apparatus had been compromised deeply. She couldn't rely on anyone for assistance: she would have to take care of this problem herself. A few meters further on another black-clad goon intercepted her. She side-stepped his attack and put her knee in his solar plexus exceptionally hard. He doubled over and she grabbed him in a headlock and then, bracing herself off one wall, leapt up into the air and used her own body's mass in addition to a well-timed twist to break his neck. No time for being subtle or elegant here.

She dispatched a total of four of them along the way: three with cervical fractures and one with massive cerebral hemorrhage when she took away a metal pry bar he was carrying and used it on him. Finally she reached another ladder that went both up and down; she figured they would be expecting her to go down to the carriage station, so she went up into the Royal Residence instead.

At the top of the stairs was another secret entrance; this one came out in the study next to the master bedroom. She rolled a sofa over to the entrance and jammed it into the access bay to slow any pursuit. She stopped for a moment to consider the most defensible spot in the residence and decided on her home office where her computers were. She had her own array of sensors linked into there that were not in the RPC network and not mapped by anyone but her. She had triple bar locks on the door and a lot of homebrew software running to control everything.

She sat at the monitor and had just managed to use her own personal account on the RPC master server to trigger a 'Royal Personage Under Attack' alarm centered on the Royal Residence when a slight noise behind her caused her to roll out of her chair to the right and come up in defensive stance. A voice from the darkness said, calmly, "Very impressive, the way you handled my minions, Miss Consort. I assure you I am quite convinced that you are more adept at martial arts than I; I have no intention of engaging you in a battle."

"The very fact that you are here, in my private quarters, means you have forfeited that option, hobgoblin scumbag."

"Such language from a member of the Royal Family and Officer of the King's Cabinet. The reason you are mistaken," he paused while a dart sped silently from a gun he had hidden in a fold of his clothing and lodged itself in her shoulder, "Is in this tiny, inoffensive dart."

She yanked the dart from the place it had penetrated her hide and was about to launch a vicious attack on him when she suddenly paused as the world went spinning.

"My very sage advice is that you restrain yourself. The poison with which you have been injected is quite deadly, but how quickly it kills you is dependent to a certain extent on your physical activity. The more you move around, the more rapidly you will expire."

"Assassin!" she spit it out at him: a label and a curse all rolled into one.

"Well, yes and no. If you do not cooperate, then yes. If, on the other hand, you do perform one simple task for me, I will administer this antidote," he waved a small blue glass vial in the air, "And you will wake up in a few hours with a respectable headache, but otherwise none the worse for the experience."

"What," she asked in a rasp, as her respiratory system was beginning to falter, "Is this 'simple task?'"

"Go to your little computer keyboard over there and use your Royal Family override code to release just one ship from embargo in Cladimil, and this unfortunate little episode will be merely one of those stories you tell your grandchildren as they sit upon your knee late in life. Fail to do that, however, and your life will end in less than ten minutes. The king will be so disappointed in you, not to mention your precious Royal Protective Corps, which I found pathetically simple to disable, incidentally."

"How did you accomplish such a tremendous feat?" Boogla gasped.

"No time for chit-chat or foolish flattery, goblin: do as I ask, or die. You have very little time left to make the correct decision. Imagine how distraught His Majesty will be if you make the wrong one."

"If you're trying to start a war between Tragacanth and Solemadrina, Aspet is far too intelligent to fall into that trap."

"I want nothing of the sort. Bad for business. I simply want you to release some goods that have been promised to certain merchants in the international market."

"Going to rather extremes just to get some merchandise delivered, aren't you?"

"My employer has a reputation to uphold. Nothing is too much effort where that is concerned."

"All right. You've convinced me." She rolled somewhat erratically over to her computer desk and logged into the Cladimil Port Authority. "Which ship are we talking about?"

"I believe you know perfectly well which ship," the hobgoblin replied.

"Yes, I know which ship by name. But something—maybe it's pollen in the air—is making it very difficult for me to focus my eyes and I need you to point out which ship that is on this Port Authority Manifest. There are a dozen or so embargoed at the moment."

The hobgoblin cautiously approached. "That one. Third down. The vessel named *Saltwater Skipper*."

"This one?"

"No, two down from that. I told you, the third one!"

"Uh, I thought that was the third one. My vision's getting pretty blurry. Can you just click on it for me? I'll enter the passcode when you do."

The hob reached across her shoulder and positioned the cursor over the correct ship.

"Much better," she said, gritting her teeth. "Thanks." She suddenly pressed a three-key combination that turned off the lights and simultaneously pushed off against the desk in an explosive move that propelled her into the hob. They fell together and landed with her on his chest. She had her fist positioned for a fatal blow to his throat when the room around them positively exploded.

Chapter the Seventh

in which a Royal vanishing act results in a visit with an ancient forest spirit

At first Aspet couldn't figure out what was happening. Everything suddenly felt wrong, but he couldn't identify precisely what that meant. It occurred to him at last that everything was moving in fast forward: the leaves were red on the trees one second and then brown, green, gone the next. The trees themselves seemed to be growing taller and giving off branches as he watched. The entire world was moving much too fast. He couldn't help but wonder how long it would be before his own death when a voice that seemed full of life, wisdom, and all of the elements in soil, rain, and sun at once spoke.

"Welcome, great king, to the Eldest Grove. I've had to pull you through the Shroud of Equilibrium in order to be able to communicate in your native time scale. Mine is much, much slower."

"I...thank you for your kind welcome. I am called Aspet; may I have a name by which to call you?"

The voice paused. "The giving of names is not a common practice here, but I suppose you may call me Arbus the Barktender."

"Well met, Master Arbus. To what do I owe the singular honor of your esteemed company?"

"You are a civil one; I'll give you that right off. That is well in a leader. I have brought you here today, as Sovereign of the Hurriers, to..."

"I beg your pardon, but 'Hurriers?' Aspet interrupted.

"Yes. We refer to your race that way because you do everything with such great speed: move, talk, reproduce, grow, live, and die."

"Ah. Apologies; do continue..."

"I have brought you here to sue for protection, quite frankly."

"Protection? What sort of protection could I give to one such as you?"

"While these woods as a whole are of varied age—some of the younger trees are scarcely a centum old—the forest at the center, demarcated by the large roots that rise up out of the ground in such glorious fashion, is actually much, much more ancient. We have achieved, as you might say, some degree of self-awareness and a desire to prolong our existence in peace."

"I believe all sentient creatures have that inalienable right. How can I assist?"

"We know that Hurriers harvest the outer fringes of the forest for wood; we have achieved peace with that. It is part of the natural order of things. However, we are very much afraid that they may eventually work their way into the center and try to harm the Eldest Grove. That, we would be forced to oppose in any ways at our disposal, for the sake of survival. Any such confrontations would undoubtedly lead to enmity on both sides; we would dearly wish to avoid such. Therefore, we are asking that you declare our little area of the forest off limits for any cutting, pruning, or burning. We welcome visitors, so long as they carry neither axe nor flame, at least with the intention of employing them."

"That is certainly not an unreasonable petition. In fact, the purpose for my visit to your forest to begin with is to create such a preserve. May I see more of the Eldest Grove, for my own edification?"

"I would be honored and delighted to show off our wonderful community, wise King. Look around you and I will move the images past."

The forest surrounding him began to flow from one scene to another. The view shifted to the tallest treetops: fully 150 meters from the forest floor. In this amazing tangle of limbs, branches, and vines—that stretched as far as the eye could see in all directions—lived a staggering complexity of animals and insects, many of which Aspet had never seen nor read about before. There were simians, avians, rodents, leafhoppers, branchleapers, buzzers, climbing reptiles, rope-reptiles, viper-worms, and more. Aspet had never stopped to consider the ecological diversity in treetops; it was an eye-opening experience for him.

Next the scene morphed into mid-tree. Here, different avians and climbers scrambled up and down the trunk, extracting insects and larvae from the bark folds. There were peckers who braced themselves against the trunk and used their heavy beaks to drill small holes in the bark, from which sap leaked. They then visited those areas periodically to harvest insects trapped in the sap. Here and there multicolored rope-reptiles curled around the trunk like vines, searching for climbers or unwary avians to make a meal of.

The roots and, below them, the forest floor were moving carpets of life. Large numbers of creepers, crawlers, scrabblers, slimers, ground-avians, various reptiles, peckers, pokers, viper-worms, and many, many others swarmed there. Also on the forest floor, mostly in and around two-meter barrows covered in heavy sod, were visible the spirits of creatures that resembled a cross between dwarves and goblins. They milled to and fro, but were not in any way threatening. Aspet was enchanted by them.

"Who are these languid specters?" he asked.

"They are the first of your kind to live here," Arbus replied, "In the days before the different Hurrier races appeared. They were closely allied with the forest; the Eldest Grove and they lived in perfect symbiosis. Because of that connection their spirits linger and we support them with our own energies."

"Master Arbus, you have more than convinced me. The Eldest Grove shall not be subject to incursion or development by any over whom I hold authority. This is a place of wonder and ancient beauty that must be protected at all costs."

"Pleased I am that a creature of such wisdom holds sway over the Hurriers," replied Arbus, "May I ask also that cutting of live trees in the margins happen only under two conditions: the trees are relatively young—say, under three hundred turnings of the seasons—and they are immediately replaced with saplings of the same species. It is not, I suspect, at all apparent to you, but each tree must fight hard for its spot in the grove; when that spot is lost giving another similar tree the opportunity to take it over keeps the forest balanced as well as possible."

"Why only young trees?"

"It takes many, many turnings for the community of plants and animals that depend upon each other to develop. Once it is fully matured, that community may remain active and healthy for millennia. Cutting down such a tree does far more damage to the forest as an organism than simply removing one tree. Thousands of creatures are left homeless and without a source of food or shelter."

"I see. Very well, your request is granted. Also, there is a group of dwarves—hurriers—who want their shrine not far from here protected. Do you know of it?"

"The shrine marks the location of a very ancient thing I do not understand. It was here before the first tree: although it manifests only rarely, the latent energy field it radiates is enormously powerful. I myself have on occasion drawn some strength from it, and that pool seems bottomless. You would do well to grant their wish if only to guard it from other hurriers who might accidentally encounter that energy pool. The last time it activated, it disgorged a creature not of this world."

"So I have been told. The dwarves call him H'esh'tuk. My brother calls him 'The Exalted One.'"

"All I know of him is that he possesses a peaceful, contemplative soul and thus was adjudged no threat to us. He disturbed nothing while here and left behind no scars upon the forest. Such a being we consider a friend and will gladly suffer. Ah, we are about to have visitors."

Aspet turned, expecting to see some spirit or other ancient forest denizen. Instead he was face to face with Tol, disruptor drawn, and a goblin mage, poised to strike.

"Greetings, brother. Welcome to the Eldest Grove. Relax: you're perfectly safe here."

"Where have I heard that before?" answered Tol.

Chapter the Eighth

in which the King's absence is keenly felt and the Palace is attacked

The RPC Field Agent in Charge (FAC) immediately set up a tight perimeter around Aspet's last point of presence. No one but RPC in or out. They had their own mages, who scanned unsuccessfully for magical activity. No unusual electromagnetic fields or quantum gateways were detected, either. It was though the King had simply ceased to exist. Sudden loss of the Sovereign for any reason had not been experienced in centums; the protocols for handling this existed but were not in anyone's daily repertoire, as it were. The RPC were ruthlessly efficient at protecting the Sovereign from conventional threats; this one, however, was anything but conventional and left them stomping around in frustration.

While the traveling squad searched every square centimeter of the surrounding forest, pulling up roots or even cutting limbs were it deemed necessary in the search for clues, they discovered something truly astounding: the damaged trees healed themselves almost immediately. One of the RPC mages noticed and talked to the FAC.

"We might want to be a little more careful. This section of woods seems to be semi-sentient and given its considerable healing powers, could potentially be dangerous."

"If it had anything to do with the disappearance of His Majesty," the FAC answered grimly, "There aren't enough healing powers on the planet to save it." It was not a threat, just a fact, as the agent saw it. Goblins did not take kindly to anyone or anything that interfered with their Royalty.

As the vanishing act had the potential for being some form of advanced magic, both the Ostia Magineer and Ballop'ril, who was still on retainer with the Royal government, were summoned, although they were not told precisely why. The disappearance of the King was a tightly controlled state secret for now: everyone except RPC who had witnessed the event was taken into 'protective custody' and had any communications devices confiscated.

Ballop'ril and Prond had made such excellent and impressive progress with the new magical gateway talismans that the Archmage felt comfortable leaving the operation to assist the RPC with whatever they were so worked up about. Prond had recently advanced to the rank of Mage Second Tier and was happy with his own progress. Together they teleported to a spot communicated to them by one of the RPC mages, also a former student of Ballop'ril's.

By the time they arrived the place was crawling with RPC, soldiers, constables, reporters, and a few onlookers, despite the remote location. The officials were pulled immediately into a secret briefing where it was revealed that the King had vanished right before a lot of eyes. During the briefing another localized commotion was set off when the King's brother Sir Tol-u-ol and some transcended mage materialized. They were also brought in.

"When he disappeared, was it a shimmering, or did he go sort of wavy first?" asked Ballop'ril.

"Neither," replied the FAC, whose name was Riddix, "I was looking right at him and he just vanished. No winking, no shimmering, no waviness, no change in illumination or light scattering: just here one second, gone the next. No aftereffects, either."

"Hmm," replied Ballop'ril, looking at Oloi for confirmation, "Temporal rift?"

"That was my first thought, too, but I've been back and forth on both sides of the continuum in the local neighborhood and while there is some form of resonance present, it isn't from a simple rift."

"Exactly where was he standing?" asked Tol.

"Right here," pointed Riddix.

Tol stared at the maze of footprints and broken twigs. "Smek. You guys may be great at VIP protection, but your crime scene etiquette leaves a lot to be desired." He sighed and got down on his knees to peer carefully at the prints.

"We were trying to find His Majesty, not secure the scene," explained Riddix with a trace of irritation. "What are you doing?"

"I'm a cop. I'm looking for clues. What else?"

"We've already been over the area thoroughly."

"Looks like you brought a herd of plainsrunners with you...Aha!" Tol pointed to something no one else could see. He followed a seemingly invisible trail that led off toward an area where giant roots popped out of the ground in an oddly sculptural way.

"What is he doing?" one of the RPC asked.

"I think he's just making it up," replied Riddix.

Tol snorted in response but kept crawling.

"Wait," said Ballop'ril, "I think he's onto something. There's a faint goblin aura overprint following that same trail."

Tol stood up. "His Majesty is still here," he announced, brushing off his pants. "We just can't see him. It's like he's in one of those parallel dimensions or something. He's still leaving tracks, although they're being made so quickly it's hard to tell."

"It's an extradimensional planar fork," Ballop'ril said, realizing it himself at that moment. "Elemental magic, not invocational."

"Of course," said Oloi, "I have to go now. Can you take care of it?"

"I will do what I can," replied Ballop'ril.

"Excellent. Thank you," Oloi said, and then sparkled out.

"Prond," Ballop'ril said, "I am going to send you along with Sir Tol to rescue the king. When you are ready to depart, cast the Ritual of Rejoining and I'll direct that stream back to this physicotemporal plane."

"Yes, Master. Planar Travel Ritual of Rejoining. I am ready."

"Sir Tol-u-ol, I can send you and my apprentice to the extradimensional space where His Majesty is, if you care to go. Prond will bring you all back here."

Tol eyed the young goblin doubtfully. "You sure he's up to that task?"

"Quite certain," replied Ballop'ril. "Possibly my most competent apprentice ever."

Tol shrugged, "Okay, let 'er rip."

Ballop'ril created a blue and silver bubble from energy flowing out of his hands and, positioning it over Tol's and Prond's heads, allowed it sink down over them. Once it was in place it, and they, vanished.

"Really, Tol, you and"... he looked at Prond expectantly... "Mage Second Tier Prond, apprenticed to Archmage Ballop'ril, Your Majesty," Prond responded sharply... "Prond are perfectly all right here. Arbus has just sped time up a bit so we can converse with him in a way more comfortable for us."

Tol looked around. "That's mighty keen for you and Arbus, wherever he is, but there is a big crowd of folks back there getting very, very anxious wondering where you are right now."

"What? Oh, yes, I suppose there would be. I thank you for your extreme hospitality, Master Arbus, but it is best if we return now. Your request is granted in full."

"For that I and the Eldest Grove thank you most sincerely. You are a wise and noble Sovereign."

"May I?" asked Prond. Aspet nodded. "Goodbye, Arbus. Long may you live in peace."

"Goodbye to you, Aspet King. Long, after the fashion of your kind, may you reign in peace and health."

Prond invoked the Ritual of Rejoining and the 'other forest' blurred into existence around them as though they were returned from an amusement park ride.

The RPC instantly encircled them, weapons drawn. Aspet said a nonsense-sounding code word and gestured with both hands on his chest. They holstered their weapons and relaxed, if only a very little bit.

A couple of hours later, after everyone had been briefed and debriefed, and preliminary incident reports filed, Aspet and Tol walked through the forest. Aspet relayed to him the incredible history of the Eldest Grove.

"Apparently this part of the forest is one big organism that has been here since the Protocene. It has even evolved a limited form of sentience," said Aspet, "That's just amazing to me."

"What's amazing to me is how poorly trained the RPC are when it comes to preserving evidence. If you had been kidnapped or otherwise assaulted by creatures from this dimension we would have had a terrible time tracking the perps. Those gobs trampled everything like a herd of grazers. I could barely see your footprints while you were making them, for smek's sake."

Suddenly the FAC spoke into his comm unit and sprinted over to Aspet. "Pardon, Your Majesty, but we have a verified Condition Violet Dee."

Aspet dropped the bark section he'd been examining. "Boogla!" He turned to Riddix. "Get everyone and every piece of equipment we have on it. Go!" The RPC shouted into his comm: "Dump it all. Everything. Red Three. Royal Direct."

Aspet grabbed Tol and started running. "We need to find Ballop'ril!"

"Why?" asked Tol between breaths.

"We have to get back to the Royal Palace as soon as possible. It's under attack and Boogla is there."

"Whatta ya mean, 'under attack?'"

"I mean an armed attack against someone in the Royal Complex has taken place, a member of the Royal Family is present—that's Boogla—and at least one fatality is confirmed."

"Smek me. What kind of suicidal idiot would attack the Royal Palace? Oh, smek me double. We may never know with your evidence-destroying goons charging around."

Aspet punched him in the arm. "There's Ballop'ril." They swerved to intercept him. They and the two RPC agents running just behind them skidded to a halt in front of the bemused bugbear, who waited patiently while Aspet recovered his voice.

"Archmage, Tol and I need desperately to get to the Royal Palace as quickly as possible. Can you teleport us there?"

"I don't know much about the Palace itself. Have you any mages handy who could give me a mental map of a prospective materialization area?"

"Can you just pull it from my memories if I concentrate?"

"Yes, if you will do just that."

"Sorry; I know you won't like this, but it's an emergency," Aspet said to his RPC contingent. "Wait, can you send a couple of them along, too?"

Ballop'ril nodded. "Great, one of you run and tell Riddix you're both going back with me and that we may land near a firefight. Okay, Archmage, I'm ready to be probed."

Ballop'ril touched him lightly on the forehead and said, "Concentrate on the area where you want to materialize. It CAN NOT be inside a building: that's too dangerous. A rooftop, lawn, or road is best. Try to pick a place that isn't likely to be occupied."

Aspet closed his eyes and pictured a little-known private rooftop garden that spanned the Palace and Residence, offering access to both with his master key. He looked to Tol. "I'm thinking about the Seclusion Garden. Help me."

"What kind of help do you need?" Tol asked.

"Just visualize it as best you can. It will give Ballop'ril an alternate view."

Tol shrugged. "Okay. I'm visualizin'." The archmage put his other hand on Tol's forehead.

Just as Ballop'ril muttered, "Got it," Riddix and Aspet's other RPC agent came sprinting up.

"Your Majesty! You can't teleport into a possibly unsecured area. That's a tremendous risk."

"That's why I'm taking a couple of agents along with me, Riddix. We'll be fine. I'll let them and Sir Tol here take care of any necessary rough stuff."

"But Your Majesty! The kingdom needs its King!"

"And I need my wife. I'm going."

Riddix looked pleadingly at Tol.

"Sorry, laddie: can't help you. Runs in the blood, I'm afraid."

The FAC rolled his eyes. "Fine. Take this, at least." He handed Tol a high-powered sidearm specially built for RPC agents. He also fished around in his pocket and produced a badge for Tol. "I hereby deputize you into the Royal Protective Corps."

Tol shook his head and handed the badge back. "No offense, but I don't need no smekkin' badge. I'm a Knight of the Crimson, a sworn EE officer, and—he's my brother. No badge can trump those."

"Point taken. Please give the weapon back to one of the RPC agents at the palace. They come out of my capital budget."

"Will do."

"Do it," Aspet said to Ballop'ril.

The RPC agents stood in front of and behind Aspet, weapons drawn and facing out. Tol stood beside him in the same posture, one hand on the king's shoulder. Ballop'ril waved his own hands and then dropped them suddenly to his sides. The party vanished.

They materialized in the empty rooftop garden. Aspet leapt to a nearby door and opened it with his key. He slammed around the corner and yanked open a drawer with a console in it. The screen popped up and he put in his Royal Access Code, then in a flurry of flying fingers pulled up a tactical alarm map with body heat signatures for the entire Royal Complex. Meanwhile his RPC detail were on their comms to their own people exchanging status information.

"Look in the upper tunnels, Your Majesty!" one of them shouted.

Aspet paged over to those maps. He followed the trail of tripped alarms to the Royal Residence. He swept went along the hallways until he saw two signatures in one room. One of them was blinking purple. "Found her! She's in her private study with another person! The windows are machine barricaded but I can override that from the panel outside the master bedroom. Tell the RPC to meet us there."

"Acknowledged, Your Majesty," replied the RPC agent.

They tore down one hallway, up another, then up one flight of stairs and continued past the entrance to the master suite to another rooftop exit. This one led to a wraparound balcony that surrounded the master suite on three sides. RPC streamed in from several directions at once and surrounded the suite from both the exterior and along the hallway inside.

Aspet held up his left hand with a finger of his right poised over the shutter override. He was waiting for the RPC to signal him that they were in position inside. When everyone was ready, he counted three by waving his arm and then pressed the last key of the override code.

Windows crashed, wood splintered, and the sounds of RPC agents shouting orders filled the air. Aspet leapt through a shattered window frame behind a couple of burly agents to see Boogla perched on top of a hobgoblin dressed all in black. She had her fist poised in a throat strike. As she looked up, startled in her infirm condition at the sudden inundation of RPC, she saw Ballop'ril and Prond, the Archmage having pulled the coordinates from the FAC, shimmer into solidity to one side and stared at the manifestation for a second, confused.

The hobgoblin took that opportunity to stretch out his arm and toss a small blue vial far into the air. It arced up and over the side of the balcony. Boogla screamed for someone to grab it, but it was over everyone's head. Prond raised his arm and a stream of silver light from a stasis spell shot out, surrounding the vial and bringing it gently toward him. Aspet raced over and snatched it out of midair. He ran back to Boogla, who had tumbled off of the hobgoblin and was lying on the ground grasping her chest in respiratory distress, and dribbled the liquid carefully between her lips until she had drunk every drop.

The hob was under close guard by the RPC, who had an even dozen weapons leveled at him, but while everyone was scrambling for the vial he had swallowed the capsule secreted in his cheek pouch. His back suddenly stiffened and he arched up in a massive convulsion. When it relaxed he was dead.

Boogla was kept in the Royal Infirmary for three days under observation with a Traumamine drip to keep her tranquil, but the antidote did its job and she was released with no apparent ill effects. Aspet personally issued an International Royal Writ of Arrest for Esfina Frem, but she had gone into hiding after the failed assassination/extortion attempt. He further notified the government of Solemadrina through official channels that their trade shipments were being hijacked to funnel illegal exports to the black market.

Dolmax called an all-hands conference for the RPC and they went over every last detail of the fiasco, looking for places where they had failed and coming up with ways to prevent them happening again. Every agent was required to take forty hours of additional training, during which they practiced responding to intrusions in the Royal Complex over and over again until it was a reflex for them. Dolmax offered his resignation in response to the RPC failure; Aspet rolled his eyes and refused to accept it.

"I have an RPC Director who just participated in the greatest training exercise ever held in Tragacanth. What kind of fool would I be to lose him now? I am safe; Boogla is safe; that's all that matters. Get back to work, Director Dolmax."

Chapter the Ninth

in which the Royal Couple take a holiday and have pleasant diversions

It was estimated it would take at least a fortnight to repair the damage to the Royal master suite, so Aspet decided to take his recuperating wife and temporarily relocate the seat of government to one of the vacation palaces. He'd been to Hikklew; that was the smaller location where he first met up with Boogla. There was another one, though: a sprawling estate called Saltchitterington on Myndrythyl Bay, about midway between Port Zog and Lumbos. Aspet had stopped there once briefly on a previous visit to Lumbos to confer with the Oria Magineer. He had been quite impressed and now felt strangely drawn to the place.

As soon as he announced his intentions, he sent into operation a long chain of events. First, the RPC headed for Saltchitterington, code-named 'Natra,' to prepare for Royal residence. As Natra was a Royal estate to begin with there was a small contingent of RPC agents assigned there full time—one of the cushiest, if least exciting, billets in the Corps—but a far larger presence was required when the King and Consort were on location. With this latest unpleasantness, the embarrassed RPC were taking no chances: the place was searched and locked down one square meter at a time, inside and out.

By the time Aspet and Boogla rolled up in the Royal limousine from the carriage station, Saltchitterington was as secure as the RPC could make it. Part of the challenge of VIP security was transparency: it was important to keep as much of the security apparatus as possible invisible or at least low-profile to those being guarded.

The estate was modeled along the lines of those popular with videoz and music celebrities: large main house with several wings, pool with waterfalls, elaborate pool house, several guest houses, and riding stables. On the rear margin of the property, overlooking the bay, stood the ruins of one of the first goblin keeps built in nascent Tragacanth, nearly four thousand years ago. It was estimated that it had been continuously occupied for at least a millennium afterwards, perhaps longer. That still left nearly three thousand years since the last inhabitants moved out, which of course led to a plethora of ghost stories also attached to it.

Aspet was fascinated by the carvings and close-fitting dressed stone accomplished with only primitive tools. Even a few of the original roof and floor timbers were still extant and in place. He liked to sit in the ruins and try to imagine life in this spot thirty-five centums ago, during the heyday of its habitation. Upon consulting with the RSCA and finding that little was really known about the everyday life of people in that era, His Majesty Tragacanth had an idea.

Aspet knew from his 'freelance' hacking days that there were a number of underground groups whose membership overlapped somewhat with the hacking community. These ranged from people who collected comic journals to those who were involved in live action role-playing games. One of these groups hosted a series of historically-themed parties annually; Aspet had attended a couple some years ago.

He contacted the head of the group, the 'seneschal,' by computer mail (voice was usually awkward, as the other end had to adjust to the fact they were talking to the King of Tragacanth) and made him a proposition: if the group would agree to use it and keep it maintained, he would fund the restoration of the site as historically accurately as possible and give the group a long-term lease for its use, provided that at least two weeks of the year in the summer they would open it to the public as a 'living history village.' The King wanted people to be able to walk through and see first-hand how their ancestors had actually lived and worked.

He knew the members of the group did their best to wear period clothing and eat and drink from period utensils, play period games, and use appropriate language to the extent practical. While the site was some distance from Goblinopolis, where they were headquartered, there was frequent inexpensive carriage service available.

Thus was the Society for Historical Re-creation propelled from an obscure urban social clique to a Royally-sponsored organization with funding and instant prestige. The seneschal was actually a gaming buddy of Aspet's named Hekka, although His Majesty had forgotten that until he was reminded. In the SHR everyone adopted names that historically could have existed, so in fact Hekka went by 'Abfabra Foe-Thumper.'He had gone by that name for so long now that even people outside the SHR called him 'Abfabra' or 'Abfab' these days.

The first step was to get a reputable history scholar out here and draw up a realistic plan for the keep and settlement. Once that was done they could choose and locate the correct materials and begin restoration work. It was during this work that the strange events began.

At first they were innocuous and easy to mistake for coincidence or just practical jokes: tools moved a meter or two from where they had been left; opened doors were now closed and vice-versa; architectural drawings were taken from drafting tables and replaced upside down or backwards; lunchbox contents were mysteriously exchanged. The workers grew accustomed to this activity and even found it somewhat amusing.

After several weeks, however, events took a darker turn. One of the workers was injured when a wall suddenly collapsed on him. The wall in question had been certified structurally sound by an engineer only the day before. Then nails began to shoot across rooms randomly, at velocities sufficient to pierce goblin hide, although no one had yet been punctured. This was the point at which all involved had to face the fact that someone or something atypical was behind these occurrences. Nails can't simply propel themselves through the air like that.

They set up conventional cameras to record the perpetrators, but got nothing. Then they tried infrared cameras and for the first time garnered some evidence in the form of cold spots, vaguely bipedal in shape, moving across the field of view. They left the cameras running for a full week and when they reviewed the video got the shock of their lives.

Aspet stared at the communiqué in disbelief, as though it had just grown lips in front of him and asked for a breath mint. "They've discovered *what*?" he asked no one in particular, who happened to be standing nearby. He continued reading. "An *exorcist*? They actually want to hire an *exorcist*?" He rolled his eyes. "Sweetheart, I'm going to take a ride to the ruins and find out what in the smek is going on down there. Wanna come along?"

Boogla thought about it. "Sure; why not? Might be interesting, given that they apparently believe them to be some manner of haunted." Aspet told the RPC where he was going and they escorted him and Boogla down to the all-terrain prams used on the estate. The RPC were a little nervous about the expedition.

"We're not sure if we can adequately guard you from this threat," the captain of Aspet's personal guards told him.

"Surely you don't believe the ruins have actual ghosts in them, do you?"

"We don't know what to believe. If they do exist, however, it is our sworn duty to prevent them from harming you. Somehow."

"Captain, if I am harmed in any way by a ghost, I will hold you and your team blameless in the matter."

"We appreciate that, Your Majesty, but it would constitute a violation of our oaths nonetheless."

"Well, I strongly suspect you won't need to violate anything today. If there are any ghosts I will sic Her Highness on them. She could probably face down the entire population of the underworld: one at a time, or *en masse*."

"Are you creating work for me?" Boogla asked, giggling.

"I doubt it would be much like work for you. More like recreation, which is, after all, why we're here."

Despite the putative supernatural activity, the reconstruction team had made impressive progress. They framed out a half-dozen buildings using hand-cut timbers, laid floor mosaics, cut a huge pile of slate roof tiles, and began manufacturing tools and utensils common to everyday life back then, at least according to the history scholar in residence. Aspet started asking around concerning the supernatural occurrences, but most of the workers were too embarrassed to admit to the Monarch that they had experienced anything of the sort.

Fortunately, the site foreman was something of an amateur ghost hunter and had kept a detailed log of the events, times, and locations. Aspet and Boogla backtracked over them, one at a time, looking for commonalities. As they studied the records, Boogla suddenly spoke up.

"Even though the events themselves were occurring pretty much all over the site, notice that they all seem to coincide with significant work being done in one area: that building in the corner." She pointed at it.

Aspet looked at her notes and nodded. "Do we have any idea what that structure was used for?"

"Let's ask the scholar."

Doctor Reoksa was Northeastern Regional Director of the Tragacanth Historical League and the scholar charged with interpretation of the site. She was not very tolerant of this ghost nonsense, but since it was the King asking, she cooperated.

"Your Majesty, my best guess based on the layout, artifacts recovered, and contemporary accounts is that this structure was a teaching facility or possibly some sort of laboratory."

"Laboratory, eh? Maybe there was a tragic accident that killed some people who are still hanging around."

"Your Majesty, may I speak freely?"

"Of course, Doctor Reoksa. Go right ahead."

"I know of no empirical evidence, much less a theory or even plausible hypothesis, which could account for a spirit somehow living on after the death of its host organism. The energy requirements and intelligence source necessary simply do not add up. It is possible that ghosts exist as something completely outside our realm of experience or scholarship, but the odds against that are rather steep."

"Agreed, Doctor, although I saw something I could not personally explain that was identified to me as representing 'spirits' in the Kopyrewt Forest. Be that as it may, we're mostly just being entertained here. Taking some time off from reality, as it were."

"Very good. There's certainly nothing wrong with the occasional flight of fancy."

"Thank you for your time and expertise, Doctor. We're going to explore on our own now. We promise not to disturb any artifacts."

"I very much appreciate that, Your Majesty." She added, after a moment, "They are, of course, yours to disturb."

Aspet and Boogla strolled away, leaving Reoksa cataloguing what looked like miniature eating utensils. Boogla wanted to take another look at the layout of the buildings; Aspet was contemplating the possible explanations for the disturbances. They stopped in the center of the unknown structure and sat on work stools brought in by the RSCA crew.

Suddenly the small stone chest Aspet was holding in his hand began to glow and vibrate. He stared at it for a moment and then decided, as the RPC looked on in alarm, it would be prudent to set it down on a table. As he did a series of differently-colored smoke trails launched from the interior of the chest, filling the immediate area with chromatic smog. Boogla came over and stood by Aspet, as did two of the RPC detachment, who all at once drew their weapons.

"There are things moving around in there, Your Majesty. Get away from them."

Aspet was too fascinated to respond. Indeterminate bipedal figures had materialized from the smoke. They weren't hidden or obscured by so much as composed of it. They gestured toward Aspet and pointed to a spot on the ground, but otherwise made no threatening moves. After a few moments a breeze came through the ruins and the smoke began to dissipate, taking the apparitions with it.

After the RPC had declared the area safe again, Aspet went over to the spot the phantoms had pointed at and began to dig carefully. About twenty centimeters down he ran into the lid of a much larger stone chest. Enlisting the assistance of some of the site workers, Aspet finally got the chest excavated. He and Reoksa lifted the lid slowly and gently, setting it with great care off to one side. There were three separate hermetic seals around the contents, which almost unbelievably contained intact parchment from, apparently, forty centums ago.

Aspet let the more experienced Reoksa handle the documents wearing gloves and a mask to cut down on moisture contamination from her exhalations. The parchments contained both text and areas of symbols, but neither was in any known language. Reoksa took detailed photographs of each page and then packed them away for shipment back to the RSCA lab in Goblinopolis.

"I'd like a copy of those documents as soon as practical," Aspet said.

"Certainly, Your Majesty. May I ask why?"

"I know someone who would find them interesting."

"That person is welcome to look at them at the RSCA archives."

"I'm aware of that, but I'd rather show them to him personally, here on site."

"I'll send them off by special courier and have the facsimiles back in no later than 44 hours, Your Majesty."

"Splendid. Thank you, Doctor Reoksa."

After she walked off with the crate of manuscripts, Boogla wandered up. "Why did you want copies?" she asked.

"I think one of Tol's transcendent archmage buddies may know something about this place."

"What makes you think that?"

"I got a good look at those drawings. Some of them resemble magical glyphs. If that is what they are, this site may have something to do with the earliest magic users on N'plork. One of those mages is over 900 years old. He might have at least heard of the place."

"Sounds reasonable. How are you going to get hold of him?"

He held up his comm.

"You can call The Slice on that thing? Talk about long distance charges."

Aspet chuckled. "No, I can't call The Slice directly, but I can call Tol. He knows how to get in touch with the transcendents. He has an amulet or something."

"Handy thing to have."

"I suppose so."

Two days later the high-quality facsimiles were delivered to Saltchitterington and an hour or so after that Plåk suddenly materialized. The RPC went for their weapons out of reflex but Plåk ignored them.

"Greetings, Aspet. Imagine meeting you again."

Aspet looked hard at him. "*Have* we met?"

"Oh yes, though I doubt you'll remember it. You had a dream injected into your mind prior to the throne challenge and I helped you navigate through the difficult parts toward the end. My name is Plåk. I'm the archmage who's over nine centums old."

Boogla giggled. "I'd like to say you're looking well for someone that age, but I don't know what your species is supposed to look like when it's old."

"I *am* quite well-preserved, thank you."

"Well met, Archmage Plåk," Aspet said, "I called Tol to have him ask you to come here. I want to show you some manuscript copies and see if you recognize them. They're probably close to four thousand years old."

"I'm excited about any artifact that makes me feel young by comparison. Lead on."

Aspet slid the facsimiles from their sheath and laid them out on a table. Plåk studied them with ever-increasing concentration, moving back and forth among several repeatedly. At length he sat on a stool at the end of the table and looked up.

"I need more time with these, but I can't stay here much longer. Can you leave them out like this? I'll come back just as soon as I can recharge in The Slice."

Aspet nodded. "They'll be just as you left them. Hurry back."

"That, I most assuredly shall. Farewell for now."

He faded away in a fine shower of sparkles.

"I wonder what he thinks we have here?" asked Boogla.

"I don't know, but whatever it is sure seems to have captured his attention."

"What did he mean by that dream reference?"

Aspet exhaled audibly. "CoME injects the neuroelectrical field of throne challengers with a specially-designed entangled stream of signals while they sleep that is interpreted by the candidate's brain as a dream. They monitor the response to the puzzles presented in that dream to determine various aspects of the candidate's personality and intellect. They can weed out psychopaths and utter lunatics quite effectively this way, even if they are adept at disguising those traits in personal interactions. There is a disentanglement trigger provided to each challenger afterwards to allow them to shed the dream from their short- and long-term memory. Otherwise it takes up so much space in the brain that it runs the risk of driving the person mad."

"So, you can't remember any of it at all?"

"I have occasional flashes of recollection; they told me that would probably happen the rest of my life. But for the most part, no."

"Meaning you don't know if Plåk is telling the truth or not?"

"Not absolutely. But I have an intuitive impression that he is. Something just... rings true about his claim. At any rate, he helped Tol out quite a bit during the Pyfox business so he's not intrinsically evil or anything, no matter what might have happened in Morianella. Hey, let's go grab some lunch by the waterfall."

"Marvelous idea, my love."

"Of *course* it's a marvelous idea," Aspet replied, grinning widely.

After a cold lunch fit for a King and his Consort, Aspet and Boogla were walking hand-in-hand along a charming gravel path that led from the fruit orchard up to the waterfall when the air in front of them began to shimmer. The RPC went on guard but Aspet put out his hand for them to stand down. Plåk was back.

"I finished analyzing the manuscripts," he said, as soon as there was enough mouth to talk. "What you've got there is a journal of the parasciencers: the 'protomages' who suspected magic existed but didn't know how to invoke it. It is, as far as I am aware, the only extant written records from that ancient period. Even during my youth nine hundred years ago these would have been incalculably valuable historical artifacts. I cannot even begin to image what they are worth now; probably more than the Royal Palace itself."

"How were you able to decipher the manuscripts? What language was that?" Boogla asked.

"The script is now called *Arcanis Symbolis Anciens*; those parasciencers probably invented it. A form of it is still in use in some esoteric magical academic circles, although it is not generally taught in arcane academies as it only applies to some very specialized magic of interest to mages who study early incantation forms and a few others. I used magic to read and comprehend it through the principal of transharmonic coupling, meaning that once I worked out the intended magical effect of any part of the writing I could derive the rest of the meaning by following the harmonic resonance lines of arcane force until I found one that coincided with another magical action on the page. When I made that connection everything between those two points became comprehensible to me. I repeated this process until I understood the entire manuscript."

Aspet shrugged. "Sounds good to me. So, what does this manuscript say that is of interest to a non-mage?"

"Apparently they had encounters with transient energy streams originating in The Slice which brought them to the realization that magic itself existed. Their early attempts to make use of it seem crude and awkward now, but you have to put yourself in that situation to make sense of them. Imagine living on a world where the air is always perfectly still at the surface. Then one day you notice the smoke from a campfire rising straight up for a certain distance before making an abrupt ninety degree turn and streaming away. You deduce from this that the air at that elevation must be moving. You have just discovered the existence of wind, although you can't feel it directly yourself. This is roughly equivalent to the philosophical impact of magic on those pioneer mages."

"I see," replied Boogla, "They could observe the effects of magic so they knew it existed; they just had to figure out some way to tap into that energy and make use of it under their control."

"Precisely. I believe that once the manuscript has been studied at length by scholars, it will answer questions that have haunted the magic user community for forty centums: how did the parasciencers make the transition to true mages?"

"Speaking of haunting, that's how we came to find the manuscript cache in the first place."

Plåk looked puzzled. "Come again?"

"Haunting," replied Aspet. "We came down here because strange things were going on that made people think the place was haunted. Objects relocated, doors opening and closing: that sort of thing. I opened a small stone box and these apparitions made of smoke led us to the place where the sealed chest containing the manuscripts was buried."

"Fascinating. I've never encountered that sort of activity before. The dead no longer have access to this plane ordinarily; I wonder what is going on? Mind if I snoop around there?"

"Not at all. I'll show you the exact spot."

They led Plåk to the hole where the chest had been. He walked all the way around it.

"There's a curious linkage here I don't understand; something magical but not quite transcendental. Oh, and there's more stuff buried deeper down, incidentally. You only uncovered the top layer. The lower layers are full of some seriously funky gewgaws."

"Thanks," replied Aspet, "I'll make a note of that for the RSCA. I suspect they were planning to excavate further, anyway."

"I believe once all of it has been dug out the 'hauntings' will cease. Rather than supernatural activity, this appears to me to be some sort of beacon left here by the earliest mages to make certain this cache was eventually found. Ordinarily such a manifestation would not turn violent, but if they instilled it with a geas to be noticed, it's difficult to predict just how far things would go to achieve that goal. And now, if you'll excuse me, I must return to The Slice."

With that he bowed and shimmered out of sight.

"I wonder," Boogla mused as she stared in a kind of semi-trance at the spot where Plåk had disappeared, "What he meant by 'seriously funky gewgaws'?"

"I expect the RSCA will discover that for us in due time."

"I don't want to wait," said Boogla, and grabbed a shovel.

"Sweetie, what are you doing?"

"I'm digging, what does it look like? Stop being a stuffy ol' monarch and help me."

"Fine." Aspet found another shovel and together they dug, to the consternation and bemusement of the RPC.

About half a meter further down they encountered what resembled a sarcophagus. Aspet was concerned: if this contained the remains of a person they needed to be extraordinarily careful with it, to avoid inadvertently desecrating a corpse and violating the customs of the race that buried it. Still, why would the parasciencers bury a body here? They had already discovered the burial grounds for the settlement; the deceased there were interred in coffins of various levels of workmanship and sophistication, but all of them were in a defined and recognizable area.

The finally agreed to pry open the lid and take a peek. The RSCA wouldn't approve of course; the opening should be performed in a more controlled environment. They did have the presence of mind to grab a couple breathing masks in case there were unfriendly microbes hibernating in there.

What they found staring back at them was something neither had ever seen nor even imagined. It was a bipedal creature made entirely of different kinds of metal: an apparent automaton, in other words. It was vaguely goblin-esque in appearance, but in size it approached ogre. They cleared out all around it, rolled over a portable crane, and hoisted the huge casket up onto the ground.

One of the RSCA staff happened by and ran in, shouting, "You can't do that! Put that down! That's property of the RSCA."

Aspet looked her in the eye, expecting a glimmer of recognition, but got nothing. She continued to fuss around, trying to undo the damage they'd done, as she saw it.

Aspet sighed and walked over to the RPC captain. When he came back he was wearing the Crown of Tragacanth. He stood in front of the casket.

"I don't think I heard you correctly. This casket is whose property?"

"I told you, this casket belongs to..." At this point her eyes went up to the crown and suddenly got very wide. "...His Majesty Tragacanth, who may of course do with it as He pleases."

"Thank you. I knew I misheard you the first time. Tell Doctor Reoksa we'll try not to leave an irreparable mess."

"Yes, Your Majesty," she bowed and backed away. After about five steps she turned and ran.

Aspet returned the crown to the RPC captain for safekeeping.

"Sometimes I enjoy doing that and sometimes I don't"

"How about this time?" Boogla asked.

"Enjoyed it."

Eventually, with the help and oversight of the RSCA, they levered the automaton out of its sarcophagus and began examining it. The RPC stood close by and fretted. It made them very nervous when Aspet put himself in harm's way by fiddling around with an ancient mechanism with unknown defensive capabilities. Previous kings had shown little interest in such matters. What they failed to take into account is that standing in front of them were probably the two top hackers in Tragacanth—and if there's one thing hackers love to do, it's take things apart and (sometimes) put them back together.

With the help of some nifty tools requisitioned by Aspet, the Royal Couple managed to open a panel on the automaton and discovered that it was a mere shell. The internal components had been removed and stored somewhere, and that somewhere now became their next search objective.

It was fortunate that they experienced such success initially, because the Quest for the Guts was a dismal failure. They did uncover a great many interesting artifacts along the way, but the automaton works remained elusive. During a rest period Aspet was exploring inside the shell with his fingers when came across something that felt like a latch. It felt so much like a latch, in fact, that he pulled it and was gratified when the entire structure popped open like a casket.

The interior was not lined with connections for wires and pipes, as they had expected, but instead padded and fitted with layers of some strange metallic fiber. They puzzled over it for some time, until Aspet suddenly perked up.

"Boogla, come here. Lie down in this."

"I'm sorry; I thought you told me to lie down in that."

"I did. I think that's what it's for."

"Napping?"

"No, no. I think it was meant to be some sort of protective garment."

"I don't want to lie down in it."

"Fine. *I'll* do it, then."

An RPC agent appeared as if out of nowhere. "Please allow me, Your Majesty. We don't know what it might do."

"Right as usual," sighed Aspet, "Carry on, then."

The agent eased himself into the shell and fit almost perfectly, as the ogre sizing was the result of superstructure in the apparatus.

"Good," said Aspet, "Now, hold still."

He and Boogla carefully set the top of the shell back on as the poor RPC agent wondered what was going to happen to him. As Aspet worked to fasten the container back up, Boogla disappeared and came back lugging a box of something.

"I found this earlier and didn't know what it was. Now I think it might be some form of power supply." She set the metal-covered object down next to the sarcophagus and was gratified when two of the short cables coming out of the enclosure matched up perfectly with posts on the box.

Aspet looked in the viewport of the sarcophagus just above the agent's face. "We're just going to activate this for a second. Please give us a full account of what you experience."

The agent nodded slightly; as much as he could in the close-fitting container. Aspet did one last check of the container seal and then signaled to Boogla. She flipped a single pole-double throw switch on the side of the box and instantly a blinding light appeared inside the sarcophagus, accompanied by a low-frequency crackling. It lasted perhaps three seconds and then died away.

They popped open the box. The RPC agent was lying there with wide eyes and a little drool coming from his mouth. They helped him out of the sarcophagus; Aspet motioned for the Royal Physician to come check him over. When he was declared to be in good health they sat him down with pad and pen and asked him to narrate his experience for them in as great a detail as he could muster. He did so in a shaky hand, without speaking.

When he finished his narrative, Aspet read over it. He opened his personal briefcase, pulled out a sheaf of pre-printed parchments with Royal Letterhead and a pen, and wrote something on one before stamping it with the Royal Sigil embedded in his ring. He handed the parchment to the RPC Captain, who nodded and took the agent aside. After a minute or so the agent grabbed his gear and wobbled off down the path.

Boogla cocked her head in curiosity. "What did you do?" she asked Aspet.

"I gave him two weeks of paid leave and a bonus for service above and beyond the call of duty."

"Generous. Exactly what did he go through to deserve that?"

Aspet handed her the notepad. She read it with increasing excitement. "So, are we going to try it?"

"I'd love to, but the RPC would go ballistic. We need more controlled conditions"

"What we *need* is a mage."

"I think I know where to find a suitable candidate."

The next morning Ballop'ril and Prond appeared at the compound, answering a Royal summons. Aspet took Ballop'ril aside and talked to him for some time, then escorted him over to see the sarcophagus. The old archmage was visibly excited.

"If what the young agent wrote is accurate, this may be the missing link; the means by which the first mages were created. If so, it is an artifact of inestimable value."

"That phrase pops up a lot in reference to this site. The Magineer Liaison and I were able to locate the original power supply and for some bizarre reason it still works after all this time." Aspet said, "Here it is." He led Ballop'ril over to the box, still hooked up to the sarcophagus.

Ballop'ril laid one hand on each side of the ancient iron container and closed his eyes. He opened them again abruptly with an almost audible snap.

"It is not a power supply," he pronounced, "It is a conduit. A network connector, if you will, to The Slice. Anyone in that sarcophagus gets transported there; presumably for training purposes."

"Visiting The Slice to get trained?" Boogla asked, "By whom?"

"The arcanelementals" said a voice down the path a bit. The RPC went on guard. It was Oloi, who had teleported some distance away to give the RPC less likelihood of a coronary. Aspet waved them off as he approached and they relaxed.

"I saw the RPC agent materialize briefly in The Slice and traced the activity to here. I've heard rumors and rumors of rumors about this device from time to time, but I was never certain how much credence to lend them."

"How are the arcanelementals connected to this?" asked Ballop'ril.

"They are creations of The Slice itself: sent to worlds enveloped by the Dark Energetic Continuum to cultivate magic use and thereby assist in bleeding off excess energy in the form of 'manna.' The Continuum has many—perhaps millions or even billions—of gravitational sinks set into it that constantly suck in matter and convert it to back to energy, most of which ends up in the form we know as manna. In order to maintain stability, most of that energy must be bled off. It is likely that The Continuum represents the first sentience in the universe. It is certainly the largest, in any case. It apparently generates these beings that we call arcanelementals to infiltrate a non-magic-using world and correct that deficiency for its own purposes."

"So, they come here and do what?" asked Aspet, "Build a sarcophagus to transport people to The Slice? How does that achieve their final goal?"

"I cannot answer that with certainty, but I would hazard a guess that once in The Slice each proto-mage was given some manner of magical reservoir—a speculum arcanis. On their return to N'plork they were able to use their new manna supply to perform magic, as taught to them by the arcanelementals."

"So, they were jump started by the arcanelementals. That explains how they went from parasciencers to archmages in such a short time."

"Yes. Creating a self-perpetuating cadre of magic-users on each inhabited planet in contact with the Continuum ensures a constant drain of energy from it and therefore its continued stability. This, I believe, is a primary self-preservation mechanism for The Slice."

"So, in essence," Ballop'ril added, "This is a transcendence-simulator suit."

Oloi thought about it. "Yes, that's exactly what it is, except the restrictions are reversed: you can only stay in The Slice for a short while before you revert."

"Do we know how long, precisely?"

"I'd make a wild guess based on the energy signature I observed of about…half an hour."

"So, they made multiple trips until they were up sufficiently educated?"

"Possibly. I think it more likely that each of them only made the trip once: that was enough to convince them that what they were dealing with—magic—was real and a force that could realistically be harnessed and controlled."

"If you think about the state of civilization then," said Boogla, "The Slice must have seemed even more exotic and miraculous than it does today. It's no wonder they were profoundly affected by the sight of it."

"This find should make Doctor Reoksa's day, if not week," Aspet mused.

"Perhaps even entire career, given the magnitude of these artifacts," said Ballop'ril. "They solve a mystery that has been haunting us for thousands of years."

"And that brings us neatly back to the question of who or what was haunting this area in the first place," said Boogla.

"I thought we'd already established they were some form of magical beacons."

"'Beacons' that move objects around and fire nails across the room? I suppose that makes *him* a beacon, too." She pointed at a glowing figure standing behind the RPC captain, who dove forward and came back up with his weapon drawn.

The figure—it looked like a malnourished goblin in a simple tunic and stitched shoes—regarded them mildly, ignoring the RPC's threatening posture. Most of the audience were just stunned and unsure of what action to take, if any, but Ballop'ril and Oloi walked over to it in fascination.

"Do you see the aura?" asked Oloi.

"Yes. It's quite strong. Some form of harmonic residual, perhaps."

"Partially, but it has a multiplanar presence that is most unusual."

"What is the geometry of the planar extrusions? Is it uniform or irregular?"

Oloi disappeared momentarily and then faded back into sight.

"The extrusion is minimal on all planes except this one and the hypertropic."

"The hypertropic? What purpose would an extrusion there serve?" Ballop'ril asked, stroking his beard.

"I have a theory," replied Oloi, "Let us test it. Give me a few seconds to situate myself in the hypertropic and then dispel the figure."

"Is not that a bit harsh? It has taken no action against us."

"I believe the effect will not be permanent."

"So, you wish for me to cast only a prime plane dispel, then?"

"No. Full-spectrum polyplanar." With that he dissolved once more.

Ballop'ril shrugged. "Sorry about this, whoever you are." He put his hands in front of him, palms facing forward, and suddenly pulled them apart. A flash of deep blue radiance erupted from the spot where his hands had begun and enveloped the specter, which faded away into nothing.

Ballop'ril stood awaiting the return of Oloi when suddenly the spectral figure itself faded back in, as though it had simply experienced a momentary power outage. Oloi reappeared a few seconds later.

"It's an anchor," he explained, "Your dispel got looped around and fed back into the energy stream that reconstituted the apparition. It's a permanent self-regenerating installation."

"That makes no sense. It would take an incredible amount of energy to establish a hypertropic extrusion that was stable for this long. What possible reason could there be for someone to go through that simply to provide a location with a permanent spook? Especially one that doesn't seem to speak or move much."

"We haven't hit the right trigger yet."

"What are we supposed to do?" asked Boogla, "Jump up and down and stick out our tongues?"

"I do not know. Try it," Oloi answered. "I'll be back," he added, fading from sight with a faint sparkle.

"That must be annoying," Aspet observed.

"What, Your Majesty?" asked Boogla.

"Having to go home and recharge every so often."

"We all do that in a manner of speaking," replied Ballop'ril, "Just on a longer cycle and with somewhat more freedom of scheduling."

Boogla walked over to the apparition and then straight through it.

"Did you feel anything?" asked Ballop'ril

"Just a slight tingle."

"That's the power flux. The thing is using a tremendous amount of energy."

Aspet was looking at something directly in the line of sight of the specter.

"This looks like some faint symbol set into the floor." He knelt down and wiped off the dust. As his hand moved across the apparition began to speak. Everyone stared in amazement.

"Ersryhestan me golspij'nemol is Qillopot selmone. Klasetgilomj'giloma. Lo kop re'sthklaju Ta'slizh'I," it said, in a slow, measured, faintly metallic voice. They all scratched their heads as it droned on, repeating the announcement, or whatever it was, in an endless loop.

"My best guess would be some form of protogoblish," said Ballop'ril, finally.

"Do we know anyone who understands protogoblish?" asked Aspet.

"Only a few academics. Come to think of it, one of them might be Dr. Reoksa."

"Let's see if we can get her over here." He pointed at the RPC captain's comm.

Half an hour later the good doctor came putting up in her little pram. Aspet explained the situation to her and led her over to the apparition, which she regarded with a mixture of scholarly curiosity and alarm. He stood on the trigger glyph and she listened intently as the specter spoke.

"It's a dialect of protogoblish known as *Noorpridic* because it was first documented from a small island a few hundred kilometers off the coast of Esmia..." She tailed off.

"Well," Aspet asked after a few seconds of silence," What is he saying?"

Dr. Reoksa scratched her cheek. "He appears to be, um, barking."

"Barking? Like a hound?" Aspet was incredulous.

"Like a carnival barker," interjected Ballop'ril, "He is trying to...sell us something."

"So it would seem," agreed Dr. Reoksa, "The translation is, more or less, 'Be welcome here in Qillopot, all goblins, and hear my words: come and try on the raiment of wonder to be transported to the energy source and return a goblin enraptured.' I'm not too sure about that last word—*re'sthklaju*—but 'enraptured' is pretty close."

"So, they constructed this amazing suit just to entertain the masses?" asked Boogla.

"I expect that is merely an afterthought," said Ballop'ril, "To provide funding for future magical endeavors. Remember that magic was a new phenomenon at the time; most people believed it to be no more than prestidigitatory illusion. In order to gain some cachet as a serious scholarly pursuit they needed to present more than simple parlor tricks. It is one thing to be told of a separate plane of existence where a previously unknown form of energy originates; it is quite another to witness it with your own eyes."

Aspet chuckled. "So, instead of turning people into amphibians to illustrate that they were legitimate they just let them peek through a window at The Slice, eh?"

"Must have worked; that's probably where they got the money to build this complex," Boogla said.

"This was probably the most exhilarating experience most of these people had ever had. Remember, we're talking four thousand years ago: agrarian economy, iron implements, simple tools. The introduction of a force as powerful as magic must have been enormously transformative," said Dr. Reoksa.

"Even with the assistance of the arcanelementals it would have taken them years to master the physical control necessary to perform magic at the archmage level. Knowledge of the process is only part of that challenge," said Ballop'ril, "This carnival act may have been the only way they could impress people enough to support their efforts."

"In some ways this reminds me of Arbus and the Elder Grove. That early era of exploration and discovery on N'plork must have been an exciting time." Aspet suddenly stopped and stared off into space. After a few seconds he grinned and walked over to Boogla, taking both her hands.

"I want to make a side trip on our way home."

"Of course. Where did you want to go?"

"Dockside. In Goblinopolis."

"Visiting your old neighborhood?"

"In this case, no. I want to meet and talk with a very enigmatic entity who lives there."

Boogla looked puzzled.

"His name is H'esh'tuk, but he is more commonly referred to as 'the Exalted One.'"

Recognition glinted in her eyes. "The creature with all the tentacles. It's funny, but one of the Sisters of the Code is a dwarf born into his sect. She left them on friendly terms when she attended Polytechnic, but she still goes back to visit every so often. She says he is a remarkable person: a 'force of nature,' in fact."

"All the more reason to pay him a visit," Aspet declared. "I ran across him from time to time as a lad, but I always thought he and his dwarven retinue were a bit strange and gave them a wide berth. I understand he and Tol are something like buddies, though. I even saw him at Tol's knighting."

Boogla shrugged, "I'm game."

Chapter the Tenth

in which the origin of The Exalted One is revealed

The next morning, bright and early, the Royal Party set off for Goblinopolis, leaving Dr. Reoksa behind to supervise the excavation and restoration of what they now knew to be Qillopot, the presumptive birthplace of magic on N'plork. Aspet had sent a message to Tol asking him to meet them at the carriage station, to provide an introduction and because Aspet knew Tol would enjoy visiting with H'esh'tuk.

In the Royal limo on the way to Dockside, Aspet quizzed Tol on the mysterious creature.

"So, what is he like? For that matter what *is* he?" Aspet asked, munching on a protein bar.

Tol accepted his offer of one of his own and thought about the answer as he opened the wrapper.

"I don't really know what he is. Not from around here, that's for sure. He can talk, but if he has any eyes, I haven't seen them. He seems to perceive his environment largely by touch: those tentacles are very, very sensitive. He also occasionally emits a high-pitched trilling noise that may be some form of echolocation. That reminds me: if you're going to meet him, he will want to run those tentacles all over your face. Better warn the RPC about that or they might get unpleasant with him."

"Great advice. I will do definitely do that. Are they... slimy or anything?

"No, nothing like that. They are dry and his touch is very light. They just brush against you, really."

"Good. That doesn't sound too traumatic or invasive."

"It isn't. It's disconcerting if you're not expecting it, but otherwise there's nothin' to it."

As luck would have it, the Exalted One was in residence at the Temple of Placidity when the Royal Convoy rolled up. Aspet's first contact with H'esh'tuk went off smoothly; the RPC, while nervous and extremely attentive, allowed him to probe Aspet without interference. As they sat in the meditation ring of the temple, sipping a herbal infusion that Aspet found delicious and a little intoxicating (although he would not say that out loud for fear the RPC would take it away from him), His Majesty decided to get down to business.

"Exalted One, may I ask your origins? How you came to be here at this place at this time?"

The barnacle body vibrated for a few seconds, tentacles flexing rhythmically, then at last a thin, wavering voice drifted out from somewhere inside the depths of the creature's bulk.

"My birth name was H'esh'tuk. I am from a world that called itself Djolda, which in my native tongue simply means 'Everything there is.' I was inducted at a young age into the Order of Salxeras, a monastic order that studied and worshipped the energies from which all living things are derived. Once every horcan, which corresponds to five circuits around our star, an elaborate ritual takes place in which the monk deemed holiest and most devout is chosen to be dropped into a swirling eddy of dark energy located on a high mountain top. In my forty-third circuit of existence I was named that most holy monk."

"So," interjected Tol, "Your reward for being the holiest monk was to be sacrificed. That doesn't sound as though it would encourage devotion very effectively."

"Ah, but do not mistake, Tol-u-ol: being chosen for the 'sacrifice' is the highest honor one may achieve in my Order. We refer to it as being 'sanctified,' rather than sacrificed."

"Well, yeah, 'cause everyone who gets it disappears into a black hole forever. It would be difficult to achieve much of anything after that."

"It requires many years of study and meditation, as well as being immersed in the culture, to understand why the sanctification is a goal to be desired," replied H'esh'tuk patiently, "Remember that we believed the energy field was a portal to paradise, not a death trap as you seem to think. We worshipped it as a manifestation of the Divine and called it the *Infinity Pool*."

"What would happen," Aspet asked, "If someone unworthy were to jump into the energy vortex?"

"We are taught that non-worthy subjects are cast into a vast plane of Limbo, forever to wander a barren and blasted landscape. They have no chance at Paradise."

"Bummer," said Tol, "I hope there's a fence around it or something."

"What was it like, to be 'sanctified' in that way?" Boogla asked.

"As I was lowered gently into the whirling energy field, I really had no idea what to expect. I pulled all of my tentacles in tight to my body and closed my eyes."

"You have *eyes*?" Tol interrupted.

"Yes, of course, Tol-u-ol. They are located on four of my tentacles, as you call them. These four." He waved four of the thicker appendages with bulbous endings on them.

"I see mostly in the realm you would call ultra-high frequency, although I can adjust the reception to a fairly broad range."

"So, you perceive the world in the radio spectrum, then?" said Boogla.

"Correct. I do not see 'color,' as I have come to understand it from speaking with my adherents, but I can distinguish between very fine textural differences that amount to colors. In other words, the pigments used to provide color often vary at the fine scale and I can distinguish between them, although I have no mental image of the different colors, per se."

"Fascinating and enlightening," Boogla replied, "Please, continue your story." Tol started to make a comment but she frowned at him and he shrank back a little in his chair, looking chagrined for her benefit.

"The air around me crackled and sputtered," H'esh'tuk resumed, "There were odors and sounds I could not identify. I fell through a hole in reality, plummeting rapidly without the sensation of falling. At last I came to a halt, at least as far as my deprived senses could tell. I opened my eyes gradually, thankful that I was still alive, or at least aware. I was in a small meadow of sweet heather and wildflowers, surrounded by tall plants with thick skin and many, many limbs terminating in clusters of delicate veined scales.

Two odd creatures with bipedal stance and only a single pair of upper appendages came crashing through the high grass, making a whistling noise I recognized as a form of music—yes, we had music on my world; it formed a very important part of our culture. I withdrew my tentacles and instinctively froze. They almost passed me by, but one of them glanced in my direction and approached, curious at what they perceived as an unusual plant form. I was unsure how to react, but I took a chance and began to hum an ancient song from my culture.

At first the creatures could not seem to understand where the noise was coming from, but they finally realized it was being generated by the 'plant.' They gawked in fascination until first one, then the other, began to hum along with me. I knew then that they were most likely sentient.

We traded songs for quite some time until they determined it was necessary to return to their homes. They seemed quite saddened by the parting, so I decided to follow them. Initially frightened, they soon realized that I was not a plant, but a sentient animal like themselves and that I meant them no harm. Over the next few months we developed a close friendship. They taught me first Dwarven and then Goblish.

That friendship evolved into a student-mentor relationship that eventually led to the formation of what I understand is now referred to officially as 'the Cult of H'esh'tuk.' I find this at once amusing and somewhat misleading, since we were only three for a good long while. Three seems a little sparse for a 'cult' to me. At any rate, after they left their homes and for my benefit lived a strictly nomadic life for some years, my companions were at last able to raise sufficient funds to build the Temple of Placidity, where you now sit."

"Your followers have petitioned me to grant protected religious status to a rather interesting arboreal manifestation in the center of the newly-created Kopyrewt Natural Preserve," said Aspet, "What say you to that?"

"That is one of the terminal nexuses for the dark energy vortex—the Infinity Pool—which connects to my homeworld. Sadly, the traversal is efferent only. The vortex provides some of the extradimensional manna the forest organism residing there requires to maintain sentience, although I doubt that organism is fully aware of this. It is a symbiotic relationship, as the vortex itself needs termini through which to bleed off energy in order to remain in an entropic steady-state."

"Wait," said Boogla, frowning, "Does that mean *every* sanctified monk ends up on N'plork? Why haven't we encountered any others?"

"No one really understands the process fully, but my best estimation from the known facts is that each sanctification creates a new terminus of the vortex at some other dark energy nexus. The possibility exists that if sufficient sanctifications take place the energy pulse may once again target N'plork, but I consider the chances of that quite remote given the dystropic nature of the event."

"What if the vortex terminus appears in deep space, or underwater, or in solid rock?" asked Tol.

"I have considered that myself," answered H'esh'tuk after a moment, "And I came to the conclusion that the vortex seeks approximately the same conditions of atmospheric composition, temperature, and gravity in order to terminate. It doesn't have to breathe or sustain biochemical reactions, of course, but the specific environmental conditions that support our form of life also combine, I believe, to form the ideal terminus point for the vortex. I also suspect this is no mere coincidence."

"It may also be intertwined with The Slice and therefore restricted to those planets where magic has been tapped," observed Boogla.

"Yes," the Exalted One replied, "That is another factor in the equation that plays a more important role than perhaps I had previously determined. Magic is a force to be reckoned with wherever it appears. The Slice and the Infinity Pool seem to share the same energy stabilization processes; it is likely therefore that they are both manifestations of the dark energetic continuum."

"Well," said Aspet, standing up, followed by everyone who wasn't already standing doing so as well, "While I've known of you all my life, H'esh'tuk, I've never really known you until now. I am granting the petition for special status of the Nexus Grove and I will issue a special limited dispensation for construction there. Please keep it to a minimum, as the area is now a Preserve and we need to limit encroachment of any kind as much as possible."

"As you command, so shall it be," replied one of the dwarves. "We will submit our plan for the shrine for your approval before any work begins. Much of it will involve entraining of plants already living there."

"Excellent and appreciated," replied Aspet, "Farewell to the Cult of H'esh'tuk and may the fates smile upon your lives and endeavors."

"Farewell, noble King. I name you *Aspet the Wise* and predict you will reign longer than any other King of Tragacanth."

Aspet was taken aback. "I... thank you for the well-wishes underlying that prognostication; many things must fall into place for it to be rendered accurate, I'm afraid."

"Nonetheless, the prediction stands."

Chapter the Eleventh

in which Tol rescues a slave beneath Hellehoell

Tol stepped off the carriage in Fenurian to quite a different picture than the previous time. Instead of tents and generators, there was a real live station house. It wasn't quite finished, but it was open for business and in comparison with the tents, quite elegant. On the ride to Hellehoell he saw other significant reconstruction efforts, including some needed infrastructure improvements to highways and public utilities. It was a far cry from the quake-ravaged landscape of three months earlier, and it cheered him considerably.

His purpose was to visit with the titan leadership and evaluate for the King how diplomatic ties were progressing. In order to encourage the titans and subject them to as little kingdom bureaucracy as necessary, Aspet had declared the occupied portions of Hellehoell an autonomous region, only nominally subject to the laws and oversight of the Tragacanth government. It was the first step toward granting them full city-state status, which was Aspet's eventual intent if they so desired it. It was a sincere offer, with no strings attached, and Tol was proud of his brother for extending it. So far CoME had offered no objections.

He drove a rented pram to the entrance to Hellehoell, now patrolled by teams consisting of both Ferroc Norda and titan guards. Tol was met by Tartag, who had been appointed Ambassador to Tragacanth by the first interim Hellehoell Council of Elders. The titan seemed quite excited over the prospect of showing off more of his beloved city to Tol. As they descended from the newly-widened entrance, the considerable progress of the titan restoration crews was quite evident. Gone were the dusty, dull stones and partially filled-in carvings. In their place were brilliantly gleaming facades of granite and marble with cunningly wrought silver inlays. The air, once musty and unpleasant, was now swept clean and cool, brought up from some deep reservoir. The streets were lit by a seemingly infinite number of gas lamps that cast a warm, yellow, inviting glow.

There was light everywhere; former murk and shadow now replaced by golden radiance. The very stone seemed alive and vibrant. As they moved even deeper the layout of the municipal complex, obscured by debris and dust during their first descent, was now revealed. A wide avenue paved with shimmering marble rolled past tall, beautiful town homes and shops to the central Plaza of the Wheel, where connecting broadstreets of quartz cobblestone took travelers to the eight outer cities, five of which were already mostly ready for occupancy as a result of the titans' hard work. Few creatures could work so diligently as titans, especially ones as strongly motivated as were these, reclaiming their magnificent birthright after millennia of dispersion.

Each of the perimeter cities, which Tartag referred to as 'Scintillas,' boasted its own unique fundamental architecture. One was based on blue bricks made from Tudmash Marsh mud; another on ironstone from the southern Masron and northern Espwe Mountains. A third boasted massive greenish blood timbers brought around in coastwise steamers from southern Galanga. Others were based on bleached sea-coral and shimmering starrock. Taken as a whole, Hellehoell represented every facet of titan society and knowledge, every social and cultural stratum—the full spectrum of what it meant to share the titan heritage.

As he toured the restorations, Tol was struck by the apparent incongruity of the huge, brutal titans of legend and these sensitive, industrious souls with the patience to carve intricate zoomorphics into ironstone columns and cornerstones. Perhaps titans who lived in the wild were somehow different, but Tol's instinct—the one that had saved his life innumerable times on the street—told him that this wasn't the case: titans had been saddled with their ferocious reputations merely because they *looked* capable of a great deal of mayhem. Of course Tol harbored no delusions that they could not tear up the landscape quite effectively given sufficient motivation, but overall they seemed peaceable creatures with little natural propensity for violence.

At the very deepest portion of the reconstruction, which now consisted of excavation of an area buried under an ancient collapse and rockslide, Tol and Tartag paused so that the titan could expound on what was known of this, the very oldest chamber, the first expansion of what up until then had merely been a wide shaft. It had been abandoned, the records said, after a sudden collapse of the roof and walls killed a number of workers. The cause of the collapse had never been officially determined, but to this day there persists in titan genetic memory the account of a creature or force awakened in the tunnels and the sacrifice of nine elite titan commandos who died holding it off while the explosives were planted to collapse the tunnel forever…or so they thought.

Tartag was rounding the corner, heading for home with his exposition, when suddenly his rumbling voice was interrupted by a shrill banshee wail and the sound of feet flying across stone. After a few seconds a large group of titans came barreling out of the newly-opened area. Tartag called to one in Titanic and seemed taken aback by the reply.

"It seems," he said in response to Tol's unspoken inquiry, "That they've inadvertently disturbed a nest of deepdrakes."

"What the smek is a 'deepdrake?'" Tol asked.

A voice from Tol's pocket suddenly cut in. "Deepdrakes were thought, at least up until now, to be mythical inhabitants of very far underground locations that serve as the transition zones between normal rock and magma chambers. They are reptiloid, ten to fourteen meters long, and associate in groups of up to twenty-five individuals."

"Thanks, Petey. Tartag, about how far beneath the surface are we right now?"

The titan did a little figuring in his head, putting his lengthy digits to good use in the process. "I'd say about a kilometer, give or take a few tens of meters."

Great. Petey, can you corroborate that?"

"It's a little difficult to be sure of calibration down here, but backtracking along my known good sensor readings and extrapolating where necessary, I would say approximately 1,037 meters."

"Well done, Tartag. At this point we only have two options, presuming all of the titans are out of there: we can push ahead and investigate these creatures in the name of science, or just re-seal the tunnel here and now and be done with it. If anyone wants my opinion, I'd say we go with the latter."

Before Tartag could answer, a small square module on his belt began to vibrate and flash red. The titan ripped it off and read the message on the small screen. He turned ashen as he sounded out the peculiar glyphs of the titan language. Finally he dropped his arm weakly, narrowly avoiding dropping the module. "There is a titan trapped in the deepdrake chamber. His emergency telemetry signal has been activated, which means he's been seriously injured."

"Decision made for us, then." Tol walked over to a row of packs with tools in them. "Would it be all right to borrow some of this stuff?"

"I can authorize that. Why do you need it?"

Tol looked surprised. "I don't think I'll be much good in there with only my bare hands."

"In there?" Tartag repeated, as though he couldn't quite make sense of the words.

"Yes, in there. Where the trapped titan is. Where did you think I was talking about?"

"But...trained extrication teams and a Special Forces unit from the Civil Guard will be here soon. We can't just go in there without knowing what we're up against."

"A titan's life is at stake. I'm sworn to protect the people of Tragacanth, and until His Majesty signs that final Writ of Territorial Transfer, Hellehoell is still nominally Tragacanth. I will do my best to rescue him or die in the attempt."

"I'm afraid I can't authorize such an expedition."

Tol whipped out his KotC and Special Investigator credentials. "You don't need to. I am already authorized by Royal Writ to carry out operations anywhere in Tragacanth or its possessions. That, as I've already pointed out, includes here. Anyone coming with me?"

It took Tartag a few seconds of mental anguish comparing rules and regulations before he agreed, albeit somewhat reluctantly, to accompany Tol. Two other titans from the crew that recently fled, Apoj and Eltiar, agreed to join the party and act as guides.

Tol picked the smallest pack of the lot, which still nearly dragged the floor when resting on his comparatively diminutive shoulders, and filled it with whatever tools looked as though they might come in handy during the mission: a pickaxe, hand axe, auger, shovel, spade, pry bar, and a couple of less readily identifiable but still strangely useful-appearing implements of high-carbon steel with sturdy nut tree wood hafts. These were all scaled for titan use, of course, so Tol felt a little like a child wielding adult tools, but he persevered. A citizen's life was at stake here.

So it was that a heroic group of three titans led by a goblin cracked and pounded and atomized their way through a dense wall of stones, boulders, and gravel on a desperate rescue mission. At length they broke through to a smallish antechamber and stopped to catch their breath and take their bearings. Tol walked the perimeter, searching for the route forward. He dropped a thin stream of dust in front of a small hole and was gratified to observe it first be drawn into the hole and then repulsed. He wedged a pry bar into the opening and started working on enlarging it.

At length he returned to the rescue party. "I think I got us a way forward worked out."

"Excellent," replied Tartag, "Did you find another tunnel?"

"Well, yes, except that I sort of had to make it myself, or at least part of it."

"You dug a *tunnel* while you were gone? One that *titans* could fit through?" Apoj seemed skeptical. "You don't look strong enough for that." It wasn't an insult; just an observation of what seemed the obvious.

"I'm not as strong as you guys, sure, but I have a tendency not to let go of an objective until it is accomplished."

In truth, while titans have at least three times the brute strength of goblins as a species, goblin tenacity is legendary. A goblin once fixated on a goal was more difficult to dislodge from it than tearing a razor-toothed swamp floater away from the carcass of a tidewater grazer calf.

The titans were impressed with the entryway the little goblin had managed to create. It was broad enough for a titan with pack to crawl through, which meant 'wide enough for a small dray to negotiate.' They lost no time scrambling through, to find themselves in a shallow, flat room of sufficient height for the titans to stand. There was a hole in the floor, through which they could hear and smell flowing water. There seemed to be a little steam curling up from time to time, as well, which suggested that the water was geothermal in origin. Best not to leap in until they could check the temperature. Tol didn't know what boiled titan smelled like, but he'd experienced poached goblin and it wasn't pleasant.

Using some rope from his pack and a rock to take soundings, Tol concluded that the water's surface lay about five meters below the opening and was three or four meters in depth. The rock came back warm, but not too hot to touch. The water was probably not only easily survivable, but in fact quite pleasant.

"Can titans swim?" he asked.

"Yes. Not quickly, but for long distances," replied Tartag.

"Perfect. We don't need speed for this, but we don't know how long we'll have to swim. I'll go first." He crawled to the edge of the opening and tied one end of a long rope around his shoulders in a loose harness. "Lower me down. Once I've determined the water is habitable, I'll slip out and you can jump in after me." The titans nodded. Tol went over the edge and they paid out the line slowly until they heard a splash followed by Tol's voice. "This is smekkin' great!" he called up to them, "Like being in a spa or something. I'm slipping out of the rope now." The line went slack and they retrieved it.

One by one the titans followed Tol into the warm, mineral-laden water. There wasn't a lot of light, but they could still see where they were going to a certain extent. They swam with the steadily-increasing current for a while before Eltiar's voice suddenly broke the silence. "Anyone else hear that noise? Sounds like a roaring or rumbling."

"I hear it, too," replied Tol, who was still ahead of the pack, "And I think I know what it is. Anybody see a shelf or ledge or anything else we can grab onto?"

They all looked around at the smooth stone walls. "No, not really."

"Then you better take a deep brea…"

The titans were surprised when Tol suddenly disappeared and even more surprised when they followed him…over the edge of a vertical falls down into total darkness.

The little party plummeted wetly for a quite a long time, it seemed to them. At last Tol touched bottom and pushed himself upwards as powerfully as possible—he had no idea how deep the channel was here. He popped up on the surface, gasping for air, and discovered after a few disorienting moments that he was holding onto a thin shelf, evidently *behind* the waterfall. He clambered up onto it and called to the others.

"Hey, guys. Over here!"

First Tartag, followed by Eltiar and Apoj, hoisted their waterlogged forms up onto the shelf with Tol. He produced a small electric torch and waved it around trying to build up some comprehensible picture of their surroundings. They appeared to be in a small shelter or anteroom hidden behind the pitch-black waterfall. Shining the torch at the far end of the space proved unhelpful, so Tol struggled to his feet and shuffled cautiously in that direction. Tartag followed closely behind.

"The tracking signal is finally getting stronger. I think we're heading in the right direction now," Tartag called after Tol.

"Can you tell how far we need to go?"

"It isn't that granular a device. It only tells direction and relative signal strength."

"Better than nothing. This looks like a sentient-built passage of some sort; at any rate it's the best shot we've got. Follow me!"

Tol scrambled down a slight slope with rock fall detritus scattered around on it and headed off into the absolute darkness of the tunnel, the light from his tiny torch bobbing here and there. The titans, despite their much larger stride, struggled to keep up. Tol was now pure detective on the trail; he was totally focused on the quarry and could move with surprising alacrity when so engaged.

The tunnel seemed to have more than its fair share of side passages as they pressed forward, but Tol barely hesitated at each one before continuing. Finally he stopped at one, looked at the ground for a moment, and indicated they were turning off to the left. "Why do you think we should go that way?" Tartag asked.

Tol shone his light down on the floor. "Because whoever got here before us did. I thought we could ask him if he knows the way out."

Tartag looked carefully at the spot Tol indicated and was astonished to see that there were very subtle indentations in the thin layer of dust. Anyone else would have missed them, even were they looking specifically for that type of manifestation.

"How did you even *see* that?"

"A lifetime of tracking down guys who thought they were too clever to be caught. It sort of hones your skills."

"I'll say it does."

They followed the narrower passage somewhat more cautiously, as it was liberally strewn with rock debris and the footing was treacherous. Every now and then Tol would point out some ridiculously obscure sign that a person or persons had recently gone before them. Tartag just shook his head in wonder. After at least forty-five minutes of steady travel Tol halted abruptly and cocked his head to one side. He made a silencing gesture to the titans behind him. "Did everyone bring some sort of weapon?" In response, the titans all drew their *yankiri*, or long-bladed glaves. The sound of sharpened metal moving against leather scabbard was strangely comforting to Tol as he stood there with his new rapid-fire disruptor, a far more powerful version of his trusty old service weapon (which he still carried in a holster under the other shoulder, as backup).

"There's something coming, and it's got more than two legs," Tol announced quietly. "Be ready to fight." Everyone stiffened and waited. There was no sound for a few moments, then without warning a swarm of huge reptilian things with very large talons and foul, toxic-smelling breath were upon them.

"Deepdrakes!" Tartag cried, as he swung his yankiri wildly. Tol fired once on the stun setting and the lizard shook it off, so he raised the power level to *perforate* and shot again.

"Apparently," he said to no one in particular as he dove behind a rock jutting from the wall, "Perforating a deepdrake just irritates it. A lot."

"They don't seem to take well to being sliced open, either," replied Eltiar, his weapon dripping with grayish-pink deepdrake gore.

"The heads do come off nice and clean," added Apoj, holding up a particularly fearsome-looking specimen by lacerated neck muscle tissue. Just then another one leapt at Apoj's own throat and was surprised to find an entire deepdrake head stuffed far down its gaping maw. As it struggled to dislodge the breathing obstacle Tartag brought his glave down with incredible force on the creature's back, severing the spinal column and very nearly bisecting the entire animal.

"Yecch. It's gettin' slippery in here," observed Tol as he slid his way into position to take a shot at the next deepdrake coming down the corridor at them. He got it right between the eyes with a full-power bolt that drove a meter-long fountain of brain tissue and blood out the back of the huge, misshapen skull. The beast kept coming at them as a result of its considerable momentum; Eltiar sliced off one its front legs for good measure as it slid by.

When the battle was over there were seven demised deepdrakes. Their opponents had suffered a few lacerations and one relatively minor fracture. They were covered in a thick layer of the same gore that enveloped their immediate environs, though. They scraped as much of it from themselves and each other as practical and headed off down the corridor, alert to the very real possibility that the first encounter might only have been with a scouting party.

They made their way among skeletons and other, less identifiable clumps of what they could only presume were deepdrake prey. The stench was nearly unbearable, even for Tol, who had a lot experience dealing with stinky places, having lived his life in Sebacea. It was becoming more and more apparent that this corridor was some sort of deepdrake larder, where choice gobbets of flesh were stashed to age for a while before being consumed. The titans looked at one another nervously: the odds were very high that they would encounter more deepdrakes—possibly more than they could handle, even collectively. Only Tol seemed unconcerned. He regarded deepdrakes as, despite their large size, inferior fighters to the vicious sewer wrats of Sebacea, and he'd taken on entire nests of those bleeders by himself before.

The passageway was taking a definite downward slant now; at times quite dramatic. The air temperature was increasing as they ventured deeper and deeper. There were multiple openings in the wall, with black, unfathomable depths behind them, but Tol seemed quite adamant that the trail they were following led straight along the main hallway. The caches of flesh and piles of bone were becoming less frequent, concurrent with a welcome decline in the odor of decay and dried bodily fluids with which they'd been forced to contend for some time.

As the incident debris diminished, the roughly-hewn walls and floor of the passage smoothed and after a while even began seemingly to glisten. They passed through an arch—an obvious artifice—beyond which the surroundings improved dramatically. The walls and ceiling moved outward and were now composed of polished marble, albeit of a different form than they'd seen in Hellehoell itself. The crude steps had morphed into an elegantly-constructed formal staircase, still leading down precipitously. The increasing warmth was ameliorated by a constant flow of cool air, although by what mechanism and even via what ventilation system was impossible to say.

A hundred meters or so further along Tol took a step that almost caused him to lose his balance. The step itself was the culprit, as the pressure from his foot caused an ancient mechanism to activate and the stairs began to descend on their own. They moved hesitantly at first, sticking and releasing noisily as though they had not been used in millennia—but then some form of lubrication apparently kicked in and the jolting died down into a quiet, fluid motion.

Tol waited until it seemed safe to do so and then stepped back on. The moving stairway carried him smoothly down, at a surprisingly rapid clip. He turned around and grinned as he watched the titans try to figure out how to address this new challenge; it was obvious none of them had ever before encountered such a mechanism. Finally Tartag took the plunge; he stepped gingerly on and was very nearly sent reeling backwards for his trouble. But, he righted himself and after a few seconds called back to the others.

"It's quite enjoyable and not at all difficult once you're here. Come on!"

The other two titans looked at each other and shrugged. First one then the other leapt on and joggled back and forth for a moment before they got the hang of it. Soon all four of them were gliding gracefully down, down, toward some unguessable destination. At least the ride was pleasant and, for the titans anyway, mildly exhilarating.

"What do you call this contraption?" Tartag yelled down to Tol.

"It's a moving stairway. Some people call it a 'stairveyor.' It's a bunch of steps mounted on a conveyor belt. They're popular in cities for moving people from one floor to the next."

"Quite a marvelous conveyance."

"Yeah, I had a lot of fun riding them as a kid."

"How do you get back up, once you've gone down?"

"They go both ways. They'll usually put two of them side-by-side. One goes up, the other down. If they break down or lose power, they're still perfectly good stairs."

"Where do you think these are taking us?"

"I haven't got any idea. We're still on the track, though."

"How could you possibly track someone on this stair-whatever?"

"There are faint footprints on the step two below mine. They're too big and the wrong shape for deepdrakes, but just the right size to be titan. The stairveyor must have cycled all the way around once before we got here, and as you can see, it's pretty dusty."

"You are quite a tribute to your profession, Sir Tol-u-ol. Your tracking skills are most impressive."

"Thanks. Comes with the territory. Often you have to get them before they get you."

"Yes, well, I hope no one will be trying to 'get you' today. Other than the deepdrakes, I mean."

"They're just walking turds, really. Nasty teeth and that, but predictable and easy to out-maneuver."

The longest moving stairway on, or rather, in, Tragacanth was finally coming to a terminus. They could see the end scant meters ahead.

"I don't think that's a very charitable characterization, in all fairness," an odd voice chimed from the darkness below.

Tol and the titans went on their guard, although Tol did not draw his disruptor. He was the first to come face to face with the voice, which turned out to be emanating from a deepdrake's body. Vocal abilities aside, it was no ordinary deepdrake: it was about a quarter again larger, with more agile front legs and paws, and deeply-set eyes that shone with intelligence. Tol regarded it curiously for a moment.

"Well, begging your pardon, but the ones we've encountered so far did not see fit to communicate, unless you call trying to rip us limb from limb communicating."

The deepdrake chuckled. "The harvesters are rather exuberant in their quest for meat, 'tis true. However, they are not representative of deepdrakes as a species: merely a primitive derivative thereof, bred specifically for their function."

"I presume that you claim to be such a representative, then?" asked Tartag; by now the titans had all reached the bottom of the stairway.

"I am indeed," the deepdrake replied, "I am Fontaric the Voluble, Harvestlord of Dzilidonia.

"I am Tartag, Hellehoell Ambassador to Tragacanth, and these are my companions Apoj and Eltiar," he said, waving his arm toward the other titans. "And this," he added, turning to Tol, "Is Sir Tol-u-ol of Sebacea, Knight of the Crimson, Special Investigator and brother to the King of Tragacanth."

"Welcome to you all. You have reached the outer limits of the Realm of Dzilidonia, home to Phaeon Timeskin."

"Thank you for the welcome, Fontaric. I'm afraid we were a little hard on your harvesters back there. We didn't feel we had a lot of choice."

Fontaric laughed merrily. "No harm done. They will regenerate in due course. We are an immortal species, created to be companions of an immortal. There are exactly six hundred and sixty-six deepdrakes in existence. Once every six hundred and sixty-six years we come together for a great celebration of our species with banquets and drink in abundance. For this reason we refer to 666 as the 'number of the feast.'"

Fontaric's curious story seemed to be over, so Tol spoke up. "Who is this 'Phaeon Timeskin'?"

"Phaeon," Fontaric replied, "Is an eternal entity created by the same event and of the same raw ingredients as the spacetime fabric itself. He was one of many cast out in dark energy bubbles, spreading across the universe at thousands of times the speed of light, at least initially."

"How did such a singular entity come to be embedded in N'plork?" asked Eltiar.

"He floated free in deep space while the first generation of stars formed and then blew themselves apart. Finally his bubble struck this nascent planet and became embedded in the molten mass. He chose to remain here while N'plork cooled and solidified around him. He has watched the rise of life on this world from the first protocell. In many ways, then, he *is* N'plork."

"Such an entity must be awe-inspiring to behold," said Tartag, "Might we be allowed to meet and communicate with him?"

"I believe," came a mellifluous yet intense, almost hypnotically lyrical sound, which they realized after a moment was also a voice, from somewhere in the middle of the room, "That can be arranged. I am Phaeon Timeskin, at your service."

They turned to face the apparent source of the voice, but there was no one there to be seen. "Where...where *are* you?" Tol finally asked.

"I am right here. I take it you all have had limited experience with brane visualization."

"I'm visualizing my brain downright confused right now," answered Tol.

"B-r-a-n-e, derived from mem*brane*. Sections of the fabric of spacetime can be peeled off, if you will, and used to create physical objects. The brane has no intrinsic color or texture, however, so you have to train your particular optical perception mechanism in order to visualize it." He knelt down and drew a circle on the floor. "Start at the circle and work up. I'm roughly the same height as the goblin. If you look carefully, you'll notice that the packet of 'thin air' just above the circle doesn't seem quite right. Now, concentrate on that area, move your head back and forth, and let your line of vision travel with it. At the edges on both sides you should eventually begin to build up an outline which, when filled in, will be me."

They stood there shaking their heads as though in collective denial as Phaeon continued.

"You will have to assign clothing, skin color, and even features from your own minds; I have none of my own. As a result, I appear differently to each person."

"So, you're some kind of personal hallucination, then?" asked Tol, who was feeling rather foolish shaking his head back and forth.

"I'm quite real; quite tangible. I'm just made from the same pattern as the wallpaper, if you want to phrase it in that manner."

"Wait, I'm starting to get something!" yelled Tartag. "You look like a very short titan to me. You're wearing an outfit similar to the ones we wore in schola. That takes me back..."

"I see him, too!" shouted Apoj. "He's got dark skin and white fur."

Soon Eltiar joined them in visualizing Phaeon. That left only Tol still in the dark.

"I can't help thinking this is some kind of practical joke being played on me. Do you guys *really* see something there?"

"I believe," Phaeon interjected, "Your lifelong detective skills may be working against you here. You see only what makes sense for you to see; spacetime aberrations such as myself do not make sense in the classical universe your brain is trained to see and comprehend. It simply edits me out."

"Yeah? What do you suggest I do to up my gullibility factor, then?"

"I suggest you look past me, to the other side of the room. Now walk in a large circle, with the circle I drew on the floor at its center. Keep your line of sight aligned with the air above the circle, but focus as far away as you can. As you rotate, at some point your brain should suddenly fill in the missing details when it realizes that the view is inconsistent."

Tol complied, but on the third roundabout he was about to declare the whole premise absurd when he caught a glimpse of something that he knew wasn't there. He stopped and backtracked. The something reappeared, although in a slightly different location and orientation from the first time. It was like a cutout of a goblin that was so thin it utterly vanished when seen on edge.

Tol decided there might be something to this after all, so he stopped walking around in circles and just concentrated. As he did, a marvelous occurrence took place: he watched in amazement as the figure of a young goblin filled in, complete in all three dimensions. He looked to be just barely a full adult, wearing one of those trendy outfits popular in the nightclub sector of Sebacea. This was, as Phaeon had explained, because his native appearance contained no relevant, useful information, as a result of which the observer's brain had to fill it all in with bits and pieces from their own experience. Tol gawked and tried to make sense of what he was seeing.

The entity Phaeon regarded them; concluded that they had each established some form of mental representation for him that would enable further social interaction.

"I bid you all welcome to my home within your own," he began, "What hospitality I have to offer is yours to enjoy."

A table set with all manner of delicacies and laden with exotic drink sprang invitingly into their midst from nowhere. They gaped at it. Eventually Tol shrugged and pulled out the goblin-sized chair. He was, as usual, rather peckish, now that the subject had been broached. The titans looked at one another somewhat uneasily, but at last followed suit.

"Nice trick," Tol observed between appreciative bites, "You must be some kind of mage, too."

"Mage?" their host asked, "Ah, no, I am not a magic-user. Magic draws upon the Dark Energy Continuum as a power source. I simply manipulate the spacetime fabric directly. Less overhead, as it were."

"How are you able to accomplish that?" asked Eltiar.

"When you read a tale, do you visualize the story, as it unfolds, in your mind?" asked Phaeon.

"Of course. It would be very difficult to derive any enjoyment from it otherwise."

"You are, in effect, manipulating that bit of the spacetime fabric that resides within your neocortex: the part of your brain where higher reasoning is located. I do the same, except as a result of my origins I can manipulate the fabric on a far grander scale. What you share amongst a few million neurons, I can bring into objective existence."

"Is this food imaginary?" asked Tartag, "That is; would it exist even were I not here to witness it?"

Phaeon smiled. "Well, in fact nothing at all exists until you witness it. This is one of the foundational principles of quantum behavior. Prior to being processed by your sensory organs, events and objects are merely probabilities with a certain n-dimensional quantum causality vector associated with them.

"Are you trying to say that if I weren't aware of this table it wouldn't be here?"

"Only if nothing else was aware of it, either. Not the air, not the floor, not the light reflecting off of it, and so on. By 'aware,' I really mean, 'impinged upon by'."

"But," Apoj broke in, "That's really the same as saying that it wouldn't exist, since by definition anything that exists will impinge upon *something* else."

"Precisely so. See how it works?"

Tol had reached his philosophical, not to mention his gastronomical, limit, so he changed the subject.

"We're looking for someone. A titan, to be exact. His tracks show he came through here within the last few hours. He is most likely injured. Have you seen anyone else lately?"

Phaeon looked thoughtful. "I have seen no one, but if he is within this realm I can locate him for you." He moved over to a wall; it transformed into a giant map covered with squiggles and brightly-colored dots, some of which on closer examination were moving slowly.

"This map shows the position of every sentient organism in or near what you call Hellehoell," Phaeon explained, "It works by detecting the slight distortion sentient brains produce on the enveloping spacetime fabric. We are…here." He pointed to a spot at the lowest point of the map.

Tol peered at it. "There's one too few dots here to account for all of us. Unless your map doesn't consider somebody here to be sentient."

"You can scarcely blame it for that," replied a faint voice from Tol's overjack pocket. Everyone looked at Tol, who rolled his eyes. "Ignore that. It's an electronic heckling machine I carry around for reasons known not even to me." The pocket chuckled.

"*I* do not appear on the map," said Phaeon, "I have no external effect on the fabric, but am rather part of it; or it of me. I blend into the background, in a manner of speaking."

"So, that's *us*?" The titans seemed truly besotted by the idea that they were represented by those little blotches. They began to walk around in the room, watching the map as their dots got relocated. Tol was not similarly fascinated by his own dot, but he was by another nearby blob. He traced the passages from their current position to that of the dot of interest, then walked over to a matching position on the wall, shrugged, and passed straight through. None of the titans noticed at first.

Tol wasn't sure why, but somehow he knew that he would be able to walk through the seemingly solid stone wall without hindrance: he didn't even flinch. Behind the wall was a rather fetching hallway lined with polished granite and lit by tasteful soft pink radiance emanating from hidden recesses along the ceiling. Complex filigree patterns were picked out in gold leaf in a series of panels along each wall. Despite magmatic heat radiating from the surrounding stones, the air flowing down the corridor was cool, dry, and fragrant.

After a hundred meters of level travel with side hallways branching off every so often, the passage abruptly assumed a positive grade, gradually increasing until it took considerable effort for Tol to continue. He persevered, stopping every so often to catch his breath and massage his tired leg muscles. Not only did the passageway slope upward, it had taken to spiraling quite tightly to the left. As it climbed, it gradually lost the polished marble walls and other artifice. There had been no spoor from his quarry in some time, but Tol remained confident that he was still on the right trail, based on what he'd seen on Phaeon's map. He realized he hadn't told the others where he was going, but he wasn't about to retrace his steps now. They'd figure it out eventually.

Finally the grade decreased substantially and the corridor he had been following opened out into what appeared to be a natural, active cave system. It hit Tol that he'd spent an inordinate amount of time lately underground. He suddenly longed to see sunlight and quaff a laden breeze off the meat-packing plant on the southern edge of Sebacea. Great. Now he was hungry again, as well.

He came to an intersection of sorts, where roughly-hewn passages led off in several directions. Tol studied the floor, walls, and cave formations for a sign he'd almost given up on spotting before a glint of something shiny on the floor caught his eye. He picked it up; it was a mineral layer inside a broken stalagmite reflecting in the dim light of the caverns. Searching around, Tol found the formation it had come from and inspection convinced him it had been broken off recently. Not iron-clad proof that his quarry had passed this way, but a clue nonetheless.

A few meters away he found much more substantial spoor: wet footprints from shoes that had passed through a water puddle on the floor in the last few minutes. He had almost caught up with the elusive fugitive. For someone who'd presumably been injured in a collapse, he sure was difficult to track.

Tol followed the prints for as far as they held out, then extrapolated that they led to a niche high up on the wall, accessible via a series of hand and foot-holds carved into the rock face. In full stealth mode he crept up the wall, pausing just below the rim of the niche to catch his breath. When he felt ready, Tol leapt up into the niche and was surprised to find a young adult titan cowering in a corner.

"Please. I don't want to go back. Don't make me go back!" the titan wailed, pitiably.

"Easy there, youngster," Tol answered, in a soothing voice. "Nobody's gonna make you do anything. Are you the one who was trapped by the collapse back there?"

"I wasn't trapped. I ran away when it happened."

"But your beacon was activated."

"I ripped it off and tossed it down a crevice, to throw off any pursuit."

"Why?"

"I don't want to be a slave anymore."

"What do mean, 'a slave'?"

"I am a half-breed. My mother was a troll who was raped by my father. Titans are rabid racial purists; half-breeds are considered abominations and forced into slavery."

"I didn't know that. What'll you do now?"

"If I can escape, I will travel to my mother's family in Aspolia. We have corresponded, and they seem willing to accept me for who I am."

"I'll get you out of here, kid. Slavery is contrary to Tragacanthan edict."

"You are a true benefactor. How may I call you, master?"

"Don't you be calling *anybody* 'master.' That's part of your problem, right there. My name is Tol. What's yours?"

"Yes, mast... Tol. My name is Korq. How will you get me out, past all these titans?"

"Piece o' cake. If we get caught I'll tell them you violated an edict and I'm taking you back to Goblinopolis for trial."

"You could do that?"

"Yeah, I'm a cop. A special investigator, as a matter of fact."

"Wow. Think it will work?"

"I hope so. If they try to interfere with a Tragacanthan edict enforcement officer in the conduct of official duties they'll seriously jeopardize their application for sovereign standing, I can promise that. Now, come on down and let's figure a way out of this hole."

Together they climbed down the wall and then began to scout for an exit.

"I came in the same way you did, so we know where that direction leads," said Tol, waving toward the corridor out of which he'd emerged. "Let's do some exploring."

Tol led the way as they investigated every possible passage out of the room, one by one. At last Tol stopped at the entrance to a small irregularly-shaped corridor that led sharply upward. He wiped his hand across the damp stone just inside the opening, sniffing it.

"This one leads to the surface."

"But Tol, how do you know this?" asked Korq, his eyes wide.

Tol held up his hand and swirled his finger around on some fine particles smeared on his palm. "See the little grains? They're pollen from plants on the surface. They were carried down here by the wind, which tells me that this passage connects to the surface. Doesn't promise that the opening will be big enough for us to get through, but we'll cross that bridge when we come to it."

"How can you tell there is a bridge?"

Tol looked at the half-titan for a few seconds with puzzlement; chuckled.

"Just an expression, kid. It means we will solve one problem at a time."

"I am seeing it now."

"Great. Let's get moving."

The going was slow along the steeply-graded passageway, with frequent stops to rest and catch their breaths. More than once Korq slipped and began to slide, forcing Tol to slide down after him and halt both their descents with a great outpouring of strength.

"I'm getting' too old for this smek," he exclaimed after one such exertion. "Watch your footing, kid. I might not be able to stop you next time."

"I will endeavor not to be so clumsy in the future, master, I mean, Tol. I am unaccustomed to traversing such pathways," Korq apologized, wringing his hands.

"No sweat, kid: you're doing fine. Just be a little more careful about where you step, and try to find handholds whenever you can."

"I will gladly comply...Tol."

During a rest break after about half an hour of steady, laborious effort, Tol's head suddenly snapped up. Korq glanced over in alarm.

"Is something amiss, Tol?"

"You smell that? It's the smell of rain in fresh air. We're almost to the surface!" Tol was practically dancing a jig. He was *really* tired of being underground.

"Yes: I do smell it now."

"Wait here," Tol commanded and scrambled up the last few meters of the passage to where it dead-ended into a pile of rubble. He scrutinized the area both visually and nasally until he pinpointed the opening to the surface.

"Hang tight to the left wall," he called back down to Korq, "I'm going to do a little excavating; I'll toss the rocks as far to the right as I can."

Korq did as he was told and hugged the left wall while Tol dislodged larger and larger stones that crashed and bounced their way back down the shaft. Finally he called down to the half-titan.

"Come on up now, Korq. Very carefully. If you slip now I won't be able to stop you from sliding all the way back down."

"I am proceeding with great care, Tol."

Korq made his way slowly up to the top of the shaft, one step and handhold at a time, until at last he stood with his goblin rescuer. Tol heaved one final boulder aside and crawled through the resultant space. He stood up and found himself unexpectedly looking out over the broad entrance to Hellehoell, sprawling some twenty meters below. He turned his head as Korq came clambering out.

"Keep a low profile, kid. We don't want to get spotted by the sentries down there."

Korq followed Tol's pointing finger and shrank back against the rocks of the cliff, trying to blend in. Tol skirted around out of sight from the sentries and told Korq to do the same. In the process the half-titan dislodged a cascade of pebbles that tumbled noisily to the valley floor below. Tol flinched involuntarily.

"Well, they know *something's* up here now. We better skedaddle before a patrol comes to check it out."

"As you command."

"It's not a command: it's a suggestion, albeit a strongly-worded one. I'm not your smekkin' boss."

"I believe your suggestion to be sound, then, and I am inclined to accept it."

"That's more like it. Now, move!"

They half-jogged, half-skidded along a steep trail that wound its way down in multiple switchbacks to a ravine hidden from Hellehoell's grand boulevard of Daludobris. At the bottom Tol motioned for a stop and suggested that Korq hide in the tall grass until he came back.

Tol stood very still at the trailhead and cranked all of his senses to full power. After a couple of minutes, satisfied that they had not yet been detected, he returned to Korq.

"Let's go, young'un. Stay close to me and keep your head down as much as you can. When I stop, you stop. And stay quiet."

They made their stealthy way along a rutted road that led, finally, to the main highway connecting Fenurian with Cladimil. Tol got out his comm, which luckily still had enough of a charge to contact the district edict enforcement headquarters, and in less than an hour they were heading to Cladimil in an EE dray.

Chapter the Twelfth

in which Tol goes unwillingly to sea and meets there a fellow knight

"They will be looking very hard for me. Titans do not like to lose track of their slaves. I am forbidden to talk to anyone about my parentage or enslavement; the punishments for disobedience are harsh indeed."

"Then," Tol replied grimly, "We'd better make sure they don't find you."

They had the EE dray drop them off at the docks. Tol went scouting for a suitable vessel and came back a few minutes later to the little dive bar where he'd left Korq sitting by himself in a corner.

"The purser of the *Grollnash* agreed to take you on as a non-manifested passenger, for a few extra billmes," Tol said in a low voice.

"What does that mean, 'non-manifested'?"

"It means the official record of passengers won't have your name on it. Passenger manifests are released to those with a need to know. They could be checked by the titans. This way no one will be aware that you are on the ship except you, me, and the purser."

"Where is the ship going, exactly?"

"It's a freighter bound for Solemadrina. Port Jool, I think. You can get to Aspolia from there by carriage. I'll pay for it. Come on, I'll get you settled in."

They tromped up the gangway, checked in with the purser, and headed down to the meager passenger quarters to find the unoccupied cabin the purser had indicated Korq could use. The bunks were not lengthy enough for even a young titan, so he and Tol improvised with mats and blankets along one wall. When at last Tol was satisfied that Korq had a place to sleep, he gave him enough money for food and sundries for the trip, as well as carriage fare to Aspolia.

"I cannot take your money, Tol. I have done nothing to earn it."

"This ain't about earning, kid; it's about gettin' you outta a bad situation. You can pay me back later, if you want. It's not like I'm exactly poor these days."

"I...I do not know how to express my gratitude for such a kind and generous act. You are my friend forever, Tol."

"And you mine. Now I better get my butt offa this boat before I end up sailing with you. Goodbye, kid. Good luck. I hope life with your mom's family is everything you want it to be."

"It will certainly be better than being a slave. Goodbye to you, Tol. Thank you again for all that you have done for me. I did not know people such as you existed in this world. I am very glad to discover that they indeed do."

They shook hands and then embraced warmly. It was a bit awkward because Korq was over a meter taller than Tol, but they managed it somehow anyway. Tol waved one last time and headed forward toward the gangplank. He passed a shadowy alcove; his danger alarm suddenly went off and he reached instinctively for his disruptor. As his hand closed around the familiar grip there was a very loud noise in his head and the lights went out.

Tol woke up with a throbbing headache in a sparse, utilitarian bunk. He rolled over and came face to face with an ogre with several livid scars wearing the uniform of a merchant marine boatswain.

"Welcome to the crew of the O.V. *Grollnash*, seacrew. Ye'll be swabbing decks and slapping on paint under me watchful eye."

"I ain't no kind of seacrew. Some smekker ambushed me. When I find him he's gonna wish he'd stayed home with his momma."

The ogre swung a ham-sized fist at Tol but he dodged it easily and reached for his disruptor. It wasn't there. The ogre chuckled.

"Where is my pistol, you ugly smekker?"

"Weapons are not allowed on board, seacrew. It was confiscated and locked up."

"It better get unlocked toot sweet."

"Or what, tough guy?"

Tol snarled and was about to show the ogre 'what' when he suddenly realized he was now on a case. The *Grollnash* had sailed from a Tragacanth port under a Tragacanthan flag, so by international treaty it was under Tragacanthan jurisdiction at all times. At least one count of illegal impressment had taken place; it was up to him to investigate. Instead of laying the boatswain out, he decided to play it cool and stay undercover.

"Er, nothing, bo's'n. I was just groggy and not thinkin' straight. Sorry about that."

"That's better, seacrew. Follow me and I'll show ye yer duties. You'll find me a fair one, so long as ye keep yer place and do yer job."

"So, do you get all your crew by bopping them on the head?"

The ogre stopped and gave Tol a look that was almost wistful.

"Truth is, almost all of the crew with the exception of the deck officers are conscripts. We're people trying to forget our past, or hoping someone else will, at least. Ye'll do best not to ask too many questions, though. The second mate, he don't like inquisitive crew."

"I can see why. My name is Tol, by the way."

"Tol it is. Mine's Fevins, but ye'll be calling me bo's'n. What did ye do afore ye became seacrew?"

"I did a lot of... walking. Mostly in Goblinopolis."

"Ah, the big city. I was there oncest. Walked around that enormous palace they got there and wondered what it would be like to be in the Royal Fam'ly."

Tol almost choked. "Probably just like any other family," he squeaked out, finally, "They put their pants on one leg at a time, same as you and me."

"I figured they had someone do it for them."

"You know that the King of Tragacanth is no longer a hereditary position, right? They have this big hacking contest and the winner gets to be king for a few years."

"So? CoME has to agree on the candidates and run the contest. The whole thing is obviously rigged."

"Ya think so? What do ya think of the current king?"

"A little snot-nosed brainy brat whose family probably bought the office for him; at least, that's what I heerd."

Tol suppressed his desire to leave the ogre a bloodied pulp and made no reply. Fortunately for Fevins they had reached the small closet where the mops were stored.

"All right, seacrew. Ye're going to learn how to push a mop *Grollnash*-style. By the time ye're through, ye'll be a regular expert at it."

He showed Tol the proper way to push, wring, and swirl. Tol took to it like a natural and had finished a quarter of the deck before Fevins could even comment.

"I ain't never seen a conscript work like ye, seacrew. Ye might make bo's'n's mate if ye keep that up."

Tol just grinned and kept working. He had a mission now, and when Tol-u-ol was on a mission absolutely nothing got in his way.

That evening after his twelve-hour shift, Tol sat in the crew mess and got to know the other seacrew. He learned over time that, as Fevins had said, they were all conscripts, beaten and kept on board by threats. They were never allowed shore leave, for obvious reasons. Tol avoided contact with Korq, who the officers probably figured to be too large and strong to intimidate and so remained merely a paid passenger, because he didn't want the young half-titan to blow his assumed cover.

The fourth day out from Cladimil the third mate poked his head belowdecks.

"Thar be rough seas ahead, swabs. Git ready on the pumps. Bo's'n, get a crew and furl the corsels. We be leavin' the topsels and gallans for maneuvering. Git yer scurvy hides movin!"

Up to now the ship's movements had been relatively benign; almost relaxing. Tol hadn't felt any seasickness at all, to his surprise. That was about to change.

Not ten minutes after the third mate's visit the roll and pitch of the *Grollnash* began to increase: gradually at first, but then in a more dramatic manner. Tol was assigned to one of the bilge pumps across from a half-ogre called Yomb. As the hull flexed and bulged with the crashing waves, water was forced between the strakes and came splashing in around the rotting edges of the cargo hatches. The job of the twelve crew at the six bilge pumps was to pump that water right back out over the side through large hoses.

The pumps could be operated by attached engines, but Fevins preferred to use manual labor to save valuable fuel. "Put yer backs into it, ye scurvy hounds. If this 'ere hold fills up with sea water we all be sleeping with the fishes tonight, no mistake."

The pumps, once primed, had to be operated continuously to maintain suction. Yomb showed Tol how they traded off resting and how to appear to be working even while you took a break.

The storm continued to escalate until it seemed the ship must surely come apart. Every swell stood the *Grollnash* nearly on end. Even some of the old hands were seasick; Tol had long since lost the contents of his stomach and was into dry heaves—but not once did he let up on the pump handle. The water level in the lower hold wasn't rising, but it wasn't going down, either. They were just holding their own, and growing exhausted in the process. All around them the boards were creaking, popping, and screeching.

Finally, after an eternity of pitching, rolling, rising, and falling, the fury of the sea spent itself and the bilge water drained to its normal level. When Fevins gave the order to 'secure pumps,' Tol felt as though he could never again raise his arms. He stumbled to his bunk and slept soundly until duty call the next morning.

When they made Port Jool, Tol sneaked up on deck to make sure that Korq got off safely. He wanted to wish him well again, but that would risk breaking his cover, so he watched the young half-titan make his way uncertainly down the gangplank and off to find his family. As he entered the port facility two trolls were there to greet him warmly. They walked off together, chatting animatedly. It appeared Korq had finally found a place he could call home. Tol felt a tiny wetness well up in one corner of his eye. He wiped it away. "Smekkin' sea spray," he muttered.

Tol began rather to enjoy seacrew life, but he realized that Selpla would be very worried about him by now, and he wanted to set these impressees free, so he had a strategy meeting with Fevins. The boatswain, who had been impressed almost four years previous, when he'd come aboard to deliver flour and meal for a local mill in the port city of Zekka down in Ovinis, had despite their early differences become his best friend on board.

"Why do you stay here?" Tol asked him one night after mess. "I saw the third mate beatin' you with that nine-tailed whip o' his. I would have kicked his goblin butt into next week and then some."

Fevins cracked a wry grin, "I ain't much of a fighter, when it comes down to it. As bo's'n I'm a trustee—I could go into port for supplies and jest not come back—but truth be tolt I ain't got nowhere to run to. That's probably why they made me bo's'n."

"You could go back to the mill in Zekka," said Tol, munching on a big crumble of hardtack soaked in weak stock that he'd smuggled back to his berth.

"Old Wikker's probably dead by now, or at least too old to run the mill. His whelp Axlo and I never saw eye to eye on much o' anythin.' I doubt he'd even take me back."

"Don't you have family somewhere?"

"Well, I guess I must have, but I don't know 'em. Me daddy run off when I was still stiff-kneed and me momma, she drank herself to death the next year. I was raised in a orphan home until I run away; must have been about eight. From them on I made me way on the streets: first in a village outside of Nar Braylov and then I hitched to Zekka. Funny thing is, I actually came to Zekka to sign on as a deck hand. This wasn't exactly the career I was expecting, but I suppose it be close enough."

"You said you weren't a fighter: is that because you don't believe in fightin' or something?"

"Nah, nothin' like that; I jest never larned. I was in a few scraps as a kid, but I got pretty good at avoidin' trouble as I got older."

"That's a mighty good skill to have, itself. Still, if you'd like to learn, I could teach you a few things about hand-to-hand. Keep you alive in a fight, at least."

"I never turn down a chance to larn something' useful. Were ye some kind of soldier or somethin'?"

"You could say that. All right, the first thing you need to learn is how to stand. Always keep your body pointed at the opponent: lead with one leg and put the other behind you, like this."

After three hours of this instruction every evening for a week, Fevins went from a raw novice to taking Tol down two falls out of five. Following one such particularly bruising bout, Tol got up and dusted himself off.

"You just graduated from the Tol-u-ol school of martial arts, my friend. From here on out we spar just to keep limber and maintain our skills."

"I got to admit, Tol, that feels mighty good. I never thought I'd be this comfortable with me own defense. I guess I don't got to run away no more, eh?"

"No, you don't. But you do need to pick your fights. If the other guy is better than you, there ain't no sense in hanging around to let him hand you your butt. Get while the getting's good."

"I owe ye a big one, Tol. Ye said yer name was Tol-u-ol? That sounds familiar, for some reason."

Tol saw the red flag and hurriedly changed the subject. "So, I've been wanting to talk about something. This seems like as good a time as any. You know that this ship is operating contrary to edict, right? I mean, impressing hasn't been legal for a couple of centums now."

"Yeah, I know that. But we ain't got no cops on board, and the captain would deny that anything unsavory was goin' on. He'd be believed, too, because he's all important. He's one o' them Red Knights and all."

Tol stopped in shock. "Do you mean the captain of this vessel is a Knight of the Crimson?"

"Yeah, that what it was. Won it during the pirate wars. Nobody would question a goblin of that stature."

"I can't believe a Knight of the Crimson would allow impressing on his vessel."

Fevins chuckled. "He don't know nothin' about it. The second mate controls all o' that: forges our writs of service and contracts. I'll bet there's one in the captain's cabin with yer name on it."

But probably not my full title, Tol thought.

"The officers is very careful not to let the captain and crew mingle. They tells the captain that we're all criminals trying to go straight, that sort o' thing. Tells him that it would be better if he lets them do all the associatin' with the crew, so as not to bust our morale by seeing how grand and glorious he is or some such bilgewater."

"That makes about as much sense as tellin' a hound not to bark when the bell gets pulled," Tol said, "I think it's time Captain High and Mighty knows the truth."

Fevins got very serious. "They'll kill ye before they'll leave ye alone wi' th' captain. I mean it. The first mate ain't really a bad sort, but the second and third are nothin' but trouble. They're both deserters from the Frespiolan Marines and neither one o' them would hesitate for a second to slit yer gullet and toss you overboard for the toothfishes."

To Fevins' surprise, Tol started laughing. "If I had a billme for every time some palooka threatened to jank me, I'd be sittin' on a pile of money instead of pumping out bilges," he said, wiping the tears out of his eyes. "I've watched those two and they ain't nothin' more than cheap thugs. You could take 'em both at once, I'll wager."

"Ye'd lose that wager, seahound, even if they was ten ov'im," came a voice from the doorway. It was the third mate, with the second standing close behind him. They both had pieces of lead pipe.

"Yeah?" replied Tol, standing up, "Why, you got real fighters hidden back there somewhere? 'Cause I don't see nothin' but scullin' maids right now."

The mates moved in menacingly. "Yer about to get sculled, all right, seahound. We goin' to hang yer hide right over there on th' wall."

At this point Fevins stood up, too. "You just get over there and watch, bo's'n," said Tol, "Ain't no reason for you to get involved here. I won't even break a sweat on these two."

"This here bo's'n knows which side his bread is buttered on. He ain't gonna git in the way," chuckled the third mate.

Tol glanced at Fevins and nodded. The boatswain moved to block the doorway inconspicuously so that no one else could get in or out.

The third mate brought his pipe up and cocked it to throw a blow at Tol's temporal ridge. "Time to die, seahound," he said, bringing the heavy pipe down.

"Not unless I have a stroke from laughing at your stupid clichés," Tol replied, dodging the swing and bringing his elbow up in the goblin's face, breaking his nose. The third mate gasped as blood ran down his chin and splattered all over the floor.

"Aw, does 'em have a boo-boo?" asked Tol, "Here, you can wipe it with this." He whirled and hit the goblin squarely in the face with his foot, knocking him back a full meter against the wall. Tol grinned and turned to the other sailor, a half-ogre.

The second mate threw his pipe at Tol; while he was ducking the mate pulled a wicked illegally-boosted disruptor from his overjack pocket.

"I ain't wasting no more time on ye, bilge rodent. Let's see ye shrug *this* off!"

He aimed the pistol-grip carbine at Tol's head and pulled the trigger. Tol waited until the last possible split-second before dropping down and plowing directly into his opponent's solar plexus, lifting him bodily off the ground and painfully smashing him obliquely into the doorframe. The second mate kept trying to shoot Tol, but the charges hit random targets around the room, once of them being the third mate's leg. The mate howled in pain and rolled on the deck as the maximum energy bolt turned his calf into a burnt sausage.

Finally Tol kicked the second mate savagely in the knee; as he bent over to grab the injured joint Tol yanked the gun out of his grip. He handed the weapon to Fevins.

"Aren't ye gonna use it on 'em?" The boatswain asked, surprised.

"Nah. I never use a gun where my fists will do just fine. Less chance of collateral damage. Right, stumpy?" Tol replied, nodding at the third mate, still clutching his leg in agony.

The second mate lunged clumsily at him. Tol stepped aside and used his assailant's own weight and momentum against him, driving his head into the end of a berth and laying him out cold. Tol wiped some splattered blood off his jack with a towel while Fevins looked on in admiration.

"You sure know your way around a fight, Tol," he said, shaking his head.

"I've been in a couple here and there," Tol answered, grinning.

"What is the all the ruckus in here?" demanded the first mate, who had suddenly appeared at the doorway. "Where are my officer..." He tailed off as he saw the second and third mates lying unconscious and grimacing in pain, respectively.

"Sorry, sir, they're... otherwise engaged at present," explained Fevins.

"Who did this?" he was almost screaming.

Tol stepped forward. "Guilty as charged. But they really had it coming."

This revelation presented the first mate a puzzle with most of the pieces missing. He looked at the incapacitated officers and back at Tol. "Why did you attack my officers. Who *are* you?"

"D'ya want those questions answered in that order?" Tol asked, scratching under his ear.

"I don't care what bloody order you answer them in. Bo's'n! Go fetch the surgeon for these poor gents."

"I took them down in self-defense, as your bo's'n will attest. My name is Tol."

"Well, Tol," he said the name derisively, "The captain will decide what happens to you. Let's go."

"I'm right behind you, mate."

"You will address me as 'sir:' got that?"

"Yes sir, got it, sir. You can still call me Tol."

The first mate did not respond, but led Tol by the arm toward the bridge.

They entered the wheelhouse and a kindly old man in a captain's jack turned to greet them.

"Ah, there you are, first mate. I have been looking for you." He stopped and regarded Tol and a strange expression passed across his face. "Have we met?" he said to Tol. Tol regarded the Knight Commander of the Crimson medallion on his pocket. "It's entirely possible. My name is Tol."

The first mate stood there in shock at this exchange. "Captain, this... person is responsible for seriously injuring the second and third mates not fifteen minutes ago on the crew deck. He claims self-defense."

The captain was still staring at Tol, as though trying to remember something. "What have you to say on the matter of battery upon two ship's officers, Tol?"

"Those officers, captain, were running an impress gang. This ship is a haven for sentient slavery."

"What? That's a preposterous charge. I have merchant mariner contracts for every member of my crew."

"Forged by the second mate," said Tol.

The captain walked over and unlocked an oak filing cabinet set into one wall. He pulled out a file and handed it to Tol.

"Here is the paper you signed when you joined this crew."

Tol laughed. "It says my full name is Tal, I was a stonemason's helper before, and I come from Fenurian. That's not even close. Neither is the signature."

He picked up a pen and signed his full name and title on the back of the contract. The captain picked it up and read it.

"Sir Tol-u-ol of Sebacea, Special Investigator, Tragacanth Edict Enforcement Bureau."

Tol pushed past the first mate and shook hands with the captain using the special Knights of the Crimson recognition ritual. The light finally dawned in the old seafarer's eyes.

"I was at your knighting ceremony in Goblinopolis! You're that new Knight-Protector."

He turned a little pale, "And...b-b-brother to His Majesty Tragacanth."

The first mate and Fevins, who had just appeared after taking the surgeon to the injured officers, gasped and took an involuntary step back. The first mate suddenly disappeared.

The captain sat down heavily in his command chair. "I'm honored to have a member of the Royal Family on board the *Grollnash*, but I...I don't know how to answer your allegations of slavery. That is not something I could ever condone."

"I always figured you knew nothing about it, Knight-Commander. You've been the victim of a sophisticated organized criminal activity perpetrated by a couple of career hoods. I'll bet when I run those lugs back in Goblinopolis they come back with a rap sheet an arm long."

"You'll have to do it *in absentia*, I'm afraid," the first mate said, coming back onto the bridge. "I just went to check on them and they appeared to have taken one of the life boats and cast off."

"What?" exclaimed the captain, "In these seas? They'll be swamped before they've made twenty lengths."

"Whatever else he may be, Second Mate Hinyak is a fine sailor," replied the first mate, "They might make it to land; the Paradiddle Islands are only a day's hard row from here."

Tol shrugged. "At any rate, you've got a hold full of unwilling crew members down there who need to be given the option to return to wherever they were impressed. I'll be overseeing that personally."

"Understood," answered the captain, "And it looks as though I need a new second mate." He stared pointedly at Fevins. "Bo's'n, I've watched you grow as a sailor over the past years. I think you're ready to take on more responsibility. How would you feel if I offered you a commission in the Merchant Marines?"

Fevins looked startled for a moment, but regained his composure quickly. "Captain, as a friend and mentor of mine once told me, when opportunity drives by, ye better run after it and jump on." Tol chuckled at this. "I'd be honored to serve as yer officer," Fevins continued.

"Excellent. Step over here and we'll sign the papers and take care of the oath."

"Oath?" asked Tol.

"Every Merchant Marine officer takes an oath to serve the nation offering the commission, which in this case is obviously Tragacanth," explained the first mate, "Ordinarily the oath is accepted by the captain, standing in for the king, but since a member of the Royal Family is present, protocol demands that you hear and either accept or deny the oath."

Tol nodded. As he did, he reflected on the changes he'd undergone in the months since his knighting. The oath-taking seemed perfectly natural now; two years ago he would have rolled his eyes and made some disparaging comment if asked to participate in such a ceremony.

"Repeat after me," the captain said, once Fevins and Tol were in place, "I, Fevins of Zekka, do here solemnly swear to uphold the edicts and customs of Tragacanth, to discharge my duties as a commissioned officer faithfully and to the utmost of my ability, to treat fairly and with due honor all whom I encounter, and obey my superior officers without question unless ordered to perform any act contrary to my oath or edict. So swear I on the honor of my

131

ancestors." When Fevins had completed the Oath, Tol looked at the captain.

"Are you satisfied with this sailor's oath and intentions, Knight-Commander?"

"Aye, that I am, Knight-Protector. He will make a fine officer."

"Then on behalf of His Majesty Tragacanth I hereby accept this oath and authorize the issuance of an officer's commission in the Tragacanthan Merchant Marine. Congratulations, Second Mate."

After the oath, Fevins signed the commissioning papers and officer's contract. The Captain then handed his insignia of rank to the first mate, who pinned them on Fevins' new officer's shirt as he stood at attention. "Welcome to the officer corps, Second Mate Fevins," said the captain. Fevins saluted smartly. "A pleasure to serve under ye, sir. I'll never let ye down, even unto me last breath."

"And he's a good hand in a scrap, as well," Tol added. Fevins was glad he'd never learned how to blush as a lad.

"Well, Mr. Fevins. You've been just been commissioned an officer in the presence of not one, but two Knights of the Crimson," the first mate said, "I can't remember another officer being so honored in all the proud history of the *Grollnash*. Congratulations."

"Being honored makes me weak in the knees, begging yer pardons. May I be excused so I can have a sit down?" Fevins asked.

"Of course, Mr. Fevins. You'll need to be moving into the officers' quarters now, anyway. Dismissed."

As the new second mate made his way to the bridge door, the Captain called after him. "Oh, and Mr. Fevins: once you're ready to report for duty, I want you interview the entire crew one at a time and get me the names and ports of call of everyone who does not want to be part of this crew. We will take them back to their chosen port and while I don't have a great deal of money, I will share what I do have among them in partial recompense for their forced labor."

"Yes, captain. Thank you, sir!"

The Captain sat down at his desk and wrote out a parchment. "I hereby declare Jovsox of Correq and Hinyak of Terimpu Outlaws of the High Seas. Any duly-appointed captain of merchant marines or registered private vessel may arrest, hold, and if necessary, execute one or both without further writ or release."

"Harsh," Tol replied.

"It's standard language," said the captain, "What it really means is that if an outlaw presents a clear and present danger to you or your crew, you can deal with him in whatever manner is suitable for the situation, up to and including the use of deadly force. It's really the same authority you have as an edict enforcement officer, except that yours is a blanket authorization; this one covers only the individuals named. We don't have cops on the high seas, so captains have to assume the duty to keep the peace."

"I can see where that's necessary," Tol answered, "I guess I never really thought much about it before."

"That's one of the reasons all certificated captains have to go through a course that covers those issues of authority and international relations. You can instigate a great deal of bother as a ship's captain if you cause an international situation. All captains must be both cops and ambassadors, as well as competent sailors, administrators, supervisors, and counselors."

Tol grinned. "You learn something new every day if you keep your eyes open. I have a lot more understanding of and respect for ship's captains than I had ten minutes ago."

"I'm glad to be a part of your education, Sir Tol-u-ol. You, in turn, have shown me precisely why His Majesty felt compelled to create an order of Knighthood just for you. You are a remarkable goblin."

Tol shook his head. "Thanks, but I'm really just an average jlok who keeps gettin' mixed up in things beyond his control."

"We all find ourselves there from time to time. It's how you handle yourself in those situations that sets you apart."

"Can we please change the subject?"

"Of course. Come, let me show you how the *Grollnash* is steered and navigated."

"Thanks. *That's* something I would very much enjoy."

Fevins walked up just then with two items in his hand.

"I believe these belong to you, Sir Tol-u-ol."

He handed Tol's disruptor and comm unit back to him.

"I found these in the Second Mate's sea chest," he explained.

Tol took them from him and switched the comm unit on. He chuckled.

"I signed these out from the EE Quartermaster and he'd chew off a good square of my hide if I came back without them."

"Of course, Sir Tol. I apologize again for them having been taken away from you. I will keep a much closer eye on the conduct of my crew from this point forward," said the captain.

"It's not the crew you have to watch," Tol replied, "It's the bilge wrats."

Chapter the Thirteenth

in which Tol encounters a rather odd but inarguably dangerous summoned creature

Tol called Selpla on his comm as soon as they were within range of a repeater and told her enough of the story to cover the major events. While he missed her more than he would have guessed, he nevertheless disembarked only reluctantly back in Cladimil. The captain had sent word ahead that Tol was safe and aboard the *Grollnash*. An EE pram met him at the docks. "The Commissioner, not to mention His Majesty, would very much like to know how you ended up at sea and what you were doing out there," the EE sergeant who was acting as his driver said

"So would I, to tell the truth," replied Tol. "It wasn't exactly my idea."

"Well, I hope you're prepared to write a full report, as soon as possible."

"If there's one thing I've learned from a lifetime in EE, it's how to write a report."

"I can't wait to read it. I expect it will be a best-seller."

"Yeah, ya know, maybe I will write my memoirs one day. They'd probably sell, at that."

"They might even make a cinematic of your life story."

"*A Hard Day's Knight*," said a mechanical voice from his overjack pocket.

"Smek me, Petey. I forgot you were in there. Did you get banged up any?"

"There were a few moments in which I expected to be flooded by salt water, but on the whole I'm still relatively intact."

Sergeant Yunbah nodded knowingly in the direction of the voice. "I, um, accidentally 'misplaced' mine."

"It's in the rear of your upper-right desk drawer, stuffed in a sealed manila envelope with the words "Do Not Open: Biohazard" written on it in red permanent ink," replied Petey, scornfully.

The sergeant sighed. "Thanks. I'll... um...look there as soon as I get back to the office."

Yunbah dropped Tol off at the carriage station. "You can take the regular cross-country back to Goblinopolis or request a Crimson express: your choice."

"This isn't an emergency situation; I'd rather not abuse the Crimson privilege. Those expresses are really expensive for both the carriage line and the taxpayers. Besides, the cross-country will give me more time to write the report."

Tol had about four hours to kill before the West-Tragacanth Limited pulled into Cladimil Central Station, so he decided to take in some of the local sights. He could only remember ever having been in the city once prior, when he was a young cop taking an EE workshop held here. He didn't have much time (or billmes) for sightseeing on that occasion, the per diem provided by the Precinct being barely enough to cover room and meals. He wasn't blessed with a lot of time now, either, but at least finances weren't an issue.

Cladimil is not nearly far enough south to be in the actual tropics—that region starts in southern Galanga, in fact—but it likes to pretend that it is. Vegetation, buildings, and even lifestyles are finely calculated to give off a tropical aura; even street vendors operate under a strict code of visual and gastronomic 'tropicality.'

Tol had never been to a tropical region, so he was quite happily taken in by the ruse. He bought some souvenirs for Selpla, ate some good seafood at a dockside restaurant, watched random young people frolicking in the surf, and was in a generally jovial mood (and slightly sleepy) when he finally boarded the Limited for Goblinopolis.

There were only two routes around the Masrons: northerly through Krubber Pass or the desert route to the south through Asga Teslu. Since the northerly route ran through Fenurian and Dresmak,

Tol chose the shorter, faster desert run, although it was less scenic. He wasn't interested in scenery so much. Besides, he intended to sleep most of the way.

Once the Limited made the Zongat crossing and swung around the southern edge of the Masrons, the landscape turned harsh but strangely beautiful. There were soaring spires of sandstone, deep canyons striped in red, yellow, and orange, and vast tabletop mesas. Giant succulents that store hundreds of liters of water and guard that treasure with motile fire thorns dotted heat-distorted horizons in every direction. During daylight hours the air was hushed except for carrion-bugs and blowing sand, but at night a cascade of activity and sounds flowed into the desert world, bringing it to life.

Most of this was lost on Tol, however, who crawled into a bunk in the sleeper coach and was snoring before the Limited was ten kilometers outbound. The arid wastelands whizzed by him completely unheeded until a curious thing happened. Without warning the brakes locked and the carriage ground to a prolonged, screeching halt. The noise finally woke Tol, who sat up in his bunk in annoyance was promptly catapulted to the floor by the final braking action.

He got up, slipped boots on, and wandered down the stairs of the double-decked sleeper to investigate. He stuck his head out between the sleeper and lounge and saw several carriageway employees walking around with torches. He jumped down and walked over to them.

"What's going on? Did we lose a wheel or something?"

One of the officials came over to meet him.

"Sorry, sir, this is a carriageway matter. Please return to the carriage."

Tol pulled out his badge and held it under the goblin's face. The official's eyebrow ridges shot up. "Sorry, investigator; I didn't know you were on board. We got a report from two different passengers that someone had jumped off the carriage."

"While we were movin'? Probably not a lot left of them, then."

"That's what we're afraid of."

"If you've got an extra torch I'll help you look."

Tol joined in the search. They had done some math and come up with the area indicated. The passenger had jumped from near the front of the kilometer-long carriage. He or she could be anywhere from this point to a half-kilometer back, assuming no rolling under the carriage itself. They formed a line and started walking slowly towards the rear. As they trudged along Tol found himself next to the official he'd first encountered.

"Did the witnesses say anything about *why* the subject jumped off a carriage moving at 100 kilometers an hour?"

"Only that the subject—apparently an elf—was very pale and suddenly screamed something about 'the curse has followed me,' just before he jumped."

"Yeah, I'd call the urge to jump off a fast-moving object a curse, all right. Not a long-term problem, though."

Just then one of the others yelled "Sir! There's something over here!"

"*Something*? By that do you mean *something we're looking for*?" the conductor yelled back.

"I...I'm not sure."

Tol and Wijuvva ('Wijjy'), the conductor, hurried over to where the other search team members were gathered. There was an elf there, on the ground. He was obviously deceased: so far, no surprises. Tol bent down and examined the body. It was completely intact: not a bruise, abrasion, or laceration to be seen. There was neither blood nor tissue in evidence. The elf looked perfectly healthy, with only one minor exception. He wasn't breathing.

The rail employees brought the body back to an unoccupied car under Tol's supervision. A company doctor declared the elf officially deceased. That just left three questions: why did the elf leap from the carriage in the first place; why wasn't he all bunged up from the high-speed impact; and since he wasn't bunged up, what killed him?

The put the deceased on ice for the remainder of the trip, as Tol had ordered him taken to the National Forensic Lab in Goblinopolis for post-mortem examination. The remainder of the trip gave Tol an opportunity to reconstruct the event. The conductor moved all passengers back and sealed off the first car as a potential crime scene. Tol interviewed the witnesses in depth. What they told him did not make sense.

The elf got on at the farming village of Upupa, the only stop between Goblinopolis and Dresmak. (The Limited made a loop, starting and ending up at Goblinopolis. One carriage looped clockwise, the other in the opposite direction.) He kept to himself up until the last half-hour, at which point he began changing seats every couple of minutes, growing increasingly agitated. He asked people if they saw someone or something following him, but no one did. Toward the end he was holding a very strained conversation with an invisible 'ghost' companion and pacing back and forth. People moved away from him and who/whatever he was talking to; he did not seem to notice.

Finally, the elf broke into a sudden run for the door, yelling something garbled about a curse. One of the witnesses said it sound like he said "ancestral curse," but none of the others could make out any details of what the elf was babbling hysterically as he ran. "Crazy as a night-screamer," Tol muttered, as he read through his notes. He was on the verge of simply calling the case closed due to 'mental aberration of the subject' when a shadow passed over, or rather through, him and it suddenly got very cold.

Tol looked around instinctively for an open window, but then remembered they were in the Asga Teslu where in the daytime it got hot enough to coagulate a red-throated rock crawler's blood. The carriages were cooled, yes, but not by any process powerful enough to create that level of temperature differential. Tol smiled as he realized once again how potent was the power of suggestion. Of course he felt cold: that was the traditional means by which 'ghosts' made themselves known. Ghosts and curses and phantoms were all manifestations of an active imagination, but that didn't make them any less real to those who truly believed.

Tol wasn't one of them. He had long since concluded that people were the only things that go bump in the night. He went to take a sip of the nice hot tea he'd been drinking while writing out his preliminary report and was shocked into temporary immobility by what he discovered. It was frozen solid.

"Wait, if it really was some ancestral curse, why would the spirit or whatever still be on board the carriage after the victim offed himself?" Tol was talking to Doctor Millmoss, the paranormal psychologist the EE Bureau used as a consultant on cases like this, on his comm.

"Residual energy? Are you on the level? I thought energy made things hotter, not colder. Negative energy? Is there really such a thing? No offense, doc, but I just can't buy into this malarkey. Thanks, anyway. Bye."

Tol sat and stared at the ceiling of the carriage in thought. He wasn't focused on anything up there, just fixated on one spot while his mind went over recent events analytically. Suddenly an impossibly black shadow moved across his field of vision. It took a second or two for it to register; when it did Tol leapt to his feet reflexively. He spun completely around, taking in the lighting and calculating the necessary position of an object in order to cast that shadow.

There was no object, and no strong source of light in the direction necessary to cast the shadow even if there had been. It must be some form of optical illusion.

Tol decided to conduct a simple experiment. He had been sitting in the same seat the witnesses said was occupied by the elf for most of the trip. He relocated to the other end of the now-empty carriage and waited. After a full hour there had been no shadows, no temperature fluctuations: nothing. He returned to the original seat. This time he hadn't been sitting there for more than a couple of minutes when it felt as though two strong hands grabbed his throat and were trying to choke him. Tol jumped to his feet and spun to dislodge the attacker. The choking sensation immediately ceased. He suddenly had an idea.

"Hey Petey," he said, taking the pen from his overjack pocket, "Got any clue what's going on here?"

"My presumption was that you were suffering from some form of neuromotive palsy," came the metallic reply, "Although your EEG readings were not abnormal. Allow me to rephrase that: not abnormal for *you*."

"Har, har. Please tell me you've also been following the bizarre little saga unfolding here."

"Yes. I see a spike in overall electromagnetic radiation concurrent with the manifestations of the shadow, but I cannot pinpoint the origin or even the precise nature of the field generated by that radiation. It is as though the source is extradimensional, which may well be the case—improbable though that sounds."

"Extradimensional...you mean like from The Slice?" Tol asked.

"Not exactly. Dark energy such as that siphoned from The Slice has a characteristic signature. This signature is very unusual in that it shows no consistent pattern; or rather, the pattern is there, but parts of it seem to be located in an energetic continuum that does not register on my sensors."

"So? Maybe you just haven't got the right sensors?"

"Perhaps, but I am equipped with sensors for the full spectrum of known radiative emissions. That means this energy is of a type unknown to engineers."

"Yeah? How can that be?"

"I have no answer for that question."

"I never thought I'd hear those words coming from your little electronic mouth."

"The number of questions to which I do not have the answer is infinite. My knowledge base only seems vast in comparison with your own."

"If the obligatory derogation period has concluded, I'd like to return to the anomaly under discussion."

"Your increased vocabulary is somewhat anomalous in itself and will, I might add, make the 'derogation periods' less frequent and of shorter duration. Returning per request to the discussion, the elf committed suicide based, apparently, on a belief that he was the victim of some form of malediction. If he experienced and misinterpreted the anomalous energy, and was predisposed to rash action based on some perceived prior intimidation, his reaction might be explicable on that basis."

"I'm not comfortable with the reliance that explanation places on irrationality," Tol replied, "Can we construct something a little more empirical?"

"I am deeply impressed. Perhaps I have misjudged you all these years."

"Nah. I really have been trying to expand my vocabulary lately."

"And you've made noticeable progress. As to the chain of events, it might be helpful if you carried me around while I scan for more encounters with the mystery energy. The more samples I have, the better a characterization I can develop."

Tol clipped the pen to an outside pocket to avoid any shielding effect from the lined overjack and transected the carriage methodically. After one complete survey they had found nothing and were considering the possibility that whatever it was had returned to wherever it had come from when Tol suddenly felt something: an intensely malevolent presence.

"You see anything on the sensors?" he asked Petey.

"Yes. 'Pegged the meter,' as you might say. An energy signature I've never seen before that isn't even possible with the limits of engineering as we know them. To put it into context, were it thermal energy this coach and in fact the entire carriage would be molten. The level is now approaching the full-spectrum radiative output of a small star. If some form of harmonic or feedback loop is established with 'normal' energy something dramatic and most likely catastrophic will occur." Petey's volume was increasing at the end to compensate for a rising thrum in the coach.

"What can we do to prevent that from taking place?" Tol yelled.

"Jump!"

"I meant, and survive the experience!"

"Oh. In that case I would suggest contacting your transcended mage friend. The energy signature here is closer to dark energy than anything else. He might recognize it."

"Good idea," Tol muttered while fumbling in his pocket for a talisman Oloi had given him. He squinted at the tiny lettering, which obligingly began to glow a bright golden as the talisman heated up in his palm. "Ulul..." he started, before remembering he was supposed to read right to left..." Veniteet ululaverunt!"

Nothing happened for a few moments, except that the oppressive feeling in the coach grew so incredibly intense that it seemed the walls themselves would surely give way. A golden swirling mist appeared and an odd bipedal creature with smooth light brownish-red hide and shocks of startling thin white fur on its head assembled itself therefrom.

"Nice to see you, Oloi," said Tol, when enough of the apparition had materialized for him to be confident that hearing was possible.

"Yooouraaaang?" Oloi replied in an artificially deep voice.

"Yeah, I guess I did. Do you feel that?"

"What, precisely, am I expected to be feeling?"

"An incredible sense of evil, oppression, and foreboding."

Oloi sniffed the air and waved his hand back and forth. "Smells like a Duellomortu."

Tol glared at him. "Whatta ya mean 'smells like?' And what the smek is a dwellomor...whatever?"

"A Duellomortu is revenant who can only be killed in a duel. With a sword. A dueling sword, to be exact: rapier, colichemarde, or sabre, usually."

"This sounds like a monster from some role playing game," said Petey, drily.

"That's precisely the origin of it, old boy. When you're an archmage with a very high fever and a very potent Artifact of Instantiation within easy reach of your bedside, these sorts of things happen."

"How do we make it go away?" screamed Tol over the almost intolerable din.

"Oh," replied Oloi, "You really can't, now. Not until you set a time and place for the duel. The best you can do is move to another coach. It won't follow you."

They all moved to the next coach in line and huddled in the first berth. "You mean that coach is now haunted?" asked Wijjy, who had joined them when they changed coaches.

"In a sense, yes. The Duellomortu will remain attached that physical location until someone completes the geas by challenging it to, and fighting, the proper form of duel."

"What happens if you lose the duel?"

Oloi shrugged. "You die and take the Duellomortu's place."

"And if you win?"

"The Duellomortu dissipates."

"How is any of this possible?" Tol asked.

The archmage crossed his legs. "Do know what a wheel boot is?"

"Yeah," replied Tol, "It's a locking collar we clamp on the wheel of prams or drays to keep them from moving until we're ready for that to happen."

"Precisely: a revenant is a malevolent spirit held in place by a magical 'soul boot,' not to be freed until a specific trigger releases it. In the case of a Duellomortu that trigger consists of being defeated in a sword battle using the rules of formal rapier combat."

"You said 'in the case of *a* Duellomortu.' Does that mean there is more than one in existence?" asked Wijjy.

"Unfortunately, yes. An artifact is so-called because of its great power. An Artifact of Instantiation burns a permanent template into the interface between the prime and arcane realms that generates whatever was programmed into that template more or less forever. It dissipates eventually, but only after millions of years. As a result, Duellomortu will continue to appear throughout N'plork for quite a long time to come."

"Well," observed Tol after a few moments' reflection, "I suppose it creates job security for the fencing masters."

"Quite so," answered Oloi. "Is this why you called me here?"

"No," Tol replied, "Actually, it isn't." He recounted the story of the elf's last moments and suicide. "We were trying to understand the rapidly building negative energy field, as well as how the elf could have leapt to his death without any apparent injuries."

Oloi smiled grimly. "You'll find the injuries are all internal. While he did leap off, he was no longer moving relative to the ground when he came to rest."

"How do you figure that?"

"One thing I forgot to tell you about Duellomortu: they aren't very patient. If you refuse to engage one in actual rapier combat, it may very well attack you with 'spirit swords' that do the same damage internally as a real sword, but do not leave any external wounds. When a person dies that way he passes through a transition stage during which his body is impervious to external forces while the spirit is being harvested extradimensionally. That's not entirely accurate: in fact, the body itself is temporarily located in another dimension. Apparently this poor fellow died just before or as he left the train and had already stopped rolling on the ground when he returned fully to the native state. *Et voila*: deceased elf with no apparent injuries."

Oloi had to return to The Slice a few minutes later. Tol sat and began to write out his report. When there was a stiff involved the paperwork got much more arduous. As he wrote the conductor sat across from Tol, waiting for him to finish. Finally Tol decided to take a 'rest his writing arm' break.

"What can I do for you, Wijjy?"

"I have some rather disappointing news. The 'haunted' coach is one of the very few in our fleet with the engine coupling installed. In other words, it's the one car we really can't do without on the Limited carriage. Without it, there's no way to attach the engines to the other coaches.

"So, I guess you'd better find a fencing master or get to training pretty hard. That's the only way I know of to get that coach back into operation, unless you want to sell tickets to the 'haunted carriage' or something."

"While that is a tempting proposition, I don't believe upper management would go for it. The insurance premiums would be prohibitive. What they *would* go for, however—and I know this because I have a message from them right here—is hiring you to take care of the problem for us."

Tol's incredulous expression morphed after a moment into a broad grin, accompanied by a hearty chuckle. "You've been setting me up for that punchline the entire time, haven't you?"

The conductor looked puzzled. "I assure you this offer is quite legitimate."

Tol's expression toned down. "I'm a special investigator for His Majesty's Edict Enforcement Bureau. I can't accept commissions of that sort. Nor can I engage in combat with a specter or anything else except in the course of apprehending a suspect or preventing a violent illegal act."

"Were not asking you to engage in combat personally, or at all if you can figure out some other approach. We're merely hiring you make this problem go away and give us back the use of our coach."

Tol cocked his head, turned away, and closed one eye. He was figurin.' At last he turned to face Wijjy again. "All right: it's a deal. I'll find someone to fight the Duello-thing and turn all of that money over to them."

"Are you sure you can't keep any of it?"

"Only up to twenty billmes from any given entity, as a gift in appreciation of service."

"Is that twenty per day, or just twenty, period?"

"I don't know. It's never come up before. Check with the EEB Ethics Office. They play craps back in the alley behind HQ on Midweeksday; otherwise they're pretty easy to get hold of."

"Thank you, Sir Tol-u-ol. This carriage is the lifeline for many people living along the tracks. Your assistance will be essential in maintaining service to those people, as well as providing transportation for many business travelers and thousands of tonnes of goods every month."

"Yeah, yeah. I've read your brochure. I'll kill the monster for you. It may take some time, though."

"Understood; please proceed as rapidly as possible, however."

"The sooner you get me to Goblinopolis, the sooner I'll get started."

"Your express carriage will be pulling up in about ten minutes."

"There's no siding here; how are you going to turn the carriage around?"

"There's an engine on both ends of most of our carriages. They can provide propulsion in synch with one another in either the forward or reverse direction of travel. When your carriage gets here the engineer will simply switch ends."

"Clever. Makes sense, now that I think about it."

"We're going to cancel all Track Warrants between here and Goblinopolis. That means any carriages on that route will have to pull into the next siding and wait for you to go by. That ensures that you will get to Goblinopolis in the shortest possible time, with no detours or stops necessary."

"I can see you are very serious about this mission. I will do my best to help you."

"That's all we can ask, Sir Tol-u-ol. May Providence be with you."

Chapter the Fourteenth

in which Tol encounters and hires an awe-inspiring bladesmistress

"Rack your weapon and go to your corner, Verax. Meditate on patience and on learning from the lesson you received today." Jadean stood with hands on hips: her 'don't argue with me' posture. Verax, her advanced student and potential cadet, was shaking with anger and frustration.

"I have practiced that attack over and over and over. I set it up right; why was it so easy for you to parry?" He was no longer shouting, but still obviously struggling to maintain self-control.

"The Attaque au Fer was effective; the initial balestra was well-timed, but your riposte following my parry was poorly executed because once again, you forgot about your footwork. You were not in an advantageous position for the reprise because I side-stepped. You should have rotated on the ball of your foot and reset for the patinando, which would have been quite effective had you been in the proper position. As executed, however, passé was inevitable and your forward recovery was inept. I could have driven my sword completely through your neck or shoulder with ease."

"What am I doing that is so wrong, Randora?" Verax was calming down now, but still shaking.

"Your footwork," she explained, "Is fine when you first attack, but once you get involved in the fight and shift focus to your blade you forget about it and begin to stumble around like a novice. You must practice footwork until it becomes second nature at all times. I want you to be awoken from a deep sleep and leap out of bed en garde and in perfect balance. Until then you will be defeatable simply by staying in tight defense until you've engaged two or three times. You are especially prone to failure during an opposition parry after multiple exchanges. The longer our blades are in contact, the worse your footing becomes. Now, go and meditate."

Jadean Zov was the Doen-ya, or Spiritual Leader, of the Academy of Fence and Defence, (AFD), on the southeast side of Goblinopolis, within sight of the immense grain fields and fruit orchards that occupy tens of thousands of hectares south of the city. She held the rarified title of Randora, which in Elvish translates roughly to "Chaos Warrior:" the first to do so in several generations. She was technically a Heterelf—a full elf, but with the blood of at least one other race strongly detectable in her genome—but the only outward manifestation of that was a slightly more muscular build and a little shorter stature. Elves are very secretive about their genetic makeup; this added to the fact that Jadean was a martial arts uber-master meant that no one ever pried into what she was unwilling to divulge freely—at least, no one who knew anything about elves and their culture. Any who did pry were soundly rebuffed in a manner that made it quite clear they would not be wise to inquire further.

Jadean had grown up in the fencing community; fencing was in her blood. Her father Sir Aqriz Zov was for a time the world's champion freestyle kumite fencer, after having first distinguished himself in the army by almost single-handedly repelling a localized orc invasion with a bill-guisarme and poignard. He was the only elf ever raised to the rank of Knight of the Crimson, in fact.

Tol had watched a number of Jadean's matches, and those of her students, over the years. He was greatly in awe of her consummate skill with any blade at all. Jadean always made the weapon seem an extension of her body, wielding a sword with the same ease and comfort as simply waving her hand. Tol was fond of saying Jadean could take out a squadron of commandoes with a spatula.

So, after spending a full day with Selpla and giving her the gifts he bought her as well as a little more, it was at the Academy of Fence and Defence that Tol found himself on the second morning after returning to his native city. "Tol?" Jadean said, smiling as he walked in the door. "I haven't laid eyes on you in years. Oh, it's *Sir* Tol now, isn't it? Very impressive."

Tol waved his hand dismissively. "Not in comparison with anything you've accomplished. Anyway, I didn't come to talk about me."

Jadean offered him a seat and some herbal infusion.

"So, why did you come?"

Tol leaned back and considered his words.

"I came to offer you a...proposition, of sorts."

Jadean laughed and batted her eyes at him.

"I'm flattered, to say the least."

Tol's own eyes got wide and he blushed a lovely blue-green.

"No...I mean...a *business* proposition. Really, more of a challenge."

Still chuckling, she took a sip of her infusion.

"What manner of challenge?"

"A sword fight. To the death. With an...unusual opponent."

Jadean's face took on a more serious cast.

"I don't fight outrance, only plaisance. Society frowns on the first; they call it murder. But you of course are aware of that. So, why ask?"

"Killing this opponent will not be murder, or in fact any crime at all, under edict."

"Is he a fugitive, then, or perhaps a convicted killer himself?"

"No. He's simply not alive and so cannot be murdered, per se."

Jadean raised her eyebrows. "Not alive? How am I to kill something that is not alive to begin with?"

"Have you ever heard the term *Duellomortu*?"

Jadean smirked at him. "You cannot be serious. Duellomortu is a fictitious magical construct employed as a thought experiment in higher-level martial philosophy teachings. It does not literally exist."

"I can promise you this one does. Experienced it myself, and saw it off an elf in Asga Teslu."

"Who told this thing you encountered was indeed Duellomortu?"

"A transcendent archmage by the name of Oloi. Same guy who helped me nab Pyfox."

She looked thoughtful.

"I believe we have met. An archmage is about the only authority I would trust to be able to categorize a manifestation of that nature correctly." Jadean stood up and sighed.

"If Duellomortu it is, then I have no choice but to accept the challenge. To do otherwise would bring shame upon myself and my scholabellum. I will want to train first. How long do I have?"

"Every day we delay brings more hardship to the people and businesses who depend on the Limited carriage to and from the Western cities. This thing is infesting one of the coaches that provide a link between the engine and passenger or freight buggies."

"Then, I will begin now."

She walked gracefully, fluidly over to a raised platform covered with a thin mat and sat cross-legged upon it. Fifteen seconds later she was absolutely motionless. She didn't even seem to be breathing. Tol was beginning to get worried when suddenly her eyes opened. She stood, and reached for two swords from a rack of over a dozen. Her entire body snapped *en garde* like a gigantic work of origami. She took three measured breaths, and then worked her way through an ever more complex series of katas until she and the blades were whirling, diving, undulating, and spinning almost faster than the eye could follow.

As the final movement of the ultimate kata, called 'flashing razor,' she turned a complete somersault while executing two entirely separate sub-katas, one with each arm, and before touching down on the mat slashed with incredible speed and precision at four thick cords suspended vertically in a large frame. Each of the cords had a thin red line encircling it at a different spot along its length. While she was cooling down on the mat, Tol examined them. Each was sliced very neatly exactly on the line: not the tiniest bit above or below.

"I will execute that master kata sequence three more times and then I will be ready."

Tol summoned his express carriage and they left the next morning. Tol and Wijjy had decided it was better to uncouple the possessed coach and leave it on a siding at the edge of the desert to minimize the chance that anyone would wander near and be injured and/or traumatized.

During their journey Tol summoned Oloi once more, to have him brief Jadean on how the challenge was issued and what to expect.

"You'll be facing a creature which has imprinted upon it the basic rules of fencing, but no native skill. It will absorb and match whatever skill you exhibit, as it was originally created partially for use as a training device. You cannot kill it literally, but if you defeat it according to its internal rules it will dissipate. It will," Oloi added, looking at her pointedly, "Most likely represent the greatest challenge of your life and if you die, you will take its place."

Jadean nodded. "A challenge skirted is a life diminished. I am ready."

When they reached the siding, they disembarked the Crimson Express and had it back away a hundred meters from the haunted coach.

"I don't know exactly how this is going to go," Tol said, "But I don't want anyone else hurt or any unnecessary damage done."

He and Jadean approached the coach cautiously. Oloi, who had been forced to return to The Slice, had given them detailed instructions on how to issue the challenge. Jadean stood in the aisle of the coach, head bowed, saber in one hand and colichemarde in the other. She looked up.

"Challenge is hereby issued to that which waits in this place. I bring lawful weapons and am prepared to do combat in the lawful style."

There was dead silence for a few long moments, then from what sounded like a great distance there came a shrill noise that got louder and lower in pitch as it approached them. At last it seemed to be emanating from the air directly in front of Jadean.

"Lllllllawful challlllenge hassss been offered annnd accepted," it hissed, "Therrrre must beeee noooo othersss."

It stopped. Jadean looked at Tol. "I think it's talking about you."

Tol rolled his eyes. "Fine; I'll wait outside." He walked over and set his pen on a window ledge before exiting.

Once Tol was gone, the voice resumed. The hissing was gone. What remained was a broken voice, guttural and dead. A spectral figure with rapier and buckler wavered in the air a scarce meter before Jade's face.

"Are you prepared to begin? This combat is outrance," it rasped.

"I am aware of outrance and ready to begin."

"Then, combat is joined."

With that the Duellomortu slashed viciously at her saber arm and before she could even react threw a solid punch toward her face with its buckler. She parried the slash and ducked out of the punch.

"That was not a lawful attack," she said.

The apparition laughed. "*I* decide what is lawful here. I judge that attack within the rules, as is *this* one."

Before it finished speaking the Duellomortu rolled right with blinding speed and came out of the spin with rapier point facing backward so that it preceded him, driving it hard at her throat. She brought the colichemarde up to parry near the hilt of the rapier, sliding along it until at the tip she twisted suddenly downward, hooking the single heavy quillion over the rapier blade and neatly snapping it in half. The upper portion was flung several meters and skittered along the floor of the coach. The specter laughed as his rapier blade magically regrew.

"I would wager," Jadean said as she launched a complex cross-thrusting lunge, "That my blades, once broken, would not be so quick to repair themselves."

The Duellomortu laughed again. "Mortal warriors wield mortal weapons."

"So, by 'lawful,' you really mean 'whatever gives you an unfair advantage,'" Jadean observed.

"It may seem unfair to you, but I was created without any skills. I must absorb and incorporate them into my makeup on the fly for every bout. That is a tremendous handicap that far outweighs any issues you have with broken blades."

Jadean thought about this. "Granted. I will cease to question you."

"Especially when I have opened you up like a fileted toothfish," it cried, launching a rapid combination of thrusts and slashes, which Jadean deftly dodged, albeit barely. She leapt completely over a sweeping cut and brought both her blades out in a crossing pattern that would have neatly decapitated a living opponent, but had no effect on her shadowy opponent.

"I *know* that made contact," she said, parrying two more thrusting attacks in rapid succession, "So what sort of rules are we playing under here?"

"The rules were set down by the master. He did not like his challenges trivial. You must land multiple killing blows on me to win. I, of course, need kill you only once. I even pointed out to him once that his rules were unfair. He responded that life was unfair and he wanted to simulate life."

"Noble of him, I'm sure. What became of him?"

"I killed him, of course. He was distracted by a vile creature who looked a lot like you."

"Oh ho! You were *jealous*, then."

"I know not this word, jealous."

"I think you do." She accompanied this with a flurry of off-hand swipes followed by a vicious rising thrust that changed direction at the last possible second and impaled the specter beneath the right arm and into the chest. Or would have, on a living creature.

"That's two," she said, grimly, executing a standing backflip to avoid the phantom's counter-attack.

"Yes. Two. What fun! Now, the only thing more entertaining than an apparently immortal opponent is..."

"Two of them!" answered a duplicate specter behind her.

True martial arts masters have two levels of defensive capability: the *kuori*, or outer shell, and the *ydin*, or core. The *ydin* is rarely accessed, as it comes into play only in life or death situations, in which people at Jadean's level rarely find themselves due to their superior skills. With the appearance of the second sword-specter, however, Jadean snapped into *ydin*.

In the core there is nothing but you and your opponents; all else fades. There is no sound, no speech, no background. Only you and the foe exist, in high-definition, ultra-clarity. Each movement is in slow-motion, each reaction exquisitely choreographed by brain strata unreachable under any but the most extreme circumstances. In this state Jadean was quite simply an unstoppable killing machine.

She leapt high into the air and in one blinding, blurred cascade of motion as she descended slashed both opponents hard across the face, feinted immediately to draw them offside, cut them both across the midriff, feinted once more as she touched down, and finally continued into a crouch and sprang forward, impaling each with a different weapon. Both opponents abruptly vanished.

She drew back into the en garde position and waited, her breathing tightly controlled. Every muscle in her body was on high alert but relaxed, ready for whatever it was called upon to do. Nothing happened for a few pregnant moments, and then the specter reappeared, more solid than before.

It stood in front of Jadean and slowly slid rapier into scabbard. It bowed formally and said, "Most impressive, Mistress. I hereby declare the malediction lifted."

With that, rather than fading away, it dissipated like smoke from a dying fire. In a few seconds there was nothing left. Sensing that the threat was past, Jadean finally dropped her guard. She stuck her head out of the coach.

"All clear. You can come back in now."

Tol returned. "So, is it over?"

"I believe it is. The apparition declared the curse lifted," replied Jadean, exhaling fully for the first time since the battle began.

Tol smiled. "I knew you were the right person for the job." He walked over to the ledge and picked up his pen. "Petey, here, probably has some amazing footage for us. Am I right?"

"You are absolutely correct, Sir Tol-u-ol. Would you care to see it?"

"Yes, Petey, that would be most appreciated."

A tight, rapidly scanning beam of light emanated from the pen to form a small cube of high-resolution video in the air before their faces. In it was a three-dimensional depiction of the battle, complete with surround-sound audio.

"That's one heck of a pen you got there," observed Jadean as they watched the spectacle. "I'm guessing you didn't buy it from some mail-order catalog."

"Yeah, it's really useful, once you get past the abrasive personality disorder."

There was a snort of derision from the pen. "Projection," was all it said in reply. Tol and Jadean both laughed at the embedded pun.

"That was an almost unbelievable display of skill," Tol said after the cinematics were done. "There is no way I'd face you in a fight, even a friendly bout."

"Well, I don't kill people—or things—ordinarily, you know," Jadean replied, "This was something of a special circumstance. Besides, you've killed a lot more people than I have, I'll wager."

"Probably so. But all of them were trying to kill me."

"The same is true for me. One never uses deadly force unless it is a matter of one's own survival. Even then it must be the avenue of last resort."

Tol reached into his pocket for a small card. "This contains your payment, as promised. I think you'll find it acceptable."

She took the card and pressed the edge with her thumb, to show the amount. Her eyes got wide. "I...I had no idea it was this much. This is enough to pay all expenses for the Academy for an entire year. I can buy new equipment and perhaps expand. Tol, I cannot thank you enough; I and the Academy are forever in your debt."

"On the contrary, Randora Jadean, the debt falls squarely on the shoulders of the Greater Tragacanth Carriage Authority. You have restored to them the use of a carriage worth ten times the price they paid you."

"And you?" Jadean asked, "What payment have you received from this victory?"

"The taxpayers of Tragacanth pay my salary, but far greater coin for me is the satisfaction I get from helping citizens in need. And in this case, I was gifted with the privilege of watching one of the greatest warriors of all time at the top of her game. That's worth more than I can even count."

"So is the number of fingers on two pairs of gloves," said a voice from inside his overjack pocket.

Jadean looked at him quizzically.

Tol grinned. "Remember the personality disorder thing?"

Chapter the Fifteenth

in which Selpla tracks her lover with the help of an archmage

Selpla took a sip of her greatfruit infusion and closed her eyes. She had just finished filming a segment on a new self-cleaning undergarments invention for the morning broadcast and now sat in the studio canteen relaxing. She was waiting for Tol to call so they could plan their upcoming date to Lake Streblor across the border in Galanga. Tol had never been and she was anxious to show it to him. Streblor was world-famous for its crystal clear waters, teeming avian and piscean life, and due to a particular mineral present in the water, it smelled like roasting meat. Avid carnivores from all over the world came just to sit on the beach and sniff.

By the time Selpla was ready to leave for home, Tol still had not called. She checked her comm to make sure she had not inadvertently turned off the alert tone. It was still on, and no message from Tol. He must have had difficulty getting that titan kid onto the boat. She called him up. It went immediately to voice record, which meant that his comm unit was unable to receive calls for one reason or another.

Selpla still wasn't too concerned: Tol was, after all, a cop who sometimes went incommunicado to get the job done. Turning off his comm accidentally wasn't all that unusual. He also did it intentionally every so often just to get some peace and quiet, although that reason probably wasn't going to apply here. He would call her as soon as he got the chance; she had no doubt of that.

The next morning she was full-blown worried. She checked her messages on every conceivable device and found nothing. She grabbed her always-ready overnight bag and headed to the carriage station to buy a ticket to Cladimil. All along the lengthy trip to the west coast she continued to try contacting Tol. She left messages at his office comm, and the Tragacanth Edict Enforcement headquarters; she even asked the Royal Residence staff to have Tol call her as soon as possible if they heard from him first.

The harbormaster in Cladimil was an old ogre named Nid. He didn't much like goblins, and he didn't have time for a pretty young female one with a bunch of questions. "You are welcome to file a Manifest Discovery Request," he said, without looking up, "Shouldn't take more than three weeks, if the Records Keeper isn't out with the croup again." He wasn't impressed that the missing person was a Knight of the Crimson, nor even that he was Royal Family. Nid shooed her out of his office; Selpla stood there in the hallway only for a moment considering her options before striding briskly away.

An hour later she was back with a camera crew from the local affiliate station. She told Nid she was fascinated by his glamorous job and wanted the people of Cladimil and in fact all of Tragacanth to know more about him. He was naturally suspicious at first, but Selpla was a difficult person to resist over the long term and eventually Nid gave her the interview, and more.

She remembered that Tol had said he was he was going to escort a young titan named Korq onto the ship and see that he was well-treated on his way to be with family in Solemadrina. Based on the slip, time, and destination, she decided the ship must have been the *Grollnash*, although that wasn't a certificated passenger vessel.

There was no Korq on the passenger manifest, but that wasn't surprising, she learned by talking with the local cargo jocks. Ships not officially certificated as primary passenger haulers were actually allowed twelve paying passengers per sailing; any beyond that would be traveling 'exconsigno' or off-manifest.

After she'd pumped the Harbormaster for all the information he apparently had to offer under the guise of interviewing him for a high-profile news spot, Selpla and her crew moved on to conducting dockside interviews. The dock denizens came from almost every race and nation on N'plork, so asking them if they'd seen a goblin get on board the *Grollnash* would have been pointless except for Korq. A titan, even a young one, was certainly a novelty even for the dock workers. Many of them hadn't seriously believed that titans existed until then.

"Bleeder was taller than an ogre on growth serum," one of them exclaimed.

"Tall en skinny ez a needle-arbor," said another.

"Did you see who he was with?" Selpla would ask them hopefully.

"Was 'e wit' summun? Dint notice," was the most common reply.

At last, one of the loadmasters indicated that he'd seen Tol get on the boat.

"Tough-lookin' goblin," he related, "Like a cop er retired soljer. Funny thing is, I never seen 'im git off—an' I was here until long after th' scow pushed away."

Selpla tried Tol's comm again. No connection made. It was either destroyed or no longer in range of a signal repeater: even when powered off, a functional comm unit sends out a "busy" beacon. No signal at all was bad. Selpla thought about the problem for a moment and then suddenly brightened. She thanked the crew for helping her little information-gathering sham succeed and raced off into the approaching darkness.

Roadway T-1 made a giant loop from Goblinopolis to Cladimil to Fenurian to Dresmak and back. T-2 wound its way from Goblinopolis to Port Zog to Lumbos. The T-3 ran almost in a straight line from the capitol city down through Ft. Ullglava and then to Tillimil. The T-4 ran from Tillimil to Dreadmost. Finally, the T-5 ran from the T-4 just south of the River Tud Bridge to Qoplebarq. There were dozens of smaller roads, of course, such as the one from Cartlug to Strix in the Southern Reaches or the road from the T-1 to Upupa in the District of Northmia. The T-level highways were maintained by the Royal Engineers; the small byways by the local Road & Bridge Districts.

Selpla took the T-3 and stopped in Ft. Ullglava to eat lunch. Despite the military installation for which it was named—the largest single active reservation in the kingdom—the town itself was surprisingly charming. A small river, the Feqlo, ran through the heart of the hamlet and emptied finally into the Bay of Sorrows, named for the abundance of sharp rocks and unpredictable gales that sent many ships and sailors to their dooms over the millennia.

The residents of Ft. Ullglava the town, originally a retirement community for soldiers but now with a thriving population unrelated to said military, had built a most marvelous shopping and dining district along the river, with multiple stone-arched foot bridges interconnecting a cohesive collection of shops, restaurants, theatres, and art enclaves that made for an absorbing (and for the proprietors, profitable) tourist experience. Selpla found a darling little cafe on the southern end of the river path where she sat with her favorites: citrus-leaf infusion and ogrecress sandwich.

Tol's comm was still dead. She had never been the pessimistic sort and swore that this setback would not convert her. He was out there, somewhere, and she would find him. Alive. Tol was nothing if not a survivor. She knew the odds were with him, whatever he'd gotten himself into. She decided to put the brake on this line of reasoning because it was scaring her a little. She did not like to be scared. This episode made Selpla realize just how much she cared about Tol. She'd never felt this way about anyone outside her family before.

She arrived in Cartlug in the late afternoon and went straight to the Mages' Lodge. She carried with her a small amulet given to her by Ballop'ril. When plugged into a slot in a ceremonial console in the Cartlug Mages' Lodgehall, it was supposed to summon the archmage somehow. After exchanging a few pleasantries with the resident mages, she was led into the corridor of ceremonies where the receptacle in question was located. Selpla slotted the carved talisman in place and waited. After a few seconds a faint glow appeared in the air before her. As she watched, it intensified until she could make out that it was some sort of command or notice. It said:

Hang On!

She was still puzzling over the meaning of this cryptic instruction when the world seemed to contract and rush toward her, fuzzing as it went. She gave out with a little scream that ended abruptly when she found herself back in Ballop'ril's elaborate mountain cavern, with the wizened little bugbear himself standing there. Just behind and to his left was Prond, with a new silver sash.

"Hi Selpla! Great to see you. I made Mage, Second Tier. Isn't that great?"

Selpla took a deep breath to clear her head and grinned at him.

"Yeah, that's super, Prond. You'll be an archmage before you know it."

"Not so much," he replied, "That will take at least twenty more years—if I'm lucky."

"Luck has little to do with it," Ballop'ril interjected, "Hard work is the key to advancement; scarce else matters. Now then, young lady: to what do we owe the great honor of your visit today?"

Selpla composed herself quickly and adopted her usual aplomb. "Greetings, Archmage Ballop'ril. Thank you for allowing me again into your fabulous home. Other than simply wishing to gaze upon all this magnificence once more, I need to trace down an inert comm unit and was hoping you could perform such a feat."

The archmage stroked his chin. "If the unit has an arcane heterodyning module it might be possible. Have you misplaced it?"

"In a manner of speaking. I have misplaced the goblin carrying it: Sir Tol."

"Sir Tol-u-ol is missing? This is most grievous news. How did such a thing come about?"

Selpla relayed what little of the story she knew.

"And you say your comm is priority-linked to his? That will simplify things a bit. Please set it on the table here, inside the circle of glyphs."

While Prond stood nearby with a full speculum for providing additional manna if needed, Ballop'ril coalesced an energy sphere in mid-air, lowering it gently onto the table until one full hemisphere disappeared into the surface, leaving the comm encased in a semi-circle of pulsating blue.

"The comm unit is now located partially in arcane space and partially in physical space," Ballop'ril explained, "A priority link uses a form of quantum entanglement: certain subatomic particles of this comm unit are inextricably tied to their counterparts in Tol's. If I initiate a 'Multidimensional Pinpoint' spell on the comm, the entangled particles should act as shunts to their equivalents in the other device and feed us the precise location of them in the process. The trick will be to cast the spell with sufficient power that the trace takes place all the way down to the subatomic level. Otherwise we won't get enough information back from Tol's comm to ascertain its exact resting spot."

Prond conjured a three-dimensional map in the air near them on which to display the tracking information. As the spell took hold the energy in the speculum began to drain away until it was merely a transparent glass ovoid. On Prond's map, little points of light began to sparkle and move about as the trace spell ran its course. A dense clump of red photoluminescence marked the spot on which they stood, where Selpla's comm rested. As they watched, small green clumps began to form and move toward Cladimil, then in a relatively straight line away to the west, across the Noorprid Sea. They met at a spot roughly two thirds of the way across that ocean, on a trajectory that would seem to be taking them to Port Jool or Woklopen in Solemadrina.

"I guess he decided to tag along," remarked Selpla after a few moments, "Odd that he didn't call to tell me, though."

"Odder still that an Edict Enforcement officer would turn off his comm. The model they use self-recharges through the Arcane Ether," Prond added. "No need to turn it off, ever."

"Way out there, though, there aren't any repeaters for the conventional signals. Those comms are meant to use arcane mode for signal boosting only: you can't make a call without the conventional radio portion," explained Ballop'ril.

While they pondered these ponderables, Ballop'ril made them all a nice cup of hot Mages Special infusion (or 'infission,' as he called it).

"Tol-u-ol is alive," he announced suddenly, voicing an answer to the question they were all thinking.

"How...how do you know?" Selpla asked, trembling a little.

"He left me this."

He held up a small crystal with a pale yellowish glow coming from it.

"This is his arcanic essence. It's like genetic material only derived from his arcane aura, not his biological chromosomes. It flooded into an empty crystal cocoon in my pocket when I touched him preparatory to teleporting him to the Royal Residence. I realized it sometime later and asked if he wanted me to destroy it. He said no, it might come in handy one day. Prescient of him."

Selpla still looked puzzled.

"Ah, I forgot the most important part," Ballop'ril continued in response. "As with the comm unit, arcanic essence is linked by a form of quantum entanglement to the person from whom it was derived. If the crystal is energized, the life force of the donor still exists. The crystal, as you can see, is glowing. Were he demised, the crystal would be a dull red. Therefore..."

"I am very happy to know this," Selpla said quietly.

"Here," Ballop'ril handed her the glowing cylinder. "Keep this in a safe place and you will always know that he is among the living."

Selpla's eyes got wide. "What if I...drop it or something?"

The archmage laughed. "So long as it is filled with arcanic essence it is quite indestructible, I assure you. These crystals possess an intrinsic inviolability enchantment that is activated when they fill."

She cradled it in her palm as though it were a fragile, precious living creature. "I will keep it close to me always." She pulled a fine, strong chain from around her neck and threaded it through a hole in the wire enmeshing the crystal, placing it back over her head.

"It will never be further away than a hair's breadth."

Knowing Tol was alive was a great comfort, of course, as was knowing approximately where he was located, but not knowing precisely *why* he was there ate at her tremendously. Back in Goblinopolis she set up her own comm unit to override any existing call with an incoming from Tol's number and made his ringtone a loud alarm sound. When she built a little shrine to him, with his picture at the center, she realized she was in love.

Chapter the Sixteenth

in which a healing ritual inadvertently creates a lethal swarm of monsters

Tol did call, at last, and relayed his adventures in abbreviated form. He was on the way to Cladimil, there to take the carriage back to Goblinopolis, back to her. She could not remember happier news. Her entire universe suddenly brightened up, as though the sun had come out from behind thick, enveloping clouds for the first time in weeks. She bought new clothes and did everything she could think of to maximize her attractiveness for him. The reunion would be, she hoped, epic.

Then the call came in from Kurg, her boss: the crew will be by in ten minutes to pick you up; the titans are having some sort of disagreement that threatens to turn violent and I want you there to cover it. No ifs or buts.

She slammed the comm down and steamed for a moment, but in the end her journalistic instincts came through and made the outcome inevitable. She sighed and picked up the 'go bag' she kept on a shelf near the door and headed out to meet the guys. The trip would only make their reunion even sweeter.

She called Tol to tell him the news and discovered that he was dealing with a rather bizarre situation involving a ghost haunting a carriage. She shook her head. He could certainly wriggle himself into interesting predicaments. The very thought of wriggling excited Selpla so much she had to conjure up something sad immediately. She remembered a treasured lapspider she'd had as a child that was mashed against the wall when a door blew open during an intense storm. Sad, and a real mess to clean up. That helped.

It was a long way from Goblinopolis to Hellehoell, so far in fact that Kurg grudgingly sprung for third-class carriage fare, which

Selpla immediately upgraded to first on her expense account. "We're not bouncing and scraping all the way to Fenurian in the third-class coach," she explained to Lom, her lighting tech; Drin, who took care of her audio; and Fob, the camera jockey replacing Prond.

"Won't mister Kurg be upset that you're spending that money, Miss Selpla?" asked Fob.

"We just call him Kurg," explained Lom, "*Mister* is wasted on him."

Fob looked bewildered. "But, he is our supervisor, yes?"

"He's the city desk editor who gives us news assignments. Supervisor is a bit misleading."

"I think he a big bully sometime," added Drin.

Selpla laughed. "Kurg is just Kurg. He's a big lug with a gruff exterior, but deep down he's really, well, still a big lug. Respect him when he's around, but don't get carried away with it."

"Yes, Miss Selpla. I will try not to get carried away."

"Don't call her 'Miss Selpla,' either," Lom said, annoyed, "Makes her sound like somebody's maiden auntie."

"I am sorry, Mister Lom. I did not mean to offend you."

"Leave the kid alone, both of you," Selpla warned, "He can call me Miss Selpla if he wants to. I think it's sweet and respectful."

"It give me stomach ache," observed Drin.

They rolled into Fenurian station just before dawn. While third class berths would have been cramped, uncomfortable, and virtually sleep-proof, the first class sleeper coach was downright luxurious. As a result, they were relatively well-rested and ready to get to work.

It was a further ninety minutes by rented pram to the Hellehoell excavation site. As they drove up, Selpla's news team couldn't help but notice that the air seemed to be full of gigantic flying monstrosities of types none of them had ever even imagined, let alone seen before. The behemoths swept angrily to and fro, like colossal agitated bloodbuzzers. No stranger to chronicling conflict, Selpla immediately found a sheltered location to observe the goings-on without unduly endangering herself or her troops. It was shaping up to be quite a spectacle, whatever was going on.

The titans appeared to be arrayed along two long, opposing fronts facing each other across the broad boulevard leading into the underground metropolis of Hellehoell. Every ten meters or so there was an outrageously outfitted shaman waving some elaborately carved staves outfitted with a wide variety of feathers, brightly colored strips of hide, and what looked like some form of dried plant materials.

Swooping majestically and at a rather disconcertingly low altitude were gargantuan creatures with multiple heads, wings, and tails: some of them spouting fire, some emitting ice clouds, some crackling with electrical charge, a few even spitting clouds of roiling toxins. While they all appeared to be bilaterally symmetric, aside from this there was no uniformity of physiognomy. The sky was the limit.

While the aerobatics of the behemoths were impossible to ignore, not so easily discernible was the purpose behind them. They weren't exactly doing combat, but neither did their intentions appear to be on the whole peaceful. The titans beneath them were silent and stony-faced, almost as though they were standing at attention in formation.

After observing the shamans for a while it became apparent to Selpla that they were each controlling one of the dive-bombing monstrosities as though they were enormous puppets. All at once the monsters stopped swooping and hovered in midair quietly. She looked over at Fob to be certain the camera was rolling. Something was about to happen.

One of the most elaborately-dressed shamans stepped forward and pounded the butt of his staff on the pavement. In the dead center of the assemblage, in the air perhaps twenty meters above the boulevard itself, a tiny but extremely intense ball of light appeared. Jiggling and wobbling, it grew steadily larger but less intensely luminous, taking the form of a sphere with hundreds of vicious-looking spines of varying lengths protruding from it. The apparition inflated to a good thirty meters across before the expansion slowed and then halted. It hung there, the air pregnant with anticipation.

Without warning the titans all began to scream in defiance and shake their fists as the monsters rose up and ripped into the glowing sphere. Fire, ice, smoke, steam, and fumes sprayed and swirled in a huge, billowing mass. The aerial creatures attacked with savage fury, ripping stalactite shards off and casting them to the ground viciously. The sphere spun wildly, reversing direction with every other blow and steadily losing mass. All the while hundreds of titans were pumping their arms and yelling in abject fury. It was the most riveting demonstration Selpla had ever witnessed, though she had not the faintest idea what it represented or what triggered it.

With one final swipe of a mighty paw the sphere disintegrated, the remaining fragments falling to the ground with glowing trails tracing their paths. As the fiery tracers died away, so too did the flying apparitions—along with the screams of the titans. Now there was but a single voice, the shaman who conjured the sphere, keening mournfully.

At length even his voice faded, leaving faint reverberances that lapped one another like pond ripples as they echoed off the canyon walls on their way to silence. When the last detectable vibration had ceased, the titans turned as though on cue and filed back into the mouth of Hellehoell. The ceremony, if that's what it was, was over.

Having captured it all with the camera and microphones, Selpla figured now would be a good time to ask someone what it was they had witnessed. She approached one of the shamans, but was intercepted by a more conservatively dressed titan who introduced himself as Tartag.

"Hello, Tartag, I am Selpla from Goblinopolis Video News. Can you explain what we just saw out there?"

"Yes, Selpla, I can. It will take a few minutes to do it properly, however."

"We have plenty of time. I just want to get the story accurate."

"A noble aspiration; very well. You are standing in the entrance to the ancestral titan homeland: the underground complex of Hellehoell. We have not occupied this demesne for millennia; the way in was lost as a result of some ancient cataclysm and we have wandered the world nationless since that event. Now that we have reclaimed our ancient homeland, we must exorcise it of accumulated negative spiritual energies and imbue it with a uniquely titan aura. So, our shamans held a summoning of the traditional titan totemic beasts and then drew the negative energy—we call it *malisucci*—out of both substrate and superstructure to be absorbed and thereby rendered inert by the totems. *That* is what you witnessed."

"It sure beat the pants off a Weekendsday ball game," Lom offered.

"I found it breathtakingly dramatic," said Selpla, "And I am honored we were permitted to watch. Is it permissible to broadcast this ceremony?"

"We have no prohibitions or taboos concerning such a thing, so long as proper context is provided and our people are shown in a positive light," answered Tartag after a moment's consideration.

"That I can promise," said Selpla, "I'll be doing the reporting and I'm certainly positively impressed."

"Amazing. Made eyes open up wide," Drin enthused.

"I had to go to 2.35:1 to keep the frame coherent," remarked Fob. Everyone looked at him curiously. "What?" he asked, "It would have worked better with a crane shot, but I didn't have the right dolly."

"He was a cinematography major," Selpla explained, quietly, averting her eyes.

Everyone nodded and regarded Fob sympathetically.

"What?"

By this time there were approximately thirty thousand titans in residence at Hellehoell, with new groups or individuals streaming in almost every day. The restoration work was progressing apace, now that an understanding had been worked out between the titans and RSCA scholars who were charged with preserving as much of the ancient cities as practical. The titans had a keen respect for their own heritage, so for the most part the cooperation was effortless.

After the Malisucci ceremony most titans went back to their labors deep inside the cities. The shamans gathered for a final ritual that would seal the cities from evil influences, the *Operimentum Malum*. That ritual had been developed millennia earlier by the first generation of titan shamans to have recognized their innate arcane abilities and formulated magical practices around them. Consequently, the Malum ritual drew upon the rawest, most primitive magical energies available.

Planets embedded in the dark energy continuum exhibit what might be referred to as a 'dark magnetic field' associated with the movement of the planet's metallic core through the dark energy stream. On worlds where magic is in very heavy use over a period of tens of millennia this field is gradually weakened by cumulative absorption. On N'plork, in contrast, significant magic use has only been in place for a few millennia and the native dark magnetic field strength is still quite high. It was on that plentiful latent energy which the Malum ritual drew. The easy availability of that energy was also the reason Phaeon Timeskin chose N'plork for a habitation. He superimposed his own personal energy absorption regimen over the existing complex of fields and energy patterns, effectively integrating himself into the cyclic energetic totality of the planet itself. Unfortunately, the Malum ritual disturbed that totality in ways no one could have predicted.

The deepdrakes were creatures of dark energetic origin. Not only were they constructed from perturbations in that field, they drew their power, their existence, from eddies produced in that structure by natural planetary mechanics. The Malum ritual temporarily squeezed those eddies; elongated them into thin ellipses that no longer conformed to the template upon which the deepdrakes had been designed. This created an unstable imbalance in the non-sentient deepdrake population that manifested itself in several significant ways, the most immediately disturbing of which is that half the population ceased to exist and the other half began to grow uncontrolled in both size and temperament.

When the deepdrakes outgrew their cave habitats, they began to break their way into larger spaces, eventually encroaching on the lower regions of Hellehoell and driving the titan reconstruction workers before them as they advanced. As the alarm spread, the titans formed ranks and began to fight the deepdrakes off, but their efforts were complicated by the chaotic nature of the energy instability that imbued each deepdrake with different offensive and defensive capabilities.

Some had grown armor plating; some sported chemical or pyrotechnic projectile weapons. Others had unusual strength or extreme resistance to magical damage. A few were even able to levitate or cling to walls like a climbing reptile. The sentient deepdrakes were not affected by the energy surge, except inasmuch as they lost any control over their feral brethren. Even Phaeon seemed negatively impacted and took refuge in the dark material plane.

Eventually the mutated deepdrakes could not be contained in the lower reaches any longer and began to spill out into the inhabited areas, bringing destruction and chaos with them. The combat was often one-on-one now, with the more aggressive monsters pushing harder and faster than the others. The civil guard was called out, but as a newly-formed unit with little actual combat experience they were minimally effective. Finally the ruling council felt it necessary to ask the government of Tragacanth for formal assistance.

"High priority diplomatic dispatch from the titans, Your Majesty," explained Boogla, holding a sheaf of parchment in her hands. "It seems they are being overrun by deepdrakes. Mutated ones, at that. They request mobilization of the regional security forces."

"Is it really so bad that thirty thousand plus titans can't handle it?" Aspet scratched his chin. "Those must be some vicious deepdrakes."

"They are formally requesting assistance, Your Majesty. What are your orders?"

"What does my Consort and Magineer Liaison think?"

"I think that if we don't send them some troops, we'll be risking both another meltdown in Hellehoell and a definite cooling of the relations between us and the ruling caste of the titans."

"Very well, I do so order it. Muster the 3rd Civil Defense Brigade in Fenurian and then march them to Hellehoell, there to be temporarily under the directive advisement of the titan Ruling Council for the duration of the crisis. Tell Colonel Goile to be respectful but exercise his tactical control firmly and at all times. We will help the titans in their time of need, but we will not meld with them."

"By your command, Majesty."

"I have another command."

Boogla giggled. "Let me transmit this directive first. I'll be back in a moment."

"Affairs of State should not be delayed. Hurry back."

Colonel Tun Goile was a career soldier who had served in a variety of capacities in the Tragacanthan military, both on land and at sea. He had been in his current command, the 3rd Civil Defense Brigade, for only a few months. Previously he had served as the executive officer to the commander of Ft. Ullglava and as Northeast Commodore in the Tragacanthan Coastal Patrol. He could trace his ancestry in unbroken line back to the first settlers of Esmia, four thousand years ago. His family had been proud members of the esteemed Society of Firsters since its inception more than a millennium prior.

His social pretensions made Goile a bit of a prima donna, but he kept it under control most of the time. The only time it manifested itself was when he was forced to deal as an equal with persons he felt were clearly beneath him in the social hierarchy. As commander those situations were mercifully rare.

He had, in the course of his military career, encountered myriad enemies, from pirates on the high seas to insane militants who wanted to impose Scarya Law—a bizarre set of edicts that basically took away all rights from people who refused to acknowledge publically that the Supreme Being was an enormous nocturnal three-legged marsupial named *Tata*—in the Paradiddle Islands. As a result, he felt fairly confident that this latest menace would prove no great challenge.

The entire brigade was currently staffed at 3,200 soldiers, but of course it wasn't going to require that amount of strength for this simple suppression action. As far as he could tell they were talking about wildlife control, more than anything else. He was a little insulted that he'd been called out by the king to serve as what amounted to an animal exterminator, but orders were orders.

When the first wave, his command pram and seven drays full of soldiers from the 16th Regiment, 3rd Brigade, pulled up to Hellehoell, Col. Goile was gritting his teeth in preparation for being placed under 'directive advisement.' He hated oversight by non-soldiers; they invariably did not understand military objectives and wanted things to run in ways contrary to the stated mission. He was pleasantly surprised, then, when the ruling council leader came out to meet him and turned full control of the situation over to him. The titan was plainly frightened and just wanted the problem solved by the most expeditious means possible.

Emboldened by this development, Goile took charge and began to deploy reconnaissance units to assess the tactical situation. He sent Selpla and her team back to Goblinopolis on the next carriage for their own protection, despite Selpla's protestations. "This is no place for civilians," he said to her, "This is a war zone."

The titans reported that only the uppermost level was safe; below that the mutated deepdrakes were running rampant. The descriptions he was getting of the size and capabilities of the deepdrakes were difficult to take seriously, so he sent photographic units in as part of the recon effort.

The first recon unit was ambushed and barely made it out sans casualties. They got only blurry pictures of fearsome creatures that were much larger and more vicious than the deepdrakes in Goile's cryptozoology reference manual. The colonel realized quickly that he was dealing with a more significant foe that he'd anticipated. He pulled the recon units back and ordered the fire teams to assemble.

Once he had four full strike teams and a reserve in place, Goile ordered them inserted but to advance no further than one kilometer without further orders. There would be two center units and one on each flank; the reserve would remain at center rear unless needed. They were equipped with high-power disruptor rifles, flame-throwers, and stunglobe launchers. The center units were under the command of Lieutenants Jawata and Soturi, both outstanding young officers only recently graduated from the Royal Military Academy. The expeditionary fire team force itself was commanded by Captain Diqlosse, who preferred to lead from the rear. "I can get a broader view of the battle front from there," he was fond of explaining. The argument would be more convincing were he not usually behind a huge heavily-armored rolling pavise.

The deepdrakes were on the move as the fire teams inserted. They appeared intent on making it to the surface, in contrast to their non-mutated brethren who preferred underground lairs. They were huge—even larger than the sentient companions to Phaeon Timeskin—and their teeth and claws seemed made of some hardened metal rather than enamel and keratin. The creatures were, in addition, fearless and insanely aggressive.

The first contact came when strike team center right was attacked by a pair of deepdrakes that appeared suddenly over a small rise in the footpath. The monsters were on them in a heartbeat, slashing and biting with great effect. Four soldiers were mutilated almost immediately, before anyone could squeeze off a shot. The disruptors offered little deterrent. Flame throwers were somewhat more effective, but the collateral damage in terms of 'friendly fire' was unacceptably high at close quarters. The stunglobes were equally impractical here. They set their disruptors on full power and concentrated on first disabling the creatures, then finishing them off with bayonets.

Once the first two deepdrakes were finally dead, Captain Diqlosse gave the order to collect casualties and withdraw. They had suffered three fatalities and four wounded. The kill ratio was unacceptably low; they needed to change tactics. Colonel Goile did not take the encounter well. He lined his troops up and dressed them down for ten fist-palming minutes, pointing to the sheet-covered litters where the casualties lay with a rage-quivering finger.

The regroup effort was abbreviated, however, because the deepdrakes finally made it to the surface and began to spill out over the countryside. Goile was under strict orders to contain them to titan lands. He sent an entire regiment after the escapees and planted another at the entrance to prevent any further monsters from exiting alive.

Fifteen hundred soldiers seems like a lot of firepower, but when two hundred five meter long flesh-rending monstrosities suddenly bubble up out of a huge hole in the ground, that perception is fluid. Not only were the mutant deepdrakes huge and well-armed, they were deceptively quick. Worse, they could tear a soldier completely in half with one bite. Goile lost a dozen troops before he could devise an effective counter-attack.

He assigned squads of five to each monster. Two aimed for the eyes, two went for the hind legs to limit mobility, and the last concentrated on severing or severely damaging the spinal cord. Once the beast was down, all five charged with elongated electrified leaf-tip bayonets and stabbed until it stopped moving. It was lethal, blood-soaking work.

At first the deepdrakes were emerging from the city entrance as singles or pairs; they were not too terribly difficult to dispatch like this. After the first twenty or so had been taken out, there was a sudden surge as they began to escape in larger, more difficult to handle groups of four and five. Groile and Diqlosse adopted hammer and anvil tactics to trap and slaughter them, but occasionally one dodged the columns and had to be hunted down individually.

As the day wore on, the seemingly never-ending stream of mutated deepdrakes finally began to thin out. The soldiers were wearing down by now as well, as the area within a hundred meters of the entrance was waist-high in gore and mutilated bodies from both sides of the conflict. They were so closely intermingled that in places it was impossible to tell whose remains you were looking at. According to the recon sergeant, only three of the monstrosities had escaped into the countryside.

Col. Goile ordered five strike teams with two all-terrain prams each to fan out and eliminate the escapees. Failure was not an option. They had highly-trained predator avians with them to act as aerial scouts. For several hours they combed the area in ever-widening circles, searching for the fugitive deepdrakes. When one was found, all forces in that sector—usually two strike teams—converged on it. Even with two fully-equipped combat units the battles were quite bloody, protracted, and casualty-laden.

When at last the final mutant drake lay twitching in its death-throes on the blood-saturated ground, the strike teams conveyed their wounded and deceased back to Col. Goile's field headquarters. The hardened battle veteran shook his head in dismay at the extensive casualty list. They had accomplished their mission, but at a terrible price. Worse, they had no guarantee that there weren't more deepdrakes waiting far down in the labyrinthine spaces beneath Hellehoell.

When what was left of the 3rd Brigade mustered in front of the entrance to the titan cities, Tartag and a small delegation came out to express their sincere gratitude to Col. Goile for the sacrifices his people had made on behalf of the titans. Goile wasn't having any of it. He just turned his back on the titan emissary and drove away. Tartag restrained his impulse toward anger, reminding himself that Goile had just lost dozens of troops and was in no mood to be sociable, or even, apparently, to exhibit basic courtesy. The colonel no doubt blamed the titans for releasing the monsters in the first place, and perhaps he had a point there. Tartag decided therefore not to lodge an official complaint against Goile's behavior.

Goile attended each and every memorial service for his fallen troops; he had done so for his entire career as an officer. He was angry at the titans, as Tartag had guessed. He regarded them as foreigners who had moved into Tragacanth uninvited and irresponsibly released a terrible plague that his soldiers had died to stamp out. There were several dozen sets of grieving relatives and friends because the titans had been careless, in his view. Colonel Goile was the consummate professional soldier: an officer who followed orders to the letter.

But he did not forget, nor did he forgive.

Chapter the Seventeenth

in which an ancient being relocates while Tol receives a secret mission

Phaeon was sorely troubled by the reports of deepdrakes taking on new forms and turning feral. They were of his making, after all, and he had not intended for them to mutate. Biology, he concluded, was easy; it was magic which added that layer of uncertainty and difficulty to creation. He dispatched the sentients to round up as many as possible and drive them into the lower caves where they could be contained. There he would root out and destroy any mutants.

In the end perhaps three hundred total mutants escaped the roundup and spilled out onto the surface, but the sentient deepdrakes managed to corral and imprison several thousand of their mutated brethren far below. After Phaeon had eliminated them—or in the case of drakes whose mutation process had stalled, reversed it and brought them back to their original condition—there were fewer than a hundred wild deepdrakes remaining, not counting the handful of sentients, who were not affected by the runaway mutations.

Phaeon was saddened by this development, but he decided not to create any further creatures here. He had not taken into account the potential for disastrous unforeseen consequences on a planet embedded in the dark energetic continuum. Perhaps he would do well simply to move on to another world, one far from magic entanglements. He sighed and looked around him.

"Come, Fontaric. Gather your brethren. It is time we migrated to a new home."

"Shall I assemble also the wild drakes?"

"We shall leave them here to live or die in this, their native world, and create a new race when we are settled on the next."

"Will they survive without us?"

"Yes. I have given them the skill and the means to do so. While they will no longer regenerate, there is abundant food for them in the lower caves, as there exist multiple colonies of the rodents on which they thrive scattered all around the perimeter of their lair. I have seen to it that the members of these prey colonies are fecund and well-supplied with fodder for at least the next few centums."

"And us? What will become of us?"

"You will revert to your base forms during the transfer. I will decide how you will appear when we reach our new home."

"Then we are ready, master."

Phaeon stretched out his hands, palms up and curled inward. He brought them slowly together. When the palms touched there was a blinding flash of light and a noise like a huge space rock hurtling through the atmosphere. When the light faded, Phaeon, the sentient deepdrakes, and the lush appointments were all gone. Only a simple, rough-hewn cave remained.

A starship approaching N'plork at that moment would have seen a ball of pure energy launch from a spot directly over Hellehoell and speed away, disappearing rapidly into the inky blackness of interstellar space. There wasn't any such ship, in fact, so no one off-planet witnessed Phaeon Timeskin, one of the oldest intelligences in this current multiverse, as he sought out a new world far from the influence of magic to call home.

Tol sat in his fancy-schmancy office in Justice Hall and watched the reports of fierce fighting in Ferroc Norda between the Civil Defense troops and what he recognized as mutated deepdrakes, although the media insisted on calling them 'dragons.' He wondered what sort of event could have prompted the mutations. The press seemed to think that the titans were somehow to blame, but Tol couldn't decide if that was based on a kernel of truth or just a manifestation of latent xenophobia. It was easy to fear the titans, especially with generations of rumors and legends surrounding them. Tol steadfastly refused to allow himself to be led down this toxic path. The titans he'd met had been intelligent, rational, and courteous. He was going to regard all titans that way unless he had good cause to change.

There was another item that caught his eye: a large, intense fireball of some sort was launched from a mountainside not far from the epicenter of the fighting near the entrance to the titan enclave of Hellehoell. It headed up rapidly and apparently was able to make escape velocity. Investigators could find no trace of the launch site, based on a reverse calculation of its trajectory. No burned vegetation, no scorch marks, no disturbed soil. The verdict? Magic. Convenient, all-encompassing, and despite that very probably accurate in this instance.

A high-pitched bell rang three times on the other side of his office: secure message coming in. He rolled over in his fancy high-backed office chair and stared at the communiqué. It made him frown in consternation:

From: Aspet I, King of Tragacanth

To: Sir Tol-u-ol of Sebacea, Special Investigator, Royal EE Branch

Assignment:

Capture or neutralize Esfina Frem. Last known location: Goblinopolis, but intelligence suggests she may have returned to Solemadrina. She is wanted for conspiracy to commit murder of a member of the Royal Family and state espionage. This is an Alpha Priority/Royal Family-only matter. You are authorized whatever funds and equipment you deem necessary to carry out the mission. You will report directly to me. A courier pouch will arrive with diplomatic credentials so that you may travel internationally under guise of diplomatic service. Remember that any false steps while deployed may result in an ugly international incident. Stay smart and be safe.

--message ends--

Capture or neutralize. That was unusual language, coming from Aspet. He guessed the king didn't want to bring himself to order Tol directly to off someone if need be. They'd known all along that this Frem was involved up to her eye ridges in the plot against Boogla; why the sudden urgency to have her 'neutralized?' Though Tol didn't relish the role of King's Assassin, he was challenged by the whole cloak and dagger thing. Very different from the overt approach he'd almost always taken as a street cop.

As Tol considered his brother's full intent, it suddenly hit him that he was automatically thinking of Aspet as his supervisor—and therefore as king—for the first time. It was an odd sort of realization, like finding out that the hat you had been wearing for many years was actually intended as a boot or an apron.

That surreal detour was mercifully brief and soon he was mentally back on mission. Tracking someone within Tragacanthan jurisdiction and outside those boundaries were two decidedly different propositions, it seemed to Tol. He really didn't know much of anything about international espionage; he was just a simple city beat cop with a fancy title. He decided to drop in on an old partner who had left the force years ago to work for the Tragacanthan squad of the Trans-national Edict Enforcement Cooperative, or TEEC. If anyone knew about this stuff, he should.

Anbat Yemmilla, or Yemmy, was ancient, and even more grizzled than Tol. He glanced up when Tol walked into his office and grunted. "Heya, youngster. Heard you went and got yourself knighted. Good work, I guess."

Tol shrugged. "Hi, Yemmy. It is what it is. I need some advice."

"Pull up a chair. What's going down?"

Tol related a condensed version of events leading up to this visit, carefully circumnavigating the nature of his orders regarding the perpetrator. "So," he finished up, "I need some tutoring on how to conduct, um, 'EE operations' OTRAG."

Yemmy leaned back, put his feet up on his desk, and regarded his former partner for a moment before replying.

"Do it quietly, in a private place, then leave the body in a position where detection of the event will be put off as long as possible. Alternatively, use a delayed-effect method like toxins."

Tol was momentarily taken aback by the old goblin's candor and the ease with which he deduced Tol's true mission, but then grinned. "So, you got any? Toxins, I mean."

"Smek, no. Those substances are illegal to possess by international treaty. I do have some small vials of liquid intended for an entirely different purpose that could, in a pinch, be repurposed by a clever and enterprising special investigator on an official mission, though." He handed a small leather pouch with six glass bottles in it to Tol. "Inside is a short description of each and its most effective route of application. Be careful: as with all other weapons, these can't tell the difference between the good guys and the bad."

Tol was thanking him when he suddenly stopped at looked at Yemmy suspiciously. "How is it you come to have these...*substances* all packed up and ready to go?"

"TEEC trains with them fairly regularly. We conducted a live exercise less than a fortnight ago and this kit is leftover from that. I honestly don't know if any of these has ever been put to use in the field by an authorized EE agent, however. Not many have been so authorized. I do know that all of these substances have been used to kill multiple people over the years. They exhibit proven lethality for all races."

"Comes with an instruction manual, eh? How handy."

"Of sorts, yes. Nothing in depth, but enough to get the job done."

Tol looked at the thin booklet for a moment before sliding it back into the pouch.

"Alrighty, then. I guess I have my weapon of choice. Now I just have to work out how to justify from a moral standpoint knocking off an unarmed, unresisting person."

"Authority to eliminate a civilian enemy of Tragacanth can come only from the king himself. He must have told you why this person warranted such action."

"Yeah, I suppose he did. I don't think I'm going to get comfortable with this sort of stuff any time soon," Tol sighed.

"Which is exactly why he chose you for the mission. Those who become comfortable with killing are no longer trustworthy to kill only when ordered. Killing a sentient being should be repugnant and difficult, no matter their crimes."

Tol left Yemmy's office with lethal weapons and words of wisdom. Now if he could just get over his misgivings concerning the mission itself. He had seen firsthand the aftermath of the attempt on Boogla's life and he understood why Aspet wanted the mastermind eliminated, but there was more to this than simple justice: Aspet really wanted vengeance. As king, however, he was by the rules of their society within his rights to seek it. Tol had one of those dumbstruck moments when it sank in that his little brother, his 'Pet,' could legally order a foreign national assassinated. He scratched his neck beneath the left ear the way he always did when the world was hard to understand and grunted at the wonder of it all.

After verifying that Frem had not been seen in Goblinopolis since the attack on the Royal Palace, Tol set sail once more for Solemadrina. This time, however, he booked a first-class cabin aboard a sleek, comfortable passenger vessel, the *Avvolli*. He'd always wanted to travel in style—and posing as a wealthy entrepreneur was a decent cover. He'd decided, rather than a diplomat, to play the role of an agricultural supplies broker. He was no expert at either, but his years of experience in the feed store as a youngster at least taught him the required lingo for the latter.

They left from the other side of Tragacanth this time, as the Arctal Current was flowing the correct way to whisk them from Lumbos to Aspolia in only six days, rather than the typical eight to ten. Not that transit time was any issue for Tol. He suspected the passenger line increased their profits a bit by not having to provide meals and services for those extra days, as the ticket cost the same no matter how long it ended up taking to get there.

As this was a rather expensive cruise, the line management felt it appropriate to provide entertainment beyond the usual musical shows, hammer-string lyre bars, and water sports. The third day out that entertainment centered around a demonstration on the Solare deck by the eccentric gnome inventor of a crazy new flying contraption.

People had taken cracks at practical flying machines for years, but none of them made much progress. There was the kobold over in Hividz who constructed this ten meter-wide framework covered in light fabric that could soar reasonably well when launched from a cliff, but on the third such attempt a microburst slammed him and it into the ground so hard that both were thoroughly dismembered.

There had been many experiments with hot-air envelopes over the centums as well, with varying degrees of success. A small group of dedicated enthusiasts held demonstrations every year and flew their 'airspheres' for excited crowds, but the concept never really bled over into either freight or commercial passenger-hauling: too many issues no one was willing to fund working out.

The gnome showing off his invention to the passengers of the *Avvolli* had hit upon something quite different, however. He lived in the rugged mountainous area of southern Tantatku where he'd spent most of his life as an independent miner, finding and exploiting small veins of various valuable minerals. One day he'd chanced upon a reddish streak that looked like nothing he'd ever seen before. Extracting a sample and heating it repeatedly in his athanor, he eventually worked out that he'd discovered a previously unknown substance that when heated generated a gas with the potentially useful property of linear thermal buoyancy: the hotter it became, the more buoyant.

The gnome, whose name was Dagyo, soon realized he had the basis for an entirely new form of transport in his hands, if he could only work out the niggling details. He spent the next three years doing just that. He used his miner's knowledge of metallurgy to create an alloy that was both light and extremely strong. From his new metal he crafted a structure that looked like a squashed ice cream cone in cross section: a semicircle sitting atop an acute triangle. It was ten meters long and six wide, covered with a stiff doped fabric. Underneath was slung a streamlined control compartment big enough to house four gnomes.

Along the keel of the craft ran a u-channel with fan-shaped burners situated every meter such that the heating would be relatively uniform across the entire length. The interior of the giant bag was coated with a thin but tough metallic foil sandwiched between two sheets of rubberized fabric. As the solid mineral Dagyo had christened 'aerite' sublimed under the influence of the battery-powered burners, it expanded into the sealed envelope. When it cooled to liquid state, the aerite ran down the sides and fed back into the trough to be re-heated. The hotter Dagyo made the fires, the lighter his craft would get.

He added horizontal and vertical planes for navigation and two curious internal fan-driven engines for propulsion, controlling all of that via pulleys and wires from a console at the front of the little passenger car. Dagyo referred to his craft as a *Zifjagga*, which translates from gnomish as 'flying jellyfish.' After two months of almost constant practice and refinement, he took his show on the road to drum up funds for further enhancements.

He landed the *Avvolli* gig after one of the line's executives brought his children to an amusement park where Dagyo had been contracted to do demonstrations to distract those in near-infinite queues for the most popular rides. The executive immediately saw the potential for entertainment, if not transport, and booked Dagyo to bring his contraption aboard the *Avvolli*.

The premise of Dagyo's Zifjagga show was pretty simple: the ship's owners had installed a large swiveling mooring point on top of a ten-meter mast on the Solare deck. Not only did the Zifjagga moor there, it was attached by a one hundred meter extra-strong tether to a ring welded below the mooring point so that Dagyo could take the AeroPram (as he named it) out and fly it around in circles without worrying about engine failure or jammed controls causing him to become separated from the *Avvolli* in the deep ocean.

The spectacle of a bag full of gas with someone suspended underneath it was quite diverting; the shows always had people lining the decks: some to marvel at the engineering, some to gaze in naked envy at the gnome who was no longer bound to the surface, and a few who secretly or not so secretly just hoped to witness a disaster. One of the latter category was a kobold named Lizgug, who happened to be distantly related to the glider creator in Hividz. He hoped the bag would explode, or maybe break apart. Kobolds are not as a race particularly empathic or charitable, but Lizgug exceeded those already low standards by a considerable margin: he was actively—sometimes even aggressively—unpleasant.

Tol saw posters for the exhibition in the dining hall and wandered up to the Solare deck to check it out. So did Lizgug. The two did not know each other, surprisingly. Lizgug was an itinerant thug-for-hire who provided muscle for collections and extortion schemes, jimmied doors for burglars, and generally accepted jobs others were loath or too lazy to undertake. The cruise was a gift to himself after a particularly profitable shakedown; it was also a way to flee to Solemadrina, well away from the long arm of Tragacanthan EE. Or, so he imagined.

After an introduction by the ship's cruise director, Dagyo waved to the crowd and ascended a portable stairway to the gondola of the gently swaying captive AeroPram. He waved again at the door, and then stepped inside. The crowd waited expectantly as he lit the burners and the aerite began to expand throughout the envelope. At last, first the right, then the left engine vroomed to life. The tail of the Zifjagga lifted, the nose slipped out of the mooring socket, and the craft moved gracefully away to the applause of (most of) the assembled passengers.

One of those who did not applaud was Lizgug. He was analyzing the setup, looking for an easy way to wreak some amusing and potentially profitable havoc. As Tol applauded he swept the assemblage, looking for anything suspicious. His glance passed over Lizgug and stopped cold. He knew that look: it never ended well. This one bore watching.

On a hunch, Tol pulled Petey out of his pocket. "Scan the crowd and look for wanted fugitives, please."

"Are you not on vacation, then?" asked Petey.

"No. It's a cover."

"I see no orders at all in the EE database."

"You won't find them there. This mission is Royal Family Eyes Only."

"Impressive. I do see an open acquisition warrant in your name. They have given you an infinite credit line, for all practical purposes. Must be frightfully important."

"It's very important to the king; as one of his knights that makes it very important to me."

"Not to mention a family affair."

"There is that."

"I have three positive matches from the facial database. Two of them are minor traffic and administrative offenses warrants, but the third is for multiple felonies, including engaging in career criminal activities."

"That's the fellow I'm after. Let me guess: kobold? Light pink shirt and green pants?"

"Correct. His name is Lizgug Trelk. Hails originally from Ubxafa, a coastal village about twenty kilometers southwest of Evcolla in Hividz. Wanted for conspiracy to commit murder, conspiracy to exploit the elderly, conspiracy to sow civic discord, conspiracy to commit grand larceny, conspiracy to engage in conspiracy, and failure to signal while in a stolen pram."

"How did a guy like that even get on an international passenger vessel?"

"False credentials. The port authority does not employ facial recognition scanners on a regular basis due to funding.

Consequently, with a relatively minor effort put forward to manufacture authentic-appearing identification documents, access is easily obtained."

"The border is porous, in other words."

"Precisely."

"He's probably headed to Solemadrina to dodge Tragacanth EE. I guess I'd better make sure that doesn't happen."

"The schematics of this ship do indicate a detainment area on deck two, just above the engineering bay."

"They'd have to keep him there all the way back. Still, at least he'd be out of circulation."

Tol watched the rest of the Zifjagga performance, keeping one eye on Lizgug. When the show was over he went into surveillance mode and established a tail on the kobold. Tol was an old hand at this sort of thing: he'd followed hundreds if not thousands of perps in his career. Lizgug headed immediately off down a corridor toward the elevator to the cabin decks. He ducked into a service area just shy of the elevator and came back out two minutes later, headed aft.

The kobold walked all the way to the aft-most staircase and took it as far up as it went. Standing on the uppermost landing for quite some time to make certain he wasn't being followed (by someone with lesser skills than Tol), Lizgug at last padded off toward the observation lounge directly below the Zifjagga mooring mast. He surreptitiously scouted the possible means of access and settled on a ladder bolted to the other side of a windowless section of wall. Carefully, quietly, he stole out the door and up the ladder. Tol followed after a moment.

The Zifjagga was unoccupied and unguarded. Lizgug grinned and considered his options. He ran his hand along the underside of the rigid envelope, obviously contemplating a few well-placed punctures. Moving on, he rotated one of the spinners back and forth while he thought about sabotaging the engines somehow. Then he spotted the mooring rope.

Tol watched from the shadows as the kobold brought out a wicked knife and placed it against the rope. After the first draw Tol had all the evidence he needed. He walked quickly up behind the kobold and whipped out his badge.

"Edict Enforcement. You are under arrest for attempted criminal mischief, not to mention multiple outstanding warrants."

Lizgug waved the knife menacingly under Tol's nose.

"I'll give you exactly one chance to drop that knife," Tol said, calmly.

"Oh, I'll drop it all right. Right into yer ugly gizzard." He took a step forward and shifted his grip on the knife to blade down, prepared for a downward stab. Tol shook his head and grabbed the kobold's arm with one hand. He twisted the wrist violently, breaking the arm and forcing Lizgug to drop the knife, which Tol kicked overboard in one sweeping motion that continued with the kobold being thrown down on the deck in a none-too-gentle manner, with Tol's foot on his back.

"Ow, you smekking lunatic, that *hurt*!"

"Hey, I have an aversion to large sharp objects being jammed into my gizzard. It's a character flaw we all have to live with." He snapped the cuffs onto the kobold's warty wrists.

"Time to get up, honey."

Tol yanked the smaller Lizgug to his feet, blood dripping down his fingers from the compound fracture in his forearm.

"You better get me to the infirmary quick. Wait 'til I file a complaint on your obvious brutality. Ow! Ow! Officer brutality!"

Tol spun him around and looked him dead in the eyes.

"You see that railing right there? If you don't shut up and cooperate, I could very easily trip while you're struggling and accidentally send you down to file your complaint with the bureau of fishes. I hear the waiting room is quite damp."

The kobold turned a little white and went quiet. About that time one of the crewmembers came running up.

"What's going on here?"

Tol flipped open his badge and credentials. "Tragacanth EE Special Investigator. This person is wanted on multiple warrants. I need to use your detention area."

The crewmember seemed taken aback. "We...we weren't briefed about any fugitives aboard."

Tol gave him that special look. "If you *knew* he was a fugitive when he boarded, you wouldn't have let him on the smekking ship. At least, I hope not."

The crewmember thought about this. "Ah, right. Well, come along, then. I'll have to get permission from the Officer of the Deck to incarcerate a prisoner, but that shouldn't be too hard with you being EE and all. Down we go."

They stepped into an elevator; the crewmember used his key to bypass the other floors and take them straight to the Bathys Deck where the brig was located.

"Sub-sub-basement," he said as the doors slid open, "Casual wear, sporting goods, and detention."

Tol smirked; Lizgug rolled his eyes.

"This has got be contrary to some high seas treaty or other," the kobold complained, struggling.

Tol kicked him. "What, arresting and locking up a convicted felon fugitive? I don't think so."

"No, subjecting a prisoner to this jlok's sense of so-called 'humor.'"

Tol cocked his head, "You may be right, at that." The crewmember huffed with pretend insult. "Mention it to the magistrate and maybe he'll knock a few minutes off your sentence."

Once the prisoner was formally booked and incarcerated in the ship's holding cell, Tol shifted his attention back to the Zifjagga. He'd been thinking about potential applications for such an invention beyond the obvious transport of people and freight. Observation of criminal activities from the air would be useful, as would delivery of EE/rescue personnel to an otherwise difficult-to-access site. He set out directly to speak with the gnome about those things.

Dagyo *had* thought of those uses for the Zifjagga, it turns out—and many more besides. He was torn between a desire to see his invention adopted widely around the world and a deep reluctance to share his buoyancy secret, for fear it would be used for what he considered evil purposes. Gnomes appear to the casual observer to be concerned only with creation and building and engineering, but most have scruples as well, after their own fashion.

Tol understood Dagyo's viewpoint and suggested that he file for a *Writ of Mine*. WoMs allowed Tragacanthans who invented something that other people might want to claim for their own the right to control that creation's use. That way Dagyo could license the floatation technology but maintain control of the actual engineering process used to manufacture it. The kobold was vaguely aware of the existence of the WoM, but had no idea how to seek it. Tol promised to help him when they got back home, in return for Dagyo adapting one of his wondrous craft for EE use.

Chapter the Eighteenth

in which Tol encounters one monster that slays another

The *Avvolli* docked in Erolossma on the north coast of Solemadrina and stayed in dock for two days before starting the return voyage. That gave Tol time to make some inquiries of local EE concerning the current whereabouts of the elusive Frem. He started at the national EE office there in Erolossma, but after an afternoon of being led around in circles by bureaucracy he chucked the official approach and hit the streets.

A beat cop, especially one who has been on the same beat for many years, has many resources at his disposal when solving crimes: stoolies, friendlies, cages, dodges, and lookouts among them. Tol did not have access to this network here by virtue of long association, yet he could sense their presence and managed to worm information out of them using the same techniques he found successful on the other side of N'plork. People were people no matter where you went, with the same drives, fears, and hopes that could be exploited when needed.

Nevertheless, it took Tol a full day to generate a solid lead on Frem's whereabouts. She was, thankfully, right here in the city, hiding out in the private rooms of an inn called *The Golden Bedpost*. He decided to take the direct approach, as he didn't have much time before the *Avvolli* sailed with his prisoner.

The *Bedpost* was in a rundown neighborhood of Erolossma. The streets were lined with older homes that might have been called middle class a generation or two ago, but now bore the unmistakable hallmarks of age-related degeneration. The residents looked equally worn and tattered; they moved about their daily business in a kind of automatic pilot, showing equal parts no joy, no passion, and no interest in much of anything. They stared dully at Tol as he got out of the rented pram and walked from the parking lot to the front door of the inn. Their listless countenance was nothing new to Tol after many years in the streets of Sebacea. Desperately poor people always seemed to take on that appearance after a while. The constant grind of bare subsistence did that to you.

The crowd in the *Bedpost*'s common room was a motley assemblage. Just about every race on N'plork other than titans was represented, with a preponderance of goblins and gnomes. In one corner there was a knot of what Tol guessed were elf-gnome hybrids, the result of one of the rarer such encounters. Interracial hybrids, or 'halfers' as they were known colloquially, tended to stick together for social cohesion and safety reasons. While most of the clientele were drinking and laughing uproariously as they staggered from table to table, the halfers sipped their razzle and talked quietly amongst themselves, staying apart from the spontaneous festivities. Tol scanned them unobtrusively; they all seemed a bit ill at ease. Given the increasingly boisterous nature of the other pub patrons, most of whom were much larger and prone to violence, their reserved behavior was understandable as a survival mechanism.

More interesting to Tol than the halfers themselves was the almost invisible door directly behind them. Most people wouldn't notice it even if they were looking straight at it, but Tol was not most people. Someone had turned on a light inside for only a moment— just long enough for Tol to observe a telltale rectangular sliver of yellow. He moved casually toward the halfer table as though he wanted to get a better look at them. He felt the reassuring hard lump of his disruptor and next to it the small cold presence of a special instrument he'd been given when he accepted the assignment. It was the most lethal ranged weapon in the Tragacanthan EE arsenal, selectively destroying the medullary neurons that controlled breathing and heart rhythm by literally shaking them apart with carefully tuned radion pulses. Only a handful of people were authorized to possess this device. Tol was not particularly proud to be one of them. Of course, in the other pocket was the pouch full of lethal toxins. Tol felt like some sort of super assassin from a spy novel.

He decided that he needed a diversion to make this work. Surveying the crowd, he spotted a table of ogres. He picked up a scrap of paper from the floor and scribbled something on it. Passing near them, he dropped the scrap on their table unnoticed. Tol retreated to a position near the halfers and waited. It didn't take long.

One of the ogres spotted the paper and picked it up. His face turned bright green as he read it before leaping up from his chair and making for the nearest group of elves with obvious felonious intent. The elves were taken entirely by surprise and scattered before the onslaught like leaves before a sudden gale. He chased one down and began to pummel the hapless fellow while everyone else either booed or cheered. When the other elves tried to defend their brother the solo beating suddenly exploded into a free-for-all, as Tol had expected. He felt for and quickly located the expected release catch under the lip of the nearby bar, slipping quietly through the cryptic opening at the height of the melee.

He found himself in a darkened corridor, narrow and musty from disuse. He had to stifle the sudden urge to cough as he crept down the hall toward a set of heavy drapes framing an opening at the far end. He parted the fabric ever so slightly and peered through into a non-descript room containing a bed, dresser, and washbasin. The furniture was plain and unadorned. Lying on the bed with her back to the door was a goblin that met Frem's general description, apparently sleeping.

It was way too easy. Tol looked around the room for subtle signs of a trap. He found them when he noticed very fine wires leading from the bed frame into the wall. The figure on the bed was only a mannequin, rigged to trigger some most likely fatal action if disturbed. It was a booby-trap; Tol was not a booby. He gave the bed a wide berth and cautiously approached the door beyond. Rather than a traditional square knob, it was fitted with a peculiar form of closure known as a spade-latch, which allowed for speedier operation when rapid exits were a necessity. Another clue that something unusual was going down.

Tol cracked the door and stepped back in case it, too, was trapped. He pushed on it carefully with a broom leaning against the wall. He left it standing wide open for a full thirty seconds and then when nothing lethal had appeared, slipped in.

The second room was larger than the first, with more elaborate furnishings. It appeared to have been recently occupied and hastily abandoned: there was a half-eaten meal on the table next to a book on the history of Tragacanth. It was lying open to a chapter on the Royal Family. Several passages concerning Aspet were underlined. Tol felt himself getting angry and his reluctance to carry out the mission receding. There was only one door in evidence—the one he'd come through—but it was obvious there was another exit.

Tol decided to search the room thoroughly. He went through the drawers of the bureau, looked under the table, rummaged through the cushions of the armchair, and lifted the throw rugs. Finally he checked out the adjoining bathroom. At first it looked normal, but something about the toilet didn't sit right with Tol. He walked over and lifted the lid. It was of the 'direct-drop' variety— where the toilet emptied straight into the sewage line—common in the lower economic urban areas where the builders sought to save a little money: hygiene and foul odors be hanged. As he stepped away, the entire apparatus vibrated slightly and caught Tol's attention. He walked back toward it and the vibration recurred. He got down on his knees and inspected the area around the toilet. It was circumscribed by a barely-visible line.

Directly in front of the toilet there was an ornamental tile in the shape of a jublybud, a common architectural motif in Solemadrina as the plants were one of the more exuberant native wildflowers. He examined it, poking and prodding around the perimeter. He pushed down hard and the tile popped up from the floor. Tol twisted it and the crack around the toilet grew suddenly wider as the entire assembly lifted. He pulled up on the tile/handle and the toilet platform swung around to reveal a hole just big enough for a goblin to fit.

He pulled the pen out of his overjack pocket and whispered.

"Petey, is there anything sentient alive down there?"

"I see evidence of two beings, probably goblins. One is three meters from the opening, the other a further two meters in the same direction. Both will be to your right if you pass through in the same orientation as present," the pen replied at very low volume.

Tol sighed. "Hold on. Could be a bumpy ride."

"Your 'rides' tend toward that direction."

Tol stood there a further moment cursing his choice of career before reluctantly dropping down into the pitch-black and decidedly aromatic opening. He swung as far to one side as possible to avoid the sewage itself. He landed on a concrete apron that formed one bank of the sewage channel.

Tol hugged the first wall he encountered and crouched. He waited for his eyes to adjust to the almost absolute dark. When his vision was as good as it was going to get, he crept forward, continuing with the wall mere millimeters to his right. He heard a slight scraping sound ahead and drew his disruptor.

No more than three seconds passed before he heard a goblin voice utter some odd words and then a flash lit up the passageway. Tol cursed under his breath as he grabbed at his left arm, which now sported a neat perforation spurting arterial blood. The projectile had pierced the muscles of his triceps and exited cleanly, without hitting bone. Some kind of magic slug, he guessed. He slapped a healing patch on it and the blood flow trickled to a stop.

Tol was in pain, but he didn't really mind. Pain kept him focused; kept out distractions. The brief illumination had given him a clear fix on his assailant's location and appearance: a relatively heavy-set male goblin, about ten meters further down. He pretended to be mortally wounded and fell heavily to the floor, gambling that the gob mage would simply flee and not try to make certain he was finished off in the blackness.

His gamble paid off: the assailant began to move away from Tol, feeling his way in the dark. Tol got noiselessly to his feet and edged along in pursuit, holding his throbbing arm. Whenever he sensed the gob had stopped, he stopped as well, holding his breath. Finally they came to a doorway with pale light spilling from it. Tol flattened himself against a wall out of the direct line of sight from within, watching and listening.

"Did you lose the tail?" said a female voice without warmth or emotion.

"I did better than that. I hit him with *Bayren's Ballistic Bullet*."

"So long as he is incapacitated."

"I am sure of it. I heard him fall."

"Good. We need to get moving. I have to meet with Honto in half an hour."

"I will locate the key to the main sewer grate. We should leave that way, in case the pub is being watched."

"I just hope there's not too much yuck in there."

"This end rarely gets any. The level has to be quite high for the main flow to reach this far out."

They walked away from the door. Tol recognized the second, female, voice as belonging to his quarry, Frem. He had found her, now he had to make certain he did not lose her. He slipped through the door and once again hugged the wall, this time on the left. He moved quietly, without audible footsteps.

The male goblin came back after a couple of minutes. "Found the key," he said.

"Good. Let's get going."

They headed for a metal door set into an irregular opening in the far wall. Tol crept as close as he dared; while he wanted to remain out of sight, he could not afford to stay so far behind that a door could shut and lock before he was able to grab it. He leapt for and caught the metal door just before it latched. Slipping in quickly, he let the door close with a loud click to reassure Frem and her companion that the way behind was secure.

They were in a brick-lined sewage tunnel with the light of day shining through a narrow opening about twenty meters further along. About halfway there two larger tunnels led off to the right and left. Tol wrapped himself in his dark overjack and crouched to stay as invisible as possible. He heard a muffled roaring sound coming from the four-way intersection: water flowing some distance away. He knew that the noise would be louder there, and waited until Frem and her companion had reached the confluence before hurrying after them. The gurgling of rushing sewage made it impossible for them to hear Tol coming up behind them.

Tol set his disruptor on *Stun*, thought better of it, and ratcheted up to *Solid Bonk*. He didn't want to take any chances. He aimed carefully and hit the male dead center back of the head. He went down like a bale of wet straw as Tol quickly flattened himself against the wall. Frem heard her escort fall and without even checking to see if he was still alive took off at a dead run down the left-hand sewage tunnel. "Touching display of concern," Tol muttered as he ran in pursuit.

Frem was in excellent shape and far more acrobatic than Tol on his best day. She knew he was following her and steadily drew further away. As she rounded a corner in the tunnel she suddenly slowed, then stopped along the bank of the sewage trench. Tol heard her stop and narrowed the distance between them warily in case she was setting him up. All those years on the street instilled a healthy paranoia into anyone who survived them. When he came around the same corner Tol immediately saw why Frem had stopped: there was something—something very behemoth-like—blocking the tunnel.

Frem was standing there gaping up at the thing, and Tol could find no fault with her response. It was huge, slimy, scaly, stinky, and pulsed indecently. It had a variety of circular indentations that could have been eyes, a horrible proboscis of sorts, and a mouth full of something very much resembling spines. That maw opened and emitted a most disturbing sound: a combination roar, whine, and gurgle. Both Tol and Frem took a step back. Frem turned to flee, but when she saw Tol standing there she abruptly reversed course and slung a wicked spike-ball at one of the creature's eyes. It roared out in pain and she breezed past Tol, shouting, "I only have to be quicker than you!"

Tol took out after her, ignoring the monster, but it was coming now too, at an alarming clip. As it closed on Tol, he wondered how something that large and bloated could move so quickly. A powerful, mucous-coated tentacle took a vicious swipe at him; he ducked but was grazed, which sent him tumbling into the odiferous muck. Tol stood up, dripping with unspeakable slime, and felt the anger building. This obese blob had pissed him off.

Heedless of the danger, Tol set his disruptor to full power and started shooting at the creature's presumptive eyes. Each time he hit one the beast would roar in pain and rage, swiping at Tol with a tentacle or spitting a high-velocity bolus of some noxious expectoration that went blasting down the tunnel and disappeared into the darkness when Tol dodged. As he obliterated the last of the eyes the monster reared up as far as it could within the tunnel's confines and then came crashing down with a tremendous wet thud. The resultant sewage tsunami overcame Tol; he floundered in the muck, gasping for air and fighting against the urge to projectile vomit.

The wave generated by the blinded gargantua carried Tol far down the tunnel, at last scraping him off against a wall a hundred meters or more from his starting point. He was bruised, battered, bleeding, and possessing of an indescribable scent, but otherwise intact. Once his wits and proprioception had returned, Tol stood up to take stock of the tactical situation. The monster was nowhere to be seen; the same was true for Frem. He scraped as much of the awful offal as he could from his body parts and limped off along the tunnel. He sighed as he realized he would probably have to start over on the search for Frem. *So close*. He would have to miss the *Avvolli*'s sailing and book another way home. First, though, he desperately needed a shower or three.

Tol figured the next sewer access hole was about fifty or sixty meters away, based on his experience in Goblinopolis. Most metropolitan sewage systems on N'plork were built on more or less the same template. As he limped along, he noticed an unusual lump in the placidly-flowing waste and stopped to examine it. He'd almost passed it up in the dim light. It was suspiciously goblin-shaped.

The body, for that's what it was, had grotesque disfigurement of the back side of the head and upper torso, as though it had been eaten away by some powerful acid. Well, this *was* a sewer and contained who-knew-what chemicals from a variety of industrial sources. This certainly wasn't the first body he'd seen disposed of in this manner. Dumping a stiff down a sewer hole was in fact a time-honored method for disposing of evidence on the run. Not his jurisdiction; not his problem.

He was about to shrug and pass on when a chance movement of sludge raised the left arm above the surface and Tol recognized it as belonging to a female. He knelt, dragged the body up out of the muck, and turned it over. It was Frem. She had apparently been struck by one or more of the monster's acid spitballs. He searched the body and found a host of useful information concerning contacts and motives. He put it all in an evidence bag, filled out the label, and signed it. Then he took flash pictures of the body and was about to send a message back to HQ to notify local EE of its location when he remembered Yemmy's advice: *leave the body in a position where detection of the event will be put off as long as possible.*

Looked like he would make that return voyage, after all.

Chapter the Nineteenth

in which Tol foils an escape plan and once more tests his mariner's skills

Less than a full day out on the voyage back Tol noticed a brace of small vessels shadowing them. The ship's crew probably noticed them as well, but there was no high seas edict being violated by such an act so long as the smaller ships did not encroach on the navigational zone around the *Avvolli*. There was a variety of reasons why the sloops might be there, but Tol had a hunch the fact that Lizgug did not show up for his rendezvous with whoever was waiting for him in Solemadrina had a lot to do with it.

Two sailing ships didn't seem like much of an immediate threat to the huge cruise liner as Tol sat and watched them. They could be scouts for some larger force, but he didn't think so. He decided to stroll up to the bridge and have a word with the captain about it. The crew were polite but firm that this wasn't the sort of thing passengers just did on a whim, but Tol was a hard gob to put off and, in a pinch, had that handy Crimson Knight badge.

"I am aware of the sloops, Sir Knight. While such traffic is not common, we do occasionally pick up sailors who use our course as their own in order to facilitate navigation, as we ply this route continually and know it extremely well. They will probably peel off at some point as we approach Esmian waters."

"Do your occasional pick-ups routinely come armed with torpedoes?" Tol asked, staring at the distant vessels through the captain's high-powered opticals, "'Cause these sure seem to be."

"What?" replied the captain, taking the glasses from Tol and sweeping the sloops. "Don't be absurd. Those are either external fuel tanks of some sort or fishing buoys. I appreciate your concern,

Sir Tol, but we have the situation well in hand here. There is no danger presented by these small vessels."

Tol shrugged. "It's your boat."

"That," replied the captain, turning back to his duties, "It is."

Tol wandered to the stern and stationed himself at one of the long-distance observation scopes mounted along the railing. He had a strange feeling about the stalkers, and his intuition wasn't often wrong about such things. Nothing he could really do about them but watch and wait; if they made a move he would, well, figure something out.

They took no action for the next few days, though: just kept their distance. Occasionally he would see someone out on deck— not fishing or sunning themselves as holiday-makers would be, but not doing anything threatening, either: just watching the *Avvolli*. Still, Tol couldn't shake the impression they were up to no good.

At dawn on the seventh morning, about a day away from docking at Lumbos, Tol went on deck and discovered that the shadowing sloops had disappeared. This fitted with the Captain's prediction, so Tol reluctantly let go of his suspicions. He was relieved but still vaguely troubled, at the same time. He couldn't say precisely why he was troubled, but something just didn't smell right. He was willing to admit that it could be himself generating the off odor: even after a half-dozen baths the scent of the Erolossma sewage system lingered faintly. Whatever the source, it left him uneasy for no readily apparent reason.

Two hours later Tol was eating a late breakfast on the forward veranda when he felt the ship's engines slow and then cut out altogether. He strolled over to the port rail and saw one of the sloops drawn up alongside. He walked over to the starboard and there sat the other one. Every alarm bell in his body started clanging. He made his way to the bridge as quickly as possible, waving his EE creds in the face of anyone who tried to intervene along the way.

"What's the scoop, Captain?" Tol asked breathlessly as he slid to a stop near the command chair.

"I'm very busy, now, Sir Tol."

"I'd guessed that. I'd also guessed that being so busy is somehow related to those sloops bracketing the ship right now."

The Captain sighed. "You would be correct, Sir Knight. They say they are armed and will sink or heavily damage the ship unless we lower your prisoner down to them."

Tol rolled his eyes. "Stall them, any way you can." He turned and ran out the door.

The Captain blinked; shrugged. "We will comply with your demand," he said into the radio, "As soon as we work out a technical issue with the winch. It was apparently...uh...not lubricated per the manufacturer's maintenance schedule."

Tol ran down to the lowest deck with balconies and headed for the aft-most access point. He slung a rope he'd picked up outside the bridge over the railing and rappelled down to the ocean's surface, out of the sight of either sloop. On the way down he heard a voice from his overjack pocket.

"What, if I may be so bold, are you hoping to accomplish by this little episode of derring-do?"

"I'm going to stop these jloks from springing my prisoner. Did you think I'd just decided to go for a leisurely swim?"

"May I remind you that you are not a strong swimmer, especially in two-meter swells?"

"I know. But I can float like nobody's business, and paddle while I do it. That's almost as good as swimming, right?"

"Again: in calm water, perhaps. But this water is *not* calm. You will experience considerable difficulty floating on it without ingesting salt water."

"I'll manage. And I have an ace up my sleeve."

There was a pause while Petey analyzed and cross-referenced the colloquialism. "What could that possibly be? Are you carrying a hidden collapsible dinghy?"

"You'll see. I'll give you a hint: check the ship's blueprints."

At that Tol released the rope and plummeted heavily into the briny drink, feet first. He went under for a longish while before bobbing to the surface like a cork on the trailing edge of a swell. He coughed and sputtered, flailing rather unproductively for a moment before finding his rhythm. He made for the *Avvolli*'s port hull and felt along it with one hand until he came into contact with something jutting out from the plating. He chuckled triumphantly as he firmed his grasp on the scraper's bracket, a C-shaped piece of steel welded every three meters along the length of the hull on both sides to which netting was suspended. It supported scrapers who removed the accumulated marine life and rust from the hull in dry dock prior to periodic repainting.

Tol propelled himself from one bracket to the next until he reached one of the sloops. The pirate had made a tactical error from Tol's perspective by staying so close to the hull of the cruise ship. It hid Tol's approach and boarding quite well. He crept up the stern ladder and held Petey up to check for witnesses.

"I see no one on the deck. There appear to be several persons on board: two on the bridge and two belowdecks. So far as I can ascertain it is clear for you to come aboard if you do not tarry."

Tol grunted in satisfaction and clambered up onto the wooden planks of the aft deck. He flattened himself against the exterior wall of the pilothouse adjacent to the entry hatch. He took a deep breath and then exploded onto the bridge. He had destroyed the radio even before the surprised occupants could react. The first one that came at him he tossed through the thick glass of the pilothouse, from which he fell to the deck and then rolled off into the pitching waves. The second drew a weapon, but Tol wrenched a navigational instrument from its moorings and hurled it at him, knocking the pistol from his hand and severely injuring his arm. Tol dragged the screaming kobold through the hatchway and heaved him overboard with his companion.

Tol looked around until he found the armory. Inside, to his grim delight, were a dozen fragmentation globes. He carried the crate over to an open access hatch for below decks, set the timer to fifteen seconds, pulled the pin, dropped it in, and then sealed the hatch. He ran back and dove over the stern just as one of the remaining crew came up from below via the other hatch and yelled at him.

The crewmember's protestations were cut short by a rapid-fire series of dull thumps from deep within the sloop, thumps punctuated by the stern and bow being violently separated from one another. Tol grinned as the bisected ship rapidly took on water and sank, leaving only floating debris to mark the spot where a few moments earlier there had been an intact sloop. He turned and made his way as quickly as possible along the hull around the stern, thanking his lucky stars that the engines were at full stop as he walked across the housing for the huge screws, and forward to the other vessel.

"I see nothing but floating wreckage, sir," reported the first mate, scanning the port side. He trotted over to starboard and focused his glasses on the other sloop. "The starboard ship seems intact...no, wait! There is heavy smoke pouring out of it!"

The Captain trained his own glasses on the remaining sloop. It was indeed belching thick, black smoke from the engine room area. The crew tossed an inflatable life raft over the side and leapt into it one by one as the sloop was consumed rapidly by the ravenous flames.

"Person overboard drill," he commanded. The first mate passed the order along as the captain continued to watch the burning sloop and its erstwhile crew. The life raft suddenly began to droop on the sides and then the sea rushed in. Within seconds it was entirely submerged and the occupants treading water. There was no sign of Tol.

After the survivors had been hauled aboard and sequestered in the now-crowded brig, the captain considered how he was going to word the communiqué that a Knight of the Crimson had been lost at sea. He had certainly gone down in glory—saving the *Avvolli* from high-seas pirates—but that didn't make the situation any less sticky. The Tragacanthans were very protective of their Knights and would insist on a full investigation. That might keep the *Avvolli* in port for days or even weeks, which would greatly displease her owners and possibly even endanger the captain's job.

He was sitting at the desk in his quarters, pen in hand, when there came a knock on the door. He ignored it. The knocking came again, this time more insistent. The Captain scowled and slammed down the pen. He had left strict orders not to be disturbed: someone was asking for six weeks of grease trap duty. He yanked open the door and was poised to rip into whoever was on the other side, but stopped in mid-rip.

Tol was standing there, drenched and grinning. "Sorry it took me so long to get back on board," he said, "Rope broke." He held up a frayed piece of nautical cordage with obvious wrat tooth marks. "You probably ought to do some about the wrat problem in your storage lockers."

The Captain looked at him with a mixture of incredulity and relief, mouth still hanging open. "Oh, and you were right about the torpedo-looking things being fuel tanks," Tol added, "Went up nice and hot."

Once in dock Tol escorted his prisoners to the nearest EE station and contacted Aspet on an encrypted comm channel.

"Frem is dealt with," he said, without formalities.

"How do you know for sure?"

"She had the back of her head and chest cavity eaten away by some smekking powerful acid. I examined her myself. Quite thoroughly deceased. I didn't have to use any of the...tools I took with me."

"Where did it happen?" Aspet asked, munching on a slice of candied greatfruit in his office.

"The sewers beneath Erolossma. Some huge smekker of a beast. Looked like a giant wooleater worm with multiple eyes, tentacles, and acid for spit. Not even a smidgen cuddly. Downright vicious, in fact."

"Did you kill it?"

"Possibly; I shot out everything that appeared to be an eye, anyway. The beastie didn't take kindly to that, but it probably saved my life." He sniffed his forearm. "Still can't quite get all of that stench out, though."

Aspet shook his head and smiled warmly.

"Tol, you've done a great service for your country and your family. We have considerable intelligence to indicate that Frem was hired to kill Boogla and quite possibly even me. She has a long history as a paid assassin."

"I believe it. She was tough and smart. I found a book with stuff about you underlined in Frem's hideout. She definitely was coming back for another shot."

"I'm very glad you took care of her," said Aspet.

"It more luck than skill, to be honest," Tol replied, "She was just in the wrong place when the monster decided to hack a loogie."

"Luck in this sort of endeavor, good or bad, is not a matter of chance. It's ultimately a natural result of pre-existing conditions established by the actions of one or more persons."

"Whatever you say, Your Majesty."

"When will you be home, brother?"

"I'm in Lumbos now. Sometime tomorrow, I expect."

"Come see me as soon as you can, please."

"I am yours to command, brother."

Chapter the Twentieth

in which an intrepid reporter uncovers a story she did not anticipate

Selpla glanced at her calendar again, just to make sure. It said her appointment to interview the newly-elected leader of the restored underground titan city of Hellehoell was the following day at ten in the morning. She looked at the name—Tartag—and realized it was the same titan she'd met the last time she was there. Tol was still on some secret mission; he didn't expect to be back for at least two more days, which is why she'd scheduled this appointment now.

The rail carriage view from Goblinopolis to Dresmak was serenely beautiful, alternating between wild grasslands and copses of a variety of large-leaved northern hardwoods. There was wildlife in abundance here, with few settlements. The only one of any size, in fact, was the village of Upupa, and it was a good fifty kilometers east of the rail line, which more or less paralleled the T-1. Some of the flocks of avians were so extensive that they blotted out the sun for minutes at a time as they passed over. This was one of the few entirely natural places left in Tragacanth; Selpla enjoyed getting a glimpse of the way her country had appeared before civilization encroached four millennia previous. Not that she wanted to give up the convenience and cultural advantages of life in the big city, of course.

After Dresmak the landscape changed dramatically. Barely ten minutes west of the city limits the ground began to rise into the foothills of the mighty Masron range. As the rails climbed, the forests fell away; in their place were majestic, plunging crags and deeply gouged rifts that scarred the mountainsides like cuts from colossal blades. Grays, browns, blues, and intense violets dominated the color spectrum here, with only the occasional smear of dullish purple from isolated patches of montane scrub.

When the carriage chugged into Fenurian that evening, Selpla was asleep. She'd nodded off after the last gorge-spanning bridge on the west side of the Masrons and rubbed her eyes drowsily as the carriage eased to a halt at the Fenurian South Station. She pulled her overnight bag down and shuffled to a waiting shuttle from her customary inn, where she crawled into a soft bed no more than five minutes after she'd signed the guest register.

The next morning she woke early and took breakfast on her balcony overlooking the seaside cliffs of Amnil Bay. The Noorprid Sea was unpredictable here: tranquil and deep green one moment, angry and electric blue the next. Whirling saltchitters and waveskimmers formed aerial vortices at regular intervals along the shallow sublittoral waters. Sailing vessels were common from here around Neaux Point into Yohkla Inlet with Dresmak at its mouth. The protected waters of the Inlet were ideally suited for those learning to handle sailboats.

At nine o'clock she left the hotel in a rented pram, heading for Hellehoell. The titans had already accomplished an impressive amount of excavation and reconstruction: the approach and entrance—they called it *Daludobris*—were now lined with marble bas reliefs and fluted demi-columns. The roadway itself was paved with shiny variegated pink and orange shellstone mined from ancient sea beds now located in wide strata deep beneath the northern Masrons. The combined effect was quite stunning. She found herself glancing unwittingly at the sky from time to time, looking for the swooping phantasmagoric beasts she'd witnessed on her first visit. Selpla had not brought any support crew with her on this occasion, so she took a number of still photographs on her own to accompany the story.

The titan she was to meet and interview, Tartag, the former ambassador to Tragacanth, had been instrumental in reinstituting the titan government of Hellehoell and in gratitude the populace had elected him their first Chief Elder, or *Odinial* in Titanic. The new Odinial was the tallest titan in Hellehoell, owing principally to his status as the last of the Storm Titans. Goblins are large, substantial bipeds, but Selpla once more felt like a toddler staring up at the lean mountain of flesh and muscle that was Tartag. *The Prayer for Protection from the Rock Titans* kept running through her head. ...*Pray, keep those titans far away*.

Far from the willfully destructive creature proscribed in the *Prayer*, however, Tartag was in contrast charming, congenial, and quite erudite. He remembered Selpla and took her on an abbreviated tour of the revitalized areas to date, pointing proudly to innovations and construction that improved upon the original designs. Titan society had obviously not stood still despite the long centums of exile. All along the tour Selpla marveled at the scale of everything. It was a doll house in reverse: the doorways were easily tall enough for a goblin standing on another's shoulders to pass through, while the benches required a boost up for her to sit on them.

Tartag related to her the tale of Tol's incarceration and escape from his own vantage point, providing details Tol himself had left out or skimmed over in his recitation. She smiled to herself over his courage and strong ethics. He was a good person through and through: very different and, at least to her, much more desirable than the shallow narcissists she had dated in the past. Selpla decided right then and there Tol was a keeper, if only she could make things work out that way. She was nothing if not ingenious when her heart was set on a goal.

For now, she had an interview to wrap up and a story to compose. As Tartag escorted her back to the entrance and her rental pram, which he had valet parked in his private garage, she promised him that she would do her part to set the minds of her readers at rest concerning the intentions of the titans in occupying Hellehoell. The titans' eventual goal was, of course, for the semi-autonomous Hellehoell to be designated a full sovereign city-state; generating goodwill amongst their Tragacanthan landlords was an important step along this path.

As she watched Daludobris recede in her rearview mirrors, Selpla could not stop smiling. Not only was she deeply impressed by the titan city and its charismatic leader, she had come to one of the most important and far-reaching decisions in her life while there. She wasn't yet sure of the best route to take to her destination, but for now she figured she'd just keep going the way she had been going and see how far that took her.

A couple of kilometers south of Fenurian lay the largest of the tent colonies supporting the labor population for the city's massive rebuilding effort. Sensing a possible story centered on primitive living conditions for the camped laborers, Selpla took an unplanned detour to see for herself. She left her pram in an area she assessed as relatively secure on the perimeter and hiked in toward what seemed, based on the density and arrangement of tents, to be the center of the temporary community.

She was looking for someone to interview, or at least from whom to pick up useable tidbits concerning life in the construction labor camp. She didn't expect to find any sort of civic leader, of course, but she did hope to encounter someone who'd been there since the beginning and could chronicle both the current and past history of the temporary settlement. As she stood scanning the area a half-ogre approached from the direction of her parked pram, flanked by two scruffy-looking companions: a hob and kobold.

"Welcome to New Fenurian, madam. May we help you?" asked half-ogre, with what appeared to Selpla a disingenuous flourish. Unlike the other two, he was dressed in fairly nice clothes, albeit out of style and in curious combination. Something about him didn't seem quite right, but he was the only person who'd bothered to give her even a second glance so far. She had to start somewhere.

"Yes, thank you. I am a reporter from Goblinopolis and I'm looking for a little history on this labor camp. Do you think you might be able to provide that?"

"Sure, doll. We can provide whatever you want, for the right price."

Selpla shook her head. "Sorry; not playing that game. If you don't want to talk to me, I can find someone who will."

The half-ogre shrugged. "Suit yourself. You get what you pay for out here. You give nothing, you get nothing."

"Thanks for nothing," she replied, walking away.

Sticker suddenly called after her.

"You said you were from Goblinopolis, right?"

Selpla stopped and turned back to him, hands on hips.

"That's what I said, yes."

"You know any cops there?"

Alarm bells were going off in her head. She chose her response carefully, picking her way through a thorny forest.

"I'm a reporter. You can't be a reporter without occasionally interacting with edict enforcement."

"I asked if you *knew* any cops. Personally."

"One or two, I guess. What's it to you?" She noticed that the hob and kobold had circled around behind her and she was now surrounded. She felt in her pocket for the reassuring mass of the comm unit Tol had given her. It had a panic button that used arcane heterodyning to broadcast a narrowly targeted signal to his own comm from practically anywhere on N'plork. It was priority linked using some form of entanglement she didn't really understand, but her encounter with Ballop'ril had reassured her that it worked.

"What it is to me, doll, is a matter of...personal interest. You see, there is one particular cop in the capitol city I'd like to meet in person. His name is Tol. Ever heard of him?"

Selpla tried to hide her shock, but the tiny jerk she made at the mention of Tol's name did not go unnoticed by Sticker. "Um, doesn't sound familiar, but it's possible. I don't remember names unless I need to. If I haven't written about them recently, I don't usually remember them."

Sticker regarded her for a moment before subtly motioning his companions away. "All right, doll. I'll let you in on a secret. I have a present for Tol. A very special present."

"Super. Give it to me and I'll look him up and hand it over to him when I get back, if that's what you're getting at."

Sticker laughed: an oily, grating series of exhalations. "It doesn't work that way, doll. This present is not one you could carry; Tol will have to come and get it for himself."

Selpla rolled her eyes. "Well, I'm sure if you contact the EE headquarters in Goblinopolis they can route your message to this Tol. Excuse me, but I have a job to do." At that she turned on her heel and walked away. These creeps made her uncomfortable in a way she hadn't felt in a long time. It took all of her self-control not to run away at full tilt. She decided that this story wasn't worth the effort and headed back to her pram.

Sticker grinned as he watched her walking. "She knows Tol, I would say. Quite well, even. I think she may be useful."

"You gonna stop her, boss?" asked Slag.

The half-ogre held up a small metal cylinder with two protruding wires.

"I already have."

The drive mechanism in her pram would not engage. Selpla cursed her bad luck and sat there for a moment, collecting her wits. She used her comm unit to call the number for the pram rental firm posted on the dashboard, but all she heard was a recorded message. She banged her head against the steering wheel a couple of times, sighed, and got out to seek help.

Sticker and his goons walked up. "Having trouble, doll?"

Selpla glared at the half-ogre momentarily before switching her pitch-up. She sidled up to him seductively and twisted her finger in his plaid lapel. "Nothing a big strong fella like you can't handle, I'm sure."

Sticker was momentarily taken aback by her new tactics, but it's hard to con a con artist and while Selpla was pretty convincing, she was dealing with a pro here. He decided to play along.

"I might be able to rescue you, doll. Depends on what you're willing to give up in return."

"What did you have in mind?" Selpla asked in reply, wiggling her eyebrows suggestively.

"We can discuss that later. First, let's see if we can fix your pram."

They all moved over to the stricken vehicle. Selpla sat in the driver's seat with the window down. He pretended to be working on the engine, his hands hidden by the engine compartment access hatch lid. "Try it now."

Selpla flipped the starter switch; nothing happened. Dross came over to stand next to her.

"Boss says to try pumping the throttle back and forth."

She pushed in on the throttle pedal several times. "Like that?" As she turned her head back to look at the kobold, he slapped a pad soaked in some strong-smelling chemical across her face, covering her nose and mouth snugly. She struggled briefly against it before her world faded to black.

Sticker reinserted the missing part, slammed shut the access hatch, and pushed the unconscious Selpla over so that he could sit in the driver's seat. Dross and Slag got into the back and they all drove away.

Chapter the Twenty-First

in which a dastardly crime is horribly botched

Tol sat at his desk reading the latest EE dispatches in some irritation. He had hurried back from Lumbos and abbreviated his post-mission debrief with Aspet only to discover that Selpla was in Hellehoell again. He knew she had a job to do, of course, but they hadn't been together much since before his accidental voyage to Port Jool and he was feeling the urge something fierce. He flipped over to the Ferroc Norda section of the dispatch log, a section he usually didn't bother to read, solely because that's where Selpla was.

The first item listed caught his eye. An armored dray loaded with currency had been brazenly stolen from in front of a money-changer's office. Witnesses saw at least one unfamiliar kobold and hobgoblin in the area, but no one actually came forward to report observing the crime in progress. Tol shrugged and wished local EE well. Not his problem.

As the day wore on he expected to hear from Selpla. He tried calling her once, but got no answer. That wasn't particularly worrisome: if she was somewhere in the depths of Hellehoell the only way she'd be reachable was via arcane mode. She may or may not have that enabled on her comm unit at the moment. He went back to writing reports and tried not to think of her. It was a hopeless task. When quitting time rolled around and he still had not heard from Selpla, Tol contacted the South Fenurian EE desk sergeant.

"Hey Grelko, this is Tol in Goblinopolis. Yeah, it's been a long time. Look, I'm trying to track down an errant reporter who rented a pram there and drove out to that titan city. Her name is Selpla and she should be either on the carriage or waiting for it by now, but I can't contact her. Can you find out if any of your guys has seen her? Of course it's official EE business. Call me back at this number. Thanks."

He slapped the comm unit down on the desk and sat there staring out an ornate window at the bustling courtyard of the Justice Center below. He shouldn't feel this way but he did, and the only person who could make him stop feeling this way was Selpla. He got up and paced the imported Nerrian rug covering the parqueted hardwood floors of his office suite. He'd never quite made adjustment to the splendor of his current work environment; one wall was covered with some of the worn and faded artifacts of his years in Sebacea. Smack dab in the middle of that wall was Selpla's nicely-framed photo.

Finally the comm unit buzzed.

"Tol here. Hey, Grelko. Whatta ya mean, you can't find her? She didn't turn in her rented pram? Did you check with the rail line? She was supposed to be on the evening carriage to Goblinopolis. She never boarded? Thanks. That isn't good. I'm on the way."

Tol was in no mood to be pleasant or negotiate. He walked into the carriage station and cut into the front of a lengthy queue, ignoring the glares and complaints of the patrons.

"Private carriage to Fenurian," he said to the clerk, showing his Crimson Knight creds, "Priority one."

The clerk started to say something about no available carriages, but Tol's expression dissuaded him. "Um, I'll find you something as soon as I can." Tol just stared at him, to the point where the clerk could not concentrate on anything else. He picked up a comm and dispatched one of the reserve engines with a single carriage. "Track four-A," he said to Tol.

Tol nodded his nominal satisfaction and walked briskly away. The clerk became aware of his own profuse perspiration and wiped it before turning back to the next customer in line. Some of the patrons glared angrily at Tol, but a few recognized him and their expressions were more akin to awe and respect than irritation. Tol didn't give a wrat's backside at that moment what anyone felt. He just wanted to get to Selpla.

He pushed the carriage engineer to take the machine to its limits. They rode down the rails as fast the carriage would realistically take them in the quickest voyage ever undertaken from Goblinopolis to Fenurian. Tol leapt from the carriage before they had even come to a complete halt and hit the platform running. He jumped in an EE vehicle that he'd called ahead to have waiting for him and sped off toward Selpla's last confirmed location in Hellehoell.

Hellehoell was actually east-northeast of Fenurian, but the only navigable approach required heading south from the city before turning east and then north. A few kilometers north of the left turn Tol passed a large assemblage of tents. It occurred to him that someone there might have seen Selpla's rental pram. He pulled over and started talking to people.

Most of the laborers were unwilling to speak at first, but Tol had many years of experience in loosening reluctant tongues. After half an hour he'd established beyond reasonable doubt that the pram had entered the tent city but had not come out. Ipso facto, it and most probably Selpla were still here somewhere. He would find her if he had to dismantle the camp tent by tent.

Such draconian measures were not necessary, as it turned out. Barely ten minutes into the search Tol spotted a pram matching the description of the one Selpla had rented. It was unoccupied, but Tol saw one of the jeweled scarves Selpla was fond of wearing on the dashboard. He was torn between anger and worry. As he peered through the window of the pram, a half-ogre approached.

"Sir Tol-u-ol, I presume," said the stranger, extending a hand. Tol did not reciprocate.

"You presume quite a lot. Who, exactly, are you?"

"You can call me Sticker."

"Sticker? What the smek kind of name is that?"

"It is only a nickname given me by some former associates, but I've been going by it for so long that it has, in essence, become my real name."

"All right, 'Sticker,' I'm looking for a female goblin who goes by the name of Selpla. Have you seen her? She was driving this pram."

Sticker stroked his chin as though in thought. "Yes, I believe I *did* see a lady goblin around here an hour or two ago."

"Can you show me where you last saw her?"

"Yes. Yes, I can. It was over there." He pointed toward a dense cluster of larger tents and headed off in that direction. Tol followed. As they rounded a corner, Tol was surprised to see an armored dray parked between two of the tents. He immediately recalled the dispatch about a stolen dray in Fenurian and put two and two together. He turned on Sticker.

"What's going down here? I'm guessing you aren't a good citizen who just happened to discover this stolen dray sitting here and wanted to turn it in to the cops."

Sticker laughed. "My good Sir Tol, you have, it seems, misjudged me. I am precisely that. This vehicle simply appeared here and is quite out of place. I was on my way to report it to the local constabulary when you quite accommodatingly showed up."

Tol stared at him, looking for sincerity. What he saw was unconvincing, but his real reason for being there suddenly pushed its way back to the forefront.

"I don't care about the dray. That's local EE's problem. What I *do* care about is that reporter. You said you saw her here."

"It is most extraordinary that a special investigator—a Knight of the Crimson, no less—should be so concerned about a journalist that he travels 350 kilometers simply to find her. I would be most interested in knowing the reasons for this."

"The reasons are EE business," Tol snapped at him, "And none of yours. Now, where is she?"

"The fate of your lady friend and this dray are inextricably intertwined, Sir Knight," replied Sticker. "All will be revealed inside."

"Whatta ya mean, 'inside?'" Tol asked with growing irritation.

"Inside the dray. She is inside the dray. If you want to rescue the damsel, you must also enter."

"I don't know what kind of game you're playing here, but I'm just about ready to start bustin' heads and I'm inclined to start with yours."

"That would be most unwise, Special Investigator, for my associates have strict orders to terminate said reporter if anything happens to me."

Tol grabbed the half-ogre by the jack and hauled his face right up to Tol's own.

"If anything *at all* happens to her," he said, biting the words out, "I will dismantle your ugly hide one body part at a time."

"There's no need to threaten violence, Sir Knight. Let us remain civilized and conduct this as a business transaction, the first step of which is for you to see what I have created inside the dray itself."

Tol rolled his eyes. "Fine. Let's see what is so smekking important about the inside of the smekking dray."

Sticker yanked opened the heavily reinforced door leading into the dray's cargo area and held it open for him. Tol stuck his head in and saw Selpla gagged and bound to a chair. He leapt in after her and Sticker slammed the door shut, bolting it securely from the outside. Tol pulled off Selpla's gag and began to untie her.

"I'm so happy to see you, Tol. Why did they *do* this to me?"

"Some kinda cockamamie kidnap for ransom scheme, I expect."

"But you walked right into their trap, then!"

"Your safety is my primary concern. I've dealt with wrats like this before. They're dumb as a box of rocks. Everything will be fine."

"How can you say that? We're hopelessly imprisoned inside a heavily armored dray."

In answer, Tol spoke into his overjack pocket. "Petey, scan this dray and tell me about the safety interlock system, please."

"The shielding effect is too strong for normal mode; I'll need to switch over to arcane. Hang on a moment," the pen said in muffled reply.

Selpla was now free and rubbing her sore wrists. She looked at Tol inquisitively.

"Every armored dray in Tragacanth has a mandated escape route so that drivers can't be locked inside accidentally and suffocate or something before they're missed," he explained, "Only the driver, the driver's dispatcher, and EE have access to that mechanism, however, and the codes change periodically or when a driver leaves. That's one of the reasons there is such intense scrutiny of prospective armored dray drivers."

"Data accessed," Petey announced. "This dray requires a transponder signal followed by a specific mechanical sequence to open. The egress portal is set into the floor, to the right, relative to the normal longitudinal orientation of the vehicle, of the driveshaft housing and just proximal to the rear axle."

Selpla looked confused. "What did it say?"

Tol chuckled and pointed to a spot on the floor. "Petey said the escape hatch is right about there." He got down on his knees and inspected the metal floor plates closely. "Here's the outline of it. Very close tolerances on these things."

"Yes," agreed Petey, "Standards specifications dictate no greater than one ten-thousandth of a meter."

"Why so precise?" Selpla asked.

"These things routinely transport hundreds of thousands or even millions of billmes, or the equivalent in precious alloys. People are very creative when it comes to robbery. Over the years the standards have grown more stringent in response to some of the more spectacular and ingenious thefts."

Selpla was quiet for a few moments. "It said a transponder signal was required. How are you going to handle that part?"

"I have a dandy transmitter on me that can probably generate the proper signal. Right, Petey?"

"Correct. I will need you to place me as near to the receiver's antenna as possible, however, as my output at that frequency is synthetic and rather limited in power. The antenna is that thin wire high on the wall at the front, across from the door."

"Super. And the mechanical part?"

"Standard three-point pressure sequence, centered directly on the escape portal. Hatch disengage will trigger when you move off after activation."

"Got it. Selpla, please hold Petey up right next to that little wire over there," Tol said, handing the sentient writing instrument to her. She complied while Tol walked over to the correct spot. He placed his right foot on the almost-invisible circle on the floor and his hands on two similarly inconspicuous spots on the wall. "Ready," he said.

"Signal transmission commencing," announced Petey. "Engage pressure sequence."

The muscles in Tol's arms and leg suddenly tensed, followed by a solid click. He stepped away and a circular section of flooring popped up far enough for Tol to get his fingers under it. He motioned for Selpla to stay quiet and in place as he removed the hatch cover silently, setting it aside.

Tol lowered himself through the opening. "Hang tight for a little while. I'll let you know when it's safe to come out."

He crouched down under the dray and after ensuring that the coast was clear slipped unnoticed into the cover of a nearby tent.

"Your Majesty, there is a high-priority call for you from the RPC Officer of the Day. She said to tell you it was Code Violet-Vee."

Aspet looked up from his papers sharply. "Thank you, Sergeant. Please patch it through to my encrypted desk comm channel at once."

"As you command, Majesty." The adjutant saluted and turned smartly on his heel. After a few seconds a light on the comm panel built into the king's elaborately carved desk blinked urgently. Aspet typed in the Royal Key that allowed the incoming message to be decrypted.

"Your Majesty," the OD's voice said, "We are in receipt of a communiqué through the Citizen's Anonymous Reporting Service that claims Sir Tol-u-ol and a local reporter named Selpla are being held prisoner. The caller demands ten million billmes and has left detailed instructions on how the money is to be delivered."

"What?" Aspet stood up in agitation. "Did you trace the comm path?"

"All we can tell by the circuit is that it originated in Ferroc Norda. The switching on this circuit is intentionally obfuscated so that people feel freer to report fraudulent activity."

"What's the time frame?"

"The caller has given us forty-four hours to get the money and deposit it on a buoy off the northern end of Yohkla Inlet."

"That's not much time. How certain are we that they were really kidnapped?"

"Selpla's employer reports that she has not been heard from since yesterday. Likewise, Sir Tol-u-ol is not answering his comm unit. It appears to be turned off. He was last reported at his desk in the Justice Hall."

"The most logical sequence of events would be that she was snatched first and he went to save her. Where was Selpla's last assignment?"

"Hellehoell, according to the managing editor. We've already notified Fenurian EE and dispatched a Crimson Knight mobility team."

"I know my brother. He will be giving these guys a serious headache. Get the money together, but don't take any further action for now. Watch and wait."

"As you command, Majesty."

Aspet sat down and put his head between his hands. Kidnapped. Tol? What kind of idiot would try to kidnap Tol? How

223

would they even go *about* it? It boggled his mind. He knew he should be worried about the safety of his brother and his girlfriend, but really he was more concerned for the perpetrators. Tol was historically not very tolerant towards edict-breakers, even less so when those close to him were threatened by said activity.

"How we gonna snag the dough, boss?"

It was an hour after sundown and Sticker had just finished a fine meal in a tent near the armored dray. He patted the corners of his mouth with a white napkin.

"I have an acquaintance who makes his living diving for marine shell meat, and as a result can hold his breath for quite some time," he replied to Dross. "The authorities will be expecting the money to be retrieved by someone in a boat. He will swim up from beneath the waves, grab the bundle, and be gone before they realize what's happening."

"That's real smart, boss."

"I know. 'Smart' is, as the hipsters say, how I roll."

"I'm gonna find just how *far* you roll," said a gruff voice coming from the shadows, "Or individual pieces of you, anyway." Tol crashed into the tent like a sudden microburst and caught the half-ogre as he tried to dive through the flap on the opposite side. Dross and Slag scattered in opposite directions, but Tol wasn't interested in them.

"You're under arrest for kidnapping, false imprisonment, and some other stuff," he said, dislocating Sticker's shoulder.

"Ow, you barbarian! Stop it!" Sticker whined as he tried to twist out of Tol's hold.

Tol put an elbow just above Sticker's neck and snapped it smartly downward. The half-ogre crumpled up like a piece of paper. He was standing above Sticker—sprawled on the floor like an ejectee from a high-speed carriage crash—with his fists poised to pummel when the Crimson Knight squad came running in, weapons drawn. Tol glanced up at them, looked back down at Sticker, sighed heavily, and relaxed. "Double smek," he muttered under his breath, "What rotten timing."

"Glad to see you are safe and whole, brother," said the detachment chief, a Knight-Commander named Foumil. "We were very concerned about you."

"Thanks, uh, brother. I pretty much had things under control."

"I see that. Where is the reporter?"

"She's safe, in the armored dray out there. There were two other perps, a hob and a kobold."

"Yes. We apprehended them just outside."

"Officer brutality...uph," Sticker mumbled from the floor, trailing off when Tol kicked him.

"What did he say?" asked Foumil.

"He confessed to everything," answered Tol. "Save it for the magistrate, smekhead," he snapped down at the half-ogre.

Local EE arrived just about then and Tol and the other Knights turned their prisoners over to them, with Tol supplying the list of charges. Tol went to fetch Selpla and after they both gave their statements they left together on the next regularly-scheduled rail carriage for Goblinopolis.

"How did you know I was in trouble?" Selpla asked him as they snuggled together in the first-class carriage. The rail line put Crimson Knights there as a matter of policy: it was still a lot cheaper for them than express carriages.

"I hadn't heard from you," Tol replied. "When a reporter doesn't communicate there's usually a good reason. Checking in regularly is in your blood, so to speak."

"Where did you pick up that gem of wisdom?"

"Just an observation. Yours isn't the first missing journalist case I've worked, you know. Remember Vidda Klertios?"

Selpla thought for a moment. "The star reporter from the old *Goblinopolis Daily Mentioner*? Yeah, I remember her. Disappeared on a story, right?"

"Right. Except what the public never was told because she asked for things to be that way is that she didn't just 'disappear.' She had a race-change operation and still lives in Goblinopolis."

"A race-change operation? I thought those were mythical."

"Oh, no: they do happen. Scaling down is much easier than the other way around, though. Vidda went even further and changed genders while she was at it. She went from goblin female to dwarven male. Can't say that I understand the attraction, but to each their own. He's a mystery writer now; goes by the name of Gervac."

"*Semna* Gervac? I *love* his books. I have one in my satchel right now. *The Case of the Pilfered Portcullis*. I would never have guessed in a million years he was formerly Vidda. Amazing."

"The reason I brought it up is that Vidda's editor first contacted us because she'd gone a full day without calling in. That apparently was unheard of, whether she was on assignment or not."

"And from that you extrapolated that all journalists are constantly in touch?" Selpla challenged smilingly.

"No, I got that from observing *you*."

Selpla acted affronted. "I beg your pardon," she sniffed, "I do *not* find it necessary to call in every few minutes."

Tol reached into his overjack pocket and pulled out a sheaf of paper. He held it out for her to see.

"Your comm records. Over the last three months you called back to the city desk on average twelve times a day. Sometimes even on your days off." That works out to...once every forty minutes or so."

"There must be some mistake with those records. I don't call in that often: I wouldn't have time to get any work done."

"It doesn't matter," Tol said, taking her in his arms, "That's not the kind of contact I'm interested in making at the moment."

Selpla clicked her comm unit onto *Do Not Disturb*. "I'll put that call through for you immediately, Sir Knight."

Chapter the Twenty-Second

in which two fugitives stir up a hornet's nest

"Land ho! I told you we would make it!" Hinyak was grinning broadly as he brought the tattered sail around to tack into the southeast wind. They had rowed for the first few hours after escaping the *Grollnash*, but a sudden squall had driven them further out to sea. When one of the oars had been washed overboard by a wave, they'd taken a sail repair kit and sewn their own clothes into a makeshift sheet. It had taken three days to make up the lost kilometers. They were starving, badly dehydrated, and wearing only their underwear. Jovsox was suffering considerably from the blast to his leg as well; it had festered and was oozing copious pus.

A crew of commercial fishers spotted them and brought them aboard the hoy they used to transport catches back to the fishmongers on shore, commenting favorably on their ingenuity at rigging the improvised sail. The ship's medic drained and dressed the goblin's wound, wisely avoiding any questions as to its origin. Fishers plying the vast southern N'plorkian oceans are a hardy and uninquisitive lot.

The northernmost of the Paradiddle Islands is a tropical paradise known as Ratamacue, and this is where the outlawed sailors at last washed up, so to speak. Although it is a small island in one of the smallest nations on the planet, Ratamacue has a well-equipped hospital as a result of its popularity among celebrities from across the globe seeking treatment for 'exhaustion.' Jovsox healed rapidly here and the pair were soon looking for further diversion.

"We need t' find a crew to sign on with," said Hinyak one morning, "So's we can get t' Balom."

"Balom?" asked Jovsox incredulously, "Why d' we want to get back t' that place? They didn't like us much there the last time, as I remember it. That one cop said he was going to throw away the key if we ever came back."

"I ain't scared o' him. It don't matter whether they liked us or not. That stretch of beach just south of the border—the one where we pulled the 'pirate treasure' scam—really *does* have a buried treasure: ours. I buried that haul we took on the carriage heist there. That's why the cops couldn't pin anything on us."

"Really?" the goblin seemed truly interested now, "I thought we lost all that dough in the landslide."

"Naw. I did use that as cover, though. The Galangan cops still think that's where the money is buried, but it ain't. It's on the beach about a kilometer north of that little lighthouse, almost right on the Tragacanth border."

"So, how are we gonna get there?"

"I figure we take ourselves over to Jessmirto or Xovcastra and sign on with one o' them coastwise tramp freighters, then just work our way up, one port at a time. Balom does a lot o' trade that way. Once we get where we're goin' we jump ship and collect the dough. We oughta be able t' live on that for a long time."

"Why didn't you think o' this sooner?" Jovsox suddenly asked.

"I did," replied Hinyak, shaking his head. "That's mostly why we signed on with the *Grollnash*. The ship's log showed several visits t' Balom in the past; I figured we were due for another one sooner or later. If it hadn't been for that stupid Tragacanth cop we prolly would have made it, too."

"That jlok was tough, I will say that," said Jovsox, rubbing his healing leg gently.

"Yeah. Guess he came by that knight thing for good reason."

"I'd sure love t' pop him, though."

"Just be patient. All things come to those who wait." Hinyak stretched out on his bed in the hostel where they were staying. "Our paths might well cross again."

Hinyak was not only a competent sailor, he also possessed the rudimentary charisma prerequisite for all who engage in the fraudster's trade successfully, despite his half-ogre origins. Within two days he had talked their way onto the crew of a tour vessel called the *SeaSpotter* that took eco-tourists up and down the western coast of Esmia, from Loppren in Asmagon all the way to Yohkla Inlet in northern Tragacanth, stopping at every sizeable port along the route. In an impressive manifestation of what might be termed Hinyak's particular genius, it was exactly what they needed to get them to Balom.

Though Hinyak and Jovsox were of different races, the paths they had separately taken to their present destination were remarkably similar. Both were orphaned at a young age and fled the orphanage after only a year or two, to make their own ways on the streets of opposite coasts in the island nation of Frespiola. Both had been in trouble on and off their entire lives, rationalizing it, as many of their ilk did, as an inevitable consequence of the position life had put them in, rather than their own questionable moral underpinning.

Both joined the Frespiolan Marines as soon as they were old enough. Hinyak was a quick study and rose through the enlisted ranks to Sergeant of the Sextant. Jovsox was not exactly dim, but his intrinsic resistance to authority interfered with promotion; when they met he was a Greaser's Mate and unlikely to progress much further.

They immediately formed a friendship. Jovsox, despite his lackluster intellect, recognized a kindred spirit in Hinyak and admired his ability to solve problems. For his own part, Hinyak saw the undiluted simplistic loyalty Jovsox was capable of exhibiting and it engendered in him a kind of familial attachment. He thought of himself as the goblin's 'big brother,' a relationship that Jovsox himself found both fitting and agreeable, and so they formed a duet that had so far endured all stresses and strains placed upon it.

Hinyak had been recommended for officer training, which meant that he would be transferred out of his unit and spend the next year at the Marine Academy in Melaman. Jovsox was clearly distraught at this prospect.

"I ain't liking that idea at all," he complained. "I might not see you again for a long time."

"Yeah, that's true. We do have an out, though."

The goblin brightened. "We do? What is it, you screw up and stay here?"

"That may or may not work," Hinyak explained, "If they get mad they might send me on one of those shakedown deployments or even boot me."

"I got another year and a half in my hitch," Jovsox said, sadly. "I guess there's nothin' we can do about it."

"Sure there is," Hinyak said, brightly, "We can desert."

"Desert? Run away? Won't that make us...criminals?"

"And? It's not like we both ain't criminals, anyway. How many times have you snatched stuff in your life?"

"Plenty, but I was mostly just tryin' to survive."

"Me, too. EE don't care what your reasons are: if they catch you at it the jig is up, no matter why you did it. Prison is not my idea of livin'."

"But you're a good Marine; not like me. *You* got a good career goin.' Why would you just give that up?"

"Eh, I ain't really cut out for military life. Too regimented for me. I don't much like workin' for somebody else. I'd get tired of being an officer after a year or two, anyway. Might as well skip that part and take off now."

"I'm game. Being a Marine ain't exactly my idea of fun, neither."

"Tomorrow night, after mess. Meet me at that shelter near the slop station. I know a way out that ain't being watched by the guards for about ten minutes during changeover. Discovered it during a 'gap-close' exercise but kept it to myself just in case I ever needed it."

"I wisht I was smart like you," Jovsox muttered, shaking his head.

"Stick with me and you won't need to be."

So it was that Sergeant of the Sextant Hinyak of Terimpu and Greaser's Mate Third Class Jovsox of Correq were listed AWOL and then finally as deserters from the Frespiolan Self-Defense Marine Force. It was the first in what was to prove a long string of governmental denunciations that nonetheless failed to end their lives on the lam.

Now, over five years later, they served together on the *SeaSpotter*. They used assumed names, as Hinyak had rightly guessed that their hijinks aboard the *Grollnash* would have earned them outlaw designation. Hinyak, or 'Halla,' as he called himself after a childhood nickname, was assigned as the Pilot's Mate, with responsibility for ensuring that the proper charts for avoiding navigational hazards were always in place on the navigator's chart board. Jovsox, who now went rather unimaginatively by 'Juvvy,' was made Rigger's Mate, in charge of keeping the ropes and cables on board cleaned and stowed properly. It was an employment that suited him well, and he was competent at it.

It took them nearly three months of sailing in and out of ports large and small, through all kinds of weather and seas ranging from glass to gale, before finally they gazed out the tiny porthole in the crew berths and saw framed by it the northern Galangan port of Balom, their destination. Halla seemed genuinely excited for the first time in a long while.

"I have shore leave arranged for tomorrow for both of us," he told Juvvy that evening at supper. "It shouldn't take more than a couple of hours to find the money."

"Unless somebody else found it first," Juvvy said, between bites of chowder and soda bread.

"Don't be such a pessimist. I hid it very well. You can't just dig and get to it."

"I thought you said you buried it on the beach."

"I did."

"Then why can't anyone that digs in the right place find it?"

"I'll show you when we get there."

"I thought this was supposed to be a deserted beach."

"It was when I buried the money. I don't remember any of that stuff being here."

"The sign says 'Balom Orc Enclave.' I thought all the Orcs were dead or something."

"Nah. Well, mostly. But they have a few little reservations where they're allowed to live under close supervision so they don't get all militant again. I guess this is one of those, but I swear it wasn't here when I buried the money."

"Looks like it was established last year *at the request of the Grand Orcish Council, with the full cooperation of the government of Galanga,*" Juvvy read slowly from a placard bolted to the fence next to the heavily reinforced and barbed wire-encrusted gate. "But this Enclave thing isn't going to mess up our digging for the money, right?"

Halla frowned. He picked up a bucket he'd brought with them and walked over to a large tree whose ancient branches hung out over the pink beach. He paced off from it and dragged a line in the sand, and then did the same from a sign warning about rip currents, but was stopped short by the fence around the enclave.

"Smek me. The smekking money is just inside the fence. I guess we'll have to get in there somehow," Halla said, irritation evident in his voice.

"Couldn't we just dig under the fence?"

"I read that orcs are good sappers, so the fences around these things go down like ten meters," replied Halla, "We're just smekkin' lucky they missed it when they were excavating for that."

"So, whatta we do?"

"Let's just ring the bell and ask if we can come in."

"Is that safe?"

"Do you want the money? Every potentially profitable action carries risk." Halla was already walking toward the gate.

A sullen-looking orc guard peered through a slot at them.

"What?" he asked, simply.

Halla had a story prepared, but for some reason he could not readily elucidate he decided for once to tell the truth. "We buried some property here before the enclave was built and we would like permission to retrieve it. It's only a meter or so inside the fence."

The guard appraised them both. "*You* can come in. The goblin stays out there."

Halla and Juvvy looked at one another. "He is my half-brother," Halla lied, "We are family."

"You are *not* related," The orc stated it as pure fact, which it was. "The goblin stays out."

Juvvy shrugged. "It's okay. I'll just hang out here."

"I won't be long," Halla replied. "Go stand at the exact spot where I hit the fence."

Inside the compound, which was sparse and institutional at least at the perimeter, Halla wasted no time in making his way to a place immediately across the fence line from Juvvy. He started clawing at the sand with his nails, which were quite long and sharp. When he had dug down about a meter, he stopped deepening the hole and spoke to Juvvy through the fence.

"Fill that bucket with sea water and bring it back."

"Whatta ya want that for?" Juvvy asked, puzzled.

"I told you the money couldn't be accessed just by digging down. Seawater has to come in and complete an electrical circuit or the lid can't be opened. It just feels like a very solid layer of sandstone when you hit it. Anyone digging here would stop at this point and go dig somewhere else."

Juvvy returned with the bucket. While he was gone Halla scooped out a little canal from the excavation to the edge of the fence. "Pour the water through the fence into this ditch," he instructed Juvvy. The seawater trickled down and pooled on the lid.

After a minute or so there was an audible click. The water in the hole drained off to reveal a rectangular sandstone-encrusted protrusion that Halla grasped with both hands and lifted up onto the sand. Beneath it was a locked metal box about the size of an overnight bag. The half-ogre retrieved it and filled in the hole. The orc watched but said nothing.

"This is what I came to get. Thanks for letting me," Halla said to the orc, brightly. The orc remained mute while escorting him back to the gate. Halla went through and turned to the guard as the gate was closing behind him.

"Why did you let me in, but not my friend?" he asked.

"You are half-orc," the orc replied, "The Treaty of the Clans demands that I admit any of the noble bloodline. Goblins are *never* allowed on orc lands," he sneered.

The guard walked away, leaving Halla frozen in place with his mouth hanging open.

"What did he mean about you being a half-orc?"

"I...I don't know," Halla replied as they sat in the dense underbrush twenty meters from the beach, counting their ill-gotten gain. "I never knew my dad. Mom wouldn't talk about him. When she died I didn't have any relatives around to tell me, neither."

"Is it possible he was an *orc*?"

"That never occurred to me until now. That orc guard sure seemed convinced. I guess I always assumed he was a goblin or kobold or something. It explains some things about me, I suppose."

"Like what?"

"Like my temper and my wanderlust. Orcs are known for both, which is why locking them in these enclaves is doubly hard on them. But the government says it don't have a choice."

"Why not?"

"Because orcs are maniacs. They seem perfectly fine and then one day they just murder everyone within reach. They've been that way for as long as we've known about their existence."

"Why do you think they do that?"

"I dunno. Maybe they have something wrong with their brains. We don't even know exactly where they came from."

"Maybe they're from some other planet."

"We don't have any evidence that life exists anywhere else, at least as far as I know. The mages talk about other dimensions and stuff like that, but I think there's something wrong with *their* brains, also."

"Yeah, I always thought that, too," agreed Juvvy. "So, are they gonna lock you up for bein' half orc?"

Halla laughed, "If they catch either one of us they're gonna lock us up, half-orc or not. That's why we gotta keep movin.' This money will make that a lot easier. I figure we go to Azlymosh, or maybe Blostt in Tantatku. No cops gonna bother us there, long as we're careful."

"Azlymosh? Isn't that a desert or something? I don't like hot, dry places."

"Neither does anyone else: that's sort of the point. Besides, Juymiz isn't that bad, they say. It's on the coast so it's not as hot as the interior."

"What about Blostt?"

"Blostt is a little further south; across the strait from Uzplenq in Nerr. If we go there we'll need to get some fake IDs made, 'cause they have pretty strict immigration policies in Tantatku. Nobody in Azlymosh gives a smek who you are. That's why a lot of guys like you and me end up in Juymiz or one of the little coastal villages."

"If we go there and don't like it, can we leave?"

"Sure thing."

"Okay, I'm ready, then. Next stop: Juymiz!"

Half a kilometer away, in the Elders' Sanctum of the Balom Orc Enclave, the elders were listening to the guard's report.

"Half-orc came to the gate and dug something up just inside the fence. Buried in a Chieftain's Casket."

"Where is he now?"

"Gone."

"Did you see what it was?"

"No. Bundle about this big." The orc held his hands out in an approximation of the object's dimensions.

The elders dismissed him and talked among themselves.

"Buried treasure?"

"Probably. Currency or jewels. It is the way."

"But he did not share."

"Diaspora sometimes forget the old ways."

"Yet he knew about the Chieftain's Casket."

"He is only a half-breed. Not all of the engrams may be there."

"What if he is the Uul? What if he has recovered the Valtir?"

"He would have declared were he the Uul. The Valtir has little intrinsic worth, except as a symbol for orcs."

"But a half-breed may not know why he finds the Valtir important to him: just that it is."

"Do we believe that this half-breed has, indeed, stolen the Valtir from us?"

"If he is not the Uul, why else would he have brazenly come onto our land and opened a Chieftain's Casket? No outsider would dare to do such a thing, as they believe us to be indiscriminate, mad killers. He was not afraid; therefore he had foreknowledge that we would not interfere with him. No one without orc blood would think that way. No, our course is clear: we must retrieve the Valtir. It was prophesied that the Uul would take it as a test of our resolve."

"If we try to go among the outsiders, they will think we are warring upon them."

"We must take that chance. The honor of our ancestors demands that the Valtir be returned to Eithmorg. It is our duty; it is our purpose in being."

"Agreed. It will be a difficult task; we do not even know where the half-breed is, or where he intends to take the Valtir."

"The sooner we start, the easier his trail will be to follow."

"We send a message to the Moreani first. We will require their assistance if the half-breed travels by sea. Employ Okung."

One of the elders went to a window and blew three blasts on a horn made from shells and hollowed-out wooden tubing. After a moment he blew twice more, before returning to his elaborately carved chair. They sat without speaking for three full minutes before a shadow passed over the open window and an enormous sea avian landed on the external sill. The elder who ordered the horn be blown wrote a message on a small strip of parchment and sealed it in a capsule attached to the avian's leg. The huge diomedean leapt off the sill and took gracefully to the skies, heading out to sea immediately.

"Now we must proceed with care. There are far too few of us to take direct action; we must be cautious and use the shadows instead of the light. It is not the orcish way, yet we will do what must be done. On this we must all agree. Any opposed say so." There was no response. "Then, the die is cast. Let us recover the Valtir or perish in the attempt, as honor demands."

Chapter the Twenty-Third

in which a student mage is promoted and encounters an exceedingly odd curse

"Tomorrow we will begin the examination for Mage First Tier," Ballop'ril announced as breakfast concluded. "Two other mages will be present to proctor besides myself: Magus Arcanis Hutreq and Magus Academicus Kjonza. They will be here just after daybreak; the exam will begin precisely at mid-morning. You should spend today in meditation and review."

Prond dropped his fork in alarm. "I thought the MFT exam wasn't supposed to be undertaken until I had been Second Tier for at least a full half-year," he exclaimed, a little shaken.

"The mentoring mage has flexibility in the timing of all exams," Ballop'ril explained, "You know that. Based on your progress in the practica and my estimation of your skills, I believe you to be ready. It is important to strike while the iron is hot, so to speak. The exam for Mage First Tier is taxing, both mentally and physically. You should get it out of the way as soon as you are prepared to do so, and I judge that time to be now. Go and meditate."

Prond stood and bowed to the Archmage before making his way back to his cell, a little unsteadily. His mind was racing and his stomach turned flips like a circus acrobat. Was he really ready for this? The First Tier exam was infamous among students of magic as the most difficult of all exams other than the Archmage trial, because it was the first exam where macromolecular structural manipulation was required. Not only did examinees have to demonstrate spell proficiency, they also had to both create and modify solid objects using only manna. He wondered why Ballop'ril was so convinced he was ready. He didn't *feel* ready.

He did not sleep that night, but this was normal for him before exams. Prond meditated most of the night, preparing mentally for the challenge ahead. About an hour before daybreak he started running through his warmup and agility rituals. By the time the other proctors had arrived, he was as ready as he was going to get.

The exam began with the traditional questions on the ethics and practice of magic, followed by a series of increasingly difficult spell-casting exercises to test Prond's memory for the incantations he would need to be able to access to accomplish more complex magical tasks. The final and most lengthy phase was the creation and manipulation of simple objects, then more complex ones, using nothing but manna.

Prond stumbled a bit at first, but Ballop'ril's insistence on constant drilling and repetitive practice, followed always by meditation for the lessons to gel, proved effective. Once he found his groove, he was unstoppable and finished the exam in a whirlwind of stellar performances. The final examination task complete, he bowed and left the room for the proctors to deliberate. They called him back in less than a minute.

Ballop'ril spoke: "Apprentice Prond, it is the judgment of this panel of proctors, all full Magi in good standing, that you be elevated to the rank of Mage of the First Tier, effective immediately. With this rank comes a golden baldric." He unrolled from an embroidered silk wrapping the most beautiful baldric Prond had ever seen. It was made from real cloth of gold, with elaborate embroidery and gems set into it. He received it reverently and gaped.

"This baldric," Ballop'ril continued, "Is a gift from His Majesty Tragacanth, in recognition of and appreciation for your help in rescuing the Royal Consort and Magineer Liaison from the assassin's poison. Without you, the attached message reads, the vial containing the antidote might have been destroyed and with it any hope for saving her life. His Majesty asks that you accept this gift as a small token of his esteem and gratitude."

It was just too much at once: passing the strenuous exam and now this unexpected and extravagant gift from the leader of his nation. Prond honestly felt he was going to faint. Ballop'ril sensed his state of mind and hurried through the rest of the ceremony so Prond could be excused back to his cell to lie down, though it was only mid-afternoon. He fell asleep almost instantly.

After a long nap, Prond awoke feeling slightly woozy and disoriented until he saw the king's gift and the day's events came flooding back. He removed his simple silver baldric and placed the golden one over his shoulder. It fit very well, with some sort of sticky fabric under the curve that caused it to adhere to his tunic, holding the entire garment in place properly at all times. He looked at himself in the mirror, admiring the beautiful work. He really felt like a mage now, more than ever. It was something of an emotional moment for him.

At the evening meal Ballop'ril was full of cheer and congratulations. He toasted Prond while the other apprentices and staff all cheered for him. He felt as though the blush would burst completely through his cheeks. As a Mage of the First Tier Prond would now be expected to assume more comprehensive training duties for the newer apprentices, as well as accomplish lesser contracts taken on by the archmage. All of this, of course, was in addition to rigorous training for the next advancement to Magus Incipius.

The step from Mage to Magus was more of a quantum leap, since it involved not just exercises and an examination, but a formal enquestation that must be solved in multiple steps, each dependent on the successful navigation of the previous. The real difference in the Magus-level exams was that wrong answers could have serious—even fatal—repercussions. He didn't like to think about that, and he wouldn't have to for some time. Prond knew he had a lot of work to do before he would be ready for advancement to Magus.

On the other side of the world, in the city of Barra Tingo on the tropical island of Grosyem, a local business owner named

Ai'go'r sat in his office and fretted over a problem he was having, which was that the vegetables he stocked in his wholesale produce mart were spoiling much too rapidly. Hardly did he get them unpacked and distributed in the proper bins for his customers, mostly restaurateurs and retail grocers from throughout the four insular nations comprising the continent of Litria, before their ripe, brown or gray flesh began to turn lurid green and rot.

He'd tried everything. It wasn't the air, or the water, or some weird microorganism resident in his premises; he'd had all of those exhaustively analyzed. The businesses flanking him in the industrial park weren't having any issues. The very weirdest thing was that his ownership of the vegetables in question seemed to be the root cause of their accelerated demise. No matter where he took a vegetable, the same thing happened to it. Ai'go'r began to wonder if it was something his own body was giving off—some odor or aura or radiation.

The problem had started suddenly, about a fortnight previous. At first he blamed the shipper, but oddly no other end-users of that same shipping company's services were experiencing the issue. He brought in various specialists, none of whom made any progress although they had no shortage of theories, from the plausible (residual vapors from extermination) to the outlandish (aliens sucking the life forces out).

Facing the very real possibility that he might have to go into some other line of work, Ai'go'r sat with his head in his hands, trying to understand what was happening. He was listening to a news report on one of the channels that specialized in off-the-wall occurrences when he heard a brief account from the Arcanical News Network about an apprentice mage in Tragacanth who had just advanced to Mage First Tier in record time. One small corner of his mind chewed on that tidbit in the background while the rest of the brain was preoccupied with feeling sorry for itself until at last it reached a conclusion. It took a bit of jumping up and down and shouting before the tidbit made itself heard, but eventually the conclusion wound its way up the protocol stack to his conscious mind: this could be a magically-induced problem. A curse, in other words.

The possibility that he had been cursed had never occurred to Ai'go'r. He knew magic existed, of course, but it didn't play much of a role in his day-to-day life so he'd mostly dismissed matters arcane from his thoughts. Being cursed did explain a lot of things. But, who would curse him, and why? He thought back to events just prior to the beginning of the strange affliction. Nothing really leapt out at him until he started flipping through paperwork from that time.

About a week before the troubles started, Ai'go'r had rebuffed a half-hearted, or so it seemed to him, attempt from a rival on nearby Hividz across the Poltoi Strait to buy him out. The rival grocer had threatened to take punitive measures if his offer was not accepted, but as such threats were fairly customary in negotiations of the region, Ai'go'r had ignored it. The only reason he remembered the interaction at all was that rival's threat had included employing the services of a mage—not a typical strategy in his experience.

Mages all were supposed to subscribe to a code of ethics that would preclude them from casting curses for money, but as with any group of people not all mages were equally moral. The promise of quick cash might prove irresistible in circumstances where a mage was in heavy debt, for example. There was also the possibility that family or clan connections—and the usual pressures thereto appertaining—were involved.

Presuming that his produce had been cursed, how did he go about lifting said curse? What took a mage to generate would, he guessed, require one to remove. He didn't know any mages, and nor had he the slightest idea how to go about hiring one. He wondered if he could take out some form of classified advertisement in the local news journal. Then one of his customers told him that SagMag, the Society of Sages and Mages, had an office in the capitol city, Coestra, about two hours' drive.

The very next day he got up before the sun and headed out in his ancient little pram. The SagMag offices weren't even open yet when he arrived; he had to sit on a covered bench outside watching the tropical rain patter steadily while he waited. Finally someone showed up to unlock the door. Ai'go'r tried his best to be patient while the SagMag official went about the rituals associated with opening for business for the day. Things moved slowly and deliberately in the tropics; Ai'go'r was well aware of this.

When at last SagMag was ready to receive visitors, the grocer stated his business and asked about hiring a mage to remove the curse. The clerk flipped through his register and shook his head sadly. "We don't have many mages willing to take on contracts these days. Most of them either have academic posts or are employed by governments; either way they aren't free to take on outside work to avoid accusations of impropriety."

Ai'go'r frowned. "You mean there are *no* mages at all who can help me?"

The clerk seemed on the verge of confirming this when he spotted an entry at the bottom of a page. "Here's one possibility: the *Arcanium*, a mage training facility in Tragacanth that accepts contracts at all levels for the purpose of providing real-world exercises for the schola's student mages."

"Tragacanth? That's a long way off," Ai'go'r said, doubtfully. "Still, if that's where I have to go, then I will."

"Well, you don't have to go there personally, of course. They do have a comm circuit listed here." He scribbled the number on the back of a business card and handed it to Ai'go'r. "Here you are, sir. Best of luck!"

Three days later Ai'go'r received a message from the Arcanium that his contract had been accepted and a Mage First Tier was on the way to investigate and, if needed, remove the curse. He breathed a sigh of relief. Perhaps the end of the nightmare was in sight. He wondered idly if the rival whom he suspected of causing the curse to be pronounced had taken similar measures against anyone else.

"You want me to go to Grosyem? I've never been there before, although I've read about it in tourist guides. Am I traveling by conventional means or translocation spell?" Prond was discussing his latest assignment over comm with Ballop'ril, who had gone into Tillimil to meet with several other high-level mages.

"Translocation," Ballop'ril answered. "The round trip would require in excess of a fortnight if you went by sea: and that's only if you took direct ship, which would cost more than the contract will be worth. Look in the archives for translocation templates to Grosyem. You want to find one for Barra Tingo, ideally. Make certain it's recent."

"Yes, Archmage. If I find one, shall I leave immediately?"

"Yes. Don't forget your 'go' bag. And while you're there, please update the templates and perhaps even add one or two, if you get an opportunity."

When Prond was ready to leave, he had the Arcanium clerical staff contact Ai'go'r by comm with the coordinates at which Prond would appear, so he could meet him.

"Good. That's only half a kilometer from here. I can be there in a few minutes."

Prond checked and re-checked the contents of his 'go' bag. It contained not only his personal toiletry items for overnight stays, but also implements and raw materials for a variety of magical spells, talismans, phylacteries, and so on. Following schola policies, he cast a 'great circle' translocation spell that would return him to his precise starting point automatically after three days if he did not manually initiate the return sooner. This was for the mage's own safety; if he were disabled by some mechanism he would teleport home without the need to take any action.

Translocation was a curious experience. It essentially created a tunnel through The Slice connecting any two points on the material plane as though there was no physical space between them. The mage walked forward only two steps: one took him into the magical tunnel and the next to the destination. While the tunnel was located within The Slice, its walls were opaque from the point of view of the mage, so the optical sensation was a momentary blurring of vision as the scene transitioned from origin to destination. Taking only one step had no effect, because the tunnel itself was a quantum object that allowed the mage to be in superposition: in both places at once. The act of taking that second step caused the superpositioning to break down and transported the mage to the far end. If the second step was never taken, the mage remained at the original location.

Prond appeared out of thin air, from Ai'go'r's perspective, on a deserted strip of land about a hundred meters inland from a rock shoreline on the eastern outskirts of the sleepy tropical town of Barra Tingo. He nodded in satisfaction at the destination and made a note to verify this template as still valid.

"Greetings, great mage. I am Ai'go'r Desnol. I presume you have come to help me with my problem?"

Prond smiled at him. "Yes, Ai'go'r. My name is Prond, Mage of the First Tier, and I was dispatched by Archmage Ballop'ril, Master of the Schola Arcanium, to fulfill the contract you have entered into with us."

"Excellent, excellent," effused Ai'go'r, rubbing his hands together. "Let us waste no time. I will take you to my warehouse, where I believe the curse to be laid." They both got into the grocer's tiny pram and chugged off. On the way Ai'go'r relayed all of the story he could to Prond.

"So, you believe this rival grocer in Hividz paid someone to cast a curse?" Prond asked. "It is imperative that I find out more about the mage who did this, if indeed it is a curse. Not only is it a violation of the Oath of Ethical Conduct, the more I can discover about the casting mage, the easier it will be to undo the malediction."

"I'll be happy to tell you everything I know about the grocer, although I have no knowledge whatever concerning the mage. His name is Riqpen and he is a gnarlignome; the only one of that race I've ever met in person, in fact. We've never been friends, per se, but up until recently we've at least been on professional terms with one another. I even helped him out once when a shipment of his got delayed by bad weather at sea. A few weeks ago—right out of the blue—he offered to buy me out. The price he named was fair, but I have no interest in selling right now. This is my livelihood and I enjoy it, to boot."

"What happened when you turned him down?"

"Yeah, well, that's why I think he's involved. He started yelling at me and swearing by 'Arfsweener' that he would get even for this grave insult. I didn't pay a lot of attention because I hear that kind of language fairly often out here. I think it's the humidity."

"*Did* you insult him?"

"Not from my point of view: I just declined to sell. It was pretty polite, actually. I wasn't mad at him; I thought it was just a business proposition. He apparently didn't take it that way."

As he stepped inside the grocer's warehouse, Prond immediately detected a strong magical aura. He winced at the twisted, haphazard lines of arcane force sprayed around the room almost at random. Every piece of produce in the warehouse was serving as a self-perpetuating maledictive locus. This was a very sophisticated curse, not just the result of some minor talisman's spell discharge, as he had expected to find.

"You have a serious issue here," Prond told the grocer, "This spell is very complex and took a long time to cast. It will be quite tedious to undo. If the mage casting it was paid at SagMag scale, it would have cost more to commission than this place is probably worth. I don't understand the motivation here. Something's going on beyond just the retaliation of a spurned business owner."

"You...you aren't going to charge me that much to undo the curse, are you?" Ai'go'r was shaking a little as he asked.

"No. We have a contracted price, and we will honor that contract, no matter how much work it takes on my part."

"That is noble of you and reflects well upon your schola," Ai'go'r answered, wiping his brow in relief.

Prond spent the rest of that day trying to map out the arcane force patterns in the affected area. It was hard work, because any movement of the produce changed everything around. Late that evening he sat in his room at the nearby inn, wondering if this task was not too much for him to handle. Ordinarily even a Third-Tier mage could remove a simple curse, but this one was anything but simple. It was a tangled mess, in fact. He fell asleep wondering why anyone would take this bizarre approach to casting a malediction.

About the middle of the following day Ai'go'r came back from lunch with a copy of the local news journal. "Look at this!" he said to Prond, waving the folded papers under the mage's nose. Prond read the story he pointed to, which detailed the sudden, grotesque destruction of a grocery in Rebrugge, Hividz by what the local EE were calling a 'magical meltdown.'

"That was Riqpen's shop!" Ai'go'r exclaimed. "That was the gnarlignome who wanted to buy my business!"

Prond sat down heavily, paper still in hand. This changed everything and nothing at all. If the curse were tied to that physical location, it would have been altered significantly by whatever happened in Rebrugge. Since nothing here seemed to have changed, the curse was free-range now: no longer anchored. That would make it much more difficult to remove, as there was no central feed point from The Slice. Prond was seriously beginning to wonder if he possessed the skill necessary to carry out this contract. He imagined how disappointed Ballop'ril would be if he came back after having failed, however, so he racked his brain for a plan.

He decided that he needed to understand what had happened at Riqpen's place first, as that might give him insight into the source and arcane mechanism for Ai'go'r's curse. As he didn't have a lot of time left, Prond contacted a mage local to Rebrugge and asked her to head over to the spot and set up for remote viewing so he could investigate without having a physical presence.

The scene in Rebrugge was shocking. There was nothing left of Riqpen's building: the very ground seemed to be disrupted. Riqpen himself had not been seen since the incident. A team of forensic mages was on the way from Coestra to investigate the cause of the disaster on behalf of EE. CoME had dispatched its own team of investigators, as well. Apparently whatever had taken place there generated harmonics on multiple arcane planes, even in The Slice itself; ripples had been detected all over the planet.

There was not much in the way of usable evidence left, however, after what was already becoming known as the 'Rebrugge Event.' Although the remote viewing connection was quite good, even the mage who set it up for Prond said that there was so much destruction and chaos all along the magical spectrum that it was impossible to make any sense of it. Prond did his best to sort through what little he did gather before thanking the Hividz mage profusely and closing the connection. He had just over a full day left to defuse the curse.

Since he had no central energy sink from which to disconnect the magical flow that maintained the curse, the only thing Prond could think of to do was disentangle the individual streams one by one. He started at the front of the warehouse and worked his way back. As the layout was sorted by produce type and variety, he effectively 'uncursed' one vegetable at a time.

As he was preparing to head back to the inn to sleep just after midnight, Prond made a disheartening discovery. Some, although not all, of the produce he had uncursed was reconnecting to the curse-generative magical energy streams. He enfolded them in a quick arcano-static field, but he knew it would not last forever. Something *exceptionally* odd was going on here. He could really use Ballop'ril's advice right about now. He toyed with an Amulet of Summoning the archmage had given him for emergencies. This problem was vexing, but it was not an emergency, he decided at length. He sighed and headed off to bed.

Prond slept for only four hours and was back dissolving the curse before daybreak. He had only six hours left before the translocation fail-safe activated and returned him to the Arcanium.

The stasis spells were still holding; he hoped that once all of the primary energy streams had been disrupted those fields would no longer be necessary. He finished up dissociating the individual energy feeds a scant half-hour before his mandatory return kicked in.

"The curse is lifted...for now," he explained to Ai'go'r as he packed up his go bag. "I don't fully understand the mechanism by which it was cast, so I can't guarantee that it has been dispelled forever. I am quite certain that the master of the schola, Archmage Ballop'ril, will be keenly interested in your curse, which is in some way I do not comprehend connected with the strange goings-on over in Rebrugge. He and possibly I will most likely return soon."

"Thank you for your help, Mage. I hope I can get back to business now."

"I see no evidence of a curse in place at the moment. It is possible that something as simple as rearranging the shelves and bins will hinder its reinstatement. Again, without knowing the precise mechanism of casting I can't be sure of that. Farewell."

With that Prond took a step forward and disappeared.

Chapter the Twenty-Fourth

in which Prond receives more education than he can bear

As Prond had suspected, Ballop'ril was very interested in the Rebrugge Event and its relationship to Ai'go'r's curse. He quizzed his apprentice about it for hours, drilling him for every conceivable detail. He seemed particularly intrigued by the persistence of the 'feral' energy streams.

"I have seen references to this kind of behavior in ancient texts, but never any modern evidence of it. This is quite fascinating," the archmage said.

"What do you suppose is the underlying mechanism?" asked Prond.

"I cannot be certain at this point, but from your account and that of the Rebrugge mage it may well have been tied to a forking in the Dark Energetic Continuum. While such events are probably fairly common in The Slice as a whole, it is so unfathomably enormous that the odds of such a thing occurring in any given location must be beyond astronomically remote. Once in a lifetime doesn't even begin to describe it: more like once in the lifetime of a *civilization*."

"A forking of The Slice?"

"Yes. It grew a new appendage, essentially. Doing so subtly redistributes both mass and energy throughout the unimaginable expanse of The Slice itself."

"Just how large *is* The Slice?"

"No one really knows. Those who have transcended report that it traverses the very physical universe itself. If that is the case, there are no meaningful units with which to express its size. It may as well be infinite, for all it matters to our limited ability to comprehend such scales."

"How can an infinite object add to itself?" Prond surprised even himself with this query.

Ballop'ril beamed at him. "Excellent question. I don't know that forking actually adds to the volume of The Slice; it may well simply be a conformational adjustment, like a river changing course. What I do know is that it requires incredible energy to accomplish and the event has a profound effect on anything attached to The Slice at that location. We are actually fortunate that N'plork and the surrounding temperospatial fabric were not destroyed *in toto* as a byproduct."

Prond sat there in stunned silence for a moment, trying unsuccessfully not to think about this. Narrowly dodging planetary catastrophe always affected him that way. Ballop'ril seemed deep in thought; suddenly he brightened.

"This is the perfect topic for your disquisition!"

Prond stared at him, puzzled. "What 'disquisition' are you talking about, Master?"

"Yours, my apprentice. You aren't just training to be a magus. I would also like for you to attain the degree of *Doctor of Apotropaic Arts*. That will qualify you to teach at any universitas, in addition to opening your own schola. Finally, having a doctoral degree will greatly assist you when at last you come eligible for candidacy as an archmage.

Prond didn't know quite how to react to this. "Um, what else do I need to do for this doctoral degree?"

"There is also a rather substantial academic component, but you are fulfilling most of that as you advance up the mage hierarchy. There are DAA's who are not themselves mages and only do research into the magical arts, but I want to see you as a leader in both theory and practice. Remember the book that 'called to you' in my library? That text was written by one of the greatest of all scholar-mages. At that point I knew you were destined for that path."

Prond looked into space for a few moments, considering.

"All right, Master. If that is the path I am to follow, then I will tread it gladly, though I know not the way." He switched to the formal language of arcane discourse because he found it easier to express himself in that manner sometimes.

"The way will be illumined even as you traverse it," answered Ballop'ril, "For you are one of the rare ones who carry with them their own light—the flame of wisdom—and a hunger for learning I have not seen for many years. The first step in your path will be to study the Rebrugge Event in depth, until you become the world's leading expert on it. It will be your life for a while."

Prond shrugged. "As you command. To do so I will need to spend some time in Rebrugge itself."

"Agreed. Pack for an extended voyage. I authorize you to use an open-ended translocation spell for this. Please report back no less often than every two days. Take copious notes and think hard on every tidbit you uncover. Make no assumptions; take every finding for what it is. In this way you will see only what is really there to be seen."

"I will follow your teachings, Master."

"Above all else, do not pre-judge. There are motives and mechanisms at work in The Slice that we as mortal creatures cannot begin to comprehend. Take the facts for what they are and draw conclusions based on what you empirically know to be true, nothing else." Ballop'ril fished around in the pocket of his robe. "Here, you'll need this," he said, handing him a small metal object on a fine silver chain. Prond was too preoccupied with preparations to ask him what it was for, exactly.

Prond paused at the perimeter EE and CoME had established around the former grocer's warehouse, now a shimmering, wavering hemisphere of surreality. Ballop'ril had arranged for Prond to have complete access to the site; the only person granted that freedom. Everyone else was to keep a healthy distance, which was not a restriction that would need active enforcement, as the very air here was disorienting and disturbed all the senses at once. It took

252

Prond over an hour of meditation to discipline his mental resources sufficiently to venture into that whirling maw of unreason.

He began his study at the outside, intending to peel the layers back one by one. His first encounter was with the interface between the phenomenon and the 'normal' universe: a wavering, multicolored barrier that resembled the skin of a sapon bubble. Prond reached out and touched it, ever so gently. It offered no resistance, but his finger and hand seemed to siphon off some of the radiance and he felt euphoria at the contact. He withdrew his hand but the radiance came with it, clinging to him like fine gossamer.

He took detailed observations and recorded them all in the palm-sized weatherproof data journal magically linked to his mind so that it would record his thoughts when he phrased them properly to trigger the transfer. This saved time and ensured that the maximum data could be gathered even when hands were busy with other tasks.

Once Prond had gathered all the useful information he could about the outer shell, he took a deep breath and pushed his way gently into the wavering barrier. The euphoria hit him full force, but he closed his eyes and willed it not to affect his detachment. After a long minute he acclimated and the euphoria moderated into a gentle buzzing.

As he wormed his way further in, stopping every meter or so to take notes and reaffirm his bearings, Prond noticed that he could no longer see the surrounding structures of Rebrugge, although the swirling envelope had seemed translucent from the exterior. The entirety of here and now was defined by and encompassed within a sphere that seemed to travel with him, yet evolve as he moved nearer to what he reckoned to be the center of the swirling, pulsing energy sink.

Prond was finding it increasingly difficult to maintain any sense of direction or even basic plumb/level proprioception. It was as though gravity, momentum, and inertia had taken on random values that changed with no logical pattern. He could not tell where he stood with respect to the ground; he could walk around a full circle in a plane perpendicular to where he estimated gravity should be. It was so disturbing that he wondered if he were going insane. He began to panic: he wanted out desperately but had no idea which way out was. Logic told him that any direction he went should take him out of the hemisphere—it had only seemed to be around ten meters in diameter—yet he walked in as straight a line as he could manage for a full five minutes and made no visible progress whatever.

He stopped and collected his wits. *Take the facts for what they are and draw conclusions based on what you empirically know to be true*, Ballop'ril had warned him. Fine. What he empirically knew to be true was that he no longer occupied the same general coordinates in spacetime as his starting point. He also knew that wherever he was now, either the laws of motion and gravity were different here or his ability to perceive the order in them had been smashed against the rocks.

Speaking of rocks, something very much like a boulder loomed up from the swirling fabric of situational reality on his right and Prond sat upon it to take some notes. At least his data journal seemed to be functioning normally. He tried to describe his surroundings, but irritatingly any one particular aspect he looked at cycled through multiple physical characteristics so quickly that he couldn't find words to pin any of it down. He was trying to describe a rainbow to a creature born without eyes. Worse, the rainbow kept changing colors, many of them completely new to him.

If this was indeed The Slice, he could not comprehend why any archmage would choose to transcend and live here forever. It was all far too confusing. Suddenly, as he stared off into the impossible convolutions of space and time that constantly enveloped him and had done so since before his personal eternity began, Prond became aware of a shape that was static. This seemed so wrong that he couldn't wrap his brain around it at first.

The shape was in no hurry to define itself, but finally it moved in a manner that brought it closer to him (he hesitated to say 'it moved forward' because that was far too determinative) and resolved into a strange smooth-skinned biped that looked oddly familiar. As this was the first geometric manifestation Prond had encountered in a while that he could come up with terms to describe, he scribbled furiously; it stood there patiently, waiting for him to finish.

"I'm surprised you are still able to think clearly in this mess," the figure said to him, finally. While Prond heard the words and could define each of them, they were not conveying any meaning. He puzzled over this new concept: that an obviously grammatically correct statement in a language he spoke employing words he knew well from a voice he recognized as such could create no cognitive impression. They just sat there, lumps in his cerebral cortex, and refused to form any recognizable mental pictures. He shook his head at the apparition helplessly.

The unknown figure, or person, or whatever it was, took pity on Prond and led him gently away. The scenery was unchanged for a moment, but then, miraculously, collapsed back down to three recognizable spatial dimensions with at least nominally consistent physical laws governing them. Prond stood there blinking, trying to get to grips with objective normality, which now seemed grossly foreign and incomprehensible.

As manageable cognition seeped back in, Prond looked around and noticed that, while height, width, and depth seemed to have returned to their accustomed duties, the surroundings to which they applied were no longer at all sane. Soaring spires, floating bags with tendrils trailing from them;seemingly solid physical structures that flowed and bent with an otherwise undetectable wind...his day was just getting odder and odder. The figure, which had finished resolving itself, was quite definitely related to that transcendent mage who had helped them out in Pyfox's cavern and the Kopyrewt. At least, he had the same creepy smooth skin and slender build, although he seemed more substantial. Prond looked at him questioningly.

"Mage of the First Tier?" the figure said in response, "I would have expected someone a little more advanced to be investigating this, to be honest. Still, it is good experience for you. A question, then: do you know where you are?"

Prond turned in a complete circle, seeing nothing whatever during that circuit that he had ever seen before. He gave the only answer that made any sense to him. "The Slice?"

Oloi, for it was he, smiled approvingly. "Yes, indeed. Well done. Someone on the material plane punched a hole in The Slice. Not a wise thing to do; such ruptures usually end up taking a parsec or so of local spacetime with them. Why, exactly, *are* you here?"

Prond still wasn't feeling very polysyllabic. "Sent to take notes." He held up his data journal, "For DAA," he added by way of explication.

"Ah, academic degree. Very salutary. I will presume Ballop'ril is the master of your schola. Virtually no one else would send an MFT to investigate an n-dimensional rift."

Prond nodded in the affirmative.

"So," Oloi continued, "How are you meant to get back to N'plork?"

Prond gave him the most completely blank look in his repertoire.

"Oh, dear. Did Ballop'ril not give you an interdimensional translocation enchantment?"

Prond thought about this and suddenly remembered the necklace the archmage had handed him. He extracted it from his pocket.

"Ah, there it is," said Oloi, beaming, "Capital. You don't have to use it immediately, but I would not wait more than a half-day. The longer you are here, the more your body will adjust to The Slice. If you wait too long, you will not be able to return to Primus.

You have not yet the skill to transcend, so you will in effect starve to death, as there is nothing here to eat but manna, which you cannot digest in biological form."

Prond turned a little lighter shade of blue-green. "Thank you. Can you help me with 'why'?"

"I will do what I can for you. I first noticed what we call a 'deep ripple'—a disturbance in the dark energy fabric, with resonances, originating outside this plane—about what from your perspective would have been two hours or so before the 'puncture' took place. I was in this area quite by happenstance or I wouldn't have known about the rift until it was fully formed, at which point every sentient creature within this sector knew due to the dramatic effect it had on local geometry. The ripple was persistent and steadily increasing in amplitude; I knew that was going to lead to a traumatic event so I dampened it as well as I could, but the energy behind the disturbance was too great and it overcame my efforts after a while. When the rift occurred I was wise enough not to be here; it took quite a bit of the landscape down, including a couple of pinnacles I found rather attractive. Pity. Still, The Slice is over twelve billion light years long, not to mention self-healing, so it doesn't really make any difference in the grander scheme."

"So," Prond replied, having finally rediscovered the compound speech centers in his brain, "What exactly happened here? I mean, I understand that someone created a rift and that said rift required enormous energy, but who could do that and where did the energy come from?"

"Excellent questions, both. The energy apparently came from another part of The Slice itself, although the opposite or positive energetic component would have been necessary to effect a rip from Primus to here, rather than vice-versa. As to who, that one has me stumped. Even Ballop'ril would not be able to create a rift of this magnitude without having devoted the last ten or fifteen years exclusively to the project. I am forced to consider the possibility, however remote, that this may be a spontaneous conformational correction initiated by The Slice, itself."

"Ballop'ril called it a 'forking.'"

Oloi looked surprised. "Really? A forking? I suppose that's possible. That in itself is a form of adjustment, but generally forkings are associated with a pool of manna so dense that it collapses in on itself and The Slice has to provide an outlet for the resulting energy burst. For a manna pool of that density to form spontaneously is almost unheard of."

"There was a correlating event on N'plork," Prond said, "Whether it was connected or not, I don't know, but I was fulfilling a contract with our Arcanium to remove a curse. Rather than a curse on a particular person or place, every individual object—a grocer's produce, in this case—in the affected warehouse had its own unique and seemingly separate energy flow. No sooner would I shut off one than it regenerated along a slightly offset path. I finally had to lock each individual stream down with a separate stasis field, Took hours."

"Odd. Not a very traditional way to cast a curse. Why do you think it might be connected to the forking?"

"Because the owner of the warehouse that was destroyed on N'plork when the rift took place was the prime suspect for the curse's origin. He was upset about a failed business deal. Once the rift took place my stasis fields suddenly became stable and the maledictive energy streams dissipated."

"Was the suspect a mage?"

"Not as far as I know. He was just another grocer. A gnarlignome, my client said."

Oloi was about to reply but paused in mid-breath. "A *gnarlignome*?"

"Yes. He wanted to buy our client's business and did not take 'no' very well. Swore revenge for the 'insult.'"

"Did he, by any chance, mention *Arfsweener*?"

"Yes! That was the name I was told he swore by, in fact. Who, or what, is that?"

Oloi sighed. "Something of an involved story. I'll give you the extremely condensed version; please don't interrupt as you do not have much time left here." Prond nodded.

"The planet on which I was born is not embedded in The Slice. Consequently, magic does not exist there. I was once an interstellar explorer: I served aboard a starship that traveled between star systems using a wormhole generator to warp the fabric of spacetime so that such voyages could be made in reasonable time frames from crew perspective. A computing device on board kept track of how much time would have passed for people outside the wormhole envelope and we went 'back in time,' as it were, at the end of each voyage to render that perceived interval reasonable.

We didn't know about the dark energy continuum—The Slice—at first. It wasn't until we visited a planet embedded in it that had sentient life who were magic-literate that we discovered it for ourselves. Most of the crew were afraid of mages, as magic seemed to contradict the laws of physics as we knew them. I was fascinated by it: so fascinated, in fact, that I remained behind when the starship left that planet and studied under one of their archmages.

On that same planet was an archmage named Avzwenr who had, I must say, more talent for magic than anyone else I have met. He was as far advanced above the usual archmage as archmage is above mage-in-training. Unfortunately, his ego was equally well-developed; he began to think of himself as some form of divinity. I personally believe that his repeated voyages into The Slice damaged his brain, leading to a form of insanity. Whatever the cause, he began to conduct more and more bizarre experiments, eventually leading to the modification of his own life-form starting with an intelligent but sub-sentient primate found in the tropical jungles of that planet. He called the creature a *szpli-hzk*, which would translate into Goblish roughly as *short servant*. He made another one, a female, and managed to get them to breed. Eventually he had a whole colony of the things going. Worse, he had managed to instill them with enough intelligence to regard him as their creator, or deity.

I was an archmage myself by this point; the other archmages and I decided that Avzwenr had gone too far and was now a danger to both society and himself. We banded together and prepared a containment spell over a period of about a year, working around the clock in shifts. In secret we surrounded Avzwenr's compound and released the enchantment. It locked Avzwenr and his buildings in a temporal stasis that slowed time relative to the external environment, to the point that he would be effectively trapped inside for as long as the planet existed.

We did not understand just how far advanced in the magical arts Avzwenr had truly become, unfortunately. While he could not override our combined stasis field, he fed its energy back in upon itself in a closed loop until the enchantment become energetically unstable and tore a hole in The Slice similar to the rift you experienced. That rift dispersed the contents of the stasis field in random directions along the path of The Slice. At least one of the *szpli-hzk* ended up on N'plork, where it interbred with gnomes or possibly dwarves and was apparently able to produce fertile offspring. That population experienced reproductive isolation, probably because other gnomes regarded them as ugly and rather primitive, so eventually an entirely new inbred race developed who became known as *gnarlignomes* by one of several putative mechanisms. They had what you might term a 'genetic memory' of Avzwenr, which got corrupted to *Arfsweener*, now the chief god in the gnarlignome pantheon."

"Intriguing," said Prond after a few moments' contemplation. "But how is Arfsweener connected to the Rebrugge rift?"

"This is only a theory, but the initial rift Avzwenr caused when he set up the feedback loop seems to have spawned a very large number of sympathetic oscillations along the central energy conduit of The Slice, and those oscillations are somehow tied inextricably to Avzwenr. I strongly suspect that he intentionally used his own name as the invocation trigger, which would be entirely in keeping with his inflated sense of self-importance. Whenever anyone located on a planet embedded in The Slice uses that name, or a close approximation, in an invocative manner, there is a small but measureable chance that it will induce one of these oscillations. I believe that is what transpired here."

Prond shook his head. "I would never have figured that out, even if I worked on this problem for a thousand years. How do I write this up as a disquisition paper? Can I relate your theory— giving you credit for it, of course?"

"Yes. If you need more detail, I wrote a monograph on the subject that you can probably find in Ballop'ril's library. It's titled *Sympathetic Oscillations in Feedback-Induced Rifting*. I'm almost certain I gave Ballop'ril a copy. If not, he knows how to contact me. You need to be on your way. I can see subtle signs of acclimatization in your aura. Goodbye, and best of luck in your studies."

Prond smiled and waved farewell as he activated the translocation talisman. "Thank you, archmage!" he yelled as The Slice faded into the common room of the Arcanium.

Ballop'ril was there waiting for him. He examined Prond's aura and smiled warmly.

"You've been in The Slice! I'm guessing Oloi was involved. Did you learn anything?"

Prond sat down heavily in one of the overstuffed chairs. "More than my brain can comfortably hold."

Chapter the Twenty-Fifth

in which a titan nation is born, with attendant labor pains

The Elder Council meeting was set to begin in ten minutes. Tartag, as Odinial, was the officiator, but he relied on two Keepers of Order, known as the Hu and Mu, to help him run the meetings smoothly. This promised to be a pivotal assembly, because the principal item on the docket was whether to authorize issuance of the formal *Petition for Sovereign Status*. This would require a vote among the current residents of Hellehoell, the results of which must be eighty percent in favor of independence or greater for the Petition to be granted by the Tragacanthan Royal Government per His Majesty Tragacanth's directive.

While Tartag was confident the titans were fully capable of self-rule, he was worried that the more militant contingent, known as the *Xarkas*, would vote against the Petition merely because they wanted to gain independence by military means. He saw this as absurd, since the Tragacanthans were willing to grant them sovereign status within the framework of their own laws: peacefully and with no strings attached. No one would have to die, and there would be an immediate policy infrastructure in place for trade relations, not only with Tragacanth but its allies worldwide. He could not allow the Xarkas to hold sway, for the good of all titans.

The chief instigator of the Xarkas was a bitter old rock titan named Luglassa, whom everyone simply called "Lug." Lug had come to Hellehoell after a difficult and strife-filled life in a mountain village on the border of Lardonica and Ovinis. He trusted no one: even fellow titans were frequently under suspicion. His only means of interaction with other races had been violence; for that reason he was a walking mass of scars and deformations. He was in all likelihood also single-handedly responsible for at least some of the negative reputation of titans in folk legend. He had a score of old grudges to settle and he wanted to settle them by winning a decisive victory over the goblins of Tragacanth. Tartag and others had tried to convince him that they could never prevail in such a battle, but they made little progress against his closed mind.

Tartag called the meeting to order and scanned the council chambers. It was standing room only, with titans visible down the hallway as far as the eye could see and many, many more watching via closed-circuit viewscreens. This was an historic moment for all titans. Since the first call had gone out, over one hundred thousand titans had flocked to the massive underground complex, more than fifty percent of which was now restored and in use. Titan society had not been so cohesive and unified in two millennia. Well, unified except for the Xarkas.

The conclave seemed to be going well until the minor business was out of the way and the topic of the Petition came up for discussion.

"The next order of business before the Council is the Petition for Sovereignty. His Majesty Tragacanth has graciously offered us a writ of full Sovereignty over Hellehoell and its environs, as described by treaty, if by duly-enacted vote of at least eighty percent of titans present such sovereignty is sought. It is the duty of this Council first to accept or deny this proposal. Are there any Council members who wish to take the floor in discussion?"

None of the Elders spoke. Tartag turned to the assembled populace.

"Is there any discussion from the citizens of Hellehoell? Please register with Hu or Mu and wait to be called upon." The two titans circulated through the hall, taking names. The vast majority of the citizens who spoke expressed their support for self-rule, and their gratitude to Tartag for the instrumental part he had played in negotiating to this position. It looked as though the measure was going to pass without any significant opposition until the name Lug was called.

The old titan stood and walked to the front, flanked by four others.

"I just have a few questions," he said. "Where did we as a race lose our courage? When exactly did we give up our honor and dignity as titans to kowtow to a little goblin scrubhound with a crown on his ugly head? Why are the most powerful and feared sentients on this planet meekly submitting to the demands of a frankly inferior race? Hellehoell is destined to rule, not be 'allowed to exist.' We don't need treaties and parchments to rule ourselves! We are titans and we rule wherever we go. This city, this country, this continent, this world—is ours to take. Why aren't we taking it?"

His followers and a few scattered titans cheered. Everyone else looked to Tartag.

The Odinial surveyed the crowd coolly, collecting his thoughts.

"We have heard a great and stirring speech by an old titan who is yet not nearly old enough to remember the last time titans fought a war. I am not that old, either, but I do have benefit of the archives from that time. Let me read a few statistics from them for your edification.

The Battle for Molikar Valley, Titan Empire Year 234: 1,470 titans killed, about 4,800 wounded. The Battle of Uqilest, TEY 557: 320 titans killed, 570 wounded. The Illogrem Incident, TEY 631: 58 titans killed, 130 wounded. The Siege of Tiwassa, Titan Republic Years 39-41: Approximately 12,000 titans killed, at least 34,000 wounded. Shall I continue?"

The assembled crowd was somber, except for the Xarkas. "Bah. You left out how many of the enemy *we* killed!"

"It does not matter!" Tartag shouted, banging his huge fist on the Council table. "What matters is that *titans died*! Mothers and fathers and sons and daughters *died*! There is no conceivable justification for dead titans except in the defense of home and family, and neither is threatened here! We can choose peace and life, or war and death. If you choose death, you are not sane. Do you hear me?

Choosing death when life and self-rule are freely offered is *insane*. As Odinial I will offer you this choice: live with us in harmony and peace, or leave Hellehoell and make war on whomever you choose—but you will do so on your own. This government will not support you in any way. Is that clear?"

"So says the coward you have chosen to lead you," spit back Lug, "A coward leading cowards. Come, little woolbeasts, follow me to safety in the goblin pens, where we can wait peacefully to be sheared and stewed."

People were shaking their heads in disagreement as the crowd was turning actively against him. Lug surveyed the room in disgust.

"So be it! We are too few to stand in the way of your placation of the goblins. But hear this: you will *all* be sorry at some point that you did not listen to the last remaining voice of titan glory and majesty. From here on out it will be titan servitude and conciliation. The very thought makes me ill." Lug made as though to spit on the Council chamber floor.

"I won't argue that you are not ill, Lug," replied Tartag before turning back to the assembled throng. "Titans! The time for speeches is past. Now is the time for decisions. All in favor of Hellehoell becoming a sovereign nation, vote aye. Those opposed, vote nay. Hu, Mu, and I will gather the ballots."

After the ballots were counted, ninety-six percent voted for sovereignty. Once the vote was validated and witnessed, the results were attached to the Petition for Sovereign Status and sent by diplomatic courier to Goblinopolis. Now, they just had to wait for His Majesty's government to act.

Meanwhile, however, Tartag had the pleasant duty of planning the celebration of the re-founding of Hellehoell. He'd had the historians working day and night to locate and bring back to operating status all of the ancient archives, so that they might get some solid feeling for how such things were celebrated in the original Hellehoell. A celebration of the new with some flavor of the old, that's what he was shooting for. The Xarkas were sulking, which Tartag regarded as something of a blessing: at least they were off his back for the time being.

Aspet opened the diplomatic pouch and smiled as he read the Petition. He called Boogla in. "Looks like the titans have decided to rule themselves. I heartily approve."

"There are elements within the government and your people at large who believe the tax revenue from Hellehoell would be a tremendous asset in the rebuilding of Fenurian and Dresmak, you know. Not everyone feels as you do about titan independence."

Aspet lost the smile. "I'm aware of that, but ninety-six percent of the titans—that's over ninety-six *thousand* of them, by our intelligence service's estimate—voted for sovereign status. Imagine nearly a hundred thousand disgruntled titans, entrenched in a massive underground complex. Do you really think we could collect taxes from them if they decided not to pay? You know how much it costs to mobilize even a single regiment. It would take our entire military, with reserves, to make any significant inroads into a fortification of that nature. The tax revenue we could extract from a conquered Hellehoell would be insignificant compared with the expense of that campaign, both in terms of expenditure and loss of life on both sides. Dead people do not pay taxes, nor do they collect them. On the other hand, Hellehoell as an ally and trading partner will be extremely lucrative. They have a lot of resources we could really make use of."

"I know and agree, love, but it was my duty to make that point."

"Understood and appreciated. I've already made a detailed report to CoME and I have their full support on this. Even old Kryptoq agrees."

"So, when will the ceremony take place?"

"I'll want the full cabinet to review and ratify the Petition; then we'll have to draw up the formal Declaration of Relinquishment, including a detailed survey of precisely what I'll be ceding to the titans. Maybe two weeks, give or take a day or two."

"How about Suns' Peak? That would be a memorable day for their independence festival."

"Great idea. I think we can be ready by then."

The survey team had a formidable task facing them. In order to determine the extent of the surface lands that would become part of Hellehoell, they first had to determine the precise boundaries of the subsurface areas. Aspet did not want a situation where the visible land belonged to Tragacanth but the caves underneath were titan. "If you can drill straight down and hit Hellehoell," he'd told the lead engineer of the survey party, "That land needs to go to the titans."

There were, mercifully, only a handful of Tragacanthan land owners who had to be placated; most of the land was rocky and uninhabited. It took a full week to complete the survey; the results showed just how big Hellehoell was underground. The surface area, including Daludobris, was just under ten thousand hectares. Given that there were effectively several layers to the cavern complex, that gave Hellehoell itself a habitable area of at least twice that.

Aspet, through his Minister for Territorial Affairs, offered the affected land owners the full market value for their land, as well as equivalent land holdings anywhere else in Tragacanth where Royal Lands were available. Most of them were quite happy with the generous deal, although a couple resisted because they had been on their current land for generations and did not want to leave. Aspet offered to negotiate on their behalf with the Hellehoell government to see if they might be able to remain as resident alien tenants of the new titan city-state.

As it turned out, the Elder Council was not particularly interested in the fate of the surface lands and had no issues with Tragacanthans living there, with the stipulation that no well drilling could take place and all subsurface rights conveyed to the titans. All water would need to be brought in via pipes and aqueducts. Since that was the way they were getting their water now—there being a titan city below them, not a reachable water table—this restriction presented no conflicts.

The only official way in and out of Hellehoell was Daludobris. The titans had their own private entrances, of course, but these were closely-held secrets and emerged on the surface in areas of tightly restricted access. Any non-titan caught using one without a titan escort would be prosecuted for trespassing. This was the way the titans controlled their borders and it worked quite effectively.

The Daludobris of old was mostly rebuilt by this point, and it was truly one of the wonders of Esmia. A broad avenue paved with colorful shellstone and flanked by intricate sculptures was carved into the bedrock; it sloped gradually down to a magnificent stone and iron archway framing massive doors that were so cunningly wrought and perfectly balanced that when unlocked they could easily be opened by a gnome child. When locked and bolted, however, the ten meter-thick iron, steel, and wood barriers could withstand even extended artillery barrages. If the titans wanted to keep you out, you weren't getting in: at least not through the front door.

Aspet announced that the Ceremony of Transfer of Sovereignty would take place at mid-day on Suns' Peak, the point in the orbital cycle where both suns rose highest in the sky at the same time. The site chosen was Daludobris itself, with the ceremonial dais being constructed right in front of the massive doors. Grandstands lined the boulevard for several hundred meters, with room for at least fifty thousand live viewers and countless others via cameras pointed down at the dais from overhead.

Aspet arrived via Royal limousine, surrounded by RPC agents who were joined by a contingent of titan honor guards, resplendent in violet, deep green, and silver. Tartag was there as Odinial, along with the rest of the Elder Council. Tragacanth was represented by King Aspet, Plenipotentiaries Boogla, Goameel Jigha, and Eqbo Dehsz, the Minister for International Relations; rounding out the Tragacanthan contingent was the High Arbiter of Edicts, the Honorable Colmnat Fespri, and Norda Magineer Imberol.

The ceremony took exactly one hour, at the conclusion of which Aspet handed to Tartag a beautifully-framed Declaration of Relinquishment of all claim to the lands described in the accompanying survey, granting them fully and in perpetuity to the government of Hellehoell. Following this, Dehsz presented the titans with Tragacanth's official Diplomatic Writ of Recognition, establishing the Kingdom of Tragacanth as the first nation formally to recognize the new City-State of Hellehoell, and a formal *Plea for Establishment of Diplomatic Relations and Exchange of Ambassadors*.

Aspet's final speech was a notice to all citizens of Tragacanth that from this moment forward, the edicts and tariffs legislated by the government of Hellehoell would be the only ones to which any were subject while on titan soil, regardless of citizenship: Tragacanthan edicts no longer applied here. With that he shook hands warmly with Tartag, wishing him and his new City-State good fortune in the coming years, and departed, followed by the rest of the Tragacanthans present.

Tartag remained on the dais until everyone else had left; it was a tradition amongst titans that a host saw the last guest depart before he himself could retire. He stared at the elegantly-lettered and illuminated documents of sovereignty and felt himself on the verge of weeping. This was a day he had never dared dream would come, at least during his lifetime. Today he stood, not only in Hellehoell, but in a Hellehoell that had regained the right to determine its own destiny. As the first Odinial for this renewed nation, he felt an enormous responsibility to chart the right course, one that set Hellehoell on a tricky path to prosperity and security while embedded, landlocked, within another country.

Scant days passed before diplomatic notices of recognition came flooding in from nations all over the globe. The restored empty quarters along what the titans had designated as 'embassy row' began to be assigned, one by one, to ambassadors and their staffs from the nations that had formally recognized Hellehoell and sued for diplomatic relations.

The Xarkas were lying low for now, but Tartag caught the occasional rumor of their activities and knew that sooner or later they would have to be dealt with in a decisive manner. While spying of any sort was frowned upon in titan society, he had asked the constabulary to keep track of citizen reports concerning any sort of rabble-rousing the Xarkas might be engaged in. He at least had to be prepared to respond appropriately.

Meanwhile, the business of running a fledgling government was promising to occupy all of his waking hours. Busy though he was, he made time on occasion simply to wander the streets and avenues, marveling at that which was Hellehoell. He could do so without bodyguards; no titan would dream of assaulting their leader or indeed anyone at all without strong justification. Here his people felt well and truly at home for the first time, as a race, in millennia. Here the art, culture, engineering, and mores of the titan race could be integrated into a cohesive society once again. Titans would emerge from the fear and distrust born of their long isolation and take their place as integral players on the world stage once again.

Now they just had to figure out how to *feed* all these titans.

Chapter the Twenty-Sixth

in which Tol takes to the sky to combat a pretentious criminal

"So," Tol said to Selpla over the intimate dinner they were sharing at a fancy restaurant in upscale Tropsalla, "I did some checking into this Lizgug character."

"Lizgug?" Selpla replied, munching on some aged Rockrunner cheese.

"Yeah, you know, that fugitive I apprehended on the cruise ship."

"Oh. The one they kept locked in the brig for nearly the entire voyage? I would've asked for a refund, if I were him."

"Hah. I'd be very surprised if he didn't figure some way to wrangle the passage for free to begin with: he used fake ID papers, at least. Anyway, turns out Lizgug has a connection, albeit distant, to our old pal Pyfox."

"One of his henches, or something?"

"Not a hench, but an associate. Before Pyfox got jacked into that crazy controlling magic scheme with Namni, he ran a pretty successful protection racket with franchises, if you want to call them that, in nearly every small town and village in Tragacanth. He also had a few overseas, particularly in Hividz, Grosyem, and Nerr. Lizgug was apparently the regional manager for those offshore operations, with headquarters in Evcolla. When local EE finally started to crack down, he beat it and ended up in Tragacanth, running some kinda operation between Lumbos and Erolossma. He was important enough to trigger that botched rescue mission, anyway."

"Funny how things connect to one another," Selpla nodded.

"That's not all there is to it. Lizgug tried to sabotage that guy with the flying bladder things—Dagyo, the one who is supposed to

271

be demonstrating an EE version here next week. I figured he was just a lowlife looking to spoil somebody's day, but I think the stink goes a lot deeper than that. He was related to this hob in Hividz who invented a contraption that glides from one place to another, using updrafts to increase the distance. Apparently he sunk some serious money into the outfit formed to commercialize the idea."

"I thought that guy got himself killed."

"He did, but the company kept on going, trying to learn from his mistakes to make better gliders."

"What sort of commercial application did they see for gliding?"

"Not sure, but I think it had to do with rapid deliveries and dropping leaflets or something from overhead. Whatever it was, Lizgug seems to have decided that Dagyo's floating bladder machine was a threat to the gliding business and wanted to make certain it was not a success. I started reading international EE reports on 'accidents' Dagyo had experienced, and most of them were pretty obviously the result of sabotage. Somebody definitely has it in for him." He fished around in his pocket for a photo. "Here's the jlok's mug shot."

Selpla glanced at it and noticed a small tattoo on Lizgug's supraorbital ridge of two crossed harpoon heads. She chewed her artisan frosja-seed bread thoughtfully.

"Years ago I wrote a piece about a quasi-governmental group that called itself the 'Grand Maritime Duchy of Litriosc.' That entity actually existed a millennium or so ago, when Litria was still a dependency of Rublosq. There is a small but persistent movement centered in Hividz to reunite Hividz, Frespiola, Grosyem, and Spleroste into a single nation, with the capitol located where the ancient one was, in Terimpu. The activists call themselves 'The Grand Duke's Mariners' and their symbol is two crossed harpoon heads, just like the ones in that tat."

"Funny you should mention that," Tol said, "There are two other guys in custody right now with that same tat. If they're all part of some nutso movement, that might explain a few things. At first glance their crimes don't seem connected, but when you look at them in the context of promoting some political cause, they start to make more sense."

"How so?"

"Lizgug was trying to eliminate competition for the glider, which was invented in Hividz by one of his own kin. Tliko, another of the perps, was running weapons for a quasi-military outfit on Frespiola. A kobold named Aglod was caught with a large quantity of counterfeit currency in the port of Vokkale on Spleroste. He was evidently trying to smuggle it into the country. It referenced a Grand Duchy on the bills, which otherwise resembled Hividz jokoms."

"So, a conspiracy. Their goal is to turn all of Litria back into one feudal Duchy? What could possibly motivate someone to do such a thing?"

"These guys speak a common language: greed. Whoever is running the show promised them a lot of moolah. Probably some power, too, but money and power are closely connected most of the time. I guess I oughta do something about this thing before it gets any worse, huh?"

"I don't know. Is it really your problem? I mean, none of this has much to do with Tragacanth, as far as I can tell."

"Lizgug has committed several serious crimes here, actually. If I see a possible connection to international criminal activities, that gives me a responsibility to follow up. I think I'll contact EE in Hividz and find out more about this 'Grand Maritime Duchy' thing."

Edict Enforcement, in Hividz known as the *Evcolla Squadron*, had extensive dossiers on all suspected members of GMD. "They started out about twenty years ago as a sort of 'living history' group, re-creating some aspects of that time," the Deputy Director of Evcolla Squadron, Chief Inspector Prujhish, told Tol over comm. "None of the original members are still involved, though. Some local thugs took over for a while and used it to cover a variety of petty crimes, but then one of them started reading up on the historical basis for the group and conceived the idea of bringing the Grand Duchy back in reality. We think he saw how incredibly wealthy the ruling elite can get in a feudal system like that and decided that was the life for him. Since then they've been mostly into high seas piracy, smuggling, smash-and-grabs on warehouses where easily transportable expensive goods are stored, counterfeiting, and buying off local politicians to pass edicts that favor their little wealth-generating intrigues."

Tol nodded. "So, what kind of threat do they really present?"

"In terms of overthrowing the collective governments of Litria? Not much. There is very little public support for their cause. While no one alive remembers any aspect of the feudal days, the average intelligence is high enough here that most folks understand they would be considerably worse off under such a system. I don't know if the GMD jokers even understand that the Grand Duchy itself was part of Rublosq and subject to the rule of their Potentate."

"I doubt it matters to them. If the rest of 'em are anything like Lizgug, they only care about how much money they could intimidate or scam out of their 'subjects.'He's a real piece o' work."

"Yes, Lizgug is one the top lieutenants to the ringleader, a half-ogre who calls himself 'Sir Jexx.'"

"*Sir* Jexx, eh? Maybe I oughta come and meet him, seein' as how he's a fellow knight and all."

Prujhish laughed. "I don't think he would receive you in the manner to which you are accustomed."

Tol laughed in turn. "So far most of my receptions have been a little lacking in the social grace department. His would probably fit right in. You tracking his whereabouts?"

"Yeah, we keep pretty close tabs on him. You're welcome to visit; maybe it'll shake him up so he makes a slip and we can nab him on something. He's been very careful about farming out all the dirty stuff so he stays out of trouble. You need entry papers?"

"I think we have a mutual aid treaty with every Litrian nation but Grosyem. So long as that's not where he is, I can get in and out on my EE creds."

"He's in Frespiola right now. Yiks Island. He has a nice compound up there, on the east side of the island, right north of Moonfish Bay. Lots of cameras and guards, though."

"That's not an issue. I'll just walk right up to the front gate. Jlok like that—calls himself 'Sir'—won't be able to resist meeting a 'fellow knight.' I know his kind: poser with a big ego and small morals."

"That sums up Jexx pretty succinctly. Let us know when you're in place and we'll provide whatever backup we can. The resident office on Yiks has been beefed up since Jexx built that compound. They routinely ship people back and forth on a Squad ferry, so he won't notice if a few extra hands get sent over. The EE forces of all four nations of Litria have limited jurisdiction across the entire area, with the agreement that apprehended perps are handed over to the locals. Also, I heard that the Frespiolans have an operative on the inside. I don't have any further details, for obvious reasons."

"Good to know; thanks. I'll take off as soon as I get the paperwork done."

"Yiks Island?" Selpla said, "There are a couple of fabulous resorts there. One of them was designed by my dad. I haven't been there since I was a teen. I want to go with you."

Tol sighed. "I'm going after a major criminal, as usual. If you're there I'll just worry about you."

"Don't be silly. I'll be in a thousand billme per night suite in the Sellestra Placidum resort. You know: the one I'm named for. They've got better security than most embassies. I'll be perfectly safe."

"Where you're staying wouldn't be an issue if you'd actually *stay* there. You tend to venture out and get caught up in... situations, however."

"I will only venture out as far as the beach. We need a good fresh 'exotic vacation ideas' piece for the Lifestyle desk, anyway. I won't need to go anywhere but the beach bar and maybe the resort club for that."

"Fine. It wouldn't do me any good to tell you not to come, anyway."

"No. No, it wouldn't," she giggled.

The continent of Litria occupies approximately the middle third of the Sea of Fleriz, roughly four thousand kilometers east of the Gulf of Honkmin and the tip of The Effluent in Tragacanth; slightly further than that west of Hagfar out on the end of Trobwed's Spit in Rublosq. It is comprised of four island nations, from north to south and in decreasing order of land mass, Spleroste, Frespiola, Hividz, and Grosyem. From Zilond on the northern end of Spleroste to Noclet on the south coast of Grosyem is right at one thousand kilometers.

Yiks Island, off the southeast coast of mainland Frespiola, is about eighty kilometers from end to end. It has some of the most pristine beaches and pricey real estate on the planet; a variety of celebrities and other people of immense wealth call it home at least part of the year. The weather is moderated by two major ocean currents and the area is spared the brunt of most tropical cyclones due to its particular location. These cyclonic systems almost always come from the south or southwest out of the Ustrad Sea, losing most of their punch as they pass over the mountains of northern Hividz.

Selpla's father Erminian had designed Sellestra Placidum over thirty years earlier for a group of investors who already owned a half-dozen leisure properties internationally. Since that time it had climbed its way up the charts for critical acclaim and now was rated as one of the top ten resort properties on N'plork. It was stunning to behold. Beautiful veinstone staircases swirled away from a broad central approach laboriously paved with individual seashells set in tiny concretion blocks. Lush tropical vegetation, much of it brought in from halfway around the world, outlined, punctuated, and occasionally obscured the dozens of elaborate columns, statues,

276

and monoliths scattered like early morning dewdrops throughout the grounds. A collection of enormous reflecting pools in various shapes rounded out the sumptuous landscaping.

The resort consisted of an even dozen buildings, the central being the largest, for a total of just over a thousand suites. There were six pools, a variety of sports arenas, and an extravagantly appointed full twenty-hole whackball course: one of the most prestigious on the IPWA tour. One could, whilst strolling the private beach or trolling the numerous bars, meet and mingle with a cross-section of N'plork's powerful and elite.

Selpla made herself comfortable at a corner table on the veranda of the main building that commanded a fine view of both the beach and the lobby. She sat there sipping a ridiculously fragrant and complex herbal infusion that cost more than a decent lunch in Goblinopolis and took notes as the beautiful people came and went. By virtue of her father's influence she had a suite in the most prestigious wing of the resort that included fresh-cut exotic flowers twice a day, a gift basket worth more than Tol's monthly apartment rent, and a panorama that was positively breathtaking, even for someone accustomed to breathtaking panoramas. Life here was good.

Tol was staying with her, of course. While being a Knight of the Crimson did not carry quite the cachet here that it did in Tragacanth, the hotel still showed the respect due a member of the 'earned nobility,' as such offices were known. The fact that he was a special investigator for Tragacanthan EE also carried some weight. By far the most important fact from the hotel's point of view, however, was that he was a member of the Tragacanthan Royal Family. That brought him preferential treatment which ranked with the most famous celebrities, because hosting Royalty meant bragging rights, which in turn translated into prestige and thus, profit. The Sellestra Placidum could now legally boast that they were "The Choice of Royalty."

Tol was finally adjusting to the reaction to his status. He still wasn't comfortable with it, but he had decided to enjoy the results since he hadn't a lot of control over them. The hotel had vast experience with celebrities of all temperaments, of course; they judged Tol's embarrassment correctly almost immediately and provided him with luxury without the ostentation: in the background, as it were. These were true professionals in the realm of hospitality.

When Dagyo had contacted Tol regarding the upcoming demonstration of the proposed EE version of his Zifjagga, he was overjoyed to learn that Tol would be traveling to Yiks Island. That was *much* closer to his workshop in Tantatku than was Tragacanth. Why didn't he meet Tol there to conduct the demo? Tol shrugged and replied that this was fine with him.

The morning of the demonstration dawned clear, with light winds from the west-northwest: excellent weather for flying. Dagyo had worked very hard on this new model, which he hoped to sell to EE and possibly even to militaries worldwide. It was slightly smaller overall than his previous version, but actually held more aerite gas for additional buoyancy and sported two significantly better engines: more efficient spinners, better intakes, increased range. He had also improved the control surfaces and their linkages back to the command car.

There was room for two goblins in the command car and a third in a cage suspended below the car that was obviously intended for prisoner transport. The lockup cage was designed to be raised and lowered with a winch attached to the rear of the command car so that a prisoner could be deposited or picked up while the Zifjagga hovered above.

Dagyo had arranged to meet Tol and Selpla at the docks on Moonfish Bay. He arrived in a ship he had designed and built himself, the *Zifswalla*, with an integral mooring mast for the Zifjagga, which he had christened the *Sir Tol* in Tol's honor, hoping that would make points for him in closing the sale. The Zifjagga was only a little smaller than the ship itself; the three of them (the *Sir Tol*, the *Zifswalla*, and the ebullient gnome) made for rather an entertaining spectacle as they approached the dock, drawing a sizeable crowd.

Tol hadn't visualized the demo being quite so public, but there wasn't much that could be done about it now. He and Selpla went up the ramp and the gnome immediately launched into a technical discussion of the features of the new craft. Tol did his best to keep up, hoping that Petey was taking notes for him. After the tour and lecture were over, Dagyo jumped into the pilot's seat and indicated for Tol to join him. He was a little hesitant, but finally Tol shrugged and climbed in. The door was shut and latched, and as Selpla watched and took pictures with her little travel camera, the *Sir Tol* slipped off the mooring mast and floated gracefully away.

The *Sir Tol* was a dirigible: a gas bag suspended in a lightweight rigid framework. The engines ran all the time at idle, but the spinners were operated with a clutch and turned only when the craft needed to change direction or propel itself into the wind, which saved on fuel. Dagyo ran through the basics of piloting the vehicle, before then allowing Tol take a turn at the wheel and pedals. Tol was nervous at first, but after a few minutes he was almost laughing out loud at how intoxicating it was to fly with the avians.

Dagyo also demonstrated lowering and raising the 'holding cage,' including the locking mechanism that could only be operated from the command car. Selpla volunteered to be the 'prisoner,' bravely riding in the little cage from the deck of the *Zifswalla* up forty meters into the air and back down again. It was the most exhilarating fun she'd had in years.

Dagyo brought the *Sir Tol* down and dropped the mooring ball into the receptacle on the ship's mast. Then he had Tol lift them off again and repeat the mooring procedure himself.

"There," said the gnome to Tol as they were disembarking, "You are now the second most-experienced Zifjagga pilot in the world. And the *only* one with a Zifjagga named after him."

Tol stroked the side of the craft as though it were a pet. He didn't really want the ride to be over, but he had a job to do and all that. He thanked Dagyo profusely and promised to give his very strongest recommendation to the EE High Commissioner...and anyone else who would listen. He also asked Dagyo in confidence if he was looking for investors. He was, so Tol gave him a bank draft for twenty thousand billmes for a stake in the new company: *AeroPram Concepts*. Dagyo was elated at having attracted his first investor, promising frequent updates and constant improvements.

Tol and Selpla returned to the Sellestra Placidum and Tol spent the remainder of the day in the suite, writing up his recommendation for a trial purchase of Zifjaggas, making it clear for conflict of interest purposes that he was also an investor in the company as a result of the success of Dagyo's demonstration. He relaxed afterward in the heated pool, accessible directly from the suite via a private channel that could be locked from the inside via a set of remotely-operated doors when not in use. It was decidedly decadent and Tol decidedly loved it.

Elegant living notwithstanding, Tol was here for a rather risky mission: to take on a venomous asp in his own den. After checking in with Frespiolan EE via an encrypted comm link, Tol set out in a rented limousine(for appearance's sake) for the estate known to the locals as Moonfish Manor. Tol had been reading up on Jexx and his delusions of grandeur and had decided to play along with him. Toward that end, he had brought some of the ceremonial trappings of his own knighthood.

As the limo pulled up, Tol pinned the lapel version of his Medal of Royal Merit on a simple but elegant deep blue pullover with the Crimson Garter woven into it: the 'business casual' attire of the Knights. He walked up to the intercom at the estate's ornate front gate and pushed the button.

"Sir Tol-u-ol of Sebacea, Knight Protector of the Crimson Order of Tragacanth, to see Sir Jexx," he said into the microphone, using his most cultured voice. There was a stunned silence while every camera in that part of the estate swung onto Tol and zoomed in. After a few moments a deep male voice replied.

"Sir Jexx is currently receiving visitors in the lower solarium. He will send an escort for you, Sir Knight."

So far, so good.

Tol had brought no weapons with him, knowing that any criminal who'd made it as far as Jexx would have multiple scanners. He didn't really need any external weapons, anyway. There were very few situations where he couldn't either take the bad guys out with his fists or wrestle a disruptor away from one of them if he really needed it. He did have Petey, but even the most paranoid crime boss wasn't likely to take notice of a pen. He had briefed Petey on where they were going and what to expect, so it was jamming any attempt to scan its circuitry. It appeared as a simple writing instrument; nothing more.

A half-ogre goon in a pinstriped jack met Tol at the gate. Given the temperature and humidity, Tol guessed he hadn't been wearing that getup all day. The goon was sweating visibly and did not look at all comfortable in those clothes. Tol laughed at him inside but was careful to maintain his external air of noblesse. The hike from the front gate to the solarium was long and warm; by the time they arrived the goon was obviously broiling. When Jexx motioned his dismissal the half-ogre almost broke into a trot heading for cooler apparel.

"Welcome to my humble abode, Sir Tol-u-ol. I must admit to being taken by surprise by your social call, although none the less appreciative for the short notice."

"Please, call me Tol. I was in the area, and I've heard so much about you that I thought it downright rude of me not to take the opportunity to pay you a visit. It is, after all, only proper that the chivalry maintain social contacts with one another."

"Um, yes. Quite so. May I offer you some razzle? I have a well-stocked bar."

"Thank you for the offer, but for the nonce I must refuse. Physic's orders, I'm afraid."

As he spoke, Tol was sizing up the room. Glass doors: double-paned but not particularly well made. Two entrances and a bookcase along one wall that might hide another. Three cameras and at least two wall decorations that would be ideal for concealing machicolations with snipers behind them. If he needed to take Jexx out, it could not be in here.

"I see," replied Jexx, "Well, one can't go around defying the orders of one's physic, can one? Tell me, Sir Tol, what brings you to our idyllic paradise?"

"Vacation, Sir Jexx. Rest and recreation. I've heard about your wonderful island all my life; I figured I'd better come see it while I'm still able to get around. Not gettin' any younger; you know how it is."

"Ah, yes. I built this estate with the same thought in mind. I've been enamored of the sea since my youth."

"You're a sailor, then?"

"Yes, indeed. I own five sailing vessels of different sizes and configurations. I very much enjoy captaining them when I can find the time."

The solution to Tol's takedown location dilemma leapt out and danced a little hornpipe.

"I imagine time would be in short supply for a business executive such as yourself. I've done a bit of sailing, but not nearly as much as I'd like. Sadly, I live rather far from the sea, so I own no sailing vessels of my own."

So close...

Jexx cleared his throat. "While I have quite a busy schedule, I believe that for a fellow Knight I could squeeze in a short cruise at sea, if you're game."

Target acquired.

"I could scarcely pass up such a generous and noble invitation. I would be honored."

"I will have one of my staff prepare the ship. Today we shall be sailing aboard the trabaccalo *Dez Klag*, which I helped to rebuild after it suffered considerable damage in an unfortunate collision. She is a fine two-master with a large rudder and excellent draw."

"I look forward to sailing upon her."

They walked down to the docks. Tol paid very close attention to the number, position, and gait of Jexx's bodyguards. He saw four, including the one in the shack at the foot of the pier. Of the three accompanying Jexx, two he discounted offhand as overconfident bullies. The third, a goblin, might be dangerous. He had a very fluid walk and his eyes never stopped moving. The only one with any real training, Tol guessed. He also looked vaguely familiar, but that wasn't too surprising, even here on the other side of the world from Tragacanth: Tol had seen many thousands of mug shots in his day from just about every nation on N'plork. His mug could well be among them.

Once at sea, Tol had to admit that Jexx knew how to handle a boat. He was obviously showing off, but it had the desired effect; Tol was impressed. Somewhere into the voyage Jexx seemed to have made his mind up about something and they abruptly changed course. After a few minutes Tol could tell that they were making for a tiny island in the bay; nothing more than the tip of an ancient volcano ringed with lush vegetation.

"This is my private island up ahead," Jexx explained, "On the nautical charts it's called *Volcano Island*, but that's woefully prosaic for such a beautiful locale, so I've renamed it *Vershulpa*, which is ogrish for 'Green Cone:' a more appropriate moniker, I believe you'll agree." Tol stared at the verdant little bump on the ocean ahead. It was a green cone, all right.

"Works for me."

They docked on the south side of the small blot of land, at a pier that miraculously rose out of the water as the *Dez Klag* approached. "I had this pneumatic lift installed because I don't want to encourage boaters to tie off here."

"I would think the huge 'Private Property: Keep Off If You Want to Live!' signs would probably take care of that," Tol replied.

"They do help, but one can't be too careful where the riffraff are concerned," said Jexx.

"You have a lot of riffraff who own boats around here, then?"

"You'd be surprised. Even though we're ten kilometers from Yiks and almost into the shipping lanes, the number of people who pile into their little knockabouts and end up way out here is considerable. I've even had to chase off a couple of jloks in a jon boat."

"How did a jon boat get all the way out here? Was there a storm involved?"

"I believe they were carried here on a wave of cheap razzle," Jexx replied with a touch of sarcasm.

"Ah. You don't approve of razzle, I take it?"

"On the contrary. I have a sizeable cellar full of it, in various vintages and recipes, as you saw. I simply don't approve of its use by people who should be concentrating on piloting their vehicle, no matter what it is."

"I can certainly get behind that philosophy."

"Let me lead you on a tour now," said Jexx, "Of this most picturesque little island."

"No offense, but you've seen one tangled tropical jungle, you've pretty much seen them all," Tol sniffed.

"Perhaps, but I think you'll find this one to have certain... attributes not common to other similar locations."

Tol shrugged. "Lead on, then."

They followed a well-maintained path to the base of the volcanic cone and then wound their way up a gentle spiral ramp cut into the basalt, pausing every so often to take in the ever-changing panorama of the dense jungle canopy framing the deep greens, blues, and whites of the ocean beyond. At the top there was, unexpectedly to Tol, no actual indentation but instead a knob of rock and vegetation.

"What happened to the crater? I thought volcanoes always had craters."

"There is a crater," Jexx replied, "But I hid it under this roof covered with stone and jungle. It forms a little workshop, hidden from curious eyes."

"Whose eyes? Sea avians?"

"I believe what I'm about to show you will answer that question, as well as provide motivation for the camouflage." He pulled a lever concealed by a hollow tree and the entire cap folded and slid to one side, revealing a crater about forty meters in diameter. In the center stood a strange concretion of wood, wires, and fabric that looked like some great avian with its wings held out parallel to the ground. It was perched on a pair of iron rails that began at one wall of the crater and terminated abruptly at the other side.

Jexx walked over to a pedestal set near the wall and pressed a button on it. The wall at which the rails ended dropped into the floor revealing a sheer cliff below it. "This," Jexx announced with a little flourish, "Is my newest and most intriguing project: a flying machine."

Tol decided to play dumb. "What do you mean, a 'flying machine?' A machine that actually flies?"

"Precisely. Not only does the machine itself fly, it does so with me in it. It glides for quite a long distance and can ride on columns of air that rise up from the surface of the land or water."

"That," Tol said in feigned disbelief, "Is amazing."

"Isn't it? While I did not develop this astounding apparatus myself, I did provide considerable funding for it. I am the only person in the world, other than the creator—sadly now deceased—who owns a flying machine."

"Really?" Tol said, suppressing a laugh, "Simply incredible."

He decided it was time to take the conversation another, more productive direction.

"I'm interested in your knighthood, Sir Jexx. To what Order do you belong?"

This question caught the half-ogre totally off guard. "Oh, um," he stammered, "It is the, um, Order of the Grand Maritime."

Tol raised his eyebrow ridges. "As in, Grand Maritime Duchy? I thought they were a role-playing group or something."

He could see Jexx beginning to bristle and his bodyguards ratchet up the alert level. He also thought he detected a slightly incongruous response from the goblin: less hostility than simple increased attention.

"Are you questioning the legitimacy of my claim to knighthood?" Jexx asked, adopting a belligerent stance.

"Sounds like *you* are," Tol replied calmly. "Legitimate knights don't usually respond that way."

"You, sir, should be more aware of the precarious position you are in. No one knows where you are. I could simply claim, with witnesses," he waved at the guards, "That you tragically fell overboard and we were unable to recover your body."

"Yeah," Tol replied, "I noticed that several of your associates suffered similar tragic fates. You must be attracted to accident-prone people."

"In confirmation thereof, you will sadly suffer one shortly," said Jexx grimly, motioning to the guards.

Tol grinned and waited. When two of the guards approached him, one on each flank, he suddenly ducked under their grasp, coming back up with a large, knobby elbow in the crotch area of each. When they ducked in pain, he brought his huge fists down on the junction between neck and skull and both of them dropped like sacks of gravel.

The remaining guard, the goblin, drew a weapon but instead of pointing it at Tol, leveled it at Jexx. The half-ogre stared at him in surprise and anger.

"Hands up, Jexx," said the goblin, "You're under arrest for murder, attempted murder, racketeering, and tax evasion, among other charges."

It was Tol's turn to be surprised, although he'd felt there was something out of place about the gob all along. He looked at him inquisitively. The former bodyguard pulled out a badge. "Detective Gilmat: Frespiola Investigations Division," he said.

Tol nodded. "I thought there was something familiar about you." Recollection flooded in: he'd met Gilmat at an international EE conference a couple of years earlier. Gilmat was obviously the 'inside operative' Tol had been told about.

Jexx suddenly leapt for the pedestal and pressed another button. A loud pop emanated from the far wall, and the crater filled with thick smoke. Tol and Gilmat instinctively dropped down to where the air was more breathable. As they did there was a grinding noise followed by a click, then the smoke swirled violently as something large moved through it. Both cops leapt for the glider, but they caught only empty air as the flying machine was catapulted out over the dropoff with Jexx in the cockpit.

Tol and Gilmat ran out of the smoky crater onto the narrow surrounding lip in time to see Jexx inscribe a wide arc above them, laughing. "Better luck next time, gentles!" he yelled and turned toward the distant shoreline. Gilmat took a couple of shots at the glider, but if he hit his target there was no observable effect. Tol rolled his eyes. "What I wouldn't give for..." he stopped in mid-sentence as he heard a familiar drone. "That!" he finished, pointing to Dagyo approaching them in the *Sir Tol*. Gilmat, who had been on the comm calling for backup from a fast patrol boat stationed just out of sight on the ocean-facing side of the island, stared in amazement at the flying sausage.

Tol motioned for Dagyo to winch down the prisoner cage. He pointed to the rapidly shrinking glider and yelled up, "I need to catch that thing!" Dagyo nodded and released the winch cable. Tol climbed aboard the cage and turned to Gilmat.

"You go after him on the water, I'll take the air."

Gilmat just nodded with wide eyes as the cage with Tol in it lifted off. Dagyo pulled up until he was sure they were free of obstacles and then pushed both throttles full open. The Zifjagga accelerated as though eager for the chase, trailing its suspended goblin cargo behind at an acute angle. Tol tried not to think about how easy it would be to fall out of the unlocked cage and plunge to a watery demise and instead concentrated on the target ahead.

The glider was swift, but it was entirely dependent on air currents for both speed and altitude. Jexx found a thermal above a small coral archipelago and rode it as high as it would take him before popping out of the spiral with renewed height and velocity. Meanwhile Dagyo and Tol had been steadily gaining on him from below. Jexx decided to go on the offense while he still had the advantage of altitude.

Whirling suddenly, Jexx aimed his glider directly at the zifjagga and pulled out a disruptor. He aimed at Tol and then at Dagyo in the command car, but Dagyo took evasive action and both shots went wide of the mark. Switching tactics, he removed a projectile weapon from its bracket in the cockpit and started punching holes in the envelope surrounding the gas bag. The zifjagga lost altitude almost immediately and seemed to be doomed to crash into the water as the gas leaked away. Jexx laughed evilly and resumed his course toward Yiks Island.

Dagyo dumped most of his emergency ballast and the plunge toward the sea was arrested. Tol looked up at one of the exit holes from Jexx's projectiles and saw the ragged edges that had been flapping as gas escaped through the opening cease to flap. *Self-sealing*, Tol thought, *Good idea*. Dagyo ignited a small heating element that ran along the keel of the ship. This gave the remaining gas more lift; they were soon at cruising altitude again. Tol couldn't guess how long the battery powering that heater would work, but he figured it would be enough to get them back to land looming about three kilometers ahead.

They gained on Jexx again. Tol motioned to Dagyo to get as much altitude as possible. They came in on top of the fugitive while matching his speed. Tol pointed at the cage, and then down. Dagyo nodded in comprehension and lowered the metal enclosure until it was right on top of Jexx, who had not heard them coming because of the rush of wind in his ears in the open cockpit of the glider.

Something suddenly tipped him off and he made a hard right turn in evasion just as Tol dropped down onto the fabric-covered fuselage behind Jexx. Tol scrambled wildly trying to hold on, and finally grabbed a spar from which control cables ran to the surfaces on each wing that controlled the turns of the glider. Straining mightily, he reached up and grabbed the left-hand wire, pulling it back as far as he could. The corresponding wing surface folded up, levelling the plane out contrary to Jexx's control inputs.

Tol realized he now had effective mastery over the roll axis of the craft. He could counteract any attempt to upset the glider and knock him off it. Jexx scowled in anger and pulled back on the wheel, which brought the nose up until the wings no longer had any effective lift, at which point the glider stalled and dropped out of the air.

Tol hung on for dear life. When Jexx realized Tol was still there, he pushed the nose forward until the craft was once again flying. After a moment he began to twiggle the vertical control surface on the tail back and forth. This slewed the tail of the glider from side to side, making it difficult for Tol to hold on. He realized that Jexx would eventually succeed in dislodging him if he stayed put, so he started pulling himself centimeter by centimeter along the top of the glider's fuselage, inexorably creeping toward the cockpit and Jexx himself.

Finally, with the glider yawing wildly and the fabric beginning to bulge and rip as a result, Tol laid one beefy hand over the edge of the partial nacelle surrounding the cockpit proper. He pulled himself into the opening while Jexx rained blows on him with his right fist. Tol shrugged them off and punched Jexx hard in the right ear. Stunned, he slumped forward on the wheel and the glider went into a steep dive. Tol tried to pull the unconscious half-ogre away from the control wheel, but the only other space in the tiny cockpit was currently occupied by Tol himself; there was no place to put Jexx.

Tol rolled his eyes. "Smek me: why isn't anything ever easy?" He clambered back out along the spine of the craft toward the control surface cable spars. With his feet anchored under the lip of the cockpit, he reached back and grabbed both of the wires leading aft to the horizontal surfaces on the tail, pulling back as hard as he could. The glider abruptly stopped losing altitude and leveled out.

Tol realized that with the half-ogre's body mass still resting on the control wheel, as soon as he released the cables the glider would resume its dive. Seeing as how they were only a hundred meters or so above the water now, that didn't seem like a good idea. Trouble was, he was already growing fatigued from the intensely strenuous effort. Tol let out his breath and rested his head against the fabric. As he did he heard a whistling noise just above him and looked up to see that Dagyo had brought the cage to within reach. He took a deep breath, tensed, then in one motion released the cables while pushing off from the cockpit frame and grabbing the front edge of the suspended cage.

The glider pushed forward and resumed its dive, crashing into the water below at high speed and fracturing into a thousand fragments. Tol pulled himself up into the cage with his final remaining strength and slumped, breathing heavily as Dagyo winched him up to decrease drag. They puttered along for a few minutes until at last the gnome hovered over solid ground and lowered the cage to a meter above the beach. Tol dropped into the warm sand and briefly considered hugging it. He looked up at the crowd gathering and quite suddenly found himself in Selpla's arms. They had come ashore at the Sellestra Placidum beach, not ten meters from where Selpla was sunning herself in a nice wooden chaise with down cushions.

"Tol! What on N'plork were you doing?"

"Landing," Tol replied, closing his eyes and smiling blissfully.

Pieces of glider and half-ogre washed up on Yiks Island beaches for the next couple of weeks. Once most of Jexx's head was discovered wrapped in seaweed, the case was officially closed. Tol and Selpla spent a few days actually resting and recreating—with emphasis on the recreating—before heading back to Tragacanth. Tol bought Dagyo a very nice dinner at the resort in appreciation for his services and promised once again to extol the virtues of the zifjagga to those responsible for EE acquisitions back in Goblinopolis.

Chapter the Twenty-Seventh

in which a number of loose ends are secured, more or less

When Tol returned to Justice Hall, there was a diplomatic communiqué waiting for him from the office of Odinial Tartag in Hellehoell. It was requesting information on the whereabouts of a titan named Korq. The Hellehoell authorities had reason to believe that Sir Tol-u-ol was in possession of knowledge regarding his current location and respectfully asked for a meeting concerning said personage.

Tol laid down the parchment and leaned back in his padded executive swivel chair. He stared at a detailed map of Tragacanth on the far wall without seeing it and thought about how best to reply. He weighed the current excellent relations with the fledgling titan nation against the specter of slavery and racial elitism. Something about Korq's story didn't sit just right with him—never had. The titans had not betrayed any trace of that repugnant behavior in front of him, even under stress. Either they were first-rate actors as a race, or there was more to this than what Korq had given him.

Tol knew he couldn't just ignore something that arrived in a diplomatic pouch. Not like the old days, anyway, when things just 'fell behind his desk.' Heads of State had a nasty habit of knocking on the door until someone answered. He sighed and poured a cup of stankabru. He knew what the right thing to do was, of course: confront the titans about the practice of enslaving half-breeds. For most of his life he would have plunged into that crusade without a second's hesitation. He was strangely reluctant this time, and that reticence itself puzzled him.

Maybe he was just getting old. No, if he ever reached the age where he no longer felt compelled to act on known or suspected injustice, he would bloody well retire. He still enjoyed putting down the bad guys as much as ever. Slavery was abhorrent in N'plork societies, no matter what race you were, so it was definitely a hot-button issue and well worthy of his attention. So, what was holding him back?

Tol was still pondering as he walked into the central case file library for Tragacanthan EE. He sat down in one of the cubicles and started pulling records. Every cubicle had a copy of the master index list; investigators ticked the files they wanted to see and the automatic retrieval system dropped them down a chute. He selected records with the words 'slave' and 'titan' combined. Nothing popped up except the report he'd filed himself after returning from the *Grollnash* adventure.

He dropped the 'titan' keyword. A dozen files relating to people who claimed they'd been enslaved by one person or institution or the other came back; most of them were just rather loose definitions of 'slave.' So, he tried just 'titan.' Only a few files there, all of which were reports of people being terrorized by something they claimed was a 'rock titan,' but which proved to be the disgruntled next door neighbor or some wild critter that came down from the mountains looking for food.

He sighed again and headed over to the Royal Library to study up on titan society. The shelves weren't entirely bare, but titans in the past were rather secretive—so much so that most of the other residents of N'plork thought they were either entirely mythical or extinct, at least until they suddenly began streaming into Hellehoell answering a summons no one else heard. There were a few slim tomes on archaeological finds with their attendant thinly-grounded speculations on function and social customs, but nothing concerning the titans' views on enslavement or interracial breeding. Was that because there was nothing to report, or had it been expertly covered up by the titans themselves?

After a morning spent reading what little there was on titan social customs, Tol realized that he was just going to have to head back to Hellehoell and talk to the titans in person. He sighed one last time for good measure and filed the travel paperwork, then sent a message to Selpla that he would return in a couple of days.

Tol spent the carriage ride to Fenurian carefully devising the approach he was going to take. It had to be direct, at which he was quite adept, yet diplomatic, at which he was really not. He went back and forth among various planned strategies but in the end decided just to wing it, as always.

Because he was responding through official diplomatic channels, Tol was met at the station by the Tragacanthan Ambassador to Hellehoell, a career diplomatic service goblin named Liloth Tigli. She discussed the slavery issue with Tol and tried to convince him to gloss over it, which he flatly refused to do. He did promise her not to be accusatory or negative about it, however. Tol merely wanted, as he told the Ambassador, to ascertain the truth of the matter. If the titans wished to legitimize slavery within their society, they had the legal, if not moral, right to do so. Tol could not be compelled to countenance that practice, though.

Tol had steeled himself for what could prove to be a nasty confrontation, but the reality was quite different. He explained to Tartag that he was uncomfortable revealing the whereabouts of Korq before he investigated some disturbing claims the young titan had made concerning treatment of half-breeds. Tartag seemed genuinely perplexed at Korq's report of being enslaved. He was the son of a prominent titan scholar whose life's work had been research into improving crop yields to maximize the number of titans fed from a given plot of arable land. Because of his father's inclusion amongst the heroes of titan society, Korq's fate was of considerable importance to the people of Hellehoell; especially given that he simply, from their point of view, disappeared without a word.

"What sorts of experiments did his father do?"

Tartag consulted a document provided by the institute where Korq's father was employed. "It says here he did selective cross-breeding, genetic manipulation, and something called 'varietal magnification.' He magnified certain nutritional attributes of food plants by very narrow and concentrated selective breeding."

Tol considered this and had a thought. He didn't know where the thought came from; it didn't seem to be from his own brain.

"Is it possible that Korq himself did a little 'experimentation' with his father's modified plants and ingested something that affected his thought processes? Specifically, generated a form of paranoia in him?"

Tartag blinked. "I...I suppose that is a possibility. I would have to consult with our experts. What made you think of that?"

Tol shook his head. "I'm not sure. I just felt when I was talking to Korq that something wasn't quite clicking with his story. He told me that titans enslaved any who were not racially pure and that, as a half-breed, he had been essentially forced labor for pure-bred titans. His rhetoric reminded me of the drug-induced paranoids I ran into from time to time on the streets of Sebacea."

Tartag was visibly shaken by this. Ambassador Tigli winced. "Your Excellency, I'm certain that Sir Tol-u-ol was not suggesting that there is slavery extant in Hellehoell. Were you, Sir Tol?" Tigli looked at him pointedly.

Tol shrugged. "I'm not suggesting anything at all. I'm just telling you why I am reluctant to divulge the whereabouts of Korq until I get some hard facts concerning his claims. Edict enforcement officers are sworn to protect the people they serve. When Korq and I left here together, this was Tragacanth territory and therefore under my jurisdiction. I was and am bound by that oath."

"Of course you are, Sir Tol-u-ol," said Tartag, "I would not under any circumstances ask you to violate your oath. You must understand that I am simply responding to a request from Korq's family to ascertain his whereabouts. They are very concerned about him."

Tol did not let up. "*He* was very concerned about being dragged back here against his will. From what I could tell, he would be considered an adult, is that correct?"

"Yes," replied one of Tartag's staff, "Korq is above the age of legal ascendency by Hellehoell edict and titan custom."

Tol thought in silence for a few moments. "I will tell you where he is, on the condition that you give me your word that he will be allowed to live his life in the way, and location, in which he sees fit."

Tartag did not hesitate. "You have my sworn word on that, Sir Tol. We just want to be sure he is all right. We believe he is most likely with his mother's relations, which would be perfectly acceptable."

Tol let out a sigh of relief. "That is precisely where he is, Your Excellency; at least, that's where he told me he was headed. I left him in the company of trolls at the docks in Port Jool. He seemed very happy."

Tartag smiled. "Thank you, Sir Tol. That news will put his father and relatives here in Hellehoell at ease. His mother passed a few years ago; her family never approved of the marriage and refuse to communicate with any on his father's side. They blame him in some way for her death, I suspect."

"Korq told me that he was the product of...rape."

Tartag put his face in his hands. "I just don't know why he would make such a terrible accusation. I knew his mother personally for a short while; she was happily married, I can assure you. Her death was a devastating blow to Dr. Rerris. This is all very disturbing." He seemed on the verge of weeping.

"I still have unanswered questions myself, Your Excellency. Would it be at all possible for me to speak with Korq's father in person?"

"I will ask him," Tartag replied. He motioned to his staff, one of whom hurried off.

"His father's name, incidentally, is Dr. Anbeg Rerris. He is senior reader and research coordinator in agricultural sciences at the Jiwqal Institute here in Hellehoell. Korq is his only child. To be perfectly frank, very few titan-related interracial assignations produce children. We aren't certain why, but those that do almost always involve a titan as the male parent. The idea that we would enslave the children thus produced is untenable for several reasons: first, since children are very rare in those cases they are usually loved even more intensely for it; second, they are *so* rare that enslaving them wouldn't really make any difference to our labor pool; third, slavery of any sort is abhorrent to titans as a society; early in our history there were cases where titans were ourselves enslaved because we were few in number, immensely strong, and feared by the other races. Ignorance quite often engenders fear, which leads to mistrust and frequently, abuse. Because we have *been* enslaved, we as a society utterly reject that practice."

Just then the assistant came back into the room and whispered to Tartag. "Dr. Rerris is willing to speak with you. He will meet us downstairs in the first floor conference area."

Tol nodded and followed him down to the indicated room. In contrast to the fairly intimate setting of the Odinial's private conference suite, the main conference facility was quite expansive. It was still well-appointed with comfortable chairs, plenty of audio-visual capability and beautiful glonkwood tables with elaborate carving. The acoustics were quite excellent, as well, especially for lower frequencies that corresponded to the titans' speaking voices. As was the custom with all titan public buildings, the walls were covered in rich tapestries depicting various scenes from the titans' long history, much of it unknown to other races. Tol felt drawn to their examination and had to remind himself that he was there on a mission.

Dr. Rerris wasn't really the talkative sort, but after a few minutes of questioning Tol got him to admit that a couple of the plants he'd developed did exhibit psychotropic properties. He verbally resisted any suggestion on Tol's part that they might have had something to do with Korq's delusions and strong desire to flee, but Tol could tell he'd planted a seed, as it were. He thanked the professor and sent him on his way.

"I think I've gathered all the information I need, Your Excellency. You now know as much about Korq's disappearance and whereabouts as I do, and I in turn have some answers, tentative though they may be. I would appreciate being kept informed about future developments concerning this case, if for no other reason than it would provide me with more tools for evaluating this sort of behavior if I encounter it again."

"Agreed," replied Tartag, "This situation has reminded me of the importance of cooperation with other races and governments. It has been many centums since titans have been in a position to consider such things; it will take time and experience to 'normalize' our collective mentality, I'm afraid."

"From my point of view you did just fine," said Tol. "You didn't rush to judgment, you didn't make any rash decisions, and you acted in a totally responsible and reasonable manner. I don't think you're going to need much 'normalizing' at all." Ambassador Tigli gave Tol a smile and a surreptitious 'thumbs up' at this.

Tartag also smiled. "You are most kind, Sir Tol. I understand His Majesty Tragacanth's decision to create a new office of knighthood for you. You are a rare combination of tough, uncompromising, and thoughtful. If you are willing, I would like to bring you back at some point to help train our own edict enforcement people."

"I am most certainly willing, Your Excellency. Training is a part of my responsibilities that, to be honest, I have let slide more than I should."

"Then it is settled. My office will get with you on topics and scheduling."

"I am," Tol said, shaking Tartag's hand, "Always at your service."

Phaeon was a native of interstellar space, or rather, spacetime fabric before it was stretched to form the current universe, but he never ceased to be enthralled and enraptured by the spectacle of stars, nebulae, and myriad other ways in which the matter-energy disturbance manifested itself. There were countless colors and forms, ranging from the breathtaking magnificence of vast multicolored dust clouds comprising stellar nurseries to the impossibly dense points of the smallest gravity wells, which appeared to Phaeon as pinpricks through which one could peer into the next universe over.

He wandered lonely as a cosmic ray for some time—not that time has any meaning when you are part and parcel of eternity—until his attention came to rest on a small blue planet whirled with white, brown, and green. It wasn't much in the grand scheme of the multiverse, but then neither is anything else. The scale is simply too immense.

This planet was well outside of the dark energetic continuum, so magic wouldn't be an issue here. Blue planets were always inhabited by one or more forms of life, usually sentient at some point in its progression. That suited him. Eventually he would provide them evidence of his presence and see how long it took them to figure it out. Once they did and were in danger of coming into actual contact, he would move on without telling them exactly why or how. It amused him, if entities born of quantum superpositional perturbation can be said to experience amusement.

As he approached the planet, the cloud of debris surrounding it told Phaeon precisely where they were in their development: very early space-age. Most races did not pay attention to how much junk they were depositing in near orbit until it began to interfere with their satellites and kill a few of them here and there. Eventually if they continued along the space exploration vector they would herd all the debris together and either vaporize it in the atmosphere or jettison it into deep space. He preferred the former, as the latter amounted to interstellar littering. The real irony came when a planet was sterilized or otherwise seriously disrupted by collision with another civilization's jettisoned space junk. Rare, but it happened.

Phaeon did not want to deal with any even remotely advanced civilization on this occasion so he slid back a few thousand local years into the planet's past. That would give him some time to settle in before they developed any significant technology.

Settling on a place to settle in was always a diverting exercise. This planet had expansive oceans: did he want to live deep beneath one? Inside a volcano? On the tallest peak? Inside the most massive peak? Decisions, decisions. Circling the planet a few times, Phaeon finally chose a broad expanse of unbroken brown and gray: a vast desert area. He descended through the burning sands and excavated a domain there, with an elaborate palace and boulevards leading to it. To mark the spot on the surface he erected three large cut stone block structures, each with four faces and coming to a point at the top. The entryway to the largest he marked with a word meaning 'Private Property:' *Khufu*.

Aspet and Boogla had just finished a sumptuous repast on the private balcony of the Royal Residence when a red light over the door leading back into their study began blinking in a particular pattern. Aspet stared at it for a few seconds and put down his napkin.

"Military alert. That can't be good," he sighed. "I'd better find out what's up." They returned to the study and Aspet pressed a button on his desk. A hidden panel slid open and a keypad popped up. He punched in a series of numbers and characters, waited until the green light came on, and entered another. The transceiver crackled into life.

"Your Majesty, we have a disturbing report from the Coastal Patrol. A patrol boat spotted a corvet sailing out of a makeshift pier north of Balom in Galanga. We have reason to believe it was full of orcs."

"Why would you think that?" Aspet asked.

"Two reasons: first, two known individuals were positively identified on the vessel. Second, the registration was archaic and belongs to a ship known to have been taken by the orcs in a small skirmish about fifty years ago in Uzplenq."

"Uzplenq? Are you telling me this fifty year-old corvet sailed all the way across the Noorprid Sea? Alone?"

"Yes on the sailing, but not necessarily alone. While we have no evidence the orcs have anything resembling a fleet, they could have as many as a half-dozen ships of the frigate class or smaller."

"Which way was the orc ship headed?"

"Out to sea, Your Majesty."

"Any idea why?"

"None. But any movement of this sort is a violation of the worldwide Treaty of Mutual Containment. We must notify the international community and be prepared to fulfill our military obligations in this respect."

Aspet sighed. "Understood. Have the Ministers of National Defense and International Relations start the notifications through diplomatic channels. I want a full cabinet meeting in one hour."

"As you command, Majesty."

Aspet turned to Boogla. "So much for a relaxing evening. Guess you better cancel the string quartet."

Appendix

The Mythologies of N'plork

CoME Cultural Sociography Series #27

in which the physiognomy, races, and beliefs of N'plork are examined

Geography

N'plork is a water-dominated world with four principal land masses hosting a total of fifteen sovereign nations, in descending order of size: Esmia (Tragacanth, Galanga, Lardonica, Ovinis, Asmagon, the Paradiddle Islands); Turmia (Solemadrina, Rublosq, Tantatku); Litria (Spleroste, Frespiola, Hividz, Grosyem); and Bazgush (Azlymosh, Nerr). The diameter of N'plork is approximately 19,125 km. Oceans cover 80% of the planet's surface. The day length is just under 22 hours, which gives N'plork a fairly rapid rotational velocity as inhabitable planets go. This creates some dramatic weather patterns that manifest themselves primarily as extremely expansive sea storms which regularly ravage the coasts of all continents except Bazgush, which is sheltered from direct effects by its proximity to Turmia, upwind.

The extensive Turmian mountain ranges, particularly the Folmnissi range with peaks exceeding twenty thousand meters, provide the nearby coast of Bazgush with considerable shelter from the prevailing winds. However, those same peaks effectively remove all the moisture from said winds as they scale to the upper limits of the atmosphere in climbing over them, so that sheltered coastal area of Bazgush is also N'plork's most arid region, with periods of as long as twenty years with no measureable precipitation.

The rapid rotation, dramatic temperature differences, and high winds aloft also create extremely active oceanic currents that are capable of carrying an unpowered vessel along in excess of thirty knots. Moreover, two major currents, the Arctal and Austral, reverse themselves about every six months for the return trip. This makes for an efficient transportation conduit that allowed for the early development of trade routes supporting quite sophisticated civilizations. These early societies were composed of numerous races: goblins, gnomes, elves, dwarves, hobgoblins, bugbears, kobolds, ogres, and trolls chief among them—with isolated populations of gnarlignomes, titans, and orcs—and each experienced its own rich mythopoesis.

Sociography and Anamorphology

The races of N'plork all evolved, scholars believe, from a distant common ancestor and developed their particular morphologies in response to the demands of the environments in which they lived. As a result of this ancestral commonality each can theoretically hybridize with the others, although the only relatively common such interracial assignations seem to involve ogres, trolls, and goblins. Half-trolls and half-ogres are still somewhat rare in the general population, but in certain densely urban areas of Goblinopolis (Tragacanth), Aspolia (Solemadrina), and Uzplenq (Nerr), they are not an uncommon sight.

N'plork as a planet is subject to dramatic geological and meteorological phenomena on a regular basis. Combine this with the active intellects possessed by all N'plorkian races and the stage is set for the development of quite robust mythologies, which are as varied and multifaceted as the races themselves.

In order to understand more fully the basis for mythogenesis on N'plork it is necessary first to establish the mechanism by which the races evolved. As mentioned earlier, all sentient races on N'plork can trace their lineage to a single ancestor in the dim past, during the era scholars refer to as the *Protocene*. It is presently unknown where the bipedal form first emerged on N'plork; there is some archaeological evidence to suggest that the heavily forested areas of Tantatku, Turmia are a prime candidate. The woodland edges grade into grasslands dotted with treed hillocks, which scholars generally agree are the ideal conditions for bipedal evolution. There were myriad species of both vegetation and small animals here in great abundance, access to which as food sources and subsequent increase in reproductive success was presumably somehow enhanced by assumption of the bipedal stance.

At some point during the late Protocene the great migrations began, as the tribes of paleocestors (pre-differentiated bipeds) began to disperse across the continents. There are two competing schools of thought concerning the impetus for this relatively sudden expansionism: one holds that food supplies were dwindling in the area and dispersal was an attempt to find new hunting grounds; the other contends that, on the contrary, food supplies were so abundant that paleocestor numbers exploded, leaving intolerably high population density as the driving force for dispersal.

Whatever the reason, the evidence for dispersion is quite clear, as there are tantalizing artifacts from numerous camps established over the next thousand years in ever-widening concentric circles with Tantatku at the center. Precisely when the anatomical divergences began is also a point of contention, but the general consensus is that the original populations dispersed into four or more geographic locations with distinctly different requirements for survival and reproductive success. It is likely that the first mariners were the group who developed into goblins, as their artifacts begin to show up on Bazgush about a thousand years after the putative primary dispersion event (PDE).

Eventually all four continents were inhabited, with the goblins dominating Bazgush and then northern Esmia. Gnomes had a small presence on Bazgush as well, but the epicenter of ancient gnome culture was on Turmia, in the region that became known as Solemadrina. About 300 years after the goblin migration to Tragacanth in northern Esmia, estimated at approximately 4,200 years ago, the gnomes followed and established colonies in what was to become Galanga, which occupies the central land mass of Esmia.

Hobgoblins and kobolds were never very numerous; they thrived primarily in manual labor niches—occupations generally ignored by the goblins and gnomes—such as fisheries, mines, timber-cutting, and produce harvesting. They were centered in two small clusters: one in Spleroste, Litria, and the other on Turmia, in the dense tropical forests of Rublosq. As with almost all the other races, they eventually established themselves on every continent and nation of N'plork.

Dwarves are quite a minority in the modern era, although ample evidence exists to suggest that they were far more common a few millennia previous. Though they have a reputation for being gruff and somewhat combative among strangers, within their family and social units they are kind, hospitable to a fault, and more inclined to laughter than argument. Dwarves are short in stature but exceedingly strong, with almost supernatural endurance. They live for the most part in forested areas, where their oral and written histories tell of massive complexes crafted from the living trees themselves, although little proof of these is known, at least to non-dwarven scholars. Legends tell of an ancient alliance between dwarves and forest titans; again there are no known historical records concerning this.

Gnarlignomes are something of a mystery to anamorphologists, the scholars who study the races and their development. They have many of the physical characteristics of gnomes, but are smaller and significantly less cerebral. There are theories that the gnarlignomes are all descended from one isolated polymutant gnome cluster in Tantatku or Rublosq, but insufficient corroborating evidence has been discovered to solidify these claims. Socially gnarlignomes tend to be loners, or to live in small, distinctly monoracial communities.

Trolls and titans are most likely related, with titans being essentially giantized trolls. There is only one race of titans, genetically, but they tended to be named by local populations according to their preferred habitats: rock, sea, forest, or canyon. There is some evidence to suggest that a fifth group, storm titans, exist or once existed, but the references are all purely anecdotal. Titans with high-quality food resources in their habitats could exceed four meters in height (there is one set of bones that seems to have been from a storm titan over five meters tall, but scholars haven't totally accepted the legitimacy of that finding as of this writing). Modern trolls range from two and a half to just under three meters. They are intelligent to a point, but do not tend to be independently creative. Once you have earned their loyalty, however, they are extremely diligent in carrying out assigned tasks, even relatively complex ones.

Trolls are obviously suited for the heaviest of labor, and often find themselves in demand at construction sites and any other venue where immense strength is a benefit. One of the most striking of all attributes of troll society is their universal devotion to the truth. Trolls do not lie. If they find themselves in a situation where telling the truth might endanger someone, they simply say nothing at all. A troll who does not want to talk is not going to talk, and anyone who thinks differently will discover how deeply ingrained this reticence is.

Ogres are probably a subgroup of trolls with smaller morphology, although genetic evidence suggests that there may be goblin and even hobgoblin blood intermixed. Whatever the case, ogres are wont to be crude and somewhat lugubrious. They often react to stressful situations with violence and as such are frequently shunned by the races who consider themselves more civilized. Ogres are tribal and live in loosely-structured enclaves, usually in fairly isolated areas, although a few groups have adapted to urban life with varying degrees of success. They possess, as a race, traits that often make them successful criminals, although they are not necessarily of criminal aspect by nature.

Orcs are the wildcard in N'plorkian anamorphology. They resemble no other race phenotypically, yet show genotypic similarities to both elves and goblins. They seem to be congenitally bipolar, as an orc can go from calmly genial to insanely, murderously aggressive in the time it takes to draw a breath. This unpredictability, combined with their militaristic tendencies, resulted in a protracted war between the orcs and everyone else they came in contact with, with the eventual result that they were virtually eradicated as a race. The paltry number of survivors were confined to a few scattered reservations that for many years were little more than concentration camps.

As time passed the concertina wire came down and the guard towers were abandoned, but any perceived movement of a group of orcs (i.e., three or more) much beyond their established territory was nevertheless treated with swift and decisive interdiction. Orcs were ostracized in mainstream society because no one trusted them, and for good reason. A very few had managed to keep their explosive aggressive tendencies under control and live on the fringes of populated areas, but even after many years there they were still treated with some suspicion.

Elves are a racial anomaly. Unlike all the other peoples, they do not appear to have experienced any significant evolutionary changes in the fossil records of N'plork. The earliest appearance of their artifacts is in the very late Protocene, and this record begins quite abruptly. There are theories—considered by most of the established scholastic community to be somewhat crackpot—that the elvish race may be descended from alien colonists, but their genetic similarity to the other races militates against that. However, explaining their sudden appearance in the fossil record is problematic, to the point that an entire sub-branch of archaeoanamorphology, Elven Protohistory, sprang up devoted to the subject.

Interestingly, most of the Elven Protohistory researchers are not of the elvish race. The elves themselves seem curiously reluctant to talk about the distant past of their kind, although relating their chronicled history is quite another matter. They are quite accomplished historians as a race and keep meticulous journals of even their most mundane activities. Most elvish children can recite detailed life stories of a dozen heroes or more.

The Dawn of Magic

Somewhere between 500 and 1000 years after the PDE, a small group of early goblin parasciencers (pre-mages) who had migrated to the eastern coast of what eventually became Tragacanth were successful in establishing a link to the vast pool of hitherto unknown extradimensional energy they named, in Protogoblish, *Ta'slizh'I* or 'energy source.' Over time this name evolved into *The Slice*.

Precisely how they managed this connection, or discovered the existence of The Slice itself, is one of the central unsolved questions of the History of Magic and has been the subject of no fewer than thirty-one disquisitions submitted to CoME by supplicants for the rarified accolade of Doctor of Apotropaic Arts. The parasciencers kept meticulous notes concerning everything they did with the exception of the actual event that resulted in first contact with The Slice. On that topic they are strangely and uncharacteristically silent, almost as though they were fearful or otherwise reluctant to chronicle it, although one reference does exist to something or someplace known as Qillopot. Its significance is unknown.

A scant two years after discovering The Slice, they had created the twenty-four Specula Arcanis Majoris and begun the process of enchanting them with inviolability spells, some of the strongest magic known even to this day. How they went from passive researchers speculating on the very existence of magic to masters of exceedingly powerful magic in this ridiculously short time is quite difficult to grasp; despite several hypotheses set forth over the ages no substantially workable theory has emerged. All that is really known is that they experienced some dramatic episode of enlightenment.

Once the Specula were in place the practice of magic began to spread: slowly at first, but then accelerating rapidly. By the third generation following discovery and connection with The Slice (an event referred to simply as the Inception), there were mages and societies devoted to magic use on every continent of N'plork. The first goblin to take the title of 'Archmage' was Bazmura, who lived over a thousand years after the Inception. If the Society of Sages and Mages in truth possesses any records pertaining to the earliest days of magic on N'plork (they claim they do not), they have not shared them with CoME or either of the principal organizations dedicated to researching and preserving the histories of magic and technology.

Deities and Pantheons

Goblins are somewhat ambiguous from a spirituality standpoint. They have a basic belief in the supernatural, but as with most sentients who have a scholarly class, that belief is tempered by skepticism about the presence of any power or entity that cannot be experienced using one of the fundamental six senses. The pantheon of Goblin deities consists primarily of Plegma, the All-Goblin or Almighty, Gammag Palindromia, the god of truth, meditation, and justice, and Mordik, the god of fertility, childbirth, and relationships. There are other minor deities worshipped by scattered cults, such as Hork, the goddess of ridicule, and Grund, the patron deity of orators, but the big three draw the overwhelming majority of goblin religious rites. It is somewhat relevant to note that goblin deities have no set gender, and may be prayed to using any pronoun one wishes, including the decidedly impersonal.

Hobgoblins tend toward functional atheism, as devoting themselves to any goal but self-aggrandizement runs contrary to their nature as a race. There is a pantheon ascribed to ancient hobgoblin society, but the only deities that have survived to this day are T'jeld, the god of stealth and thievery, and Kleska, the goddess of luck and gamblers. Worship of these holdovers is concentrated in a very small priestly class who operate more like bookies than spiritual leaders. For a sliding scale fee they will intervene with the gods on behalf of an applicant, but no promises of success are given. You roll the dice with god in Hobgoblin society, as you do with every other aspect of their culture.

Elves subscribe to a complex, deeply interwoven belief system that is based on the principle of Zar'bux, or concentric layers of spiritual growth. Progressing through these layers of self-awareness and improvement requires meditation, control over both the physical and mental bodies, and copious quantities of a drink called k'ppajeau (known to goblins as Aylis Tea) made from boiling the dried leaves of the Red-tipped Lysergia, a shrub found natively along semi-arid streambeds in Nerr, although it now was raised in vast greenhouses on every continent. Elves begin their spiritual journeys at the age of twenty, about five years before they reach sexual maturity. They spend two hours a day in meditation, preceded and followed by a large bowl of k'ppajeau.

As Elves progress through the spiritual levels, they are expected to worship different entities (they aren't really classified as 'gods' in the traditional sense) who represent stages along the continuum to mastery of the living soul. Primulat oversees the bottom rung, Precept. Most elves traverse Precept in two to four years, depending on their natural abilities and the level of support from their familial environment. Upon completion they are allowed to use the title *Prellus*.

The next level is Procept, ruled by Sofricia the Beneficent. The upper boundary of this stage is as far along the path as most adult elves choose to travel. Those who have mastered Procept are considered fully mature and ready to lead lives of quiet contemplation and doing good works. Successful students take the title *Mellus*.

The third level is Concept, under the protection of Belfragos the Blind. During this phase of the journey, students must look only within themselves; the outside world ceases to exist for them. They are brought their meals and do not leave their small, windowless cells. For this reason, and because attainment can take as long as twenty years, only priests and those who seek high levels of spiritual enlightenment for other reasons will customarily enter into Concept. On average ten to fifteen students per year are admitted into the stage; of these only three or four will complete the training. Those who attain all aspects of Concept are addressed as *Stellus*.

There is a rarified fourth level, Transept, which has no patron deity. Stella who enter into Transept will serve as their own instructors and spiritual guides. They shed all possessions except a hooded robe and a walking stick they harvest and carve from a tree that grows only above ten thousand meters on two adjacent peaks in the Folmnissi Mountains of Turmia. Once they get their breath back, they then wander N'plork as beggars, meditating all the while. The Transeptian Pilgrimage, as it is called, may take the entirety of a candidate's life to complete, if indeed it is completed at all. Those vanishingly few who do complete Transept are designated *Elevatus* and treated as demi-gods. As of this writing there are only three known living Elevata. None of them are able to walk very far on their own.

Dwarves are 'reformed monotheists' in that they once worshipped the god Acerbicon as a race, but after mass prayer failed to halt an epidemic that virtually wiped that race from the face of N'plork, the survivors turned their back on their deity and became confirmed agnostics. Now they get up on worship day and play 'Supplicate *This*,' a game involving hitting the many statues and stone murals of Acerbicon with as large a rock as possible while cheering and jeering. It does not seem to have brought about any further mishap to them. If Acerbicon exists and is watching, he may in fact be entertained by the ritual.

Gnome spirituality is not easily understood by outsiders. To the other races agnosticism, or rather strict antitheism seems to be an instinctive gnome behavior, but that is driven more by privacy than theology. Gnome domestic life can in fact be fraught with spiritual content, but is of a type that manifests in myriad superstition-like activities that are easily overlooked or misinterpreted by the unindoctrinated. Instead of formal worship rituals, for example, gnomes leave food, drink, and used ('blessed') containers for their domestic deities on designated altars called t'Vtraiz. To casual observers this simply looks like sloppy housekeeping. Gnomes invoke their deities by name only when agitated, ecstatic, or grieving. Unfortunately, researchers have been unable to make out what is being uttered on these occasions and so that aspect of gnome culture is still unknown to the rest of society. It may be that no one has thought simply to ask them. Gnomes can be rather terse when they think you are being too personal, which is almost always.

Gnarlignomes and their deities are interchangeable, for the most part. Both are short, wrinkled like an ancient boot left propped against the garden all winter, and irascible to a fault. While there are reputedly at least five gods in the gnarlignome pantheon, the only one routinely invoked is Arfsweener, the "Protector of the World," as he is sometimes called because of an inscription on an ages-old stone megalith in Tantatku. At least one scholar who specializes in ancient engravings insists that the text actually reads "Expectorator." With gnarlignomes the distinction hardly bears discussion.

Bugbears tend to worship the Deep Ones, gods of the N'plorkian subsurface regions. The origins of the association between underground structures and bugbears are not immediately obvious. While it's true that most affluent bugbears choose caves or cave-like dwellings to call home, the historical record does not show any particular evolutionary connection between bugbears and the subn'plorkian lifestyle. It may be simply that underground spaces were a niche not already occupied by the other races. Bugbears are smaller, on average, than any race but gnarlignomes and not at all warlike in disposition, so they might have seen the as-yet undisputed realm of the cave and cavern as quite attractive.

Their above-average intelligence and peaceful, studious demeanor is ideal for developing magical prowess, yet few choose the mantle of mage (although those who do often reach considerable heights within the profession; see for example Archmage Ballop'ril of Qoplebarq). The vast majority of bugbears are, not surprisingly, miners; a few choose to farm the numerous species of fungus used in their own and some other races' cuisines. As an aside, a race reported by early goblin voyagers to the cavern-rich regions of Litria, a race that spent all of their time underground and were capable of "clawing the rock with their own hands," whom they designated as *deep gnomes*, were almost certainly bugbears. The goblins had never before encountered the heavy tool-laden gauntlets habitually worn by bugbear miners and were therefore excused for mistaking them for their actual hands. Today the title 'deep gnome' is still bestowed upon the class of bugbear miners who do the most expert work in cavern-building, creating underground masterpieces without disturbing the native rock formations or the natural cave ecology, which all bugbears regard as sacred.

Ogres are too primitive and easily angered to have much of a spiritual life. Any deities they worship would need to be ones impressed by clubbing wildlife, hitting stones together, and clubbing other ogres. Although ogres are capable of language, some of the more intellectual among them achieving a vocabulary rivaling that of tropical mimic-avians, they choose to communicate with gestures—and by 'gestures' is meant 'aggravated assault.'

After tens of thousands of years of clubbing one another incessantly, ogres have developed protective bony plates or plaques embedded in the space between their epidermis and dermis. This adaptation has enabled them to avoid succumbing to blunt force trauma long enough to reach reproductive maturity and keep the species going, despite most unbiased observers' strong advice to the contrary.

There is one archaeological find relevant to ogre theology: on the southern tip of Nerr, children playing discovered an ancient barrow that contained an altar and numerous artifacts—presumably of a religious nature—of workmanship that could only have been ogrish in origin, owing principally to their having been shaped by bashing various raw materials with a club. The simple engravings showed great skill in that engraving anything at all with a club is difficult to say the least. They invoked the god Imo (eye' moh) in some form of retributive curse: "Imo kill Gug," "Imo beat Huk" and "Imo take Dob female" among the most legible. Scholars who study ogres (from a distance) are divided as to the origin and ultimate relevance of this site.

Trolls are not deeply intellectual, but they do possess a superficial intelligence that seems anomalous when coupled with their enormous frames. This intelligence lends them a benign outlook on life and society, which is fortunate for the rest of the races because an angry troll can do a lot of damage in a short time. The Trollish approach to religion is equally benevolent: trolls believe they were put on N'plork as protectors or guardians of their smaller brethren.

They worship only two deities: Blok reigns over the domain of solid matter, such as stones, soil, mountains, and so forth. The aqueous realm—which includes air and other gases—is the dominion of Plisj. There is a small priestly caste in troll society, but their role seems to be limited to divining the gods' moods and issuing the occasional demand or warning on their behalf. Most of these demands involve the priests' own subsistence, as they are supposed to be provided with the necessities by the troll population at large but trolls, while extremely diligent when devoted to a cause, are likely to forget what they're doing in mid-activity under other circumstances. Providing for their priests does not inspire devotion, it seems.

Kobolds are something of a mystery in all aspects of their lives, spirituality being no exception. They are extraordinarily insular; their interactions with the other races are by necessity only, although there are enclaves in major urban areas that are social to an extent. They mostly frequent taverns and similar venues, and the primary purpose in these excursions seems to be looking for other kobolds with whom to mate, since their traditional social outlets require a certain infrastructure lacking in the artificial setting of polyracial cities.

In their native villages, kobolds are tribal, with the average tribe consisting of 75 – 100 individuals. The Great Tribes are exceptions to this rule; as remnants of the earliest tribal affiliations they accumulated larger membership by dint of their long existence, and by aggregation of tribes that could no longer sustain themselves as independent groups. The three Great Tribes are Galga, Hinza, and Klaba. Each of these tribes boasts in excess of 1,500 members, although an exact count has never been released to the outside world by the Kofewalda, the grand moot of tribes that meets every ten years. Each tribe must send a representative to this moot, bearing certain mandated statistics and chronicles, including a tribal census.

In likewise fashion, the precise number of tribes existing in the Kobold nation, or Kabout, is uncertain. Most demographers place it at around 700. Lesser tribes are primarily geographically-oriented, although by tradition the Great Tribes were founded as trades guilds: Galga for wagoneers, husbanders, and artisans; Hinza for miners, laborers, and charcoalers; Klaba for sailors, dockworkers, fishers, and shipwrights. Members of the Great Tribes still primarily cling to these professions, although the percentage of 'outers,' as those who follow other paths are called, is growing steadily.

Orcs are of primitive mindset and seem to be mentally ill from birth as a racial characteristic. Their insanely aggressive personalities, triggered by seemingly random events, make them very difficult to study. It is thanks to a pair of dedicated scholars who risked life and limb hiding in the bushes for months that we possess the body of knowledge we do.

Orcish culture, if that word may be fairly applied here, dictates a strong hierarchical society with the leadership at each level consisting of those who can gain and maintain their positions by force of arms. Despite this warlike disposition, there is some evidence to suggest that quite remarkable works of art and artifice have been produced in orc compounds. The circumstances under which these artifacts were created are still a mystery.

Spiritually, orcs fall solidly in the shamanistic belief system. A shaman (Teg-Neg) is 'called' to his or her profession in a fit of religious ecstasy, which appears to be a seizure brought on by consumption of one or more of several psychoactive plants common to orc horticultural traditions. When one shaman challenges another for the title of Teg-Neg, a series of contests of wit and skill known collectively as the Lud-a-lud takes place, with the loser being forbidden ever to practice shamanic rituals again on pain of exile. Given that the other races both fear and intensely dislike orcs in general, exile is tantamount to execution, as lone orcs seldom survive more than a few weeks.

Orc gods are gods of basic drives: Al-Dat is the chieftain of the gods, and preserves his preeminence against the almost constant stream of challengers by right of arms: for orcs believe that only the strongest may lead.

The god of combat (personal or in battle; orcs do not distinguish between them) is Wup-Dat. To him is also assigned the patronage of athletic competitions, illustrating that in orcish culture warfare is sport and sport is combat.

The god of knowledge and wisdom, such as exists in orc society, is Wuz-Dat.

The god of sexual relations (romance is an unknown concept to orcs) is Gyump-Dat. He is called upon, rather obviously, when one orc, almost always the male, desires to arrange a tryst with a recalcitrant member of the other gender. To balance things out, there are twin goddesses named Stawp-Dat and Slugg-Dat the females seem to invoke rather often, presumably when the advances of the males are undesired or poorly executed.

They only additional deity that the researchers heard reference to was one presumably involved with agriculture, cuisine, and food supplies, who the orcs called Chyawmp-Dat. There is also reference to a sacred artifact known as the Valtir, but its nature and purpose remain a mystery.

Titans, despite their immense size, are secretive and aloof. Little serious scholarly work has been done on their culture or even basic habits, as they are powerful, seemingly intelligent, and jealously guard their privacy, both individual and collective. Nevertheless, sites they have occupied extensively and then for whatever reason abandoned contain a wealth of inferential information. [Editor's note: this monograph was written prior to the re-occupation of Hellehoell]

Arcanelementals

No treatise on mythology would be complete with mentioning the so-called Arcanelementals. Evidence for their presence is spotty, although they are accepted as having lived without question by a vast majority of the inhabitants of N'plork. They figure in many folk tales and lay histories, yet they left only a few tantalizing clues as to their origins and in fact objective existence.

The composite folk story of the arcanelementals is that they were the primary inhabitants of N'plork long before our ancestors evolved sentience and the races diverged. They were "seeded" to N'plork by The Slice itself, although as far as scholars can ascertain there was no connection between the two realms prior to the parasciencers' pivotal achievement. They were creatures of flesh and bone, but with an intrinsic, seemingly limitless, conduit to The Slice. Some researchers do believe that their primary or even sole purpose was to nudge those parasciencers along the right path to establishing the magic markers. This hypothesis, while not universally accepted, does help to explain how those goblins made the enormous leap from non-magic users to archmages in the incredibly short span of about two years.

What impetus would The Slice have for providing these magic mentors? The Slice, at least as current research would suggest, is almost as long as the universe itself, wrapping around the physical structures in chaotic patterns undetectable by any current astronomical instruments. Nevertheless, it has mass and contributes to the overall mass of the cosmos as what some call "dark matter," although The Slice itself constitutes only a small percentage of that phenomenon. It has been conjectured that other as-yet-to-be-discovered overlapping dimensions containing energies totally unlike any known to N'plorkian scholars may account for the balance of this unseen mass.

The Slice itself is a vast regenerative organism, the largest living structure in the universe so far discovered. It generates manna on an almost incomprehensible scale and this magical energy pools into vast reservoirs that at length begin to destabilize the structural fabric of The Slice itself. In order to keep the manna accumulations down, it must be siphoned off somehow. The most expeditious means of accomplishing this seems to be creating colonies of mages on nearby planets who act as 'relief valves' when they draw manna for magical use. N'plork rests in a dense pocket of The Slice and so is an ideal candidate for providing such an outlet.

Another fact that lends credence to the arcanelemental theory is that the historical record and physical evidence supports the assertion that they went 'extinct' less than a centum (perhaps even within a few years) after the last Speculum was set in place. It could well be that, their mission over, they simply returned to their native habitat.

It is hoped that one day sufficient hard evidence will be uncovered to solve the mystery of the arcanelementals once and for all and fill the gaps in our understanding of the origins of the force we call magic. That day, when it comes, will represent a significant intellectual milestone for all the races of N'plork.